Shake the Middle Tree

JANET GODDARD

Copyright © 2011 Janet Goddard

All rights reserved.

ISBN:1456591045
ISBN-13:978-1456591045

LCCN:

DEDICATION

for Grace

ACKNOWLEDGMENTS

Special thanks to Jill O'Reilly for her unwavering support of my writing, her generous readings and her excellent sense of humor. Thanks to Linda Wendling and Denise Bogard—most excellent writing partners—who, during our summertime workshops, offered me great insight, motivation, and direction.

PROLOGUE

The older kids in the neighborhood all claimed to have seen it. Thatcher and Philip claimed not only to have seen the bottom of the quarry, but to have climbed down and actually walked there. They said you could get to it from the other side, but the other side was farther than any of us younger kids were allowed to go—a block away and all fenced in. I grew up familiar with the sounds of dynamite blasts—blasts that were strong enough to rattle the china in my mother's buffet table and sometimes even break a piece or two. I walked the chain-link fence many times growing up, collecting handfuls of wild blackberries into small plastic bowls, trying to peer past the wooded ridge that blocked my view of the bottom.

I was told there was gold at the bottom—that's what they were really blasting for. I was told that greedy people climbed down to fill their pockets with the gold that lay there only to lose their balance and fall to their deaths as they tried to climb back up with their heavy, bulging sacks. I was told that bad guys and murderers camped on the quarry bottom at night, once the blasters went home for the day, and that if you listened really hard, you could hear them.

One of the older kids down the street said the bottom of the quarry was really a passageway to hell with the devil and fire and everything evil, and that a constant blanket of cold, black fog covered it. I tried hard not to picture that one at all, though sometimes, late at night when everything was dark and I couldn't quite sleep, the image snuck into my restless dreams.

I didn't really believe all the claims and stories I had heard, but I wondered. It was a fact that two men had taken their lives in the quarry at different times. Both climbed the fence and plunged over the edge. I tried to imagine it, that first step which was to become their last. I tried to imagine that defining, forward movement which led to nowhere but descent. I tried to imagine falling, as they must have felt it, unable to stop, unable to take back the decision, unable to avoid the final confrontation.

A time came, though, when I did see the bottom—or at least I think I did. I was eight.

A spring thunderstorm had caused a great flash flood on Old Warson Road not even a quarter-mile down from our house. The ground at that edge of the quarry had given way under the pressure of the water, creating a gaping hole under a section of fence. The fence dangled over the hole, exposed and naked of any support. The flood water crashed through the mighty breach and the noise echoed loudly in the canyon below, bringing out neighbors instantly.

The storm-gray sky painted the dusk. Everyone gathered at the edge of the floodwater and watched in awe as the hole swallowed a small dark sea before us. Voices were soundless beneath the bellowing rush. The adults held their arms out like paper-chain dolls to keep all of us children from getting too close. In less than fifteen minutes, the floodwater was gone and the road was left unprotected from a hole that was big enough to swallow a passing car.

The opening seemed to glow in contrast to the dusk-light and dark earth. I craned my neck to see around the arms and waists of the adults, straining to finally see the bottom. I tried to push my way in front of the adults but was reprimanded by serious looking neighbors. I fell back and circled behind the adults and went to the side of the crowd. A policeman stood in front of the hole, making sure everyone stayed away. When he turned his back, though, I stepped forward. Now I would see for myself. Ten short steps separated me from the truth.

The glow of the white rock showing through the darkness of the earth seemed to call me. I stepped closer, my view increasing with each step. It was more immense, I realized, than my imagination had conjured, more open, more vast. My eyes began to blur at the sudden shift in perspective and dimension. I sucked in my breath, feeling dizzy and light-headed. I saw the steep wall of rock on the other side of the quarry. I saw the shadow of a straight and narrow-looking road that was carved from that wall and that led, in a long and steady angle, deep down into the pit. I followed the wall down with my eyes, anticipating the view coming to rest on the bottom.

And I would have seen it, too, if Mrs. Crogh hadn't started screaming. The focus of the entire crowd turned from an inattentive, general buzz into a surging voice of gasps and yells. I looked at the policeman, who was now looking into the crowd trying to figure out why everyone was screaming. I stepped closer to the hole. One more second and I would see it. I bent my knees and leaned forward, craning my neck to see the deepening rock turn darker shades of gray. My eyes followed the wall further down into the shadows.

"Hey! Hey!" The cop grabbed me roughly by my arm. "Are you crazy? Get away from there!"

He pushed me back into the crowd, asking where my parents were, yelling at the crowd to please stay back or better yet go home. My head, however, remained turned toward the hole. My gaze remained fixed. I was so close—so close to having the mystery uncovered, so close to the secret of that magnificent pit.

But a sea of hands reached for me, pulling me far away. Parents scolded me and called me foolish while their children gathered around, reaching out to touch me and tap me and shove me to attention.

"Why'd you do that?" they wanted to know.

My older brother Thatcher cut through the crowd with uncharacteristic speed and agility. He grabbed my wrist. "Stupid," I heard him say, but I paid no attention. I felt as if I were walking in my sleep, as if I were spinning on the very edge the truth! But there I was being pulled away, taken off in the wrong direction while my mind remained firmly at the edge of the pit. Thatcher dragged me from the crowd and led me home, pulling my arm to make me walk faster.

"You're lucky that cop didn't arrest you. They can send you to jail for that, you know," Moffit said. Moffit was just a kid. He didn't know anything but was always acting like he did.

"Hey, did you see the bottom?" Donika asked. She lived in the big white house next to ours and was one of the only real friends I had growing up. She swung the heavy white cast on her right arm like a windmill—she'd fallen off the jungle gym at school the week before.

I tried to stop walking to tell her, but Thatcher wouldn't let me.

"I think . . .," I said.

Thatcher jerked my arm again, and I yelped like a reprimanded pup.

"Get lost," he told her.

"Your sister's a freak, man," Joe Baker said. He looked at the other kids for support.

Thatcher stopped and let go of my wrist, and when he turned to face Joe Baker eye to eye, we all stopped, silent and staring. Baker had forgotten his place. He was thirteen and one of the top dogs around the neighborhood kids, but Thatcher was nineteen—practically an adult—and there was simply no competing with that.

"What'd you call my sister?" Thatcher took a step toward him.

Baker took a step back. He looked at the other kids and then looked at the ground.

"Nothing, man, you know." He shrugged and lifted his hands to show innocence. "I didn't mean nothing."

From the safety of my immediate position, I stuck out my tongue at Moffit. Before I could put it back, though, Thatcher had me by the arm again and dragged me home like a ribbon in the wind.

If pressed, it would be hard for me to say honestly whether or not I actually saw the bottom of the quarry that day—if, in those last seconds before I was snatched away, I truly saw the depth of the gap. I had my *doubts, but I like to believe that I did. I like to believe that I didn't have to take anybody else's word for it anymore, that on that very day, I saw the giant truth for myself.*

CHAPTER ONE

May 15, 1982. Saturday. Finally. Ronnie stepped off the edge of the concrete patio and walked to the middle of the small, fenced-in back yard. She pushed her bangs from her face and squinted at the brightness of the morning sun. Thatcher was in the middle of the yard looking at a picnic table he'd just picked up from a garage sale. He stood with his hands on his hips, considering his bargain. She walked toward him, glancing at the white azalea bush that grew near the fence. It was getting ready to bloom and when it did, she would study the blooms and try to paint them accurately. The wet grass was cold and chilled Ronnie's bare feet.

"They wanted ten for it, but I talked them down to eight," Thatcher said.

It was one of those small, round picnic tables with a hole in the middle for the pole of a sun umbrella to go through. The green paint was peeling off the top, but the wood beneath was good and solid. Its legs were partly hidden in the overgrown grass.

"You gotta pay for the paint," Ronnie said.

Thatcher nodded. He took a pack of cigarettes out of his shirt pocket. He cupped his grease stained fingers around the flame, moving slow, his every action careful and deliberate. He always moved that way, slow and deliberate, and it drove Ronnie crazy. But then a lot of things about Thatcher drove her crazy. He walked to the patio, and she followed him.

"How do you want it painted?" she said.

He blew a cloud of smoke into the air, then turned his head and spit into the grass. "I don't care." He smoothed his hand over his unshaven jaw.

It was a good day to paint, Ronnie thought: clear sky overhead, not too humid, not too hot, not too much to think about.

"Hey," a voice called from the fence. "Hey, T. Is that you?"

Thatcher and Ronnie looked up. Ronnie jumped at the sight. Standing at the gate was the tallest man she had ever seen—tall as in unbelievably tall, tall as in giant sort of tall. He was enormous—enormous and frightening! Ronnie stared in disbelief. Long stringy brown hair hung in his face. The broad ridge of his brow bone hung over dark, wide set eyes--eyes that in the brow-bone's shadow looked small and sunken and beady. His cheekbones were broad, high, and definite, and seemed to be responsible for the oddly long distance between his eyes. He looked fake, Ronnie decided, like he had to be standing on stilts and wearing a Halloween mask—only he wasn't fake for there he stood, smiling at them, the corners of his mouth curling up. A humongous hand rested on the gatepost that was attached to Thatcher's garage. Ronnie realized that the top of the man's head was more than a couple inches higher than the top of the garage door. She couldn't look away from him, though she wanted to. She kept turning her head in Thatcher's direction to see his reaction, but her eyes remained fixed on the giant.

Ronnie followed the giant's form downward, to his neck, to his shoulders covered beneath the yellow t-shirt . . . and it was at that point Ronnie realized that the giant had breasts, that this he was not a he at all. Ronnie took a step back and put her hand on Thatcher's forearm absently pushing into him. He peeled her fingers from his arm and shook her off.

"Stay here," he said. He flicked his cigarette into the grass.

"Don't . . . " Ronnie whispered, but Thatcher was already walking away.

Ronnie was about to say his name, about to call out to him, when he turned back to her as if she *had* called out, as if he *had* heard her thoughts. His expression was peculiar, like he was both seeing her and not seeing her at the same time.

The giant started to let herself into the yard as Thatcher walked toward her. Ronnie's arms and legs felt suddenly heavy.

"T.," she said and bent to hug Thatcher.

Ronnie expected him to duck or run or push her away, but he stood there, his arms by his sides until he suddenly seemed to realize what she was doing and hesitantly raised them up to hug her back—only it was too late. Her awkward hug was over, and he was left holding his arms out to the air. He looked short standing next to her, which was odd. Thatcher was just over six feet tall and towered over Ronnie who was only five foot three and three quarter inches, but the giant looked to be at least a foot taller than Thatcher. Ronnie shook her head and blinked, trying to make sense of it.

They walked toward her. Thatcher looked pale. He was a strong looking man, lean but solid, long but not lanky. His arms hung listlessly as he walked, his legs moving in stiff, mechanical jerks as if he were consciously commanding each lift and step, lift and step. The woman seemed to be moving in slow motion, her long limbs swaying, slow and steady, back and forth like heavy pendulums. She was saying something to Thatcher, but Ronnie couldn't hear her. He stared straight ahead as he walked, but then suddenly stopped. They both looked at Ronnie, and Ronnie felt like she'd been caught in a spotlight. Thatcher looked startled by the sight of her, as if, for a moment, he'd forgotten about Ronnie altogether. The look in his eyes was so strange. Ronnie's face began to tingle, and her hand went to her cheek.

"You must be Veronica," the giant said.

Ronnie realized that the giant was talking to her. How did she know her name? She came across the yard toward Ronnie. Her voice was startlingly soft and surprisingly familiar. Where had she heard it before?

Ronnie didn't move, didn't speak. The giant's thick lips were parted and her dull brown eyes covered Ronnie in an expression of mild curiosity. Ronnie looked away from the giant's face to her blue jean shorts that were cut off just above the knee. Her knee bones were as big and round as Missouri cantaloupes.

"You've got freckles!" the woman said, suddenly smiling as she looked at Ronnie. Her voice sounded hollow and thick, like bubbling tar, boiling slow in a tar pot. "Angel kisses!"

Ronnie looked at Thatcher. Their mother had always called freckles angel kisses.

"I brought you something, Veronica," the woman was saying, "because I know you got a birthday coming up."

Ronnie focused on the woman's middle, on her elbow joints, on arms that hung long against her torso like the arms of an orangutan.

There is a giant standing in my back yard, Ronnie thought.

"It ain't nothing, but you don't find them many places. You should keep it. Never spend it," she said. "Maybe it'll be a collector's item someday."

She held out her immense hand. Ronnie looked at Thatcher for some kind of sign, but Thatcher was blank, staring off toward Ronnie but not at her, like maybe he was thinking they were in a dream as well. Ronnie reached her hand out slowly toward the woman to take the gift she offered. Her hand was shaking.

"Go on. Take it," the woman said. "I don't bite."

Ronnie unfolded a two-dollar bill.

"You don't find them everywhere, you know. You can't go to the store and expect someone to give you a two-dollar bill as change." She laughed. It was a quick, deep, one syllable "huh" sound, and for a second, Ronnie thought the woman was choking.

Thatcher took a quick step back.

"You just ain't going to see that happen, you know? Do you see what I'm saying? It's unusual."

Ronnie turned the bill over in her hand, rubbing the paper between her fingers. Yes. It was unusual.

"I guess you're pretty surprised to see me," the woman said. "I'm . . . do you mind if I sit down for a second?"

Thatcher said no a little too loudly. She sat on the old bench Ronnie had painted last summer. She had painted it white and then painted strands of ivy along the sides. The giant made the bench look small and unsteady which was odd, as Ronnie had always thought of it as being big and sturdy.

"My boy is sleeping out in the car," she said.

"You got a kid?" Thatcher said.

The giant leaned forward, resting her elbows on her knees. She wore raggedy looking, black, high-top tennis shoes on her giant feet. Ronnie looked at Thatcher's feet. The giant's were bigger.

"Yep." Her eyes closed as she smiled and lifted her face

slightly toward the sky. "You know how stupid young girls can be," she said, then opened her eyes and looked at Ronnie. "I mean . . ." she started, apologetically, but then stopped.

She looked at Thatcher.

"We've lived more than half our lives away from each other now, T."

Thatcher nodded but didn't say anything.

"And I'm looking at you here now." She looked at Ronnie. "And I'm seeing . . . oh all them freckles! You're just as cute as you can be, Veronica . . . I'm seeing . . . that you don't even know me at all." She slapped her knee trying hard to be casual. "You don't, do you?" she said, and Ronnie saw that giants showed sadness in their eyes, too.

Ronnie's mouth opened but no sound came out. She shook her head no, her mouth gaping in disbelief.

"This is Juanita," Thatcher said, only his voice didn't sound like his voice at all. His voice sounded scratchy and caught in his throat.

Ronnie squinted her eyes at Thatcher, thinking, trying to put the pieces together. Juanita? She looked at the huge woman who sat not five feet across from her on their little painted bench on their little concrete patio. Was he kidding? Ronnie wondered, really, was she dreaming? She'd read about lucid dreams in an English class. It would make sense if she were dreaming; after all, she had dreamed about Juanita many times before when she was younger, but in her dreams, Juanita—the lost sister—was beautiful, like the princesses in fairy tales, with golden hair and a china doll face. In her dreams, Ronnie welcomed Juanita. But this was something else. This was something new. This was a nightmare.

Ronnie had never had a nightmare about Juanita before. The hair on her arms stood in a chill, though the air was warm in the morning sun and the sky was still and clear and blue and the grass still held a kiss of dew. This was no dream.

"I drove to St. Louis," Juanita said, "because I told Bean—that's my son—that I'd show him the zoo up here. I live in Cabool. You know where that is, T.?"

Thatcher shook his head no.

"It's a ways away," she said. "About four hours south of here, I guess. Just a little town. Anyway, I stopped in Leasburg to get gas and, I don't know why, but I just decided to look in the phone book when we got up here, you know?" She rubbed her hands together absently. "And I didn't have no plan or nothing. I mean, I would have never gone to Momma's, of course, but I just wanted to see something, you know? I just wanted to see . . . I don't know what." Her voice got thicker and thicker as she spoke.

"And then I seen your name with your own address . . . and I seen Momma's under it, and . . . and I don't know, I just came here. I just came here and here I am and I don't know if it's a good thing or a bad thing." Her face scrunched up. Her eyes turned watery, and she kept blinking them and making faces.

"And it's like we're strangers now, and I don't know what's been done."

Thatcher raised a new cigarette to his lips.

"I . . . I . . . could I have a glass of water?" she asked.

Thatcher looked at Ronnie, and she jumped up like a flea. Her knees shook as she walked into the house, and she nearly dropped the glass as she got the water. She stood at the sink a minute, trying to take it all in.

Juanita.

When she went back outside, Juanita was openly crying, her wide face wet with tears that made it look like her nose was running. Ronnie's bangs fell into her eyes. She handed Juanita the water and stepped back quickly, pushing her hair back and nervously wiping her hands on the sides of her frayed denim shorts.

"Thank you, Veronica."

They stood there, Thatcher and Ronnie, watching Juanita drink the water. Ronnie felt stupid. What were they supposed to do? What were they supposed to say? Thatcher's expression didn't offer a thing, and Ronnie wondered whether he knew she was like this, wondered if he was happy to see Juanita or not. He seemed so cold, so stiff, so matter-of-fact, but when he looked up and their eyes met, Ronnie glimpsed the truth--Thatcher was not surprised by what he saw. He knew Juanita. He had always known her.

Juanita started to get up.

"I gotta check on Bean. He was so tired from all the driving."

"Go check on him, Ronnie," Thatcher said.

Ronnie looked at him like he was crazy, but she realized Juanita was watching. Juanita stared at Ronnie for a minute and then smiled turning her face toward the sky again, her mouth open, her eyes squinted shut. It made Ronnie think of a pumpkin head.

"You know, that would be so nice," she said. "I guess he'll be scared if he wakes up and don't know where he is." She turned her head sideways and nodded at Ronnie. "You're awful pretty, Veronica," she said. "You're so small and dainty looking." She held her hands up and looked at them. "I must be a real shock to you." She laughed her grunted "Huh."

Ronnie started to nod yes, then started to nod no. She didn't know what to say. She tried to smile and took a step toward the gate until Juanita's voice stopped her.

"Uh . . . I'm thinking again, Veronica," she said. "I'm thinking I better go check on him myself. He don't know you and I don't want him to be scared. I'll check on him myself."

Scared? Ronnie thought. Of me? Compared to you?

Juanita stepped off the patio and into the grass, then stopped and turned around.

"T., should I come back? I mean, if you want, I'll leave. I can just leave right now."

Thatcher didn't answer. He was staring at the old holly tree in the middle of the yard.

"T.," Ronnie said to jar him.

He looked at her and then looked at Juanita as if shaken awake.

"Yes!" he said. "Yes! Come back!"

She took a hesitant step, but then continued. Her gait had a clumsy rhythm to it—the top of her body swayed in an overly exaggerated motion to counter-balance the swing of her long, lanky legs. When she went out the gate and to the front of the house, Ronnie went to Thatcher.

"I can't believe you never told me about her," she whispered. "Did you see the size of her feet? My God. She's . . . "

"Shut up, Ronnie," he said.

Ronnie was startled by the strength of his voice.

"I'm just saying . . . "

He turned his head and burned a cutting line from his eyes straight at Ronnie, turning her confusion into hurt. Her mouth dropped open, but she remained silent. Thatcher turned away from her and walked toward the house.

A picture Ronnie had seen in the paper a few days before popped into her mind—a woman from Illinois who stood dazed amid the wreckage of her home. A tornado had hit, taking with it everything she owned. Ronnie was still standing there, still thinking about that picture, when Juanita and her boy came back. Thatcher was inside, and Ronnie realized that she was going to be alone out there with Juanita and her kid.

"I'm . . . Uh . . . I'll be right back," she said. Before

Juanita could even respond, Ronnie was in the door. She walked in so quickly that she nearly bumped into Thatcher. He was standing at the kitchen window looking out.

"I am *not* staying out there alone," Ronnie said.

"I can't believe she's got a kid," he said absently.

"Well, I hope *he* looks normal," she said. "This is too weird for me."

Ronnie took a step, intending to go to her room until Juanita left, but Thatcher blocked her way. She looked into his hard, cold glare. Thatcher grabbed her arm and pushed her roughly toward the back door.

"Hey!" she said trying to pull her arm away. "Stop!" She jerked her arm from his grip and walked out the back door.

Juanita stood in the grass with the boy standing in front of her. The tip of his head reached almost to the top of her thighbone. She leaned forward just enough to rest a large hand on the top of his head. Leaning like that made her shoulders look hunched. He needed a haircut. Half of his face was hidden beneath straight, brown, stringy hair that looked just like his mother's. His face was thin; his nose was long and straight: his skin was olive-tan: his eyes were dark and beady. He looked like a smart-aleck kind of kid to Ronnie. He was barefoot and his feet looked dirty. The t-shirt he wore once had a picture on the front, but it was so faded, the image was unrecognizable.

"Come on up," Thatcher said as they stepped out the door

Juanita pushed the boy forward. He stepped up onto the patio and went to the old picnic table.

"This is your Uncle Thatcher and your Aunt Veronica," she said.

She pointed at them as she said their names, drizzling them slowly over the little boy. He didn't react.

"This here is my boy, Benjamin. We call him Bean."

The boy kept looking toward the ground.

"I don't know why we call him Bean," she said. "We just do." She puckered her lips and looked sideways at her son.

"Hey, Bean," Thatcher said to the kid. He walked to him and stuck out his hand for a shake. Bean took a step closer to his mother.

"You thirsty?" Thatcher asked the boy. "You want a soda?"

He didn't answer, but looked at his mother.

"It's all right, Bean," Juanita said. "You can have one." She stroked the top of his head.

"Get him a soda, Ronnie," Thatcher said, matter of factly.

"Why don't you go with her, Bean?" Juanita said. Ronnie looked at Juanita, but she was looking at Thatcher as she spoke.

Ronnie waited a second, but when Bean didn't move, she held her hand out to him.

"Come on," she said. He didn't take her hand, but followed Ronnie inside like a puppy on a rope.

Inside, Ronnie opened his soda for him.

"You want a glass?"

He shook his head no. Ronnie leaned against the sink, staring at the kid as he drank. A memory flashed through Ronnie's mind—her own mother standing at the sink, washing dishes. Ronnie was four, maybe five years old.

"Momma," Ronnie had said. "T. said I got a sister named Juanita."

Her mother had stopped washing the dishes. Her hands rested, lying still in the soapy water.

"I told him he's a fat liar, Momma, but he says it's true. Are you gonna whip him for lying?"

Vivian had turned to Ronnie. She had turned to her

quickly and the slap she delivered sent a spray of water across Ronnie's face. It didn't hurt. Her hands had been wet and slippery and warm. But Ronnie had been stunned, stunned that her mother had turned on her like that. *She* hadn't been the one who was lying.

"You ever let me hear you say that name again and I'll put a belt on you," she said. "You understand?" She was looking down at Ronnie, pointing her index finger so that it nearly touched the tip of Ronnie's nose. Then, just as quickly, she walked out of the room, yelling Thatcher's name.

Ronnie stared at the boy. Bean. What kind of nickname was that? Thatcher came into the kitchen.

"Your Mom's ready to take you to the zoo," he said.

Bean got up and went to the back door. Ronnie noticed that the kid's hair and Thatcher's hair was almost the exact same shade of brown.

Thatcher followed him. Ronnie followed Thatcher.

"See you later," Thatcher told the boy, but the boy kept walking toward his mother.

Juanita had a goofy grin on her face. It made Ronnie think of the distorted and crazy fun house mirrors. She could hardly stand to look at her. Juanita stood there, rocking her body from side to side, a small giant step to one side and then back again, looking antsy in an elephanty sort of way.

"Well, let's go, Bean," she said. "We'll come back this afternoon, then. Right, T.?"

"Yep," he said. He was looking at the ground.

They stood there, Thatcher and Ronnie, planted like ivy, and watched their giant sister and her normal little son walk through the gate and down the driveway.

She waved to them twice before the house blocked her from view. "Okay," she said. "See you later then. See you later."

After Ronnie heard Juanita's car pull out of the driveway, she started toward the gate.

"Where do you think you're going?" Thatcher said.

"Out," Ronnie said.

"I thought you were going to paint."

"Things change, don't they?" Ronnie glared at him, daring him to try and stop her. He stared down at his shoes, nodding absently. Ronnie started to say something stupid like, "Why didn't you tell me," but she didn't even get out the first word. She knew better than to try and talk to Thatcher. He never talked about anything. He kept everything inside. He always had. And Juanita? He had kept the truth about Juanita locked away from her for 17 years. What did she expect now? Ronnie looked back at him for a second, but then walked away. It didn't matter anyway. Nothing he could have said would have prepared her for the reality of Juanita.

CHAPTER TWO

"Where *is* Cabool?" Donika asked.

Ronnie shrugged. She had walked the two streets over to Donika's house and told her everything. Now they were walking up the street to the Quick Shop.

"I would be so freaking," Donika said. "A giant sister."

"I am," Ronnie said.

She pushed the door open to the Quick Shop. Gayla stood behind the counter smoking a cigarette, even though it was against the rules for the rest of the cashiers. She was in her fifties with a couple of grown kids of her own and no husband in sight. Gayla managed the Quick Shop six days a week and had been working there for as long as Ronnie could remember. When Ronnie was 15, Thatcher had talked Gayla into hiring her as a stock girl. His mechanic shop was on the corner of McKnight and Manchester, just a few doors down from the Quick Shop, so he and Gayla knew each other pretty well. Over time, Ronnie had proven herself to be a good and dependable worker. When she turned 16, Gayla promoted her to cashier. It was an all right job as those sorts of jobs went. Gayla was nice enough, even though she saw it as her duty to give Ronnie (and anyone else who would listen) advice that she never asked for. It was better than the alternative, though, better than having to deal with her mother. Vivian was not the milk-and-cookie sort of mother, and it was always a good decision and never a wrong one to avoid her whenever possible.

"Good afternoon, Gayla," Donika said. Donika wriggled her fingers at Gayla and smiled. Ronnie admired the way Donika used her smile and spoke softly to charm people. Ronnie considered herself plain, ordinary, with too many freckles, too straight hair, and a nose that had too much sway through the bridge. Donika was not ordinary. Donika was beautiful. Ronnie admired her smooth brown skin and slightly curved nose, her voluptuous, heart-shaped lips that curved demurely at the corners. When she smiled, her eyes sparkled with a light as pleasant as the light of a firefly on a moonless night. People responded to her beauty—both men and women. Ronnie had noticed it for a long time, and at one point had even studied Donika, trying to understand what it was to be beautiful. She never went out of her house without makeup, her nails, and her hair done perfectly and made even simple outfits stylish by her choice of shoes, or a belt, or her jewelry. And there was something in Donika's walk—Donika always walked slowly and with her head held high, as if she were on display, even if no one else was around.

For a time, when Ronnie was in the 10th grade, she decided to try and be beautiful, too. She tried to act like Donika—to always wear makeup, to always have her hair combed and looking nice, to always talk to customers in a soft, feminine way. She tried it, and in all honesty, it worked. Everyone started paying attention to her—even boys—which made Ronnie extraordinarily nervous. In the end, she realized that she did not like being the center of attention, and besides that, it just took too much energy to present herself well all the time. She went back to just being herself, pulling her brown shoulder length hair back into a messy pony tail, wearing baseball caps, pinning her overgrown bangs (which she cut herself in front of the bathroom mirror) up with a barrette, not wearing much makeup unless it was a special occasion—which it hardly ever was—wearing cut-off jeans, plain t-shirts, and tennis shoes more than anything else.

"Hey, girls," Gayla said. She looked at Ronnie. "What you doing here on your day off?" Gayla smoothed the front of her sky-blue smock.

"I need my check," Ronnie said.

"Oh, I still got 'em in back. Will you watch the front for just a second?"

Ronnie nodded and stepped behind the counter.

Gayla came back out and handed Ronnie her paycheck.

"You know where Cabool is, Gayla?" Donika asked.

"Cabool?"

Gayla waved a long boney finger in the air as if to conjure the answer. She shut her eyes—eyes that Ronnie thought might have actually been pretty except that Gayla wore blue eye shadow, which sort of cancelled out anything nice about her eyes entirely. "Let's see . . ." Gayla said. "Cabool . . . hmmm. I heard of it, but I don't know." She fluffed her hair, trying to revive something that had never really been alive to begin with. Gayla's hair was the drabbest, grayish brown non-color of hair Ronnie had ever seen and though it was bone straight, Gayla kept it permed in a tortured, frizzed-up sort of way. Vivian said it was a sin what Gayla did to her hair—holding it hostage like that—and Ronnie agreed. Despite her being cosmetically challenged, though, Ronnie liked Gayla. She always talked nicely about her children.

"Some little po-dunk town somewhere, I guess," Gayla said. "Here. I'll find it." She walked toward the map stand and unfolded a Missouri map, mumbling the names of various towns as she looked. "What's in Cabool?" she asked.

"Ronnie's sister," Donika said.

Gayla stopped and looked over to Ronnie. "Are you kidding me?" She asked slowly, like she didn't trust them. "You never told me you had a sister."

"I had never met her before."

Gayla stared at Ronnie. "You *met* your sister?"

Ronnie nodded.

"When?"

"A little while ago."

"Are you kidding me?" she said again. "Cuz you don't have the gift of humor, let me tell you."

Ronnie opened her palms skyward. "Why would I kid you?"

"You seen Juanita," she said, stating it as a fact.

"How did you know her name?"

"Holy geez," Gayla said. "Juanita was here?" Gayla walked over to Ronnie and leaned in toward Ronnie to give her a test. "What does she look like?"

"If you have to ask that, you've never met her."

"I can't believe it," Gayla said. She slapped her hand down on the counter, banging a big turquoise ring that was too loose and always turned the wrong way on her finger. She immediately stopped and turned the ring up, checking the stone to see if it had been hurt.

"So you know her?" Ronnie asked. "You knew all this time I had this weird sister but you never said a word about it?"

"I don't go getting in other people's business. One thing I learned early on in life. Don't get in other people's business." She pointed to Donika. "Do you well to remember that."

"Why you pointing at me?" Donika said.

"I ain't pointing at you," she put her finger down. "I'm just saying."

"So you knew her?"

"Well, no. Not like . . . I knew who she was. Everybody did around here. I mean, ain't every day you see a kindergarten kid who is five feet tall, you know? Hey. Does T. know?"

"Know what?"

"That she's here. That she's in town."

"She was just at my house an hour ago, Gayla," Ronnie said. "It almost made me sick to look at her."

"Well ain't that something, honey," Gayla said.

* * *

Ronnie didn't want to see Thatcher when she got home. She didn't want to see his quiet stare or the sadness that always lingered behind his eyes. She had always assumed his pensive and many times taciturn personality was the result of always having to deal with Vivian. It had never really occurred to Ronnie that there was something else, that there was an entirely different reason for Thatcher's reluctance to show enthusiasm over anything. And now that the possibility had shown itself, it scared Ronnie. Thatcher hadn't been the least bit surprised by Juanita's appearance. He had been surprised by her showing up, yes, but not by her appearance, and frankly, Ronnie didn't know what to make of it. If she hadn't known something as big as this about her own family, what else did she not know?

The driveway was empty when she walked up to the house. She tried to make herself busy by lying on the couch and flipping through channels on the TV, but her mind kept drifting back to Juanita, so she finally pinned back her bangs with her favorite blue butterfly barrette, got a soda out of the refrigerator, and went to the garage to see what kind of materials she had for the table in the back yard.

She walked toward the table holding two sheets of sandpaper, intent on working, but everywhere she looked, she saw Juanita—standing at the fence, sitting on the bench resting her giant elbows on her giant knees. She remembered Juanita's gargantuan hand reaching out to her with that two dollar bill . . . Ronnie reached into her front right pocket, half expecting the bill to be gone, that she had imagined the whole thing, but there it was, the grainy feel of paper money between her fingertips. She shook her head, trying to push it out of her mind, and focused on the table, on running her hand over the dimpled top, on paying attention to the way that some areas on the table were chipped and peeling while other areas were bumpy and bubbly.

She picked at a chipped spot, trying to see how many layers of paint sat beneath. Getting a smooth surface back wasn't going to be easy, but sometimes old paint could be deceiving. Sometimes a rough and bumpy surface would sand smooth with hardly any effort, and sometimes it resisted. It all depended on what the circumstances had been like when the previous layers of paint had been applied, and what kinds of sins those layers were covering. You can cover things over with a pretty coat of paint, that was for sure, but it didn't mean the things that existed beneath it simply went away.

Ronnie ran the sandpaper across the top of the table. Her nerves jangled at the harshness of the first few scrapes. The image of Juanita—of her face lifted toward the sky as she laughed—covered Ronnie's thoughts like a gallon of green paint. She scratched across the wood until the paint began to give way and began to offer a comfortable cushion of dust. She stopped and rubbed a finger over the spot, thinking that it would be hard work going down to the wood, getting down to the bottom of it all. She thought of the look on Thatcher's face when he'd seen Juanita standing at the fence. He didn't give information easily. Ever. Ronnie knew one thing—she was in for hard work all around.

She threw down the sandpaper and went back to the garage for a more coarse grain. When she came back and started rubbing again, she used all her strength, leaning into it, taking the strength from her shoulder rather than just her wrist. Her arm muscles began to burn and beads of sweat began to form on her forehead and above her lip. Hard work, she thought. The words moved through her mind with rhythm, like the tic-toc of a grandfather clock, like the low and steady drumbeat measuring the song of a chain gang, or the steps in a warrior's march. Getting to the bottom of it would be hard work.

When Thatcher's truck pulled into the driveway, Ronnie kept sanding. She heard his car door slam and heard the swing of the front door being opened, but kept working. She heard the rustle of bags being set on the kitchen table, and the refrigerator being opened. Still she sanded, hard work, back and forth. She looked up only when she heard silence and felt Thatcher's stare from the dark, screened window. Ronnie looked at him, at his silhouette, but he turned away, and she could hear him unpacking groceries again. Hard work.

Eventually, he came outside. He and Ronnie glanced in the other's direction, but neither of them were willing to look the other in the eye. Thatcher turned his back to Ronnie and pulled the lid off the barbecue pit. She watched him, though she continued to sand —now in short, inattentive movements that accomplished nothing more than making a scratchy noise. Thatcher grabbed the bag of charcoal that was propped against the side of the house and started filling the old pit.

Silence. This is how it was with them. This is how it had always been. When things went wrong, it was their way of remaining a family. She looked at the table only to see that all of her effort had hardly made a dent in the paint at all. Maybe it wasn't worth it. Maybe all hard work brought was disappointment. Maybe it was all just one big giant waste of time. She dropped the sandpaper onto the patio and walked toward the back door, focusing her attention a bit too intently on smacking the paint-dust off of her arms before she went inside.

CHAPTER THREE

    This is what Ronnie remembered about her childhood: Vivian working a split shift at the Train Station Saloon, coming home every afternoon for few a hours, bringing cheeseburgers, bowls of chili, or toasted ravioli from the bar for their supper, and then going back to work around seven in the evening. At 10:00 o'clock each night, she called home to make sure that Ronnie and Thatcher were home and that they had finished their homework.

    Ronnie never knew how late into the night or morning Vivian worked because by the time she came home, Ronnie was usually asleep. Thatcher and Ronnie slept in the two bedrooms upstairs while Vivian had the bedroom in the far end of the basement. Sometimes Ronnie was awakened by the sound of her mother bumping into furniture as she made her way through a dark house. Sometimes she heard Vivian retching behind the closed door of the bathroom. Sometimes she heard the murmur of heavy whispers and stifled giggles trailing from the front door, through the kitchen, and down the basement steps. And in the morning, sometimes Ronnie found herself facing a strange man across the breakfast table, a man who tended to sip his coffee too loudly and who acted as if his presence in their kitchen was not only normal but also desirable.

Ronnie never knew what to do, but Thatcher did. On those mornings, he slammed his bedroom door when he came out of his room, walked straight past the kitchen without so much as a glance, went through the living room, and out the front door with another loud slam. Ronnie stared after him as she ate her cornflakes, wishing he would stay, but also admiring the way he showed his disapproval. Ronnie hated those men, but she was still young, still loyal to Vivian.

The outer room of the basement had a couch and chairs, a TV, and a small bar with its own little refrigerator and ice-box. Vivian kept little jars of cocktail onions, green olives, and cherries in that refrigerator, and while Thatcher only went into the basement to do his laundry, Ronnie liked being down there while Vivian was gone. She would sneak cherries and sip cherry juice straight from the jar, and then curl up on the tan couch and watch t.v. or read a book, waiting for her mother's day off to come.

On those days, Vivian and Ronnie had "cocktail hour" together in the late afternoon and watched movies late into the night. It was Ronnie's favorite treat, her favorite part of the week. Vivian made Ronnie kiddie cocktails of white soda with a cherry and a splash of cherry juice. Ronnie watched her mother closely and tried to imitate the way she sipped her drink, the way she rubbed the tip of her tongue on the lip of the glass for an instant before she took a sip. She would nod at Ronnie and smile at her and tell her that she was a good girl, a pretty little girl, and Ronnie loved it. She loved having Vivian all to herself—even though most of the time Vivian drank too much and fell asleep before the movie was even over. When Vivian was home, Thatcher either stayed in his room, blasting music, or simply left. That's what Ronnie remembered.

CHAPTER FOUR

Ronnie turned off the blow-dryer. She could hear the sound of voices coming from the living room, and knew it was Juanita. She heard the thickness of her low voice and knew without even seeing. Ronnie looked at herself in the bathroom mirror—at her eyes, her brow, her chin, her mouth—afraid she'd see some sort of resemblance to Juanita. But Ronnie's features were delicate, her brow was smooth. Ronnie took a deep breath. She didn't want to see Juanita again and stood there, staring at her reflection, waiting for some divine intervention, or instruction on evasion, but nothing came. When she heard their footsteps travel through the dining room and kitchen, she opened the bathroom door and stuck out her head. The mumble of Juanita's low voice trailed away as Ronnie heard the back screen door slap shut. Ronnie tried to cat-walk herself down the hallway, intending to stay in her room until Juanita was gone, intending to stay there all evening if she had to. But as she darted toward her bedroom door, a head peeped around the corner of the doorway from the dining room.

"Bean!" she said, jumping back. "You scared me!" Her hand was on her chest.

"We went to the zoo," Bean finally said.

"Hm," Ronnie said nodding politely, but looking past him, over him, to see if anyone was coming. She started to walk past him.

"You want to know my favorite animal?"

She stopped and turned around, surprised that he was talking to her, wondering what had happened to the shy kid from a few hours earlier.

"What," she said.

"Phil the Gorilla."

"Phil's dead," Ronnie said.

"I know, but he's still my favorite. He's like the big, Papa gorilla," he said. His eyes got big and he spoke excitedly. "You want to know why he's my favorite?"

Ronnie reached for the knob of her bedroom door. "Uh . . . not right now, Bean. I . . . . I gotta do something."

But Bean continued speaking as if he hadn't heard her. "Hey, you know, I like him because you can just stand there right in front of him and just look at him as long as you want to and he won't move. His hands are this big!" Bean held his hands up in measurement. "And you can see his fingernails real good. And his face. And he looks mean, but not if you look at his eyes. I looked at his eyes." Bean watched her. "You know it?"

Ronnie's hand rested on the knob of the door, but she looked down at Bean thoughtfully.

"He's so cool." His voice sounded dreamy and light.

"So your favorite animal at the zoo is dead, huh?"

"Yeah!" Bean saw the absurdity of it and started to giggle, covering his mouth with his hand as he laughed.

Ronnie laughed in spite of herself. Then her stomach growled loudly. Bean pointed at her and started laughing even harder. Ronnie looked over him, toward the kitchen.

"Bean," she whispered, "Is your Mom and T. outside?"

"Uh-huh."

"Are you sure? Go check for me."

Bean disappeared behind the corner and then a second later came running back.

"Yeah. They're out there just sitting there watching the grass grow," he whispered back.

Ronnie was surprised at the kid's wit. She found herself beginning to like him. She walked cautiously toward the kitchen, listening for the creak of the screen door opening. Bean followed her. She saw buns and paper plates and paper napkins and a bag of potato chips on the kitchen table. She opened the fridge and saw three containers from Pop's Deli. She lifted the lids on each: slaw, potato salad, and macaroni salad. Ronnie felt a nudge on her shoulder. Bean was standing right beside her as she squatted down. She put the last container back and leaned in to get a soda from the bottom shelf. Bean leaned in too and watched as she grabbed a Dr. Pepper. They stayed like that—shoulder to shoulder—for a second. Ronnie gave him a sideways glance. He wiped his nose absently with the back of his hand, his gaze remaining intent on the row of soda cans.

"You want one?" she asked him.

He nodded yes without taking his eyes off the cans.

Ronnie was reaching back into the refrigerator when she heard the familiar creak of the screen door. Her stomach flopped, and she shut her eyes. Shoot! Shoot! Shoot! She thought.

"Bean?" It was Juanita.

Ronnie sat frozen, squatted down in front of the refrigerator, hidden behind the open door. Maybe she'd just peek in and Bean would answer and then she'd go back outside. Ronnie stayed still, but when she heard Juanita's voice again, it was closer.

"What are you getting into?"

She felt the door jerk back a bit.

"Oh!" Juanita said, surprised. "Veronica, it's you!"

Ronnie stood up holding two cans of soda. She could feel her cheeks flushing, and tried to gulp her embarrassment down, but when she saw Juanita standing there, her embarrassment was immediately replaced by the renewed shock of seeing Juanita again. Her size in that little kitchen was incredible. She filled the room. Ronnie wondered how she'd even gotten through the doorway.

"Thatcher and me was just wondering where you were," she said.

Ronnie tried to look at her, but her eyes wouldn't go any higher than her middle, which was above the top of the refrigerator door.

"I'm a . . ." she started to say, but found herself speechless.

"We're barbecuing hamburgers," she said.

"Oh," Ronnie said, "Well, I'm not too hungry . . ." she couldn't look up. She just couldn't. She spotted a trail of grape juice that had been splashed on the inside of the refrigerator and hadn't been wiped down. She followed the trail down the side wall, until it disappeared behind the fruit drawer.

"We bought a peach pie for dessert. I mean, it's store bought, but . . . well maybe you'll want dessert."

"Oh. Yeah, maybe later."

"Oh. Okay then," Juanita said.

"Mom?" Bean was holding up the soda can, seeking permission.

"Well, I hope I see you later," she said to Ronnie. "I'm so happy to finally see you."

"Yeah, me too," Ronnie lied. She walked away, toward her room, feeling stupid, feeling guilty. But what else could she do? She didn't want to sit out there with them.

She was lying on the bed watching the portable t.v. Vivian had given her last year as a Christmas present. Mary Ann, Ginger, and Lovey were standing on a stage singing, "You Need Us" when Thatcher barged through the door.

"Hey!" Ronnie said sitting up. "Don't you come in here!"

And when she looked at him, she realized that he was drunk. Either she had missed it when he first came home, or Thatcher had been slamming them down while she was in the shower, but Ronnie saw it clearly now. His eyes were red, and he swayed ever so slightly as he stood in front of her. His upper lip curled into a lazy sneer under the anesthetic of alcohol.

"Geez, T." she said in disgust.

She started to lie down again, to dismiss him through her action, but he grabbed hold of her arm and pulled hard.

"Ow!" she slapped his shoulder, and tried to yank her arm back, but he didn't lessen his grip. He glared at her. Phil the Gorilla, Ronnie thought. Mean and ugly.

"We got company," Thatcher said. His face was inches from hers, and he doused her with the smell of beer and cigarettes.

"Let go." She jerked her arm from his grasp again, and this time he released her. "*You* got company," she said. "Not me."

He took a step back.

"You better get your ass out there, Ronnie."

"Screw you," she said. "I'm not going anywhere."

He pointed his finger at her and then tapped on her shoulder. "She came to see you."

"I don't even *know* her, T." Ronnie shook her head. "I can't even stand to look at her. I mean, what is she?"

"She's your sister."

"She's a freak," Ronnie whispered angrily, looking toward the door to make sure she wasn't around.

Thatcher's mouth dropped open and his shoulders stiffened. He clenched his fists and closed his eyes. Ronnie took a step away from him. He stood like that for a minute, a statue of offense, and then sat on the end of Ronnie's bed with a hard, sudden thump. Ronnie walked quickly over to her bedroom door, but she turned back to him, turned back to see what he was going to do. She expected him to say something mean. She expected him to call her a name, or threaten her. She did not expect to see the burdened droop of his shoulders or the weary look of defeat that had spread across his face, like a soldier contemplating the truth of war, like a firefighter handing a house over to flames. She did not expect her angry brother to drop his head into his hands.

He rubbed his face in his open palms. "Look," he said in a slow voice. "She's our sister."

Ronnie didn't say anything.

He stood up and stared at her. "You know what?" he said, "I don't have to care anymore. As a matter of fact, I don't care. You do whatever the hell you want to do."

He pushed past her, and she stepped aside.

Didn't care anymore? Ronnie thought. Thatcher didn't care about anything to begin with.

"I *will* do what I want, " she called after him.

But she went to her bed and sat down, stewing over his unexpected retreat. What a joke. *Do what you want.* As if that had ever been a real option. Ronnie had been hearing that phrase her entire life from both Thatcher and her mother. They said it as a last resort, to pour on the guilt and make everything her fault. If Ronnie did what she wanted, she would have asked about Juanita all those years ago when she was told to be quiet. If she did what she wanted, she would be living as far away from Thatcher and Vivian as she could. They were just a couple of drunks anyway. If she did what she wanted, Ronnie would never see Juanita or Bean again—what were they to her?

CHAPTER FIVE

It took a while, but eventually the guilt worked. Ronnie went through the kitchen and stood inside the back door, resting her arms on the screen door frame. She hated Thatcher. She really did.

He and Juanita were sitting in the adirondack chairs. Bean sat on one of the rough sanded benches for the picnic table. He was playing with a handful of rocks. He moved them around on the table, talking to them, arranging them in a circle, lining them up in an even row, then arranging them in a circle again. He looked up at Juanita.

"Can I watch t.v.?"

"I guess," Juanita said. She took a sip of beer.

Bean ran toward the screen door, and Juanita's eyes followed him, but when Bean got to the door, her eyes landed on Ronnie. Hair fell into Juanita's eyes, and she brushed it away with a slow sweep of her fingers.

"Veronica," Juanita said.

Thatcher looked up but remained silent. His hard stare showed no sign of mercy or relief or forgiveness or anything else at Ronnie's acquiescence to his demand that she come outside.

Ronnie opened the door, and Bean ran past her. Ronnie stepped out of the doorway and stood for a second, unsure of where to go or what to do, but then walked toward a lawn chair that leaned against the holly tree in a patch of ivy near the edge of the patio.

"There's plenty of room over here," Juanita said.

"That's okay," Ronnie said quietly. She glanced at Thatcher, nervously, worried that he would say something cutting, that he would somehow bring Ronnie's feelings into center ring. "I want to be in the shade," she said, trying to sound casual, trying to make her voice light and carefree though it felt scratchy and stuck in her throat.

Thatcher stood up and went to the barbecue pit.

"It smells good, T.," Juanita said.

"They're ready to go," he said, picking up a plate from the picnic table and taking burgers off the grill with a fork. One fell off and into the flames.

"Aw shit. I dropped it," he said grinning and looking over his shoulder. "I'll jus' give that one to Ronnie over there." He pointed to Ronnie with his fork and shook it.

"Oh, wait," he suddenly said. "I got stuff in the refrigerator." The word refrigerator came out sounding like "friger-ator."

"Go get it, Ronnie," he said.

Ronnie didn't move. She may have given in, but that didn't mean she was going to help him. But when Juanita said, "I'll do it," Ronnie felt a flush of fire rush to her cheeks.

"Oh . . . uh, that's all right." And walking inside, she realized that she had an opportunity to escape the scene for a minute if nothing else. She looked at the kitchen windowsill over the sink, wondering how many beers Thatcher had so far, not that it mattered, not that she could do anything about it. His keys rested on the sill, as always. She took the key to his truck off the ring, put it in her pocket, and returned the rest. It was bad enough having to sit out there at all, but the fact that Thatcher was drunk made her seethe all the more—and now she figured she had to babysit, too.

Ronnie took her time, bringing everything out in three trips when she could have easily done it all in one.

"T. was telling me he runs Oliver's Mechanic shop," Juanita said as Ronnie put ketchup and mustard on the picnic table.

"Own," Thatcher said raising his hand. "I own it."

"Hey!" He sat up straight and leaned toward Ronnie. "She even remembers Mr. Oliver."

Juanita tried to smile, squinting her eyes up at the sky. "Yes," she said, nodding.

"Yep. Me and Philip own it."

And he told her all about it, how Thatcher and Philip had started hanging around Mr. Oliver's shop up on Manchester Road when they were in middle school. How Mr. Oliver tried to run them off at first, but they went to that shop every day and pestered that old man for such a long time, he finally put them to work, making them prove themselves in small ways like running errands and sweeping the floors. Ronnie had heard the story a million times. How, as time went on, Oliver let their responsibilities grow. How he let them run the cash register or fill out inspection sheets. How he showed them how to take a car apart and put it back together again, showed them how to figure out what was wrong with a car, and then taught them how to fix it. How Oliver didn't have any sons, only one daughter. Yaddy yadda. Ronnie perched again on her chair in the ivy.

Thatcher took a long drink from his beer and shook his head slowly. "Tell Ronnie what you do," he said to Juanita.

Juanita smiled at Thatcher. "It's so good to see you, T.," she said. Her eyes got watery and she was quiet for a minute, but then she turned to Ronnie. "I sell flowers," she said.

"No, no, no," Thatcher said. "Tell her the whole story like you told me."

Juanita raised her eyebrows and looked at Ronnie, suggesting with her eyes that she would humor Thatcher.

"Well," she said glancing at Thatcher and then back to Ronnie, "Daddy lives down the road from me, back home. Not real close or nothing. You can't see his house from mine, but it's just about a half a mile away, if that." Juanita took a sip of beer. "He bought this chunk of land a long time ago—after we left—and raised cows."

The word "Daddy" started to sink into Ronnie's skin like tick fangs, along with the words, "after we left." Who was she talking about? Their father? *Her* father? Juanita talked about him as if he were real, as if he had existed all the time. What was this?

Juanita looked at Thatcher with a curious grin. "Ha!" she burst out. "Can you believe that? Cows!" Thatcher started laughing again. He was sauced, and Juanita was talking about cows, but Ronnie was still thinking about the word, and the effortless way it fell from Juanita's lips—father. A foreign concept, or an abstract one, like the Easter Bunny or Santa Claus at the very least. Never actually seen, yet supposedly real and out there somewhere.

Ronnie had never really tried to latch on to the idea of a father as if it had anything to do with her. Like Juanita, mentioning him had been off limits—only no one ever had to tell Ronnie that. She knew that one by instinct. But now Juanita was there, talking about her father . . . the man that would be Ronnie's father, too. In a way, the idea of a father was even more mysterious to Ronnie.

"And there was this little white house down the road," Juanita was saying. "It wasn't part of the property, and it wasn't big or nice or nothing. Just a few acres or so. But when the old man who lived there died, Daddy bought the house and the land behind it. It worked out real good. He let me rent the house real cheap. I worked at the lumber yard then." She laughed her one syllable laugh. "Ain't very lady-like, I know, but I'm pretty strong and they paid me all right." Juanita was laughing. "And so after awhile . . . when I . . . after I had Bean . . . ," Juanita looked down at the table and frowned for a second, her heavy brow furrowing over her deep-set eyes, "Well . . . I started up my flower business."

She looked up and smiled at Ronnie in a humble sort of way, with her chin tucked in. "I got a little plant nursery behind the house now," she said. "I love flowers. Had a greenhouse built, and it does all right."

"Ain't that nice?" Thatcher said mimicking Juanita's slow talk. His tone was off. Ronnie snapped from her paternal reverie. He was making fun of the way Juanita talked, and when he turned away, Ronnie saw his smirk. He was testing Juanita, waiting to see if she'd react, but Juanita didn't seem to notice at all. Juanita looked mild and peaceful and must have still been thinking about all the pretty little flowers because it was clear that she didn't have a clue to what had just happened, a fact which both relieved and irritated Ronnie. Thatcher walked into the house. "Ha!" They heard him chide from the kitchen. Ronnie bit her lip and looked at the grass. Why did he do that to Juanita?

Something had shifted in Thatcher while Juanita was talking. Ronnie knew it well, like the click of a telephone being disconnected, like the snap of a television being turned off—instantly off, instantly dark. The idea tasted sour in her mouth. This was Thatcher stepping into the mean side of his drinking, and Ronnie knew it meant nothing but trouble.

She sat up straight, unsure of what to do. Juanita didn't know this side of Thatcher. She didn't recognize the shift in him. He was like a sharp blade gone dull and jagged. Everyone knows that a dull blade hurts more than a sharp one, and now came the danger of it being swung carelessly. The laugh was the thing—the taunting swing of the blade, the invitation to trouble, the dare. It sat before them—only Juanita didn't know. She didn't know that when Thatcher got like this, you simply backed off. You stayed away from him, and he stayed away from you. No harm, no foul.

Ronnie peeked over at Juanita. Their eyes met, and Juanita tried to smile, but Ronnie could only shrug her shoulders and bite at her thumbnail. She would just wait and see. Maybe everything would be all right. Maybe it was no big deal, though history and her heart warned her otherwise.

Thatcher came back with new beers and handed one to Juanita. It wasn't like Ronnie suddenly let go of all of her feelings and now cared about Juanita—she didn't. But Ronnie didn't have the heart to leave *anyone* with Thatcher when he turned. He was a jerk, and she seemed to be the only one who could deal with him. It would be cruel to abandon Juanita now, like putting a lightening bug in a jar overnight. Ronnie didn't know what to do, but she knew she couldn't do that.

"Daddy's been good to me, T.," Juanita said quietly.

Ronnie sucked in her breath, wanting to stop her and not stop her at the same time.

Thatcher stared at his older sister for a minute, his chin jutting out like a rebellious child. "Yeah, well," was all he finally said. "Hey, why don't you get your boy and let's eat."

"You know what it was like for me," Juanita said. "You remember, don't you?"

Thatcher turned back to the door and yelled Bean's name. Something deep and scary and bottomless sat right in front of them, an abyss, a giant hole that led to places they had never been before—well, places Ronnie had never been before. Thatcher and Juanita—they already knew the truth, they'd been to the bottom of it, but not Ronnie. Ronnie didn't know anything, but she realized that if they kept talking she just might get a good glimpse of the giant story no one had bothered to tell her.

She sat quietly, leaning forward and listening intently. If she were careful, she could sneak up to the edge of her own family and take a quick peek at the truth before anyone even realized she was there. Ronnie wanted to hear what they had to say more than she cared about sparing Juanita's feelings. She sat on her hands, rocking back and forth, back and forth, waiting for the secrets and stories and answers to flood onto the path before them and break the barrier that kept her from the truth.

"You remember, T.?" Juanita was watching him.

But Thatcher refused to respond. He turned his back and started flipping the burgers, his shoulders taut, his movements stiff and angry. Juanita didn't say any more. She looked down at her hands and then stood up.

"I . . . I'll get Bean," she said to no one in particular and then walked into the house.

Ronnie closed her eyes. She couldn't believe it. All this talk. All this tension, all leading to nothing. Nothing now. Nothing new. Nothing for her to do but wait.

CHAPTER SIX

The afternoon light began its daily routine of fading from the dazzling yellow-bright into the softer, clear blue-tinged light that comes a good way before the grays of dusk. Ronnie watched Juanita as she ate. It was not an attractive sight—the slow smack of lips, the swing of an oversized jaw, the disturbingly deadened, unaffected glaze that filled Juanita's far-set eyes. Ronnie's own appetite had long ago dissolved into a vague notion, taking a back seat to her immediate revulsion. How could the situation in front of her be real? How could this woman be Juanita? How could so many different emotions be swimming in Ronnie's head at once?

Thatcher stood at the grill, eating a hamburger, not bothering with a plate or a napkin or any condiments, not bothering with any of the side dishes. He wolfed his meal as if eating were a nuisance. When he finished, he wiped his hands on his blue jeans and fell into the chair across from Juanita with a satisfied sounding thump. He pulled an after-meal cigarette from his t-shirt pocket.

"It's really good, T.," Juanita said with a full mouth. Her tongue poked out to lick of blob of potato salad from her lower lip.

Ronnie covered her face with her hands, wondering how long this torture would last. Her nerves stretched tight across her gut like a piano wire. Bean sat silently beside Juanita, ignoring his dinner and playing once again with his small colony of rocks. Juanita pointed to his plate.

"Bean, eat your supper," she said.

Bean nodded but continued playing.

"You know," Thatcher said out of the blue, pointing a finger at Juanita, "I don't even want to hear about him, okay?"

"Bean," Juanita said to her son but looked at Thatcher as she spoke, "I told you to eat your supper."

"I don't want to hear it. I don't want to hear it. I don't want to hear it," Thatcher said. His voice slurred like mud water on the inside of a bucket.

"Okay, T.," Juanita said quietly, humoring him. "I understand. I agree. We won't talk about it right now." Her stare sent a clear message that Bean's presence was an issue—but Thatcher's eyes were shut, and his head was turned toward the yard. Juanita turned to Ronnie, and her eyes went from hard to soft.

"Ronnie," she said, trying to change the subject, "You're sure awful quiet over there."

Ronnie shrugged.

"She's always quiet," Thatcher said. He stood up and went into the house.

Ronnie's face tingled with anxiety, and she bit her lower lip. She was alone with Juanita and Bean.

"I guess you and T. are pretty close, huh?" Juanita asked.

"Not really," Ronnie said. She bent down and pulled up a handful of grass and started picking through the pieces, throwing the shortest ones out and moving the longest blades into a small pile on the palm of her cupped fingers. She focused on each blade, looking at the greenness of them against her peach skin.

"How long have you lived here? I mean, away from your mother?"

"I don't know," Ronnie said, not looking up. She balanced the longest blade of grass on the top joint nearest her fingertips. "Since I was 12 or 13, I guess."

"This is odd," Juanita said. She sighed loudly. She tucked her chin into her chest, but her eyes rolled upward, looking toward Ronnie. "I don't think T. likes me here." She tried to smile, but her face scrunched, twisting her lips into more of a wince than a smile.

It dawned on Ronnie, momentarily forgetting about her own feelings, that this visit, perhaps, burdened Juanita, too, that this was just as difficult for Juanita as it was for Ronnie or Thatcher. And if Juanita thought she knew Thatcher before, it was quite clear that she didn't know him now—not like Ronnie knew him, anyway. Juanita was just as ignorant about Ronnie and Thatcher's life now as Ronnie was about Juanita and Thatcher's life in the past, and that fact made a small dent in the armor Ronnie had placed over her feelings so far.

"He just drank too much is all," she said and dropped the handful of long blades to the ground.

"I guess it wasn't fair of me to drop in like this. I was just hoping . . . well . . . well, the truth is, I don't know what I was hoping. I wasn't thinking."

Ronnie nodded. Juanita stood, long arms, long body, long legs, all looming large

"This is pretty." Juanita bent over the old bench Ronnie had painted a year before.

Thatcher opened the screen door and stood still in the doorway.

"Do you drink this much all the time, T.?" Juanita said, turning to face Thatcher fully.

Ronnie's jaw dropped at the bluntness of her question, but Thatcher laughed.

"Well," he said, "It's a party, isn't it? A reunion. Nothing's wrong with drinking at a party," he said. He leaned against the doorjamb defiantly, his arm stretching to keep the screen out of his way.

"You remember the parties?" he said to Juanita. He walked out onto the patio and slumped back into his chair. "You remember them decoy ducks that one year? New Year's Eve? Remember? Him trying to throw them ducks over the roof?"

Thatcher looked off into the distance, seeing the memory in his mind. He lifted his arm and threw an invisible decoy. "Wha," he said for sound effect. He grinned, lost in a memory, watching an imaginary duck sail over the roof. "You remember?" He looked at Juanita. "That was the one time Mom had to scrape Dad up off the floor wasn't it?"

Juanita pursed her lips, but didn't respond, but Ronnie hung on every word.

"And that," Thatcher said, picking up his beer, "was exactly one week before you left." He tipped the beer toward Juanita in the gesture of a toast and then took a long swallow.

Juanita frowned, her face dark and creased, her chin quivering. Tears welled in her eyes and fell over the brims, rolling down and across her broad cheekbones. But she remained silent, caught in Thatcher's momentarily merciless stare.

Bean coughed and Thatcher glanced over at him, and whatever he saw there, whatever he saw in that boy stopped him. His face softened and the harsh light went out of his eyes. Perhaps he saw something he recognized in the boy. Perhaps he saw himself. He shook his head, clearing his thoughts to a softer patch of grass.

"He's cute, you know," Thatcher slurred.

All eyes went to Bean, but Bean was immersed in an epic battle between rock piles, and it made Thatcher smile in confirmation. He said it again, "Your kid is cute." And this time Bean looked up at him.

Juanita nodded. The three of them—Thatcher, Juanita, and Ronnie—watched Bean collect his rocks one by one into an awkward fist and carry them like treasure to the back door. Thatcher took a step forward and held the door for him. Juanita wiped her mouth and her cheeks with her open palm and then smoothed the hair from her heavy forehead.

"I paid three dollars for that bench." Thatcher said, pointing to an old painted bench that sat against the house. "It looked like a piece of crap, but Ronnie fixed it up. Give her a piece of crap and she'll paint it. Make it look brand new, don't you, Ronnie? She paints everything." He made a careless sweep of his arm and didn't seem to notice when some of his beer spilled onto the patio.

"Now she's gonna paint this." He pointed to the old picnic table Bean had been sitting at. "I got it this morning for ten bucks."

He looked at Ronnie and smiled, but then stopped himself. "No! Wait. They *wanted* ten, but I only paid eight!" He sat on the newly abandoned bench. "We should go get some paint right now so you can start painting. You can show Juanita how good you paint."

Ronnie rolled her eyes and turned her head to the yard. Angry idiot, she thought.

"I'll take you," he said. "Come on. I'll drive you right now."

Ronnie looked at him, unimpressed, and shook her head. Juanita froze, looking between them, first at Ronnie, then Thatcher, then Ronnie again.

"He can't drive now," Juanita said to Ronnie. Her mouth fell open and she sat up straight.

"I don't even know what color I want it painted yet," Ronnie said, her voice mild and even.

"Hey," Juanita said.

"That doesn't matter," Thatcher said to Ronnie. "You can pick a color when we get there."

"I don't work that way," Ronnie said.

"You gotta see her paint." Thatcher turned to Juanita. His red eyes had become bleary and he swayed when he tried to stand up. "Come on, Ronnie." He stood with not a little effort and held a hand out to Ronnie as if he were asking for a dance, as if she were going to take it and off they were going to go, just like that.

"You can't drive, T.," Juanita said more insistently, but neither Ronnie nor Thatcher seemed to listen.

"I'm not going with you," Ronnie said.

"Well, then okay," Thatcher said. He jutted his chin out. "Then I'll just go pick it out myself and you'll be stuck with whatever I pick."

"Veronica," Juanita said, slowly standing up.

"Then you can paint it yourself," Ronnie said to Thatcher.

"I will," he said.

"Then do," she said back.

"Well okay."

Thatcher tried to take a step forward, but stumbled back instead and had to take a quick step to keep his balance. He walked inside and grabbed his keys from the windowsill.

"T., you shouldn't drive." Juanita was beyond alarmed. "Right, Veronica?" She looked at Ronnie, but Ronnie threw her hands up.

"Shouldn't, couldn't, wouldn't . . ."

" . . . but will," Juanita finished for him.

"Yes!" Thatcher pointed at her, laughing! "Yes! You remember!"

But Juanita wasn't smiling.

Ronnie raised her eyebrows in surprise. Shouldn't, couldn't, wouldn't, but will. It was a line they had heard Vivian say a hundred times growing up.

"It's okay," Thatcher said as he walked toward the gate. He held a hand up to assure Juanita.

"Veronica," Juanita said. "You got to do something." She started toward the gate and when they heard Thatcher's truck door slam, she turned back to Ronnie, angrily, "Veronica!"

Ronnie reached into her pocket. "It's okay," she said, holding up the ignition key. "He isn't going anywhere."

Juanita looked at Ronnie, her anger turning to confusion. A minute later they heard the truck door slam again and Thatcher walked up to the gate. "Ronnie. Give it here."

"If you can't see it on the ring you shouldn't drive."

"I swear I'm going to make a copy and then *I'm* gonna hide it from *you*!"

Thatcher walked into the yard, walked across the patio to where Juanita stood. "I put up with this kind of crap from her." He pointed at Ronnie and then shooed his arms toward her and walked into the house.

Juanita followed him to the door. "Bean, come here!" she shouted. She turned and looked at Ronnie. "Bean!" she shouted again. When Bean came outside, Juanita told him to stay on the patio.

"Look," she said to Ronnie, "That ain't funny. That ain't a game you're playing."

But she was wrong. It was a game, a game they had played many times before.

"I ain't trying to tell you how to live, but . . ."

"It *is* a game," Ronnie said.

Just a game. All of it. Everything. Ronnie saw that clearly now, just like it was a game that Thatcher had never told her the truth, and just like it was a game that Vivian had never allowed her to ask the simplest question. And now, Juanita showing up out of the blue, playing the long lost sister? That was nothing but a game, too. And it didn't matter, Ronnie decided. None of it. They would all just keep on spinning and spinning around in circles forever and ever, getting nowhere.

Ronnie and Juanita stood regarding each other, Ronnie feeling resigned to never knowing and Juanita feeling alarmed and confused, two sisters from different worlds with nothing to say. Finally, Juanita nodded in a kind of deference to Ronnie's silence and walked over to the bench. She sighed, looking down.

"It's clematis," she said absently. She leaned over and rubbed her large hand across the painted top and then turned to Ronnie. "Did you know that?"

Ronnie shook her head no.

"So you knew he would do that? You knew he would try to drive?"

Ronnie nodded.

"And would he have drove if he had the key?"

"No."

Juanita wrinkled her brow. "You know that?"

"He's just messing with us," Ronnie said, feeling sort of guilty that she'd put Juanita through a fright—but then, she deserved it, showing up and acting like she knew Thatcher.

"You know, I think it's time for me to go," Juanita said.

Ronnie followed Juanita inside, watching her duck her head to go through the doorway. In the living room, Thatcher was splayed out on the couch in front of the TV passed out. Bean sat in front of the TV, watching a cartoon, his rocks spread out in front of him on the carpet.

"See?" Ronnie said. "He'll sleep it off."

"He's . . . is he like this a lot?"

"Not too much. Every once in awhile."

Juanita nodded, wanting to believe her.

"T.," she said softy, in a whisper, not to wake him, but to simply say his name. She turned toward Ronnie. "What else do you paint?"

"Just stuff like that mostly . . . well . . . except my room, but I'm not finished with that yet."

"What'd you do in there?"

"I'm painting a wall."

"Can I see?" Juanita asked.

"It isn't done," Ronnie said.

"That's okay. I'd like to see it if you'll show me," Juanita said.

They went to Ronnie's room.

Ronnie walked quickly to her bed and threw the top cover over the mattress in an effort to make it. Her clothes were scattered on the floor, and she reached down and picked up the shirt and shorts she had worn the day before. She put the clothes on top of her desk, on top of scattered school papers, next to a couple of empty soda cans and dry paint brushes, feeling embarrassed about the mess.

"Oh, Veronica," Juanita said. She stood in front of the inside wall, staring at the different shades of greens, and browns, and yellows that made up the jungle mural with flowers here and there for color. She looked even bigger in the smallness of Ronnie's room. She reached out a long arm and ran a long finger along the curve of a palm leaf at the top—a place Ronnie had needed a step-ladder to reach.

"It's beautiful."

"I'm not finished," Ronnie said quickly. "I was thinking of adding some animals, but I'm not sure." She looked at the fern-looking plant in the left corner, thinking it needed some black to define it. She felt the heat of Juanita's eyes on her, but concentrated on a space on the wall she had started to fill with grass.

Juanita took a step to the other side of the room to where an old easel sat with a blank canvas.

"And you paint pictures, too?"

"Oh, that's just kind of a joke. . . . T. gave it to me." He had picked it up for a few dollars and given it to Ronnie along with the canvas for her birthday the year before. "I don't . . . No. I don't paint pictures." The truth was, though, that it was the first canvas Ronnie had ever owned, and it scared her. She didn't mind painting on walls or benches or stuff like that, but to paint on a canvas . . . that required something real, something true . . . that required real knowledge, and Ronnie didn't know anything.

Bean came into the room.

"Momma . . ." he said, pulling at Juanita's shirt bottom. "There's nothing to do."

"Oh, now, shush," Juanita said. "We're leaving right now, but look what your Aunt Veronica painted."

But Bean kept pulling on the bottom of her shirt as if he actually had a chance of moving her.

"He's tired," she said, apologizing. "We're getting ready to go right now, Bean. Go find something to do for a minute. I want to talk to Veronica."

Bean sulked out.

"I just . . . ." Juanita looked like she was about to cry. "I don't know what it's been like for T. since I left. I never really thought . . . ." She wiped her eyes. "I just thought about myself, but it ain't all about me." She took a deep, shuddering breath and tried to smile.

"He's fine," Ronnie said.

"And you, too . . . I just . . . I don't mean to start nothing bad here. I'm just . . . I'm just glad to finally see you."

Ronnie nodded, not sure what to say.

When Juanita and Bean left a few minutes later, Thatcher was, of course, still passed out cold. Juanita bent down low to hug Ronnie, and it took all of Ronnie's will not to back away, not to tense her body to the point of breaking.

"You keep that two-dollar bill in a special place," she said. "I hope I can see you another time, Veronica. I would really like to get to know you."

Ronnie offered nothing more than a noncommittal nod. She watched Juanita and Bean from the front door. The street seemed to be unusually active that day, though it took her a minute to realize why. Mr. and Mrs. Knoll were sitting on their front porch. They never did that. Tom Gibson was washing his car when Ronnie knew she saw him wash it just two days earlier. Mr. Horseman was peeking out his window, and the Welch kids were stopped on their bicycles, staring at Juanita from half way down the street. Ronnie's face burned red—though she wasn't quite sure who she was embarrassed for—Juanita, or herself. She couldn't really blame the neighbors. She would have come out to see the giant woman, too. Juanita bent her long limbs, folding them into the truck, making Ronnie think of circus clowns getting into those crazy little cars. The truck was big, but Juanita filled it up.

She backed out of the driveway, grinding the gear from reverse to first, and started down the street. Ronnie and all the neighbors watched as the giant drove away, becoming smaller and smaller in their fields of vision until she turned the corner and disappeared from sight completely, perhaps, Ronnie thought, forever, leaving Ronnie stuck somewhere between relief and dread.

CHAPTER SEVEN

It wouldn't be an unusual thing for Vivian to stay in bed all day on a Sunday, so Ronnie didn't really expect to see her when she walked to Donika's house the next morning. Still, Ronnie was careful. The Wilsons lived right next door to Vivian. Ronnie walked the back way—cutting through yards, and climbing a couple of fences instead of walking down the middle of the street like usual. It would be harder for Vivian to see Ronnie this way if Vivian were outside or just happened to be looking out the window. Ronnie jumped the last fence, into the Wilson's backyard, and walked along the chain-link, close to the bushes and under the shade of the tall pin oak that grew on the side of the yard furthest from Vivian's house. Ronnie kept a cautious eye out as she walked. Vivian's curtains were still drawn. That was a good sign. Ronnie relaxed, walking toward the Wilson's swirl-patterned, two story, white stucco house.

Thatcher had moved out of Vivian's house the first chance he got, which came finally when he was 19. At first, he lived not even two blocks from them over in the apartments across McKnight Road, but it was far enough. Ronnie was nine, and Thatcher was always nice about letting her come over and just be there. She liked life better at Thatcher's place and, generously, he seemed to understand that. Ronnie didn't like being home alone at night, and she didn't like waking up with strange men in her house either, so she spent a lot of nights sleeping on Thatcher's couch. Thatcher didn't seem to care about that either. Vivian sure didn't care as long as she knew where Ronnie was. A few years went by and Thatcher moved into the small, two bedroom brick house where he lived now. He bought a twin bed and a dresser and told Ronnie she could stay there if she wanted to. Vivian didn't like that so much. As a matter of fact, she didn't like that idea one bit—though that's exactly what Ronnie decided to do.

The Wilsons, though, they were Ronnie's model of a *real* family. Their house was always alive and filled with people. Mr. and Mrs. Wilson had eight kids and eighteen grandkids and they visited on a constant, revolving basis. Philip was the second to youngest Wilson and the same age as Thatcher. He and Thatcher had gone through grade school and high school together and did everything together. Philip still lived at the Wilson's, along with his older sister, Sharon, who wasn't around much because she worked all the time. Sharon was Donika's mother, and they had been living with the Wilson's ever since Sharon divorced her wife-beating husband.

When Ronnie was young, her mother had worked out a deal with Mrs. Wilson. If Thatcher needed any help, or if he needed to go somewhere without Ronnie, Ronnie was supposed to go to Mrs. Wilson—although most of the time Ronnie was over at the Wilson's house anyway, playing in the back yard with neighborhood kids, and grandkids, and any other kids Mrs. Wilson babysat. They were good people, good friends to Ronnie and Thatcher, folding them into their own family like a couple of lost sheep.

Ronnie undid the gate and walked along the driveway to the front of the Wilson's house. Mr. and Mrs. Wilson were sitting on the front porch steps. Mrs. Wilson was on the top step. Her eyes were closed and her face was lifted to the morning sun. Her profile was outlined with a line of white light that defined her sharp chin, full lips, and high forehead. She wore a breezy, sleeveless summer dress that made Ronnie think of an African Queen. Her hair was turning gray at the temples and was pulled back into a high, tight, bun. Mr. Wilson sat a step below her, his thick forearms resting on his thighs, both hands wrapped around a steaming mug of coffee. He looked like he was trying to be content and relaxed, but his legs jittered slightly, open and shut, open and shut. A few weeks back, he had retired, suddenly finding himself a busy man with time on his hands—time that he didn't quite know how to fill.

"Hey, Pretty Girl," Mr. Wilson said when he saw Ronnie.

Ronnie smiled at his deep and grumbly voice. He'd been calling Ronnie and Donika "Pretty Girls" for as long as Ronnie could remember. "There go those pretty girls," he'd say whenever they walked by.

Mrs. Wilson smiled. "Hey, sweetheart. Donika's downstairs, I think."

"Thanks," Ronnie said and walked inside.

Philip sat at the kitchen table eating a pile of toaster waffles.

"Hey," he said. His mouth was full.

"Got enough syrup there?" Ronnie said, looking at his soaked waffles.

"Where's T.?"

"I don't know." Ronnie started toward the basement steps.

"Hear you got company," he said.

Ronnie stopped.

"How do you know?"

"Because I know everything."

Ronnie stood there for a second. She bet Philip didn't know about Juanita being a giant freak. She decided to ignore him and started toward the basement door again.

"So?" he asked.

"So, what?"

"So, what you thinking?"

Ronnie reached for the knob.

"Nothing," she said and walked through the basement door. But her knees felt shaky as she walked down the steps.

She heard music coming from Donika's room and walked in without knocking. Donika looked up, alarmed and ready to complain about her rights to privacy, but relaxed when she saw it was only Ronnie. She was sitting on her bed painting her toenails dark red.

"It doesn't really change anything," Donika said. They were talking about Juanita. "I mean, I can see where you'd be upset and all—especially if she's a freak like you said, but it isn't like you didn't know, right? I mean, you said yourself you knew all this time you had a sister, so what's the big deal?"

"If you ever see her, you'll know what I mean. She's gross."

Donika nodded sympathetically.

Mr. Wilson knocked on the bedroom door and peeked in.

"I'm digging a tomato garden," he said in his booming voice. "You girls come up and help me."

Donika shook her head. "Uh-uh, Grandpa," Donika said. She wriggled her fingers in the air. "I just painted my nails. I can't do it."

"You can do it, and you will," he said.

Donika moaned and continued shaking her head, but Mr. Wilson expected people to do what he said. He'd been digging holes in the yard lately, throwing seeds in them, and calling them gardens. He didn't care if the ground was muddy or if it was rock hard; he would dig, dig, dig all the same, then look around and change his mind and start digging a new hole somewhere else in the yard. It was like a minefield back there.

Donika looked at Ronnie, then looked at her grandfather.

"You gotta make Ronnie help too or I'm not going."

He walked over and put his arm around Ronnie.

"Don't need to ask that pretty girl. She'll help me anytime, and I don't even have to ask, now do I?" He shook Ronnie in a semi-hug.

Ronnie sure didn't want to be in the backyard, and if it were anyone else in the world besides Mr. Wilson she would have refused, but she would do whatever he asked. Ronnie had spent her life watching the way Mr. Wilson treated his kids and grandkids. She yearned to belong to someone that way, to be treated that way. While he treated Ronnie very well, it made her envious that she wasn't his own. Ronnie was just an add-on, a charity case. Donika didn't know how lucky she was. Mr. Wilson was right—Ronnie would do anything for him because he included her, because it felt good when he put his arms around her like that and treated her like she was his girl, like she belonged even though she knew she didn't.

In the back yard, Donika held her shovel out in front of her, keeping her fingertips spread out so as not to wreck her nails. She put on her flip-flops and walked on the heels of her feet to keep her newly painted toes from touching the grass. They stood in the back of the yard by the fence.

"I'm going to outline this garden," Mr. Wilson boomed. "You just stand there for a minute and then you can help me dig up this sod."

"Whatever, Grandpa," Donika said. She looked at Ronnie. "Come on."

They walked over to the swing-set with Mr. Wilson calling over his shoulder that they needed to stay there. Donika sat on a swing and looked at her fingernails. Ronnie knew she would do them again later if there were even one nick in the polish. Ronnie sat on the other swing and looked nervously across the yard toward Vivian's house.

"If she sees us she's going to come out," Ronnie said.

"So what if she comes out? Who cares?"

Ronnie looked at her. "You would if she was your mother."

"Maybe," Donika said.

They were watching Mr. Wilson dig up dirt. "Almost ready," he kept saying to us. "You girls need to come over here."

"Okay, Grandpa. Just a sec," Donika kept replying, though it was clear she had no real intention of moving.

Mr. Wilson stopped, rested his arm on the tip of the handle, and looked at Donika.

"It's my nails, Grandpa. I can't help it," Donika said, but she rolled her eyes as soon as his back was turned. "Two days ago he wanted to go to the mall with me—I mean with me—like walk around with me and hang out with me." She held her hand up toward him and shook it as if to rub him from sight. "Uh-uh," she said. "I don't think so."

"He wouldn't be bad to go shopping with," Ronnie said.

"Oh, please."

"Ronnie!" It was Vivian's voice coming from across the yard.

They looked up. Vivian stood at the fence in her short satin robe, a cigarette dangled from her fingertips as her wrist rested against the fence. She flagged Ronnie impatiently with the other hand.

Mr. Wilson stopped digging and turned around.

"Morning, Mrs. Geisel," he said.

"Morning, Marvin," she said and then looked at Ronnie. "Ronnie, you come over here right now."

Ronnie blew all the breath from her lungs and handed Donika her shovel.

"Hey! Watch my nails," she said.

Ronnie walked the length of yard between them with the enthusiasm of a criminal going to court. When she had left home to live with Thatcher, when it was finally clear that Ronnie didn't want to stay with Vivian at all, Vivian had become bitter toward them—though Thatcher assured Ronnie that Vivian had been a bitter person all along. It hurt her when Ronnie left, and she didn't let Ronnie forget it.

"Hey, Mom." Ronnie tried to sound cheery, like she was happy to see her mother, though her insides rolled.

"So? What?" Vivian crossed her arms over her chest quickly, her cigarette smoldering. Her hair was messy and her eyes were puffy and bleared with make-up from the night before. "You can come over to the Wilson's but you can't come over and say hi to me?"

"I didn't want to wake you up if you were still sleeping," Ronnie said. "I was going to come over when I knew you were awake," she lied.

"Oh." She took a quick drag off her cigarette. "Well. I'm awake."

Ronnie looked over her shoulder. Mr. Wilson was busy digging up grass. Donika had gotten off the swing and was standing next to him though she still wouldn't shovel.

"I kinda told Mr. Wilson I'd help him right now," Ronnie said.

"Well," she leaned back, but grabbed the fence, as if to keep from falling. She looked at Ronnie and smirked, then leaned forward, in Mr. Wilson's direction.

"Hey, Marvin. Tell me. You don't mind if my own daughter comes over here and visits with her own Momma, now do you?" She sent the words out as a challenge—a challenge to Mr. Wilson, a challenge to Ronnie, a challenge to anyone under the sun who dared to think that she wouldn't get her way.

Ronnie's teeth dug into her lower lip. She looked at the ground.

"Now, of course not." Mr. Wilson stood up. "We'll manage for a bit."

"Well," Vivian said. She slapped her arms quickly to her sides. Smoke, like a dragon, poured out of her nose and mouth as she spoke. "Well come on over here and say hi to me. Jesus." She shook her head at Ronnie and turned and walked toward the back door. All Ronnie could do was walk toward the gate and follow.

The shades in the house were drawn and Ronnie was greeted with the stale smell of old cigarettes.

"I'll get us some coffee."

"I don't drink coffee."

She turned to Ronnie with a confused look then shook her head as if to throw out an unimportant idea. "Well, it's all I got right now. I'll put sugar in it so you like it."

"I don't want any. Really."

"You can't even have a lousy cup of coffee with me?"

Ronnie looked away. The fringe on her mother's couch cover was beginning to unravel.

"I just don't like coffee."

She waved her hands and turned to the kitchen. "Well, Jesus," she said. "It's time you started." She walked out of the room.

Ronnie sat in the rocking chair. Vivian had asked Ronnie to paint it last year. It was an old wood rocker with a carved head-rest and lathed back spindles. Ronnie painted it black and then used touches of sage and gold to make it look like old copper or something. She rubbed her hands on the smooth arms. It looked good.

Vivian spilled Ronnie's coffee on the table as she set it down and cursed and ran into the kitchen to get a towel. Her expression was drawn and sour when she walked back into the room. Ronnie was used to seeing Vivian this way, but some days were worse than others. Her eyes looked old and tired. Her skin looked sallow and unhealthy. When she realized Ronnie was looking at her, she tried to smile, but it looked forced and painful. Ronnie would look in the mirror later that day. She would stand in front of it and try to paint years on her face, try to see if she was going to look like her mother when she got older. Vivian sat on the couch and fired up another cigarette.

"So, what's new?"

"Nothing," Ronnie lied.

"Oh, come on, Ronnie."

Ronnie's stomach turned and knotted.

"You're going to be eighteen in two weeks!" She seemed annoyed with Ronnie's lack of enthusiasm. The foot of her crossed leg bounced up and down in an angry tap. "My baby is going to be eighteen." She took a drag of her cigarette, leaned her head back, and gave a sharp, short laugh.

Ronnie felt the jar of a thousand pins run through her spine, realizing that she had heard that laugh, that single "Ha!" the day before, only then it had been thicker and slower—but sure enough it was the same laugh, only Vivian's version was quick and crisp. Ronnie looked at her mother closely, seeing her with new eyes, looking for other proof that she was, indeed, Juanita's mother as well as her own. She stared hard at her mother's eyebrows.

"You gonna have a party?" Vivian asked.

"No."

"Hey!" She sat up straight, her eyes suddenly glowing with animation. "Let's have a party right here. You can call all your friends up and they can come over here . . . It'll be fun." She looked toward the ceiling and shook her head in affirmation of her brilliant idea. She leaned forward conspiratorially. "I'll even buy you beer if you don't tell no one," she said. She dragged her cigarette and smiled. "We'll have a *real* party."

She smiled smugly and sank back into the couch. Then her eyes turned sharp and aimed for Ronnie, daring her to find fault with such a generous plan. This was the very type of conversation that would have gotten Thatcher and Vivian into an immediate fight. Thatcher would have had an answer. Thatcher would have sparred back, but Ronnie said nothing.

"Or, I could just take you out to dinner," she said, but then waved her hand as if to shoo away the dullness of that idea. She leaned forward and stared at Ronnie, and Ronnie had the feeling—like she's always had the feeling—that she was supposed to say something in particular to Vivian, that she had some secret string of words stashed somewhere in her subconscious that had the power to make Vivian happy. Ronnie stared at her. Vivian was waiting, but Ronnie just didn't know what to say.

"Well, take a drink," Vivian finally said. She motioned to the coffee on the table. "Coffee is too expensive these days. It'd be cheaper just to start the day off with the good stuff."

Ronnie knew she meant vodka. She took the cup of coffee in her hands. The bitter taste was overly sweetened. Vivian pointed her finger at Ronnie's expression and offered another sharp laugh.

"Hey. I got a new boyfriend," she said. "His name is Andrew and he has horses. Can you believe that?"

"Hm," Ronnie said, nodding as if she cared. It probably wasn't even true. He was probably a loser like all the other guys her mother hooked up with.

"We've only been out like twice, but I'm thinking sometime he could take you out and show you how to ride a horse. Wouldn't that be great? We could all go out. It's in Eureka, so it isn't too far away. It'd be fun. Honey, he's a real nice guy."

Ronnie forced herself to take another sip of coffee to show Vivian just how agreeable she was.

"Well," Vivian said. Her expression darkened as she lit another cigarette. "What's your brother doing?"

"Nothing. I don't know."

"Does he got another girlfriend?"

"I don't know."

The truth was, Thatcher always had a girlfriend but they never lasted. The longest Ronnie had ever seen Thatcher with the same girl was for three weeks—she had been a dancer he'd met at some bar in Illinois.

Ronnie stood up. "Well, Mr. Wilson is expecting me."

"But you didn't even finish your coffee."

"I'll take it with me," Ronnie said trying to smile, trying to show herself as gracious and grateful. "I'll bring the cup back later."

"Fine," Vivian said. "Excuse me for wanting to visit with my own daughter." She stood up and waved her hand. "Go on and help Marvin with his stupid garden. The man is an idiot with a bunch of idiot kids and an idiot wife."

"Mom . . . "

"Go on. Go," she said. "You and T. are two of the most selfish people I have ever met. I gave you everything and you can't even sit here for two minutes." The ashes from her cigarette fell to the floor. "Shit," she said. "Nothing like being there for your own mother." She glared at Ronnie. "You sit down. You sit down and talk to me."

Ronnie felt a wave of nausea. She took a step sideways to round the table. Vivian stood up and did likewise toward the other side, as if to block Ronnie's way if she tried to pass.

"Who the hell do you think you are?" she asked. "You're worthless," she muttered.

Ronnie didn't quite know what happened after that, but her heart suddenly pounded and blood rushed to her face, making it burn. What made her say what she said next she'd never understand because she knew her mother. She knew that she was being baited into a fight. She knew that Vivian operated in a realm of drama, but today it was just too much and the words were out of Ronnie's mouth before she could stop them.

"What about Juanita, Mom? Is she worthless too?"

Ronnie stepped back and stared at Vivian defiantly, though she knew that she'd just made an awful mistake, a terrible mistake. Vivian stopped moving. She stood in shock, her mouth open, blinking her eyes in disbelief at Ronnie. Ronnie's insides began to rattle, and she walked suddenly and quickly around the table and to the front door, her body filled with electric adrenalin. She didn't look back. She went to the front door and stepped through it quickly. She wanted to avoid the fallout, the green radiation that would surely swallow her up if she stayed. She jumped off that porch, her head down, her heart pounding and walked—half walking, half running—down the center of the street, fighting back her feelings that jumbled together like the pieces of a jigsaw puzzle being shaken in the box, fighting off the hate and anger and confusion she felt. Her sandals slapped the pavement in quick tap, tap, taps.

What was she thinking? She would probably never see Juanita or Bean again. After she had pulled out of their driveway to go back to wherever it was she came from, things would have gone back to the way they were. She was a fool. She'd opened her mouth to the very person she knew she could never trust with anything real, and more than that, she knew that she would pay for it. It would come back to her, these stupid words—in one way or another. If Ronnie knew anything about Vivian, it was that. Juanita was gone, but because of her big mouth, Ronnie knew this was only the beginning.

CHAPTER EIGHT

Ronnie heard Thatcher's work van pull into the driveway. His truck had been there earlier so she knew he had gone to the shop. The van was blue and had "Oliver's Automotive" painted on the side in black letters along with the shop's phone number. He also owned a little white Volkswagen Beetle that he had bought when he was 17, but he never drove that. He kept it parked up at the shop.

"What are you doing?" Thatcher said when he walked in.

"What's it look like?" Ronnie was lying on the couch in front of the TV.

"Getting ready for work, maybe?"

"I'm working tomorrow."

If she wasn't working or going to school, Thatcher always made her feel like she was wasting time. He stood there, looking like he had something else to say, but when he remained quiet, Ronnie went back to staring at the TV. He would never say anything. Ronnie had given up on that idea long ago. Thatcher had spent his whole life saying absolutely nothing to her. If Juanita hadn't shown up, he would have gone to his grave never having said a word about her. He didn't talk about what he was thinking or about how he felt—like most people. He was a clam, and that's all there was to it. Ronnie stared straight ahead, condemning him in her mind. Vivian was really the one to blame, though. She was the one who really screwed everything up. Though Ronnie was sure learning how to screw things up herself. She tried to push away the thought of Vivian, the thought of their last conversation.

"How come you ain't working on the table?"

"Because I don't feel like it." Her voice was harsher than she'd meant it to be.

"Well, what color you gonna paint it?" He finally asked.

Ronnie sighed. The table. The table they could talk about. Something safe. Something that didn't really matter. This was Thatcher's idea of a good conversation.

He walked across the living room, rifled through the mail that was sitting on the dining room table, and then headed through the kitchen and toward the back door. Ronnie got up and followed him. He ran his hand over the top of the picnic table. The creases of his knuckles and the lines on the palms of his hand were etched in grease and his fingernails were outlined around and underneath in black.

"Don't get it dirty."

He pointed to the sandpaper.

"You ain't going to get *that* paint off with sandpaper," he said.

"Well, then how am I going to do it?" Ronnie picked up the piece of sandpaper and absently tore it in half.

"You'd need dynamite to get that stuff off. Just paint it. Just rough it up and then cover it over."

"No. I don't want to do that. I want to get it down to the wood. It'll be perfect then."

"That table is never going to be perfect. Just paint over it."

"No. The wood is good under there. I know it. That's how I see it in my head, and that's how I'm going to do it."

"You'll have to strip it, then," he finally said, "and that shit is nasty."

"Well, it's not like I'm asking you to do it." She glared at him.

"Just paint it." Thatcher started to walk away. "That stuff will burn your skin right off."

Ronnie threw the pieces of sandpaper onto the patio.

"Fine. You know what? You paint it. I'm not touching it. You bought it. You can paint it. Do it your way."

Thatcher turned back, surprised. He spoke quietly. "You don't know anything about stripping paint."

"Yeah, well, I don't know about a lot of things." She met his eyes like a head on collision, and he looked away. Ronnie smirked. Talking to him was a game of chess.

"Here's a lesson for you," he said. "Once you open that can and start the process, you're going to have to go through with the whole thing. You can't stop. You can't start it and then turn back when it gets ugly."

Ronnie pursed her lips. "Or I can just paint over it, be done with it, and move on, right?"

"That's right."

Ronnie's chest tightened and she could feel the blood flowing through her temples. She took a deep breath, trying to slow her breathing, trying to calm herself. It was just like Thatcher to want to cover everything up, paint over the whole damn thing, paint over their whole damn lives. She and Thatcher and Juanita and Vivian, all buried beneath layer after layer of secrets. Ronnie wondered if there was some sort of stripper for people, something that would take away all the secrets and leave the bare truth.

The table would be better for the work, better for the effort, but what of this family? What if the truth, if the skeletons, turned out to be something worse than what she knew now? It was true, they could just keep on going, be done with it, forget about Juanita and Bean, forget about the father she knew nothing about. But how exactly did a person go about doing that once the door had been opened, once the secret came into view? How did you paint over a giant woman and her son? How did you paint over the shadow of a man you'd still never met? Ronnie's anger burned at the base of her throat.

"Cover it up," Thatcher said as if he'd made the decision. He started walking toward the gate, but then stopped and turned around. "Trust me. I've tried to strip something down to the base before, and it's just not worth it."

Ronnie flinched. Maybe he was talking about paint, but his eyes cut to the heart of her as if he were some kind of prophet or fortune-teller, as if he were trying to warn her and offer her a way to escape both dilemmas. She didn't know how to respond, and so, as was usual in such situations, she said nothing. Thatcher shook his head and walked away, shifting the mood, clearing the fog from the crystal ball so that all that was left was Thatcher and Ronnie, talking about nothing more than paint on a table.

CHAPTER NINE

By late afternoon, Ronnie was out on the driveway working with the table and benches while Thatcher slept on the living room couch in front of the TV. She was excited about the table, excited to be learning something different with the stripper, and nearly forgot about Vivian and Juanita altogether, though they popped into her head every once in awhile. But she pushed them out. She set her mind on the table and this new process. She focused on reading the directions. She focused on the brush strokes and watched and waited to see the chemical begin to bubble the surface of the paint.

Her hands were covered with yellow latex dish gloves, so when the telephone rang, she didn't jump to answer it. Instead, she stepped inside the open gate and stood outside of her open bedroom window listening to the answering machine that sat on her desk.

"Ronnie, Jesus, Ronnie." Her stomach dropped. It sounded like Juanita with her thick, slow voice, but then the voice said, "Pick up," and Ronnie realized that it wasn't Juanita at all. It was Vivian, and the similarity between their voices was startling--the only difference being that Juanita's voice sounded slow all the time. Vivian's voice only sounded like this when she was drunk. Ronnie recalled the expression on Vivian's face when she had said Juanita's name. She recalled her own breathlessness, the thick sound of blood pounding in her ears as she had walked down the street away from Vivian. And Thatcher . . . as of yet, he knew none of this. Ronnie panicked. She ripped the gloves from her hands and threw them in the grass, running toward the house, past the phone in the kitchen, around the corner, through the dining room, and to her bedroom.

"I'll get it. I'll get it," she called, looking to the couch as she ran past.

Thatcher didn't move. He was in a deep sleep.

" . . . what you're saying . . . " Momma was saying into the recorder. Ronnie ran to pick up the phone.

"I'm here. I'm here," Ronnie said loudly. She pushed the off button on the machine and silence filled the room. Ronnie looked over her shoulder.

"Ronnie?" she finally said. "Is that you?"

"It's me."

"What in the hell are you talking about, Veronica." Vivian drew her name out long and slow and Ronnie felt, once again, the unsettling similarity between her mother's voice and Juanita's. Vivian rarely called her Veronica.

"What do you mean?" Ronnie said carefully.

"Well, if you don't know what I mean then, well, I'm not talking," she said.

"Okay, then."

There was a long silence. Ronnie imagined her body falling headlong into that deep quarry. Maybe that was it. Maybe that was how it felt to take that first step off the edge that led to the bottom. Ronnie hadn't even thought about it. She had simply opened her mouth and said Juanita's name to Vivian, and now she couldn't take it back. She felt a deep burning in her chest and leaned her forehead against the wall, waiting for the awful thud. She'd been through mother's drunken conversations many times before, but this one was different. This one was her fault.

"I'm here all by myself," Vivian said, and then she laughed. "Christ, what do you care about that, right?"

"Mom . . . " Ronnie said.

"Where's your brother?" The lining of anger edged her slurry voice.

"He's kind of busy."

"Busy my ass. Go get him."

"He's asleep."

"Ronnie, I swear to God I'll call all night long if you don't get him right now, and don't you think I won't. I'll come over there this minute if I have to."

Ronnie knew Vivian would do what she said. She knew she would call all night. She knew she would get into a car and drive over there.

"Okay, okay. Wait a minute. Just wait a minute." Her heart pounded. She looked from the receiver in her hand, to the doorway that led to Thatcher, trying to figure out what she should do, trying to figure out some way to extinguish the fire she had started, to take back the step she had taken.

She lifted the receiver back to her ear.

"Mom . . . ."

"Get him," Vivian pleaded.

She sounded so awful on the other end, so sad, so alone, so angry, so drunk. Thatcher had grown up and left her, but Ronnie . . . when she'd left, a clear message had been sent. Ronnie thought of Juanita, and realized that she and Thatcher weren't the only ones who'd left Vivian, that Vivian had been abandoned before.

"I'll get him," Ronnie said into the phone. "I'll get him for you. Just hang on."

She went to the living room and stared at Thatcher's lifeless form on the couch. Her stomach churned and for a second she thought she was going to throw up. "What is the worst thing that can happen here?" she asked herself. Vivian wasn't right here in front of her, but Thatcher was. At least she could stall from having to face him.

She turned and walked back into her room.

"He won't wake up," Ronnie said into the phone. There was silence on the other end. "Mom?" she asked cautiously.

Maybe she had put the phone down, or maybe she had passed out.

"I'll get him myself, then," she slurred and hung up the phone.

Well, that plan had worked for a whole second, Ronnie thought. A part of her wanted to just be silent about it, to let Vivian get into her car and try to come over. Let her crash on her way over and kill herself. Let her run into a tree or a telephone pole and end all the misery she passed around like holiday appetizers. As quickly as those thoughts rose in Ronnie, though, the saner thoughts, the truer thoughts that Vivian could really hurt someone, filled Ronnie's mind. Vivian wasn't the kind to go down alone—and if it happened, Ronnie would be the one who had to live with it.

She nudged Thatcher's shoulder.

"T."

He shifted on the couch and grumbled.

"Mom's drunk, and she's coming over."

"What?" Thatcher winced and sat up slowly.

"She was on the phone. She's trashed."

"So what's new?"

"No . . . she's looking for you and she's going to come over."

"Shit," he said. "Call Philip and if he's home, tell him to go over there and stall her and we'll be there in a minute."

When Philip came to the phone, Ronnie said, "Go to my Mom's house, okay? She's trashed, and we'll be there in a minute."

"Huh?"

She heard Thatcher start his van. "Okay, Philip?"

"Okay, but . . . "

But Ronnie didn't hear what else he said because she had already hung up. She got into the van, and Thatcher turned and looked at her seriously.

"Listen. Don't tell her Juanita was here. I ain't dealing with her crap."

Ronnie's panic grew, though she nodded dumbly. She closed her eyes, knowing she should tell him right then, but she couldn't. Thatcher raised his hand to put the van into reverse, and Ronnie suddenly opened the door.

"Wait," she said, jumping out. She couldn't do it. She couldn't go over there and face that.

"What are you doing?"

"I'm not going."

He looked at her.

Ronnie shook her head. "I . . . I got that stuff on the table!" she faltered. "It'll wreck it." At least she wasn't lying.

Thatcher glared at Ronnie for a second. "Great," he said sarcastically. He slammed the gear into reverse and started to back up. He backed up into the street, slammed the stick into drive, and sped off toward Vivian's. Ronnie stood up straight, took a deep breath, and walked toward the table. Sometimes the best defense against an imminent attack was simple and stoic resignation.

CHAPTER TEN

"What the hell is wrong with you?" he said.

Ronnie couldn't look at him. She was getting ready to strip the last section of the table-top and pulled on her rubber gloves. She had been thinking while Thatcher was gone, thinking and formulating how she would respond to him when he came back. Her plan was simple and honest.

"It's not my fault," she said.

"Ha!" Thatcher leaned his head back and looked up at the sky. "God," he moaned.

He turned around and went back into the house, but came back a minute later with a cigarette in one hand and a soda in the other.

"No. This is not my fault," she said again, only this time she meant it. Ronnie pointed, and took a step toward him. "*You* should have told me about her." She picked up the putty knife, planning to go about her business with cool, but her anger welled up so suddenly and so completely within her that she threw the knife to the ground. "*You* should have told me!"

And then she was crying—something that was not at all common for Ronnie. She was crying and then angry at her lack of self-control. Thatcher's glare softened, but Ronnie didn't care. This was not a part of her plan, and she shook her head in disgust. "You're just like Mom," she said. "You're just as screwed."

"Oh you think so?"

He set his soda down hard on the porch and came to the fence. The way he looked, the way he was walking . . . for a moment she feared him. She feared him and thought, "if he opens that gate, I'm running." She stared at the hand he laid on top of the fence, his eyes burning into her.

"I don't see you living with her, and I don't see her putting up with you."

Ronnie tried to wipe her eyes on her upper sleeve, tried hard to gain back her control. "I can't help that. I can't help any of that." She turned away so that he couldn't see new tears fall.

Thatcher stood still for a minute, but then retreated back into the house. Ronnie stood there, staring at the burning paint, bubbled and gooey looking. She picked up the putty knife and rubbed the flat side of it in a circle, pushing hard, watching as the first layer began to change and mix with the different colored layers of paint beneath. She kept rubbing, though her tears continued to fall, and watched the paint turn into a drab, green-gray color. She *was* in over her head. She used the edge of the knife to scrape over the top and peel the paint away. It went up the blade like wood shaving, leaving a section of raw wood behind. It looked to Ronnie like an open wound. That's what all of this was, she thought, some old wound that had been ripped open the morning Juanita showed up, and now that it was open, there was nothing anyone could do.

CHAPTER ELEVEN

Gayla knew Ronnie didn't have school on Monday. It was a study day for final exams, and so she had asked Ronnie to cover an early half-shift for her at the Quick Shop. Ronnie needed to study, but she needed money more. She still had three exams to take that week, but then she'd be finished with high school forever—maybe *all* school forever. She didn't know what she was going to do after graduation. Everyone else did, but not her. At school everyone was talking about either what college they were going to, or what a great new job they were going to start as soon as school ended—even Donika knew that she was going to Sally's School of Beauty next fall.

Thatcher had been telling Ronnie to go to the community college, but why would she do that? Why would she go and spend money she didn't have when she wasn't even sure what she wanted to be? Thatcher told her that was why you went—to find out. It seemed like a waste of time to her, though, and the truth was, it didn't matter right then anyway. All she had to do at the moment was get through her exams. She had planned to study all weekend. Of course, with Juanita showing up, that never happened.

Ronnie stood behind the counter, listening to Orange-Juice—that's what Gayla called the woman who came in every morning all dressed up for work but with her hair wrapped and pinned around small orange juice cans that she used for curlers. Ronnie guessed the woman didn't think the people who worked at the Quick Shop noticed things like orange juice cans hanging from a person's head. She was buying a cup of coffee and complaining about the expiration date on the cream. Ronnie usually worked nights, so this was the first time Ronnie had ever actually seen Orange Juice—though Gayla had been talking about her for three months. Gayla had left off one part about Orange Juice in her description, though—she was a complete bitch.

"Where's Gayla anyhow?" Orange Juice said.

Thatcher walked in. "How come you're working?" he said to Ronnie.

Ronnie shrugged.

Orange Juice turned her head and when she saw Thatcher, she changed instantly.

"Hi there," she said in a suddenly friendly voice. "How are you?"

Thatcher nodded toward her, but looked at Ronnie. "Where's Gayla?" He and Ronnie hadn't really spoken since their fight—not that they spoke to each other much anyway.

"Oh, I was just wondering the very same thing," she said, brushing his arm with her fingers. She acted as if they were sharing something special.

Ronnie rolled her eyes. She knew Thatcher was cute in a rough looking sort of way. She could see how a girl would like the looks of him with his dark eyes and high cheekbones and straight nose, but really, the way they drooled over him was annoying. Girls flirted with Thatcher wherever he went—even girls who had orange juice cans hanging in their hair.

The worst part, though, was that whenever Ronnie was with him, she would get these piercing looks from women who were trying to figure out if she was Thatcher's girlfriend or not—evil eyes that she didn't deserve. It made her feel downright hostile toward a large number of her own sex. Orange Juice was a perfect example—though she didn't like her anyway. Orange

Juice didn't know Ronnie was Thatcher's sister, but if she found out, Ronnie knew that suddenly Orange Juice would suddenly treat Ronnie like she was some kind of chum—chum as in pal, not as in fish guts, though Ronnie was amused to realize that she was chum either way: fish guts or friend depending on the situation. Ronnie knew one thing about Thatcher and women: any woman who was interested in Thatcher was no friend of Ronnie's. Thatcher's string of girlfriends over the years had taught her this. They were false and dishonest and she had yet to find even one that she liked.

Thatcher was equally annoying because he treated the whole thing like it was a big game. He didn't take any girl seriously. He turned his charm on and off like a faucet when it suited his purposes and went through girlfriends like they were candies sitting in a box. He wasn't mean that Ronnie knew of, but she also knew that he had broken a lot of hearts. Girls would fall hard for him, but he never got serious about anyone. And when he'd had enough of them and had stopped responding to their calls, they'd come to Ronnie all pouty and red-eyed. It was pathetic.

Not that she had boys knocking down her door or anything, but Ronnie vowed, long ago, that she was never going to act like those girls or go out of her way for some jerky guy. No way. She'd be damned if she was going to let anybody treat her the way she saw Thatcher treat girls—or the way men treated her mother for that matter. It was ill, and Ronnie wasn't playing. Anyone who did was nothing but a fool.

Orange Juice was busy giving Thatcher the eye, and was so completely oblivious to how ridiculous she looked that Ronnie had to look away to keep from laughing out loud.

"Ronnie," Thatcher said again, growing irritated, "Where's Gayla?"

Orange Juice looked at Ronnie and pursed her lips, assessing the fact that Thatcher knew her by name.

"I don't know," she said. "I'm just filling in until twelve."

"Hm," Thatcher said.

Orange Juice took a step toward Thatcher. He tried not to smile by looking toward the floor, excused himself, and headed for the coffee machine. Orange Juice followed him with her eyes.

"Well, see you," she called after him.

"Bye," Ronnie said to her.

Orange Juice looked at Ronnie just long enough to shut her eyes in a second of irritation and then walked out the door.

He came back with his coffee. Gayla always let him have it for free. She even told Mr. Darren—he was the owner—that it was good PR since they had a business next door and their customers always came over and that as much money as Thatcher and Philip spent on snacks and smokes, they could give up a cup of coffee.

"How come you're alone?" he asked.

Store policy said that there always had to be at least one employee old enough to sell cigarettes and alcohol, so Ronnie usually had to work with someone else. Fat-Baxter had gone home from the night shift after the early morning rush ended.

"Gayla said it was close enough," Ronnie said. She was talking about her birthday.

He pulled three dollars out of his pocket and laid it on the counter. "Bring home some milk, would you?" And then walked out the door.

Ronnie didn't know what happened between Vivian and Thatcher—not that it mattered. She knew that they wouldn't hear from Vivian for a week or so now. That was her way. She'd get drunk, hurt a few people (mainly Thatcher and Ronnie) and then lay low. She let enough time go by for the impact of her words and actions to wear off. Then, when she made her re-entrance into their lives, she acted as if everything was perfectly normal. It happened time and time again, like an old record needle stuck on a scratch. They knew better than to bring up their wounds when they saw her because if they did, things would turn ugly all over again—only somehow it would be their fault. Thatcher and Ronnie had learned to ignore all the mean and hurtful things Vivian ever did or said over the years, never talking about them with her, or even with each other. Live and be quiet: that was their family motto.

CHAPTER TWELVE

    Ronnie was happy to discover that studying for her exams ended up being a pretty good way of drowning Juanita right out of her thoughts. Every time she imagined Juanita's dull eyes or her thick voice, Ronnie filled her mind with facts on Bacon's Rebellion and past participles.
    By mid-morning on Friday, Ronnie had finished her last exam. She was free from school forever. Free, free, free. She took all of her notebooks and threw them in the trash without a second glance. She started to look in her folders, opened one and rifled through the papers, assessing their importance one last time, but then dumped them all with a smile of triumph. She felt like a dove let out of its cage. No more. No more stupid teachers telling her what to read and what to think and what to do. No more exams to take. No more homework. No nothing. She took the now full trash outside to empty into the can on the driveway, trying to figure out how she would spend her first free afternoon. When she walked outside, she saw the table, half finished and waiting, and that was where she ended up staying all afternoon.
    She had originally planned on stripping the entire table, but after she had cleaned up the mess of just doing the tabletop and bench tops, she decided it was too much. She brought the

radio outside and sang along as she worked. She roughed up the legs with sandpaper, just enough to make the paint stick. Free. She tried to imagine how it would feel on Monday morning—how she would wake up late and really know how it felt to never have to go to high school ever again.

By the time Thatcher walked up the driveway, she was painting all the legs with primer. Thatcher was carrying one of Mrs. Wilson's casserole dishes. Neither of them cooked much. They were take-out and scrambled-eggs-for-dinner kind of people, so when Mrs. Wilson cooked for them (which she did every now and then), it was a real treat.

"What is it?" Ronnie asked.

"Lasagna." Thatcher lifted the tray high into the air, as if it were an offering of some sort.

"Hey," he said looking at the table. "It's about time."

Ronnie looked down at the paintbrush in her hand. "It's just primer."

"You look happy. School's out for good, huh?"

"Yeah." She couldn't help but smile and lifted her face to let the sun shine on it.

"Well, we can celebrate," he said gesturing toward the casserole. "When's the ceremony again?"

"Friday night, T."

He knew that. He also knew it was her birthday on the following Tuesday. She had told him five times to keep Friday night open, though she was worried about Vivian being there.

"I'm going out with Donika after," Ronnie said. "There are some parties around."

"Really?" He looked at Ronnie for a minute. She didn't hang around with very many people from school, and she could see that he was skeptical. "Well, don't get in any trouble," he said as he walked into the house.

By the time Ronnie came inside to clean out her brush, Thatcher had taken a shower. He was bent over the refrigerator, looking in. Ronnie turned on the kitchen faucet and put her hand under the flow, waiting to feel the cold water turn from cool, to warm, to hot. She put the brush under the water and began alternately wringing and fanning the bristles. A white stream formed in the sink and disappeared down the drain.

"Mrs. Wilson wants us to come over on Saturday. She's having the family over for a barbeque for you and Donika," he said. "Graduation and all."

"Really?" Ronnie was surprised.

She put down the paintbrush, and started washing her hands, scraping her fingernails against the primer that was decorating her skin. A party for her and Donika? Ronnie shook her head. Of course it was a party for Donika more than her—she was sure that Mrs. Wilson was just being polite and was including her because she was Donika's best friend. Still, it felt good to her that Mrs. Wilson was thinking about her. She didn't want to make more of it than it was, though. If it weren't for Donika, Ronnie knew there would be no party. She had learned long ago to keep her expectations low about the "big deals" in life. In their house, events like Christmas and birthdays, and now graduations, she guessed, were better off downplayed. If you don't let your expectations rise, you would ever be disappointe—that was Ronnie's life philosophy.

Ronnie turned off the water and dried her hands, went to the stove, took the cold tray of lasagna, and popped it in the oven door.

"So?" Thatcher was waiting for her to answer, but she'd forgotten what he was asking.

"So . . . how long is this supposed to cook?" Ronnie didn't want him to think that she thought the party was a big deal.

He had an odd half-grin on his face. "So, that's okay?" he said. "Tomorrow is all right? I'm supposed to let Mrs. Wilson know if there's a problem . . . "

"Yeah, yeah." She nodded, trying to be casual. "That's fine."

Thatcher pulled out one of the kitchen chairs and sat down. The chairs were metal with the backs and seats covered in a heavy, marbled-looking pattern of coral and gray colored vinyl.

Ronnie hated them because they didn't go in the kitchen at all, and Thatcher was too cheap to buy new ones.

"I wish Mom wasn't going to the ceremony," she said.

"Yeah, well . . . dream on, cuz she'll be there."

"She told me *she'd* have a party for my birthday," Ronnie confided.

Thatcher laughed, but when he stopped, Ronnie realized he was grinning at her.

"What?" she asked. "What are you looking at?"

He shrugged. "I'm just sitting here."

She considered the moment, considered Thatcher sitting there, smiling. She considered whether or not to take the risk. He seemed willing to talk, but if she said the wrong thing, she knew he would leave. She leaned her back against the sink

"So . . . what did she say when you went over there?" she asked cautiously.

Thatcher groaned. Ronnie winced.

"I wanna know," she said.

Thatcher peeled the label off his Gatorade bottle. He looked up at her for a second and then looked away.

"You know how she is. She just blabbered on." He gave a slight shake of his head. "She was toasted." Thatcher took in a deep breath and then blew it out again. The air puffed out his cheeks for a second. "Same old shit."

Ronnie waited, being careful not to cut him off and stop him from talking.

"She said I've been telling you lies about her."

"Her who? Momma or Juanita?"

"About them. About them both."

Ronnie laughed. "You've never told me *anything*."

Thatcher nodded and leaned his elbow on the table. He looked suddenly weary, resting his head on his hand. He ran his fingers slowly through his hair. "I don't know," he said. He shook his head quickly and held up his hand for a second, trying to brush his thoughts away.

"What was it like, T.?" Ronnie asked.

"What?"

"Living with Juanita."

Ronnie sat down across the table from him but she didn't look at him. She looked at the speckles of gray and white in the formica tabletop and ran her finger back and forth on the smooth surface. The hair on the back of her neck felt tingly and when there was no response, she looked up. His brow crinkled in surprise.

"I don't know . . . " he finally said. "It was a long time ago . . . "

Ronnie waited.

"People made fun of her. I mean, people that didn't even know her. Once they got to know her they were fine—like in school. That was okay. People who didn't know her, though, they would stare and point at her and say mean things right to her face."

"Did they tease you?"

"I definitely got into some fights over it," he nodded. He looked up at Ronnie for a second and then looked back to the table. Thatcher was good at downplaying anything dramatic. Ronnie knew that the fact that he had answered so quickly and admitted getting into any fights at all probably meant that he'd gotten into a lot of them.

She thought about Joe Baker. She thought about that day when she'd looked into the quarry and how he had called her a freak. Thatcher had stopped dead in his tracks that day. She remembered it clearly. It was the only time she had ever seen him defend her so forcefully. It had been a proud moment in her mind, him standing up for her like that—like a moment of love or something. She thought about the word he had used. He called her a freak. Ronnie didn't know it then, but Thatcher *did* have a sister who was a freak. She studied Thatcher's face as he sat there. Yeah, she could imagine him getting into a lot of fights.

"What about Mom?" Ronnie asked.

"She couldn't be nice to her." He laughed. "Like that's a big surprise, right? She could hardly even look at her. You know how she treated you when you were little? Always dressing you up and fixing your hair and stuff?"

Memory flashed through Ronnie's mind like a slide show: her mother brushing her hair, calling her baby doll, the daffodil-yellow ruffled dress Vivian had gushed over one Easter. Ronnie saw herself sitting in front of her dresser mirror, trying to put on lipstick and eye shadow so that she'd look like Vivian.

"You're such a pretty little thing," Vivian would say. Pretty *little* thing. Ronnie had never noticed it before, but Vivian had never called her just pretty. She was always pretty and little.

"She was happy you were normal," Thatcher said.

Ronnie didn't ask him anything else because, suddenly, every thought she had, every seemingly trivial memory that was coming into her mind was being refocused through a new lens— the lens of Juanita. Everything she thought about herself, she realized, had less to do with who she actually *was* and more to do with who she *wasn't*. Suddenly her major claim to fame seemed to be that she wasn't Juanita.

CHAPTER THIRTEEN

It wasn't like she'd never had a drink before. Donika and Ronnie took wine coolers from Vivian's fridge every once in awhile for kicks, and sometimes she'd have a beer with Thatcher, but for the most part, Ronnie didn't really like beer and just wasn't into drinking. She'd seen Vivian and Thatcher drunk too many times. The whole idea was more or less a turn off. Still, she was strung tight the day of her graduation. Thankfully, the ceremony had been uneventful. Vivian went, but didn't cause any trouble. Thatcher looked handsome in his only suit, and more than a couple of the girls in her class asked her who he was. Ronnie had spent the day feeling that surreal, euphoric feeling, that natural high that comes with an accomplishment. So when Curtis and Todd picked up the girls for the graduation parties, equipped with a couple of cases of beer, Ronnie was ready to go, ready to celebrate.

Donika had been dating Curtis for a few weeks and Todd was one of his friends. She didn't really know Todd, but guessed he was all right enough. His nose was big, and he was kind of short, but other than that, he was okay. They weren't a couple. It didn't matter. They were just going to go to a few parties together—though in her ultra-happy state she found herself smiling at Todd a bit too brightly, and working hard to be attentive to him. She wanted to have fun. She wanted to let go and celebrate and love the world for once, even if it were just for the night. She wanted to smile and laugh and keep the feeling of freedom and lightness alive.

And so she drank whatever anyone handed her. She drank beer on the way to parties, more beer at the parties, and then more on the way to the next party. By the time they left the first party, she cast off completely the isolation she had sometimes felt in the hallways at school. Suddenly, she was warm and charming and feeling all fuzzy toward people who had never given her the time of day—or to whom she had never given the time of day. Suddenly it was important for her to know them, to say something that would bind them together and show that they had, indeed, shared something over the past four years—regardless of the truth. The truth didn't matter—Ronnie was sure of that. So she hugged the snobby girls who always sat at the fourth table in the lunchroom. She danced with the guy who sat two seats behind her in history and didn't mind when he put his hand on her ass. She gave congratulatory kisses and got congratulatory kisses from boys she had never even seen before—one even slipped her the tongue and tried to get her phone number. She stood out in the backyard with the pot-heads, and even took a hit off a joint that was being passed around.

She was free from caring about anything. She and Donika laughed at each other until they cried—especially when Ronnie fell out of the car door when they pulled up to the last party. Ronnie was above it all, above school, above her family, above Juanita, just flying high. Of course, it all ended poorly, though Ronnie was too drunk to know or care—she and Donika more or less spilled out onto Thatcher's front lawn early in the morning, left in the hopes that they could make it inside.

She didn't know what time it was, but Ronnie woke up with her clothes still on, Donika's bare foot in her face, and her head feeling like a bulls-eye at a dart tournament. She tried to look at the clock, but her head throbbed like a bass drum in her ears, forcing her to lie back down.

"Ronnie, get up."

It was Thatcher. She wondered if he heard her stumbling into the house (though she didn't quite remember it) and throwing up (though she didn't quite remember that either—just vague images jumbled into the awful rhythm of the bass drum). She didn't want to hear what he would say. She lifted her head and looked to see where Donika was, but Donika was gone. The clock read: 12:47.

"Get up," Thatcher commanded. He stood in the doorway. Ronnie sat up and squinted at him, her hands pushing into her temples.

"You got a party to go to," he said.

CHAPTER FOURTEEN

He didn't say a word about her condition. Not one word. And she appreciated that. He just grabbed a twelve pack out of the fridge and told her to get in the truck. Just the sight of the beer made Ronnie feel sick to her stomach. When they pulled up to the Wilson's house, a group of kids were standing around one of the Wilson grandkids as he bounced up and down on a pogo-stick on the front walkway.

"Ronnie and T.'s here!" one of them yelled over her shoulder. Pain shot through Ronnie's head.

Donika was sitting on the front porch with Philip. She didn't look herself, but Ronnie thought Donika at least looked like she felt a heck of a lot better than Ronnie did. She was all made up, as usual, whereas Ronnie had just put her hair back in a ponytail and gone without any makeup. She knew her eyes looked tired and her skin looked pasty. She didn't think putting makeup on would have changed that—but seeing Donika looking half-way decent made her sorry that she hadn't gone to the trouble.

Philip clucked his tongue at Ronnie. Thatcher opened a beer and handed it to Philip.

"Did you sleep at my house?" Ronnie whispered as she sat on the other side of Donika.

"Yes. I tried to wake you up when I left, but you were like trying to raise the dead." She looked at Ronnie and shook her head. "Girl, you look awful."

Ronnie closed her eyes.

"Well, hey now," Philip said, standing up. "I think these two fine, responsible girls have a party to go to." He held his arm out, motioning for them to go to the house. "Everyone is here waiting to take a look at the proud graduates."

Ronnie and Donika glared at him, and he laughed out loud.

"You need to eat something, Ronnie," Thatcher said. They went inside, and by the way the room hushed, Ronnie knew that everybody knew they were hung over. There would be no mercy here. A few of Donika's aunts and a couple of her uncles were sitting in the living room with their babies playing on the floor and children running here and there.

"Hm," the women all said, shaking their heads and hiding their amused smiles behind stern tones as they called Ronnie and Donika things like "young fools," and "puppy dogs," while the uncles cleared their throats and made deep chuckling noises, agreeing with the women. Ronnie stepped around two of the babies, wanting to get out of the room quickly. Donika's cousins stared at them silently, frowning. No mercy.

"Hey, hey," Charles said, suddenly blocking the doorway. Charles was the oldest of the Wilson clan—middle forties, tall, broad, and solid with a mustache that curved down around the corners of his mouth. Football player perfect. Actually, he looked just like Philip, only bigger and older and in shape.

"There she is . . ." he said looking at Ronnie. He took a step forward, held Ronnie at arms length and gave a few "uh-uh-uhs" before swallowing her up in a bear hug that she thought would make her faint.

The baby on the floor strained her neck and twisted her body, trying to see them, though her mother was trying to change her diaper.

"Hold still!" Ruthie said to the baby. She fought the baby to lie still, but as soon as she took her hand away, the baby twisted her body back again. When she turned over for the third time, Ruthie pulled the diaper away and waved her hand. "Fine! Go naked!" The baby stood up naked, clapping her hands and smiling like she'd conquered the world.

"You get that baby diapered," Charles said.

"Just a minute."

"Don't let that baby pee on the floor."

"I'm just giving her a minute, Charles. You can come right down here and do it yourself if you're so worried."

"Ha!" one of the others laughed. "I'd sure like to see that."

"Well," he said looking at Ronnie, "I think I'll go where it's safe." Charles walked toward the front door but then turned back. "But you put a baby on that diaper!" he said shaking his index finger at Ruthie.

"Put a *baby* on that *diaper*!" someone mocked and the women burst into loud laughter.

"Oh," Charles said. He closed his eyes and waved his arm in exasperation. "You know what I mean!" He walked out of the front door to the sound of the women still laughing.

Philip pushed Donika toward the kitchen, who in turn pushed Ronnie toward the kitchen. Mrs. Wilson stood at the table, mixing a big bowl of potato salad with two long wooden spoons. Gayla sat at the long kitchen table, next to Sharon.

"Oh boy," Gayla said looking at Ronnie and then nodding to Sharon. "Sure as shit, she is."

Mrs. Wilson shooed away two grandkids who were intent on sticking their fingers into one of the two sheet cakes that sat on the corner counter and then turned around.
Ronnie felt ashamed, being hung over and having to face Mrs. Wilson, but all she had for Ronnie was a warm and sympathetic smile. Ronnie lingered in it for a second, lingered in her kind eyes. She put the spoon down and hugged Ronnie, keeping her hands up so she wouldn't get any potato salad on her.

"Look at her being all nice," Sharon said.

"This kind of stuff is your problem, not mine." Mrs. Wilson put her hands on Donika's shoulders.

"Well, Donika's grounded, Ronnie, so don't you even think about going anywhere soon with her, you hear?" Sharon said.

Ronnie bit her lip and nodded.

It was odd. As bad as she felt, she also suddenly felt good, standing in that kitchen being chastised by Sharon, not being overlooked, no one going out of their way to be polite—like family. They didn't have to be this way; this family didn't have to open their home to her like they did.

"Ronnie needs something to eat," Thatcher said to Mrs. Wilson.

"Look on the table outside," Mrs. Wilson said. "Oh, and take that cooler outside, too, would you, T.?"

Ronnie started to follow Thatcher out the back door when Mrs. Wilson put her hand on Ronnie's arm. "Your Momma's out back," she warned.

Ronnie grimaced.

Kids were running around the yard and lawn chairs were situated in a rough circle holding various in-laws and a few neighbors. Mr. Neuss, who lived across the street, was leaning close to Philip's newest girlfriend, Vanessa, trying to hear something she was saying, but Vanessa was leaning away, probably to get away from the sour smell of his cigar-smoking breath.

Ronnie heard Vivian laugh and felt her jaw tighten. Vivian stood in the very back of the yard by the barbecue pit with Mr. Wilson and one of his sons, Bobby. She wore short satin shorts with high heels and a tank top with an open teal colored blouse over it. The blouse clashed with Vivian's hair, which was now colored red. She had a beer in one hand. Her other hand was on Bobby's arm. Mr. Wilson was tending meat on the grill. When he closed the lid on the kettle and turned around, he saw Ronnie and Thatcher standing on the back porch. He called their names and waved them over. When Vivian looked up, she immediately began walking toward them with quick, small steps that her high heels demanded. Ronnie felt a rush of heat in the pit of her stomach like a flash fire in a kitchen frying pan. Thatcher tapped her shoulder and handed her a bun.

"Eat it," he said.

It dawned on Ronnie that Thatcher was really being nice to her, even trying to take care of her. She took a small bite and braced herself for Vivian.

"Oh! There they are," she said loudly. She threw her arms around Thatcher and held out an arm to Ronnie, looking over her shoulder at the same time, her eyes scanning the yard mechanically, assessing exactly who was watching them, trying to measure exactly how much the moment counted. Dark circles supported her eyes and her skin showed pasty and yellow through the mask of her too-dark makeup. She looks worse than I feel, Ronnie thought.

"You changed your hair," Ronnie said. The red color clashed with the color of her skin.

"Oh," her hand went to her head. "You like it?"

"It's . . . yeah, I like it."

Vivian didn't seem to notice Ronnie's condition, or else Ronnie didn't look as bad as she felt—though that was hard to believe.

"Andrew likes red," Vivian was going on.

"Andrew?"

"Oh," she said shaking her head apologetically, "Andrew can't be here right now. I'm so disappointed because I wanted you both to meet him." She frowned a baby-like pout. "He said he's going to try and come a little later. One of his horses got hurt. Poor thing. Poked its eye on a stick . . . you understand, don't you?"

Thatcher rolled his eyes and leaned over to get a beer.

"Mom, I've never even met him," Ronnie said.

Vivian looked confused. "Well he knows all about you, baby. It's like you're family to him already. Really."

She pressed her hand on Ronnie's arm and looked at her like she needed comfort over missing the stranger she'd never met. "This," Ronnie thought sarcastically, "is a special moment."

"Where'd I leave my cigarettes," Vivian said taking her hand away and spinning her body around. She took a step toward the circle of chairs. "I think they're on the table over there." She held her hand up. "You stay here, you two. You stay right here because I want to tell you all about Andrew. He's a real gentleman and . . ." she leaned close and whispered, "he's loaded on top of it!" She smacked Ronnie's arm with the back of her hand and laughed, nearly giddy. "He's got a big place out in Eureka—forty acres, he says. And horses and all . . . . We'll take you riding. Wouldn't you like that?"

Thatcher opened his beer and took a long drink.

"I'm . . ." Ronnie started.

"No!" She said. "Don't say anything else. Stay right here. Just wait a minute." She hustled off toward the tables.

Mr. Wilson walked across the yard. He shook hands with Thatcher. His smile was warm and comfortable like an oversized sweater on a cold day. He wore a dark blue polo shirt, a pair of khaki walking shorts, and white tennis shoes. He was growing a beard—again. His face was flecked with black and gray whiskers. In the past two months, he'd tried to grow a beard three times. He'd give his beard a week, then get sick of it, go back to the razor for a while, and then try it all over again.

"Hey, Pretty Girl," he said to Ronnie. He shook his finger at her before he hugged her.

Ronnie looked at the ground.

"Celebrating a little bit hard now, aren't you?"

Ronnie didn't say anything. His look softened.

"Hear you got a birthday coming up this week. Gonna have to call you pretty *old* girl soon. Not everyday you turn eighteen, now, is it?" He rubbed his face and stuck out his chin, then turned his face side to side.

Ronnie tried to smile at him.

"It'll look good if you actually keep it," she said.

"Why, what do you mean?" He had long dimples on both sides of his mouth when he smiled, though Ronnie realized his whiskers were beginning to hide them.

Thatcher nodded toward Vivian. "She getting obnoxious yet?"

Mr. Wilson waved his hand. "You got no worries from us, son."

Vivian never came back to them—not that they were really waiting for her to. Some of the Wilson siblings had come outside and were sitting at the tables. Vivian had found a place and sat in a lawn chair, talking and drinking and smoking. Every so often, her too-loud laugh would fill the air like the sudden jar of a police siren going off. Ronnie walked past the tables quickly and without getting too close.

Ronnie and Donika sat on the swings, Donika balancing a paper plate on her lap, Ronnie taking small bites of lime jello from a paper cup. She was feeling better since she'd eaten. Thatcher was right. She watched Vivian from across the yard, talking to Vanessa. She watched as Philip walked over to her with a plate of food, watched him work a trade on Vivian: a hamburger for his girlfriend. Vivian took the plate, but set it on the table where it remained untouched.

"I want some more jello," Ronnie said. "You want more?"

"Nope."

Ronnie was going up the porch steps into the kitchen when she saw Mitchell walk through the side gate and into the yard. Mitchell had been working part-time at the shop for the past month. Now he was worth getting excited about—Ronnie mentally compared him to Todd. Mitchell was 21, tall and so fine looking with his deep wavy brown hair, his long side burns and blue eyes. Whenever Ronnie saw him, her insides ignited. She had never actually talked to him but sure liked the look of him. She stepped into the house and checked her shirt to make sure she hadn't spilled any jello on it and went into Donika's room to check her hair and put some makeup on her eyes and lips.

When she stepped back outside, Thatcher was talking to Mitchell. Mitchell was scanning the yard as Thatcher spoke and his eyes came to rest on Ronnie. She stood on the porch, flustered, feeling her face grow hot. She looked away, then looked back. Now Thatcher was watching her, too. He gave a half-smile when he realized she was looking at them. She looked back to Mitchell, whose eyebrows were raised in an expression of curiosity. Ronnie tried to smile, but her mouth felt like a tight rubber band on a shoe-box guitar. She looked away, feeling stupid, feeling caught, and headed down the porch stairs.

Donika walked up to her. "This is a snore-fest," she said. "Let's go to my room."

"I was just down there," Ronnie said.

"Well, come back then because I want to give you your birthday present."

They stepped into her room to find two of her little cousins sitting on the floor.

"Okay, you guys," Donika ordered. "Get out."

"We're not hurting nobody," the girls protested.

"Out."

Donika closed the door as the girls went chattering up the steps. She went over to her dresser and pulled out a small wrapped box.

"Okay, this is stupid, but . . . well, here." She sat on the bed holding the box out.

Ronnie looked at her and smiled before she tore the yellow paper from the box, appreciating how much she loved her best friend. Inside there was a silver ring. It was a flat band with tiny hieroglyphic looking symbols on it.

"Oh, Donika," Ronnie said slipping it on. "It's so pretty."

"It's a friendship ring," she said.

"I love it, and look—it's perfect." She held up her hand.

"It's no great thing, but, you know." She looked down at her own hands, brown and beautiful. "Happy Birthday."

"Thanks, Donika," Ronnie said, hugging her.

"Oh listen. New album," Donika said. She walked over to her turntable.

When Mrs. Wilson knocked on the door, twenty minutes later, Ronnie was lying across Donika's bed, staring at the ceiling. She was starting to feel like her old self again, and was thinking about getting something more substantial than jello to eat.

"Hey, you girls. Everyone is looking for you. There's a bunch of cards out here with your names on them," she said.

Donika jumped up quickly.

They stood next to the picnic table, opening cards and small congratulatory gifts from the family. Donika squealed over every card and gift and ran straight to the gift-givers to give them a hug. It was odd for Ronnie, though. She didn't quite know what to do or how to act. She couldn't go running around like Donika, giving hugs. She just wasn't like that and these weren't her aunts and uncles. Instead, she felt self-conscious and a little overwhelmed by the attention. She wasn't a niece, but they were sure treating her like one. By the time she had opened all the cards—more than a couple of them handmade by the kids—she was nearly a hundred dollars richer. She stood there feeling shy and grateful and thanked everyone from where she stood.

Ronnie guessed Vivian hadn't expected everyone to give her such lavish treatment because when she saw everyone giving Ronnie money, Vivian came up and put fifty dollars in Ronnie's hand in an ostentatious display. She was half crocked—the fact that she handed Ronnie that much money showed it.

"I was gonna wait until your actual birthday," she slurred, "but what the heck, right?"

Ronnie tried to feel grateful—it was, after all, a lot of money—but she knew Vivian was doing it for show more than anything and found it hard to take. But Ronnie told herself that Vivian was being generous and tried to concentrate on that. "Thanks," she said as Vivian pulled on the back of Ronnie's neck for a hug. Ronnie tried to resist the tensing she felt in her own body, tried to respond to her mother's hug and even hug her back, though she wasn't quite successful.

"Okay," Mrs. Wilson said from across the yard. "Everybody needs to go out front." She stood next to the gate.

"Oh!" Donika clapped her hands and grabbed Ronnie's arm. "Come on!"

Thatcher stood alone on the sidewalk out front.

"Come on," Donika said again, pulling Ronnie along.

Donika knew something.

"What's happening?" Ronnie looked around at everyone standing there. She looked back at the house. Mr. and Mrs. Wilson stood on the front porch. She walked past Ruthie and Philip and Vanessa and all the kids. The older cousins stood in the yard surrounded by all the younger cousins, who were running around, doing cartwheels and somersaults in the grass. She looked for Vivian, but didn't see her.

"What's going on?" Ronnie said again to no one in particular.

Suddenly, Mr. Wilson started singing "Happy Birthday" and everyone joined him.

Ronnie looked around. Her birthday wasn't for a few days still. Her face grew hot, and she tried to maintain her composure, but she could feel her knees starting to shake. She looked around at everyone, incredulous, and then her eyes fell on Vivian. She was standing with Charles and Philip at the edge of the driveway, her hand resting on Philip's arm. She leaned into him.

Thatcher walked up to Ronnie. He put his hand on her shoulder and turned her toward the street. A car was coming. It was a dark red Volkswagen with a big white bow tied to the hood. Ronnie's mouth dropped open, and she looked at Thatcher. His arms were crossed over his chest, and his smile was as wide as a smile could be. Everyone started hollering as the car came closer.

"What is this?" Ronnie asked. "What is this?"

The car came to a stop in front of the house. Mitchell was behind the wheel. He honked the horn. Ronnie couldn't move. Everyone started walking toward it, closing around the small car in a circle, only stopping long enough to pat Ronnie on the back.

Thatcher pulled Ronnie to the car. She couldn't believe what she was seeing. She touched the hood of it.

"It's yours now," Thatcher said.

Ronnie looked at him. "This is *your* bug?"

He nodded. Thatcher's Volkswagen was old, with a dull paint job and more than a couple of dents and dings. This Volkswagon looked perfect—shiny, red and gleaming.

Donika ran up to Ronnie and grabbed her shoulders.

"Did you know?" Ronnie asked.

She laughed. "Shoot, everybody knew."

Thatcher was looking at the car.

"Philip and me did it," he said.

Ronnie craned her neck over the people, toward the end of the driveway, to get a glimpse of Philip, but she couldn't find him. He and Charles and Vivian were no longer there.

Mr. Wilson stepped up and rested his hand on the top of the car.

"What year is it?"

"'65," Thatcher said.

Mr. Wilson walked around the car. He acted the role of the great inspector, though Philip always said he didn't know a thing about cars. Mr. Wilson went to the back and opened the engine cover.

"Take it for a drive, Ronnie," Mrs. Wilson hollered. She was still standing in the yard.

Everyone cheered. Ronnie looked at the car.

"I don't know how to drive a clutch," she said.

"You'll learn," Thatcher said. He turned away. "Hey, Mitch, take her for a ride, will you?"

Donika squeezed Ronnie's shoulders so hard she had to wriggle free.

"Jump in," Mitchell said from behind the wheel.

Ronnie couldn't look at him though she tried to. Her heart was beating so fast, and her whole body started to shake.

"Where's Philip?" Ronnie stammered.

"You can talk to him later," Thatcher said. "Go on. He's busy anyway."

Ronnie knew Philip and Charles were taking care of Vivian. Ronnie's smile faltered for a second, but Thatcher nodded. "Go on," he said.

It was okay. Ronnie was not to worry. Thatcher was pleased for her. She felt a ball of emotion land in her throat, bittersweet and brimmed with fear and excitement and sadness and happiness all mixed together like a very strong drink. She was simply overwhelmed. In spite of Vivian, in spite of everything she knew or didn't know about her family, Ronnie saw that she had something good here in front of her—she had Thatcher. She gave him a sudden hug, which, by Thatcher's expression, took him by complete surprise. He took a step back to keep his balance but his smile was wide and satisfied. He led her to the passenger side of the car—her car—and opened the door.

"Happy Birthday, Ronnie," Mitchell said leaning over toward the open door.

Ronnie couldn't say a thing to him. She was overwhelmed by Thatcher's gift, but she couldn't ignore the fact that she was sitting in a car next to Mitchell. She thought of all the boys she'd kissed the night before, and wished more than anything that one of them had been him.

Thatcher shut the door, and leaned in the window. "Have fun." He stood up and smacked the roof with his hand.

Mitchell drove down to the end of the dead end street and turned around. He drove slowly past the party, and as they went by, everyone waved and cheered. Those closest to the car smacked the hood and roof as they went by. Ronnie waved back feeling utterly foolish—and then she saw her. Vivian. She stood on the sidewalk between Philip and Charles—they towered over her, standing stoic like bodyguards, though Ronnie knew it was not Vivian they were protecting. Vivian glowered as they passed.

Her glare seemed especially severe against the smiles and laughter of everyone else. She stood like a lone storm cloud, dark and menacing, that fought to dampen the brilliance of the afternoon sun.

CHAPTER FIFTEEN

"She's passed out in bed," Thatcher said when Ronnie came back.

The Wilson crowd had begun to thin. The brothers and sisters who had babies and young children had started saying their good-byes and packing themselves into their cars while the rest of the group sat in the back yard.

Donika and Ronnie sat at a picnic table over in the corner away from the circle of lawn chairs. They weren't talking much, just sitting there, watching the flame of the citronella candle that burned on the table and listening to snatches of conversations around them. Thatcher was standing across the yard, spinning some yarn and making everyone laugh. He was feeling pretty good—and Ronnie didn't think it had everything to do with alcohol. He was proud. He was proud of his gift and satisfied at the joy the moment had brought all of them. Mrs. Wilson was sitting in a lawn chair next to Mr. Wilson. They were talking with Ruthie about mortgage rates.

Ronnie was surprised when Charles came over and sat next to her. As a child, she had been afraid of him. He was so much older, and so tall, and carried such an air of authority, and had that deep, booming, deep voice. But he had always been kind. He had always gone out of his way to speak to Ronnie.

"What you thinking?" he asked her.

Ronnie shook her head. "It's pretty cool," she said. "I can't believe it."

"You're next, Chops," he said pointing to Donika.

"And I can't wait," Donika said. "I want a little red fancy sports car—you can tell that to Philip."

"Well all right, then." Charles smiled, shaking his head as he looked at the table.

"Donika," Sharon called from the back door. "Come here and help me."

Donika groaned and stood up. Ronnie started to stand up, too, but Charles said, "Where you going? Sit and talk with me. Let Chops do it."

Donika smacked Charles lightly on the shoulder, but then leaned over and kissed his cheek before walking away. Charles patted the table-top, and Ronnie went to the other side and sat across from him.

"T. said Juanita was here."

Ronnie looked at Charles. He smiled at her surprise. "Caught you off guard, didn't I?" He laughed, but then said, "I knew her when we were kids, you know. We all did." He leaned into the table and folded his hands in front of him. When Ronnie didn't say anything, he looked at her. "I just want to know what you think about it."

She shrugged, trying to think of an answer. She watched the flame of the candle. The flame bounced and reached first one way, then another. "I don't know."

"You didn't know about her."

Ronnie stayed focused on the flame. "I knew I had a sister," she said.

"Yeah, but she ain't what you expected, right?"

Ronnie looked at her hands, small and white, and remembered Juanita's big hands, her long fingers, her thick knuckles.

"Yeah," Charles said to himself, nodding. "It was a hard thing, back then." He waited and when Ronnie looked up to see what he had to say, he was looking at her earnestly. "And T. was right in the middle of it all."

They both looked in Thatcher's direction. He was still at the fence, talking to Philip and Vanessa.

"He's seen some stuff."

"And I haven't?" Ronnie stated.

"You have. You have," he said. He reached across the table and cupped both of Ronnie's hands in his own. "But this was different. It was hard before Juanita left, but I'm telling you this, it was even harder for Thatcher after she left. I don't believe he would have stayed except for you."

Ronnie frowned.

"It's true. You think about it," he said. "He and Juanita were close. He lost something there."

Ronnie thought of all the years of Thatcher walking out in the middle of a fight with Vivian, slamming the door behind him . . . all those times she let herself worry about him jumping into the quarry or just leaving and never coming back . . . just leaving her there . . . . But he never did. Thatcher always came home. And when he moved out, he never once turned Ronnie away.

"I'm just saying T's in the middle of it all—between you and Juanita and your Mom. Being in the middle ain't an easy place."

Ronnie didn't respond. She didn't know what to say.

"But you're upset," Charles said for her.

She looked at him helplessly. "Well, wouldn't you be?"

Charles nodded. "I believe I would. But this is about more than how you feel."

Ronnie pulled her hands away from Charles and crossed her arms.

"All I am saying is you have a chance of maybe getting to know your sister."

"I only saw her once."

"Well, if you saw her once, you'll probably be seeing her again," he said. His eyebrows were raised, and he looked at her from the corner of his eyes, like he was getting ready to tell her a secret.

"We were friends, you know."

Ronnie looked up. She tried to imagine Charles and Juanita as children.

"I was older, but, you know . . . we all kind of looked out for her. Our mother made it clear that Juanita was special no matter what anyone said about her—and I'm telling you, people were outright mean to her." Charles' eyes got dreamy looking, and said in a reminiscent voice, "We used to run all around the Honda Trails. All day long."

"The Honda Trails?"

"Yeah," he said. "You know about the trails back there?"

"You mean the Bridle Trails?"

He smiled. "Yes, only we called them the Honda Trails because a bunch of older kids in the neighborhood used to ride their mini-bikes around back there when we were kids."

They sat quietly for a minute.

"I wonder if them trails are still there?"

Ronnie shrugged.

"Listen. . . . " Charles said after a minute, "Now, I don't know her anymore, but she was all right, Ronnie." He held his hand up and spoke passionately. "I haven't seen her in a long, long time, but I'm telling you, I'd be happy if I did. You know my mother is always right. You know that, don't you?" He tapped the table and smiled at Ronnie. "You got to see past the way she looks, is all."

Ronnie exhaled loudly at the thought of seeing Juanita again. Charles stood up. He walked around the table, put his hands on her shoulders, and squeezed. "You might find she's not all bad," he said and walked across the yard to where the adults were sitting.

CHAPTER SIXTEEN

Todd Carter called Ronnie the next day, asked her if he could come over. Ronnie wished it were Mitchell calling, but she told Todd she didn't care, and when he asked her to smoke a joint with him, she decided there was really no reason not to. Thatcher had brought her car home before he went into work, and Todd was standing in the driveway checking it out.

"Where you wanna smoke this? Inside?"

"No!" Ronnie said. "T. would kill me."

"He seems pretty cool to me."

Ronnie laughed. "Shows what you know."

"How about on the patio?"

She shook her head no. "My neighbors might see."

She got an idea.

"You wanna go for a walk?"

He shrugged.

The opening to the Bridal Trail used to be at the end of a gravel drive that bordered the pasture next to the quarry. It had been six years since Ronnie had been there, but after her conversation with Charles, she wanted to go back. When they got there, though, bush and vine had covered the old entrance. Ronnie pushed back the branches and peeked into the woods.

"Where are we going?" Todd asked.

"Just come on," Ronnie said.

"I just want to smoke some weed," he was saying as she pulled him into the woods.

The smooth and beaten path she had known as a child was gone, and a light rush of panic passed through her—everything had changed. She debated for a second whether or not they should go forward, whether or not she would be able to find the way, but then she went ahead and pushed her way through the overgrowth. She slapped at branches and sticks, trying to keep them from scratching her bare legs. Todd complained as he walked behind her, but she didn't pay him any attention. If she remembered right, if she just kept going straight, regardless of whether she stayed on that old path or not, she'd hit the creek, and once she hit the creek, she felt sure she would find her way.

The overgrowth was a sea of green that locked around her and forced her to keep her eyes down, focused on her feet.

"Come on, Ronnie. Why are we going through all this?"

"Stop complaining, would you?"

Her focus was so narrow—one foot in front of the other—that when she came to the small and sudden drop off, she was dizzied by an unexpected, airy openness. Ronnie rested her hand on the nearby tree trunk, looked below, and laughed out loud when she saw that down below the trail was alive and perfect and recognizable. Only the entrance had changed.

"Look," she said to Todd.

His mouth dropped open, but then he nodded and smiled. "A doobie spot."

Ronnie frowned at him. "I used to play here when I was a kid," she said, irritated.

She walked ahead quickly, filled with confidence and sure recognition. She looked for the old, twisted tree that sat at the top of the small, steep path. Surely, she couldn't be far from it. She walked a few steps along the small ridge, and then she saw it. She was off the old trail, but not by much.

"Old tree!" she said, and rushed toward it as if its branches reached toward her in reply. She touched its knotted and gnarly looking trunk and looked down the hill that led to the creek and clear trails below. Where she stood was no longer the bare, dirt packed hill she'd known as a child, but the old, exposed root was still there, sticking up, waiting to play the old tripping game. "Old root!" she said. She tapped it lightly with her foot, appreciating their inside joke.

She looked around. The light from the afternoon sun filtered through the branches, creating shafts that poked into the shadows like fingers. Everything was green and alive and the air smelled of sweet, clean trees with living leaves. She went down the hill, toward the creek. The sound of the water soothed her like a cool cloth on a hot forehead. She hesitated, but then waded across an ankle-deep spot, not bothering to take off her tennis shoes.

"Hey. Ain't this a good enough spot?" Todd asked.

"Come on," she said, smiling.

Todd followed.

It felt like home to her, this spot in the woods. She had forgotten what a friend it had been to her growing up.

Ronnie picked up the trail on the other side of the creek and followed it up a small hill that she knew would open to a giant field of leaf piles. This was where the city dumped all the lawn waste—acres of dead leaves; piles and piles of leaves so high she couldn't see over them. She and Todd had to walk a considerable length to get around them, the pungent smell of smoldering, organic breakdown hung thickly in the warm air.

Ronnie and Donika had found wild pumpkins in that very field one time. It had been autumn, and they were trying to walk the leaf piles without falling through when they discovered a whole patch of wild pumpkins growing at the edge, at the base of a leaf-pile that sat next to the woods. The timing was perfect because Halloween wasn't far away, so they had gone back for a wagon, brought it down the trail as far as the old tree, then spent the rest of the afternoon plucking pumpkins and toting them from the pile, across the creek, and up the hill to where the wagon waited.

They must have carried twenty pumpkins home that day, some so big they had to roll or drag them. It was hard work and their homes never seemed so far away from the trails as they had then, but they didn't care—they had struck it rich with wild pumpkins!

They kept the roundest and prettiest and tallest pumpkins for their own front porches. With the rest they set up a pumpkin stand at the top of the street and held up signs with the word "Pumkins!" colored in red crayon, and chanted, "Pumpkins for sale," whenever a car drove by.

They sold them for $1.00 each and while Ronnie couldn't remember how much money they had gotten, she did remember that she had ridden her bike up to the dime store and spent all of her money on penny candy. She had been so proud and happy that day. She had worked so hard. She had accomplished something.

Vivian had come home for her break that day, and when she saw all the candy Ronnie bought, she told her that she was a fool—that soon she would have all the candy she wanted for free.

Donika had come back over later in the evening, smiling and happy, sitting on the front porch next to the fattest pumpkin and draping her arm over it as if she were putting her arms around someone's shoulders. She leaned in and ran her other hand over the belly of the pumpkin, rubbing her palm in a wide circle like she was rubbing the belly of a Buddha, her brown arm contrasting nicely with the orange of the pumpkin skin.

"We really did something, didn't we?" she had said, looking up at Ronnie and smiling.

Ronnie had stared at the pumpkin, at the way Donika sat next to it with her sideways embrace, and tried to remember, tried to capture the feeling again, but all she could hear was her mother's voice.

"I dunno," Ronnie finally said, getting on her bike and riding away. "It's kind of stupid really."

Donika had sat there, frowning, her arm still resting on the orange treasure that for Ronnie had tarnished.

"Hurry up," she said to Todd, pushing the memory aside. She quickened her pace.

They went across the field and between the piles, the smell of decomposing earth strong in the air. They met up with the creek again on the other side of the field and crossed it again as the trail continued. Ronnie knew that if they took it far enough, they would end up at the limestone shelves. The trick would be remembering when to leave the path and cut back down to the creek. Ronnie wondered if Juanita and Charles had ever come this far, if they had ever crossed the field of leaf piles and picked up the trail on the other side.

She heard rushing water and stopped suddenly. Todd bumped into her back. She couldn't see the creek from this spot on the trail, but at the shelves, the water was deeper and rushed in a gentle rapid. She peeked through again and saw the slabs of rock to her left. They had gone too far. Ronnie turned back and cut down through the woods, down to the creek.

"Oh!" she said. Her eyes basked in the vision of the rocks and trees and water and shelves.

"Hey, this is cool," Todd said. "How'd you know this was here?"

"I told you," she said. "I used to play down here when I was a kid." Now that she was at the shelves, she was sorry she had brought Todd, because now all she really wanted was to be alone.

She sat at the edge of a shelf and took off her wet tennis shoes and socks. She set them in a sunny spot to dry and dangled her feet over the edge and dipped them into the chilly water. She cupped her hand and bathed the scrapes on her legs, then laid back on the rock, her feet still in the water. Her eyes fell into the patterns of leaves swaying above her. She sighed. It was good to be there, good to feel the familiarity of an old comfortable place.

Todd sat next to her.

He lit the joint, but when he tried to hand it to Ronnie, she didn't want any.

"You mean you brought me all the way down here and don't even want none?"

She looked over at him. "Sorry." It was good, just lying there.

The blue sky peeked in and out of view and the light of the sun tickled Ronnie's eyes open and shut. The sound of the water, the warm air around her, the warm rock beneath her, and the light of those leaves swaying so gently above, lulled her away.

It's a good thing, Charles had said about Juanita coming back.

Todd and Ronnie lay like that, him smoking his pot, her just being, both of them staring up at the light coming through the trees. She began to drift, listening to the rustle of the leaves above, listening to the secrets of the whispering trees. She began to dream. She dreamed that Juanita sat next to her on the shelf, dangling her long legs and dipping her huge feet. Juanita looked at her and smiled, but then her expression became one of mocking—mocking Ronnie in her ignorance. Ronnie woke instantly, unnerved by the dream as well as a sudden pressure on her lips. Todd was kissing her.

"Hey!" she said sitting up and pushing him away.

He held up his hands, laughing. "Sorry!" He said. "You just looked so pretty."

Ronnie rolled her eyes at him, and he laughed even harder. She must have been asleep for only a minute because he was still puffing away. He held it out to her encouragingly, but Ronnie was irritated with him. He was like a dumb dog, really—thoughtless and simple.

Ronnie started putting on her shoes.

"Let's go," she said.

"Hey, I wasn't trying to make you mad," Todd said. "What's the hurry? It's nice here."

"I know," Ronnie said. She couldn't shake the expression Juanita wore in her dream. "I'm not mad. I'm just ready to go."

This trail, this wood, this rock, this water—they held no answers for her.

CHAPTER SEVENTEEN

"Happy Birthday, Veronica."

It was Vivian.

Ronnie sat up and squinted at the alarm clock on her night table. 10:57 a.m.

"I . . . hello?"

"I know your birthday was a couple days ago, but I didn't want to bother you . . . . "

It wasn't Vivian.

"Juanita?"

Ronnie's head was foggy with sleep. She tried to swallow and lick her lips, but her mouth had gone completely dry. She pulled the phone receiver away from her ear, looking at it. Was she dreaming again?

"Veronica? Are you still there?"

Ronnie nodded yes.

"Hello?" Juanita said again.

"Yes," she said. " I'm here."

"You're like talking to one of the cows out back," Juanita said.

"Cows?"

Juanita sounded so much like her mother when she had been drinking. Ronnie remembered hearing Juanita's voice for the first time, remembered that odd feeling of having heard it before. Now she knew why.

"Are you all right?"

"I just woke up," Ronnie said. "I'm not really awake yet."

"You just woke up?" There was silence for a second and then the sound of Juanita's short laugh that was loud enough to make Ronnie pull the phone from her ear.

"Well, I'm . . . ." Ronnie started to explain that she was finished with school.

"Well hey, Veronica," Juanita cut in, "Is T. home because I kind of wanted to talk to him."

"Uh . . . I don't know if he's home, Juanita. I mean . . . he's probably at work . . . I . . . I really don't know."

"Well, dang it," Juanita said.

"I'll tell him you called."

"Veronica . . . oh shoot. Well, I got something to ask you, but I wanted to talk to T. about it first."

"Uh-huh."

"Well, this might be a stupid idea, but I was thinking that maybe you and T. would want to come and visit me in Cabool maybe."

"Cabool?"

"Yep. It's were I live, and, you know, I was just thinking . . . . I mean, if T. has to work . . . but you could come by yourself. For as long as you want to. I mean, you could stay for a day or you could stay for a week if you wanted to." She was speaking pretty fast for Juanita.

"I don't know, Juanita . . . " Ronnie said carefully. Ronnie's mind may have been foggy a second before, but she was completely awake now.

"I think you'd like it here . . . " Juanita was saying.

"Oh. Well, I . . . um . . . ."

" . . . and I think we could get to know each other a little bit."

"Oh."

"But I haven't talked to T. I need to talk to T. about it first. I shouldn't have said nothing yet."

"Well, I just don't know . . . you know . . . I just . . . I don't know," Ronnie said, though she was thinking, "No way. No way am I going to Cabool."

"I'll talk to T."

"I don't think he's here right now."

"Well, sure. You're right. I'll just call later," she said. "Yeah. That's what I'll do. I'll call later."

Ronnie was tongue-tied.

"Okay. Goodbye, Veronica."

"Okay . . . " Ronnie managed, but before she could say the word goodbye, Juanita had hung up.

CHAPTER EIGHTEEN

"Where is Cabool again?"
Donika and Ronnie were walking to *Oliver's*.
"I don't know."
When they got as far as the Quick Shop, Ronnie heard the familiar "Zap, Zap" of an impact wrench coming from Thatcher's garage. They walked between the garage and Quick Shop buildings.
"I want to stop in here," Donika said and walked in the entrance to the Quick Shop. Ronnie followed her.
"Morning Gayla," Donika said. Gayla stood at the register.
"Morning!" Gayla smoothed the front of her smock. "Why, girls, it's one o'clock in the afternoon!"
"Like morning to me," Donika said. She looked toward the door. "Philip been over here lately?"
"About an hour ago, I guess," Gayla said.
Donika walked over to the cigarette rack.
"How's that car doing?" Gayla leaned on the counter.
"I haven't really driven it yet."
"What? What's wrong with you! Darling, darling," she said. "If somebody gave me a cute little red car, I'm telling you I'd be driving it all over the place."

"I don't know how to drive a clutch."

Gayla shooed the answer away as silly.

"T's going to take me out in it later," Ronnie said.

"You are so stupid," Donika said. "I told you, you ought to get Mitchell to teach you."

Ronnie glared at Donika to shut up. Gayla had a big mouth.

"I tell you what, eighteen is an exciting time," Gayla said, "But don't you go getting pregnant, hear? Biggest mistake you can make."

"Gayla," Ronnie said trying to stop her from one of her famous lectures.

"I mean it," she said and pointed at Ronnie.

A man walked up to the counter with a Big Slurp and a bag of chips. Ronnie stepped aside. Gayla kept talking while she rang him up.

"It'll wreck your whole life. That's $2.37," she said to the man. "I found that out the hard way," she said.

The man put three dollars on the counter and looked over at Ronnie while Gayla got his change. Ronnie shrugged at the man and touched one of the $1.99 roses in a green vase that sat next to the cash register. A handwritten sign was taped to the vase that said, "I love you. $1.99."

"They're all sons of bitches and not one will ever stick by you," Gayla said. She pointed at Ronnie. "I know."

The man raised his eyebrows, looking at Ronnie.

"That's 63 cents back," Gayla said to him. Her frown turned into a practiced smile. "You have a nice day today, now," she said to the man.

The man didn't say anything but looked from Gayla to Ronnie again, then took his chips and his Big Slurp and walked out of the store. Gayla watched him leave.

"Sons of bitches," she said again, lifting her chin toward the door, toward the man who just walked out.

"Okay, look, Gayla," Donika walked up to the counter, laid her hands flat on the top—no nonsense—and leaned forward. "I'm gonna buy me a pack of cigarettes, but I don't want you telling Uncle Phil about it, 'kay?"

"You're *smoking*?" She looked at Donika.

"I'm gonna pay for them right now, and then I'll walk over and get them off the rack and put them in my pocket, okay?" Donika kept looking at the door.

Gayla looked at Ronnie.

"Are you smoking too?"

"No way," Ronnie said.

Gayla turned back to Donika.

"Don't you start walking the wild walk, Donika. You start smoking, next thing you know you'll be getting pregnant."

"Hey, I'm a customer here."

"Well hey back. I know your mother. You might not want to forget that."

Donika stopped and rubbed her hand across her mouth. Gayla laughed and turned to get a cigarette for herself from the open pack on the back counter. One of those disposable tin ashtrays sat next to the pack. She turned back to us, crossed her arms over her chest, and exhaled a cloud of smoke.

"Go on then," she said to Donika.

Donika took a step forward and then stopped. "You ain't gonna tell my mom are you?"

"You ain't my kid, Donnie," Gayla said.

"It's Donika."

"I know," Gayla said. She knew Donika hated to be called Donnie. Donika didn't want the two of them to be known as Donnie and Ronnie, and Ronnie agreed.

"So, you ain't gonna tell her?"

"Well, I don't know. What time does she get off the bus?" Gayla asked.

"I'm going next door," Ronnie said walking away from them.

"Bye, now, honey," Gayla said smiling at Ronnie. "See you tomorrow night."

Ronnie left Donika and walked to the front of the shop's double garage. Both doors were open. One stall had a red car of some kind in it, the other stall had a blue work van, lifted high in the air. Thatcher was standing under the van, reaching up and working on something. He didn't see Ronnie as she walked by him. She went into the small waiting room attached to the side of the garage.

Philip was standing behind the counter that sat right next to the door. He was talking on the phone.

"Your brakes are shot, John," he was saying. "I can't pass it like that, man."

He looked up and nodded to Ronnie.

If people waited for their cars, they had two choices: either sit on a long bench-couch covered in orange vinyl, or sit in one of the two black, high backed plastic chairs that sat on either side of a cheap end table. It was not a comfortable room, and most people didn't wait. The table had today's *Post* on it and a few magazines like *Missouri Life*, *Time*, and *People*. There was a vending machine and a soda machine, side by side on the inside wall of the room. Ronnie looked through the open door that led to the garage, past the red car and over to the blue car. She couldn't see Thatcher.

"I could have it ready for you this afternoon," Philip said. "Around four would be just fine. Uh, huh." He hung up.

"Well, hey, Ronnie" he said. "What are you doing?"

"Nothing."

"You ain't looking for someone are you?" He was smiling at her with that here's-some-trouble-for-you kind of look. "Let me guess. Kind of short—oh, wait–kind of tall compared to you, with black hair and dark brown eyes . . ."

"Oh, shut up, Philip," Ronnie said. He was talking about Mitchell—and Ronnie knew Mitchell's eyes were blue, not brown.

"He ain't here today, ma'am. I shall, however, tell him you was up here after his butt." He laughed.

Ronnie rolled her eyes.

"Oh, wait," he said. He walked around the counter to the front door. He craned his neck dramatically, though the whole room was surrounded in glass. "You drove up here in your new car, didn't you?"

"You know I can't drive a stick."

"Yeah? So? Something as silly as that wouldn't of stopped me back at your age."

Ronnie sat on the orange couch.

"Is T. really busy today?" she asked. Thatcher did *not* like people coming into the garage when he was working on cars. He was clear about that.

"Of course he's busy. Can't you see the man's working in there?"

Philip started back toward the counter but stuck his head in the doorway to the garage.

"T!" he shouted then he turned back to Ronnie and smiled.

"Thank you," Ronnie said.

Thatcher walked in the door from the garage. He was wiping his hands on a red work towel.

"Hey," he said when he saw Ronnie, then turned to Philip. "What do you want?"

"I don't want anything," Philip said.

"You called me."

"Yes, I did."

"Well, what?"

"Nothing."

Thatcher looked over at Ronnie for a second, but then turned back to the garage. Philip raised his hand to keep Ronnie still, so she just sat there on that orange couch watching the two of them. When Thatcher got all the way around the hood of the red car and was almost back to the blue car, Philip said, "Oh, wait. It was your *sister* here that might of wanted something, I think."

Philip looked at Ronnie, and she smiled.

Thatcher walked back into the waiting room and looked at Ronnie, this time ignoring Philip completely.

"What," he demanded.

"Well . . . " Ronnie said. She stood up.

"I gotta a car to work on here," Thatcher said impatiently.

His terseness ticked Ronnie off. She went there to tell him something important, to tell him about Juanita calling, but the way he was staring at her made her angry.

"What?" he said again.

"Geez, never mind," Ronnie said.

He looked over his shoulder toward Philip who was leaning on the counter. Thatcher shifted his weight from one foot to the other.

Donika walked into the waiting room.

"Hey, ya'll," she said. "Uncle Phil," she tapped her fingers on the counter. Thatcher looked at Donika.

"Hey, T.," she said.

Thatcher didn't answer. It wasn't that he didn't hear her; he was just careful to never encourage Donika with friendliness. "The key to her is small doses," Thatcher told Ronnie once. It was funny, because, Ronnie felt the same way about Philip. She liked Philip well enough, but it got on her nerves, the way he was always teasing her and testing her. It wore her out to be around him for too long. When she got right down to it, though, she guessed Philip and Donika were pretty much the same, personality-wise. Ronnie wondered if Donika and Philip ever felt the same way about Thatcher and her, that maybe they were more alike than they knew.

"Ronnie, say what you have to say or I'm going to go back to work."

Thatcher began wiping his grease-covered hands on the towel again. He looked up from his hands, but didn't quite raise his head, just his eyes. The smell of the shop—of oil and sweat—hung heavily in the air.

Ronnie shook her head. "Forget it," she said. She made her voice sound light, as if she didn't care, as if what she had to say was not important.

Thatcher dropped the towel on the counter. Philip and Donika watched them, their eyes moving back and forth as if they were watching a tennis match.

"So okay, then." He turned and walked back to the garage.

Ronnie watched Thatcher go around the trunk of the red car. Philip and Donika stared at Ronnie, waiting for her response. Her face grew hot.

"Let's go," Ronnie said.

Philip stayed leaning on the counter and watched them walk out the door without saying a word.

Ronnie heard the zap of the impact wrench again.

"What a jerk," she said.

Donika looked at her. "Where you want to go?"

"Let's go to the shelf," Ronnie said.

"The shelf? God, what made you think of that? It might not even be there anymore."

"It's there," Ronnie said.

Donika stopped and looked at Ronnie curiously for a second, but followed her as she started walking.

"Remember the pumpkins?" Ronnie asked.

Donika threw her head back and laughed. "Oh, man I forgot all about that!"

Ronnie smiled, and they walked along, talking about pumpkins and the leaf piles and the days in life when things were simple.

CHAPTER NINETEEN

"I think you should go," he said.
Ronnie felt her muscles tense at the sound of his voice. Juanita must have called up at the shop, or called while Ronnie was at work.
"No," she said without turning around.
"I think you should."
"I don't care what you think, I'm not going."
His hair hung in his eyes, and for a minute, Ronnie thought of Bean with his beady, dark eyes and his dirty little face looking up at her as he sipped on his orange soda.
"You need a haircut," she said, trying to get him to drop it.
He hadn't taken a shower yet, and he hadn't shaved either. Ronnie looked back to the section of the table she was painting and focused her attention on that. The problem was with the vines. They were too viney or something. She picked up a bottle of green acrylic and squeezed a drop of paint onto one of their small ceramic kitchen plates. She took her detail brush to one of the leaves, but then she started looking at the vines. Maybe there was too much brown on them. Maybe that was the problem.

"I mean it, Ronnie," Thatcher said. "I think you should go." His voice was quiet, but definite.

"I think you can't tell me what to do."

"I think . . . "

"There you are, T.," a voice said. It was Rochelle. She was Thatcher's latest girl friend. She'd been hanging around and calling off and on for nearly a week. Ronnie thought she dressed like a slut, wore too much makeup, and had a bad haircut. Ronnie had gone to school with one of Rochelle's sisters.

Thatcher smiled at Rochelle as she walked up to him. Ronnie found herself staring at Thatcher's expression. He didn't smile much, and when he did, it was almost never directed at her. When she did catch him in a smile, though, Ronnie found that she couldn't look away. It was such an unusual look for him, a lightness that she wasn't used to seeing. It was both beautiful and strange to her. She looked at Rochelle, feeling a jab of jealously that a stranger could make Thatcher smile like that. He put his arm around Rochelle's waist and gave her a kiss on the lips.

Ronnie turned back to her painting, disgusted. She won't last, Ronnie thought.

"Oh Ronnie, that's so pretty," Rochelle said in an overly enthusiastic voice.

"All I'm saying," Thatcher cut in, "is that I think it might be good."

"Good for who?" Ronnie said, ignoring Rochelle's statement completely.

She put down her brush and turned back to Thatcher.

"All of us."

Rochelle looked confused.

"Do you want me out of here, T.?" Ronnie suddenly asked. "Because if you do, just say the word and I'm gone."

Thatcher's mouth fell open in confusion. "What?"

"You heard me," she said.

It was like a math equation suddenly went off in her head. Graduation + eighteen years old + her own car = move out. It popped into her head, just like that. The time was coming, and suddenly Ronnie knew it, and it felt cold and hard and utterly terrifying.

"I just . . . " Thatcher was saying.

"You just what?"

He didn't finish the sentence and they stood there in the silence. Ronnie picked up her brush, threw it in the rinse jar and walked into the house.

Ronnie turned 12 the same week Thatcher had bought the twin bed for Ronnie and put it in his house. In the middle of the night, on one of her last nights in her mother's house, Vivian had gone into Ronnie's room, and sat on the edge of Ronnie's bed, whispering slurry-sounding words into Ronnie's ear.

Ronnie had been facing the wall with her back to Vivian. She opened her eyes at the sound of her mother's voice but didn't move. Vivian rested her hand on Ronnie's arm to steady herself. Light from the hallway cast the silhouette of Vivian on the wall in front of Ronnie.

"You go on and stay with T. as much as you want, Ronnie, but I'm going to tell you something. It ain't gonna last. He's full of it. You really think he's gonna want you staying in his house all the time?"

Ronnie lay still. She could smell the alcohol on Vivian's breath—a distinct smell that reminded Ronnie of black olives. She watched the screen of light on the wall in front of her as it filtered through the shadow of her mother's teased hair.

"He's gonna get himself some girlfriend, and they're gonna want to be alone. Do you know what I'm saying? He's gonna want to be alone. He's not gonna want you there. You can count on it."

She tapped her fingers on Ronnie's arm lightly, but Ronnie remained still.

"But you listen. I say stay with the son of a bitch if you want. He'll get tired of you hanging around and causing trouble. He doesn't know. You're a kid. He'll send you back the second he gets tired of you, and when he does, you just come on home, baby."

She was quiet for a minute, but then Ronnie heard the unmistakable sound of Vivian's snuffled crying. A part of her wanted to turn to her mother, to comfort her and tell her it was all right, that she wouldn't leave—but Ronnie didn't turn. She *couldn't*. She couldn't help the way her mother was and she wouldn't let herself feel sorry for her either. Ronnie knew that if she had turned to her mother then, it would have been like losing some sort of a chance.

Vivian sniffed loudly, trying to sit up straight, trying to pull herself together, only she ended up nearly falling off the bed.

"He's such a . . . such a jerk, Ronnie," she mumbled. "They all are. But you . . . you can always come here." She walked to the door. "You listen to me," she said. Her shadow was pointing toward Ronnie. "You can."

When she turned the hall light out, her shadow disappeared. For a long time after she left, Ronnie stared into the darkness of the empty black wall in front of her. That was the first and last time Vivian ever said a word to Ronnie about her moving in with Thatcher.

Ronnie tried not to give her mother power over her, but Vivian's words had a way of crouching behind the shadiest corners of Ronnie's mind. They dallied there, solid yet untouchable, only to pounce on Ronnie at the oddest times: *he'll send you back the second he gets tired of you*. Ronnie had wondered, for a long time back then, when her mother's words would come true, but in all the time she had lived with Thatcher, he had never even once hinted for her to leave.

Things were changing now, though. Things were happening that were beyond Ronnie's control. She was getting older. She was finished with high school. Juanita had shown up, and Rochelle was starting to hang around the house—Thatcher never had girls come to the house.

But hadn't he just given her a car—not just any car, but his *first* car? Hadn't he just proved that she meant something to him? Ronnie's thoughts rambled back and forth. Maybe he gave her the car, not to prove his love, but to make leaving easier. She just didn't know. All she knew was that everything was changing and changing fast.

She woke awhile later to a knock on her bedroom door.
"I ordered a pizza," Thatcher said.
Ronnie looked at the clock. She had meant to just get away from Thatcher for a little while, but had ended up falling asleep. Now it was already dinnertime.
In the kitchen, Thatcher was already eating. Rochelle was gone, and Ronnie could hear the television on and unattended in the living room. Ronnie went into the kitchen.
"I'll go with you," Thatcher said after they'd been sitting there for awhile.
Ronnie looked at him, but didn't say anything.
"Why are you fighting this?" he asked.
"Leave me alone, would you? You go. I don't want to. She's a freak."
Ronnie looked up at his silence.
There was a moment of silence, before Ronnie was jolted by the sharp crack of a half full soda can hitting the wall behind her. Thatcher had thrown it with all of his force, and it took Ronnie a full second to realize what had happened; it took another full second for her indignation to kick in.
"Hey!" she shouted turning back to him, but the cold, dark look on his face jolted her in another way entirely, made her feel like she was outside on a cold December night, a night without the whiteness of snow or a glow of moon. Instantly, she regretted what she'd said and knew she had gone too far. But for him to act that way . . . . it was the way he used to act with Vivian when he was younger. The two of them stood, glaring at each other, neither willing to retreat, their eyes holding strong and

defiant, regardless of what their hearts were whispering in the background.

Finally, Thatcher turned and walked out the back door, leaving Ronnie alone in the kitchen, the wall behind her splattered in spidery trails and the floor covered in an angry puddle. Maybe it *was* time for her to leave. Maybe she was the real problem. Maybe she had driven Vivian to act so crazy, and now she was doing it to Thatcher. She went outside, feeling suddenly panicked, like she was about to lose the only thing in life that mattered. Thatcher was in the garage bent over the old yellow lawn mower.

"T.," Ronnie said, her voice thin with timidity.

He did not look up.

"I'm sorry."

He turned his back to his workbench and began rifling through a tool-box, clanking socket wrenches and screwdrivers and whatever else he had in that box.

"I'm sorry," she said again.

Silence. His back straightened and his hands stopped searching for whatever they were seeking. She wanted to tell him that she was going to leave, that she didn't know how yet, but that she knew it was time. She wanted to say this, but didn't—couldn't—because in her heart she was too afraid that he would agree.

Instead, she said, "If you'll go with me, like you said, I'll go."

His shoulders relaxed, but he didn't turn around.

"She's a person," he said quietly.

"I know, I know," Ronnie said. "I'm sorry. I really am." She just wanted him to stop being angry with her. She just wanted everything to be okay between them.

"Ronnie," he said, "you don't know anything."

CHAPTER TWENTY

They left town late Friday afternoon, heading west down Highway 44, out of St. Louis, past Wet Willies water slide, past Six Flags, past the town of Pacific. Ronnie pointed to the Catawissa exit which led to a large slough off the Meramec River where Thatcher had taken her fishing once. Catawissa wasn't far. Not even an hour from home. Cabool was four hours away, though, with many towns between. They would go west until Rolla, Thatcher said. West then south, he said.

Where they went and how they got there didn't matter to Ronnie. She leaned back and watched billboards pass by: "Meramec Caverns—See Jesse James' Hideout!" "Onondaga Cave—See the Natural Wonder!" She watched the clouds. She watched other cars pass them by. She watched the people in the cars. She watched the reflections of truckers in their side mirrors as they glanced down to see Thatcher's old pickup truck passing them. She searched for rock and roll stations on the radio, wading through the waves of static, and finding more and more country stations and less rock-and-roll.

They rode with the windows down and chased the sun west. They watched it descend gracefully lower and lower into the horizon. Ronnie watched the hills, deep with trees—treetops blending with treetops like billowing green clouds—a green sky on the ground around them. Outlines of tree-lined hilltops shadowed against other tree-lined hilltops. Ronnie watched the valleys, the meadows, and the pasturelands. Cows stood on hilltops, stood in clusters under shade trees, stood next to small ponds, stood alone in the open, stood still, looking slow and lazy. She watched the farm houses, nested into the land—one had a red barn sitting alone on a hillside. She thought about painting, about that empty canvas that sat in her room and wondered if she would ever be able to paint scenes like that red barn. She thought about the country and wondered what it was like to live so far from neighbors, so far from friends, so far from the mall, so far from the city.

She saw the pink and yellow and white wildflowers that grew between rock cliffs, grew on the sides of the roads, grew in open fields, trying to cover the ground in a beautiful blanket. She watched turkey buzzards in the sky making slow and careful circles. She saw a hawk soaring gracefully, straight and steady and hunting strong.

"What if we don't like it there?" She shouted over the sound of the wind rushing through the windows.

"Then we'll leave."

"What if I don't like it there and you do?"

"Then we'll leave when I'm ready."

It was getting on twilight when they neared Cabool. About sixteen miles outside Cabool, they passed exits for Willow Springs. They crossed over Hog Creek, then crossed over Potter's Creek. They crossed the Big Piney River, then crossed over Elk Creek. They passed signs that read "Rez-Nod Vintage Tin and Auto Sales," "Coyote Crossing Flea Market," "Caboodle Antiques and Collectibles—Old and New," and "Feeder Pigs by Telo Auction." They passed "The Sugar Shack" and the "Hayloft Restaurant."

"Can't we stop and eat before we get there?" Ronnie said. "I don't want to get there and be hungry."

Thatcher glanced in her direction. They were pulling off of Business 60 and crossing the overpass.

"Is this it?" Ronnie looked around, seeing a house or two, but not much else. "Is this Cabool?"

"This is the outside of it," Thatcher said. "I think the center of town is up ahead."

He drove on, leaning forward and looking out the window in Ronnie's direction. "There should be a gravel road coming up on the right," he said. "Juanita said if we get to the gas station, we passed it." He pointed past Ronnie. "There it is."

A white gravel road glowed in dusk light.

"Did you hear me?" Ronnie said. "I'm hungry, T."

"Relax!" Thatcher glared at her, and Ronnie glared out to the nowhere sitting beyond the truck's windshield. "Let me see where we have to come back to before we go on," he said.

Ronnie's stomach started to ache, though she knew it didn't all have to do with being hungry. They were in Cabool. Of course she knew they would get there eventually, but until now she had pretty much avoided narrowing it down to an actuality. She had expected them to get there in that vague, uncommitted sense people have about things like having to go to the dentist. But there they were on the outskirts of Juanita's home town.

Thatcher drove past the road. "*Now* we can find someplace to eat."

They passed a two-pump gas station. Houses began to dot the road more frequently. They passed a few big, old, well-kept houses with nice flowerbeds and big front porches. One house had a tractor wheel laying in the front yard, painted white and pretending to be a planter. Small, old, unkempt houses with rusty chain-link fences that enclosed things like overgrown weeds and broken down cars nestled in the town here and there. A row of houses made with oddly shaped stones of brown, red, and tan, that fit together like pieces of a jigsaw puzzle stretched on the right side of the street. What looked like a motel or a one-story apartment building sprawled alongside a good section of the road, the bottom half of the building covered with the same kind of stone as the jigsaw houses, the top half covered in white swirled stucco—just like the Wilson's house. They drove by the Family Center Grocery and the small Presbyterian Church with a sign outside that read, "Let your light shine."

"Here," Thatcher said. He pulled into a parking lot next to a small, beige-painted, cinderblock building with a plate glass window on one side of the door and a small wood window on the other side of the door. The roof to the building was flat and angled high in the front and slanted down toward the back, making it look more like a big shed rather than a small restaurant. The hot pink neon sign in the window glowed "The Pink Lemonade."

"Oh, come on, T." Ronnie frowned. "Can't we find a McDonalds or something? Or let's try the *Sugar Shack* or *Hayloft* at least. This place is a dump."

"What's wrong with it?"

"*Look* at it."

"Yeah, well, Juanita said it's good barbecue."

Like Juanita would know anything, Ronnie thought.

"Can't we just drive on a little farther and see what else there is?"

Thatcher was out of the truck before Ronnie even finished the sentence. She crossed her arms tightly across her chest to show him her displeasure, but all he did was tap the hood of the truck with a fingertip as he walked around it toward the door of the restaurant. As he grabbed the doorknob and began to push the door open, someone from the inside pulled the door open so that Thatcher was unceremoniously pulled across the threshold, nearly bumping into an older man in cowboy boots and blue jeans.

Both men looked toward the ground, Thatcher backing up against the doorjamb, so the man could get by. The man held a Styrofoam cup in his hand and excused himself as he passed.

Thatcher went into the restaurant and Ronnie absently watched the man pass in front of the truck. She sighed. Either she could sit in the truck and starve, or go inside and eat. She got out of the truck and slammed the door, cursing Thatcher in her mind, cursing that she had to be in this dumb town to see her giant sister and her scroungy looking kid. Ronnie stood just inside the door and looked for Thatcher. He was sitting in one of the two rooms in the restaurant—the smaller of the two, that had just four round tables. The place was as small on the inside as it looked on the outside. The bigger room off to the side had cheap looking, false-wood paneling and three rows of long, cafeteria-type tables that sat end to end. Not one of the many old looking wooden chairs surrounding the tables matched.

Five older men sat along two of the tables at the far end of the room—every one of them with a baseball cap on: two greens, one white, one blue, and a red. One of the green hats was reading the paper. The other green hat was eating. The blue and white hats sat across from each other, both drinking coffee and fiddling with a pile of dominos that lay on the table in front of them. The red hat lifted his coffee cup for a re-fill while the waitress poured. They all looked up when Ronnie walked in.

In the back of the room was a counter with a cash register and a couple of old metal stools. The idea of a kitchen peeked through the swinging doors behind the counter and a lighted menu hung on the wall above. Ronnie went over to Thatcher and cleared her throat. She was going to tell him again—to whisper to him so that the waitress and the hats wouldn't hear—that she didn't want to eat there, that she wanted to leave, but he told her to sit down in a firm voice and nodded to the chair across from him.

The chair legs screeched on the mud-brown, painted plywood floor. Ronnie looked around. The waitress came over. She set two glasses of water on the table and then slipped two menus from beneath her arm. She set Ronnie's menu on the table in front of her with barely a nod, but handed Thatcher his menu.

"Here you go, sweetheart," she said, smiling at him.

"Thank you," he said, looking up at her and smiling back.

She looked to be about forty-something and was short and thick. She wore faded blue jeans, a gray t-shirt, and sneakers.

A white apron with two pockets on the front was wrapped around her waist.

"You here to see the rodeo?" she asked Thatcher.

"Rodeo?" he said.

"Well, *yes*," the waitress said. Her eyes stayed on Thatcher.

"Uh . . . no," he said.

"You *with* the rodeo, then?"

"Ha!" Thatcher laughed at the idea. "No, ma'am," he said.

The waitress looked disappointed for a second and then shrugged.

"Well, I'll give you a minute and come back to see what you want."

Ronnie tapped her fingers on the table to get Thatcher's attention.

"Are we really going to stay here?" she whispered.

"Stop it," he whispered back. "I like it here."

"Well, it sure isn't very crowded for a Friday night, T. That's got to tell you something," Ronnie said.

"Did you hear her? The rodeo's in town," Thatcher whispered back.

Ronnie heard a newspaper rattle. One of the hats coughed.

"Katie, I'll have a piece of that delicious peach pie, I think," the red hat said.

The waitress laughed and flipped her short bleach-blonde hair from her eye. "Yeah, right, Eddie. And I'll call Maysie for your letter of permission."

The greens, blue, and white laughed.

"I don't know why I come in here. You don't serve me what I want, and you smart off."

"Cuz you love me," Katie said.

A fat woman appeared from the kitchen counter.

"Hey, Eddie, I made a sugar free chocolate pie just for you."

"You did?"

"Yes, I did."

"You are on the Lord's list, Yolanda."

The fat woman disappeared back into the kitchen.

Eddie looked at Katie. "I believe I'll have that pie now."

The old men started talking about baseball. Thatcher and Ronnie looked at their menus. Katie came back a minute later and pulled her order pad from one of her apron pockets.

"What are you going to have, hon?" she said leaning in towards Thatcher.

"I think I'll have a pork steak with baked beans and a salad," he said.

"Oh, good choice," Katie said. She glanced at Ronnie, but then looked back at Thatcher.

"And what's she gonna have?" She nodded her head sideways towards Ronnie.

Thatcher looked at Ronnie. He was amused.

"What are you gonna have, Ronnie?" he said.

Ronnie started to order a cheeseburger and fries.

"You can have that if you want," Katie said, "but we're famous for our pork steaks. You should get a pork steak."

Ronnie frowned. What was this woman's problem? She looked at Thatcher for an explanation.

"Get whatever you want," he said.

"I guess I'll try a pork steak," Ronnie said and closed her menu in a huff. Katie didn't notice.

Thatcher asked for a soda.

"Well my gosh, don't you see our name?" Katie said. "We are known for our pink lemonades." She leaned in closer to Thatcher. "I personally guarantee you'll love it."

"She's right," the blue hat said from across the room.

Katie looked over her shoulder and frowned at the interference.

"Well, okay then. Two pink lemonades. Okay, Ronnie?"

"Whatever," Ronnie said.

Katie raised an eyebrow at Ronnie and took the menus. "I'll be back in a flash."

Thatcher lit a cigarette and leaned back. Ronnie looked around the room. Everything was beige: the walls, the ceiling, the windows, the paneling. It looked like the windows in the small room had been painted shut. Small pictures hung hodgepodge and on the wall behind them—all pictures of sailboats that looked as if they had been torn from travel magazines and framed.

"I have to pee," Ronnie whispered to Thatcher.

He looked around. There was a door with a rest room sign in the corner behind the wall that separated the two rooms. Ronnie had to pull a chain hanging from the ceiling to turn on the single bulb hanging down into the tiny room. At least it was clean, though she was sure not to touch the walls. She sat down and heard voices from the other room.

"Where you from?" one of the voices said.

"St. Louis," Thatcher said.

She heard them clearly and worried that they would hear her. She hurried, flushed, washed her hands, and walked out feeling embarrassed and self-conscious though no one seemed to be paying any attention to her.

" . . . cousin up there," Eddie was saying.

Thatcher nodded.

When Ronnie sat down, the door opened and a cute guy walked in. Ronnie watched him.

"Hey Joey," Katie said. She went back into the kitchen.

Joey gave a hey back, and waved half-heartedly to the elders. As he walked across the room, he looked in Ronnie's direction and their eyes met. Ronnie looked away. She hoped he'd sit down so that she could keep watching him, but he didn't. He went to the counter.

"Yolanda's getting your stuff together," Katie said as she walked by him with Thatcher and Ronnie's plates. He nodded. His eyes followed Katie back to Ronnie's table. He had to bend forward a bit to see around Katie. This time when their eyes met, he smiled at Ronnie.

"You puppy," Thatcher whispered, watching them.

Katie set their plates down.

"I brought you fries instead of beans," she said to Ronnie. "You looked more like the fry type to me."

Ronnie was pleasantly surprised. "Thanks."

"Well, I try to please. I'll be right back with your lemonade."

"See?" Thatcher said. "It looks great."

Yolanda came to the counter and handed a paper to-go sack to Joey, and when Katie came back around with their drinks, she said, "Joey, watch this. First timers."

Thatcher and Ronnie exchanged glances as Katie set the two glasses on the table. The lemonades were slushy and had cherries sitting on top. A straw and a spoon were in each glass.

"Try this," she said.

Joey, who had paid Yolanda for his order, walked toward the door, but stopped in front of Ronnie's table and stood next to Katie. He was smiling and Ronnie thought she was going to die from self-consciousness, but she sucked on the straw and tasted the most delicious lemonade that ever existed. It was sweet, but not too sweet, and slushy and cold.

Katie and Joey smiled, nodding their heads. The hats were all watching, too.

"Good stuff," one of the hats said.

"Man, that's good," Thatcher said.

Ronnie reached for her cherry.

"Uh-uh," Joey said looking at her. "You gotta eat the cherry last."

Katie was nodding. "House rules," she said.

Ronnie looked at them to see if they were kidding but took her hand away from the glass.

Katie looked at the table for a minute, waving her hand over it to see if she was forgetting anything. She looked at Joey. "Okay, now shoo before your mother thinks you got lost."

He gave Ronnie one last look, said, "See you," and then walked out the door.

Katie looked at Thatcher. "Let me know if you need something."

"Can we get a couple of steak knives?"

Katie leaned down and rested her palms on the table. "You can have a steak knife if you want one, but your butter knife will cut that steak just fine. They are tender as can be."

When she walked away, Thatcher leaned toward Ronnie. "Feels kind of like we're the entertainment for the evening, don't it?"

Ronnie looked at the door wondering if any other cute guys would come in, but realized quickly that Katie was right. The Pink Lemonade had some of the best food she had ever eaten.

"This is better than Thanksgiving," she whispered to Thatcher. He nodded with a full mouth.

When she was slurping on the last of her pink lemonade, the men started speaking to them again.

"Where you headed?" the blue hat asked.

"We're visiting my sister for the weekend," Thatcher said.

"She live here?"

"Yep," Thatcher said.

"What's her name?" the blue hat asked.

Thatcher looked at Ronnie, then at the blue hat and his gang.

"Juanita Geisel," Thatcher said.

There was a moment of silence before one of the man let out a long whistle. They passed looks to each other like plates of holiday dishes, and then looked at Ronnie and Thatcher in curious consideration. Katie was the only one who truly looked surprised. She turned to them sharply—maybe because she wasn't old like everyone else, or maybe because she had never played poker and had been taught to keep a straight face like these old men probably had.

"You say you're Juanita's family?" Katie asked.

"Uh-huh," Thatcher said. "You know her?"

"Juanita?" The blue hat said and smiled at the other men as if it were a stupid question. "Everybody knows Juanita, son." He pointed toward them. "That's her chair right over there behind you."

They both turned. Ronnie hadn't noticed it, but in the corner was a wooden two-seater bench sitting next to an unusually high table.

The men looked at each other, then looked back at Ronnie and Thatcher.

"How tall is she?" A green hat said.

"What?" Thatcher said.

"You know, if she's your sister and all, how tall is she?"

"I don't know."

There was a group response, a sort of mutual leaning back in unison.

"Well, *I* know how tall she is," the red hat said.

"Yep," the white hat said. "Me too."

Thatcher and Ronnie exchanged confused glances.

"We all do," Eddie said.

"I know she's tall," Thatcher said a bit defensively.

Katie turned to the men. "What are you all giving these customers of mine trouble for? Leave them alone." She took a step closer to Thatcher so that she was between him and the men. "Don't mind them," she said. "We're just kind of protective when it comes to Juanita."

Thatcher nodded dumbly, as if he understood, but when he looked at Ronnie, it was clear he did not. He was as lost in all of this as Ronnie was.

Katie leaned over the table. "Eighty-seven and a half," she whispered. She raised her eyebrows and smiled at him, her eyes lingering on his stubbled face.

"What?" he whispered.

She stood up straight again and laid the check face down on the table. "That's how tall she is. Eighty-seven and a half inches. That's seven foot three and a half inches tall." She nodded at us and then walked away.

Thatcher had an odd look on his face. He took the check, pulled out his wallet, and said, "Let's go."

They stood up, and Ronnie followed Thatcher over to the cash register.

"Well," the man wearing the blue hat said. "Who's your father?" He rubbed his jaw and eyed the two strangers.

"What?" Thatcher said.

"Your father. What about him?"

"My . . . Fa . . ."

"Is his name Ray?"

"Oh, now don't tell him for God's sakes," one of the men said, scoldingly.

They all stared at Thatcher.

Thatcher cleared his throat.

"Holy moley," Eddie said. "He does sort of look like him, don't he?"

"I haven't really . . . I haven't seen him in a long time," Thatcher finally said.

"Well, I guess not," blue cap said. "Otherwise you'da known him."

"What do you mean?" Thatcher asked.

"That was him going out when you was coming in," Eddie said.

"You almost knocked into him," the blue hat said.

"I didn't see . . . that was him?" Thatcher looked over his shoulder at the door.

They all nodded. Thatcher and Ronnie looked at the door, too, trying hard to remember the face of the man with the Styrofoam cup.

CHAPTER TWENTY-ONE

Thatcher's face had gone pale and his lips were tight. Ronnie had spent the last couple weeks trying not to think about any of this—and certainly hadn't thought about the possibility of meeting their father down here. Of course, she knew in the back of her mind that he would be there too, but the thought of Juanita alone was overwhelming enough, so Ronnie had forgotten all about the idea of him. But Thatcher . . . surely *he* must have thought about the possibility of seeing their father. This sudden revelation, this unexpected encounter was weird.

It was dark by the time they came out of the restaurant. They sat in the truck. Thatcher was silent behind the wheel, staring out the window. Ronnie wished she had taken a better look at that man. She wished she'd been paying attention. But who would have thought . . . it was just a man coming out of a restaurant. But Thatcher should have known. How could he not recognize his own father? Could time really do that? Could time have let Thatcher forget so entirely? And what about their father? How could a man not recognize his own son?

Ronnie looked over at Thatcher. She sat, waiting. Maybe it would be too much for him. Maybe he would call the whole thing off, and they would go back home. He started the truck. His chin was tucked and a thin white line outlined a tight top lip. He looked straight ahead with both hands gripped too firmly on the steering wheel. Ronnie sat sideways on the bench seat, facing him and fiddling with the seat belt buckle.

"T.?" she said quietly. She didn't really know what to say, but she wanted to say something. She wanted to take the darkness from his eyes and let him know that she was still there and that things were still the same and that seeing their father didn't really matter—even though, of course, she knew none of what she wanted to say was true.

He turned his head slowly toward her. His expression intense, like a bull staring at the color red. Ronnie pressed the back of her head against the rolled up window behind her. She didn't say anything. He reached in his pocket for a cigarette, and when he lit it, she saw that his hands were shaking—just barely. He glanced in her direction again, and Ronnie looked away, looked at her lap. He exhaled deeply and started driving. Ronnie rolled down her window, letting the sound of wind fill the silence.

The white gravel road seemed to glow in the dark. They couldn't miss it. Thatcher could make no mistake now unless he wanted to. He turned left.

"There's the graveyard," he said. His voice came low and thick to Ronnie's ears and the wind from her open window carried his voice past her and off into the cooling night air.

Out Thatcher's side window, the gravestones stood out like white shadows floating in the darkening dusk—a place where ghosts could certainly be real. Of course she didn't believe in ghosts, but isn't that what Juanita and her father had been for so many years? Ronnie didn't want any more surprises. Her eyes stayed on the graves until they drove past and the graveyard disappeared behind a bend of road. Gravel crunched steadily under the tires, making a cloud of dust behind them. A house was up ahead—a small, white boxy looking house.

"Here it is," Thatcher said.

The lights were on, making the house shine like a beacon in the surrounding darkness—a house alone in the middle of nowhere. Thatcher pulled in the drive and cut the engine. Suddenly they found themselves deep in the middle of a country night. The air was thick with the sound of a thousand crickets and frogs and whatever else was out there, offering waves of noise that did not relent, but grew louder, then softer, then louder still. Thatcher got out of the truck and stood with the door open. There were no streetlights to illuminate anything around them, though Ronnie tried to see beyond the house, to the sides of the house and across the road from the house. It was too dark. All she saw were shadows and darkness interrupted by the steady blinks of lightning bugs. She thought of the gravestones up the road, imagined them floating toward them, following them.

The front door of the house opened. Ronnie reached for the handle on her door, but when she looked out the window, she was suddenly afraid.

"Wait," she said to Thatcher, and slid across the seat to his open door. She jumped out and stood beside him. Juanita stepped out onto the porch. She blocked the doorway behind her and the porch light that hung above her was so close to her head that the light shined on her as if she were wearing a halo. The struggling light distorted the contours of her brow bone and cheekbones, distorted the sockets of her eyes that, from where Ronnie stood, looked like black, empty holes. Ronnie had the surreal feeling of being caught in the middle of a bad dream. The gravestones were still on her mind and when Juanita reached a long arm toward them, she thought of zombies walking slowly in the dark, arms out, slow and steady with dead intent. She heard a rustling off to her right, something just beyond the truck that stood apart from the din of the buzzing insects and croaking amphibians. She took a step back and placed herself between Thatcher and the truck.

"Hey!" Juanita said in her thick voice. "Hey! You made it!"

More than anything in the world at that moment, Ronnie wanted to be at home in her room, listening to the radio and working on her mural or on the table. She wanted to grab Thatcher's hand and push him back into that truck and get out of there.

"Was it hard to find?" Juanita asked.

"No," Thatcher said. "We stopped and had dinner."

"Oh, well good. I was worrying about my directions."

Ronnie looked cautiously past Juanita to the house. Bean was standing in the doorway.

"Veronica!" Juanita said. "You came!"

Juanita stepped closer. Ronnie took a step back, but her back hit the side of the truck. There was no place to go.

"I'm real happy to see you."

They all stood for a minute, not saying anything. Juanita was nodding her head up and down, smiling at Ronnie, not like a zombie, but like one of those bobble-head dolls that you stick on the dashboard.

"Well, come on inside." She clapped the palms of her big open hands.

Thatcher followed her up the porch steps, with Ronnie close behind. She reached out and tugged Thatcher on the arm. He stopped and when Ronnie stood at his side, he put his hand on the middle of her back. "Come on," he whispered. His voice was comforting as he pushed her gently in front of him. The porch light glared down on cracking concrete that had once been painted red, but now was faded and splotchy. A giant pair of boots sat in the corner next to the door. Bean had disappeared. Ronnie walked up the steps behind Juanita and watched as Juanita hunched down to go through the doorway. She followed the giant woman inside, and her eyes were drawn immediately to the gigantic rocking chair that sat in the living room.

"Now listen, Bean tells everybody that's his," Juanita said, smiling and nodding toward the rocker, "but don't you believe him. That's my chair."

Thatcher laughed. "Where did you get that?" he asked.

"A furniture maker two towns over was nice enough to make it for me. Cost Daddy a fortune, but I don't know what I'd do without it." She watched us. "I know you want to sit in it," she said looking at Ronnie. "Everybody does."

"Me?"

Thatcher grinned at Ronnie.

"It's okay," she said. "Really."

"You have to kind of climb up onto it."

"Oh, no . . . " Ronnie said, staring at the chair. It was the biggest chair she'd ever seen, the seat wide enough for two, the arm rests as thick as two by fours.

Juanita laughed. "Suit yourself."

The house was small and simple, even dingy-looking. The living room and dining room were really just one long room, separated by a waist-high wall that stuck halfway out into the room. Most of the furniture in the room was normal size—an old blue couch in front of the window, an end table, a brown recliner in the corner next to an open closet—but as Ronnie looked, she started to see the various adjustments that had been made to accommodate Juanita's height.

"It ain't much," Juanita said, "but let me show you what's what."

Juanita walked over to one of the two bedrooms that opened directly into the living room. As Ronnie looked around, she felt like she had run up the Beanstalk and was looking through the giant's castle—only this was no castle, and not everything was giant. The wall space above each doorway inside the house had been cut out and plastered so that the entrances to each room went all the way to the ceiling. The doors were regular height, though, so when they were closed, there was a peculiar looking open space above them. Juanita walked over to and bent down to reach for a doorknob. Ronnie couldn't imagine how she existed in such a small space. Juanita peeked into the open space over the top of the door.

"Bean," she said, "Why are you being shy. Come on out and see your aunt and uncle."

Ronnie looked at Thatcher. He looked amused.

"This is nice, Juanita," he said. "It's all made comfortable for you."

"Yeah," she said. "I dream of having a house with fourteen foot ceilings and everything made for my size . . . you know there was a couple in the 1800's did just that. They were really tall, though—almost eight feet. They traveled with the circus but had this house built with everything made just for their size. That'd be nice. I got some stuff, but a whole house? That'd be real nice." She turned back to the closed door.

"Come on now, hon," she said to Bean.

"That's my room there," she said pointing to the other closed door. Ronnie had been caught up in the curiosity of the house, but as she looked at Juanita, as she looked at the way Juanita shifted her weight from foot to foot, Ronnie realized that she was nervous, that this was not an easy thing for her to do either—having them there—that as she gave them her freak tour, she was taking a risk too, that she didn't know what Ronnie and Thatcher would think, or what would come of it, or what it all really meant.

"Bathroom's there," she said pointing toward her left, but then continued on into the kitchen. The bathroom had a curtain hanging down to cover the open space above the doorway.

"And the kitchen," she said, walking in front of them.

The kitchen was, by far, the most interesting room. The sink and the counters were very high, as high as Ronnie's chest, but only to Juanita's waist. The stove sat on a built up platform, and the cabinets hung from the ceiling.

"How's Bean get around in here?" Thatcher asked.

"Yeah," Juanita said, looking at him. "It's hard, you know? I got a stool for him." She pointed to a wooden stool sitting in the corner, "but you know that don't really help him too much. See that?" She reached down and opened a cabinet that was from the floor to the counter. "I gave him this one so he could put all his stuff in it. Like it has glasses and dishes for him so if he needs something he can get it. But I guess it's going be awhile before he can do the dishes for me!" She laughed. "All this was put in here before he was born, and I tell you what, it's made my life a whole lot easier."

"I bet," Thatcher said.

Ronnie looked at Juanita, wondering what the story was with Juanita having Bean. Where was his father, and why wasn't

Bean a giant too? She made a mental note to ask Thatcher later, to see if he knew anything.

When Ronnie was little, she was teased every once in awhile because she didn't have a father. She made up lies about him. She said he died in a plane crash, or had been murdered. Just stupid stuff. Everyone knew she was lying, and she didn't deny it, but saying something got them off her back, shut them up. She wondered if people teased Bean, but then why would anyone bother teasing a kid about something like not having a father around when he had a mother like Juanita?

"Besides," Juanita was saying, "I think most of the rest of the world is going to be normal size for him, so he's just got to deal with it. Things will get easier for him as he grows."

Juanita turned to the screened-in porch. "It's a mess in there. Just a place to do laundry and such. Ain't a basement in this house, so what you see is what you get."

"I wondered how you got along all these years," Thatcher said. "Now I see. It's nice."

"Yeah," Juanita said, turning her face upward and smiling.

"Well, I want you to be comfortable," she said after a minute.

"We'll be fine," Thatcher said.

"Can I get you something to drink?"

"I could go for that," Thatcher said.

He seemed so comfortable. There they were, standing in weird world, and Thatcher wanted to sit and have a beer.

"What about you, Veronica? Do you want a soda or something?"

"I'm fine," Ronnie said.

"Well, go on and sit," she said, pointing to the dining room.

They walked out of the kitchen with the high cut door, and Juanita went to the refrigerator.

"Bean!" Juanita called from the kitchen.

One of the two doors on the inside wall of the room opened just a crack. The crack was dark, but Ronnie saw one of Bean's eyes peeking out. When his eye met hers, the door shut.

Juanita came back holding two beers.

"Veronica, you sit down now," she said. "Come on now. Don't be timid." Still holding the beers, she made a gathering motion with her arm. Ronnie took a step over and sat on the edge of the easy chair. Juanita smiled at her, satisfied, and gave Thatcher his drink. Ronnie found it impossible not to stare at Juanita, especially in the context of such a tiny house. It was like watching a two pound bass try to get around inside of a ten-gallon aquarium.

Juanita walked around the table, and Ronnie assumed she was going to sit in one of the chairs, but she went over to the wall. There was a big cushion sitting on the floor and when Juanita started to sit down, and when Ronnie saw how high Juanita came up to the table in spite of being on the floor, Ronnie realized the floor *was* her chair.

"I'm real glad you're here, Veronica," she said. "I guess this is pretty weird for you."

"She's not the only one," Thatcher said.

"No," Juanita said. "That's definitely true—for me, too. I don't think I slept good one night this whole week—course I don't sleep so good anyway."

Ronnie cringed at the sound of her laugh. It was one thing to take a side-show tour of a giant's house, but they were supposed to stay there for two days? No way. That became clearer to Ronnie with each passing second.

Bean's door opened a crack again.

"Bean, you come on out and stop being foolish. We got company here."

"Hey, Bean." Thatcher twisted in his chair.

Thatcher seemed so calm and so comfortable. Ronnie didn't know what had come over him, but it irritated her.

"I got something for you, kid," he said. "Come here and get it."

There was silence for a minute, and then the door opened half way. Bean stood back from the light that crept into his room from the living room. He looked fuzzy, like he was half dissolved between the darkness and light.

"Come on, Bean," Juanita coaxed.

Bean walked into the room. He looked at Ronnie. She tried to smile at him, though smiling was not easy for her at the moment. He walked past Thatcher and stood next to Juanita. Thatcher laid a Payday candy bar and a Spiderman comic on the table.

"Oh, look, Bean," Juanita said. She was smiling at Thatcher.

Bean stared at the table.

"Well, that's perfect, ain't it, Bean?" Juanita said. Bean nodded and leaned into Juanita's arm. He was so tiny standing next to her, even though she was sitting.

Bean reached out for the candy bar and comic book. Juanita and Thatcher sat quiet for a minute. Tears started rolling down Juanita's cheeks.

"Well, say thank you and then get on," Juanita choked.

Bean didn't seem concerned that his mother was crying. He just whispered thank you and then walked across the room and sat on the end of the couch. Ronnie leaned back in the easy chair, crossed her arms over her chest and watched Bean as he tried to open the candy bar without ripping the wrapper.

"Why you being so careful?" Ronnie said.

Bean looked up but said nothing. Ronnie imagined that his opening presents on Christmas morning probably took forever. She watched him, how his overgrown, mouse brown bangs hung in his eyes and made a screen between them. He would glance at Ronnie every minute or so, then go back to unwrapping his candy bar again.

"You need some help?" she finally said.

He shook his head no.

"How come you're being so shy?"

His hands lay still in his lap, holding the half opened candy bar.

Juanita and Thatcher were talking—small talk—and after a minute, Ronnie didn't bother listening. She felt fidgety, but didn't want to get up. She didn't want to call any attention to herself or give Juanita any reason to start talking to her again. Bean went to the side of the couch and dragged out four small blue plastic mesh looking containers that were stacked on top of each other. As he pulled them apart, Ronnie saw that each container was divided into twelve sections, and each section contained a Hot Wheel. Bean looked at her from over his shoulder to see if she was impressed.

Ronnie took in a long, slow breath. It was going to be a long weekend. She watched silently as Bean "drove" a few of his cars to the center of the living room floor, lining them up on the carpet. Ronnie tried to stay focused on him and the little cars, but her eyes kept going back to that oak rocking chair and to the big gaps in the doorways.

"You like my cars?" Bean asked.

"Yeah."

"Wanna see?" He held up a pumpkin orange car with a blue roof, blue stripes on the hood, and the words *Revin Rebel* in white on the side.

"Nice," Ronnie said just to be polite.

"They don't go good in here," he said, looking at the carpet. "But they go real fast in the kitchen."

Ronnie looked at him for a minute and then moved to the floor. Bean handed her another car. Ronnie looked toward Thatcher and Juanita. They weren't paying attention to them.

"We can make them go through the town," Bean said. "Okay?"

"What town?"

"I got to make it still," Bean said. He turned the car containers over, arranging them into some order that apparently became the town.

"I'll just watch you," Ronnie said.

Bean shrugged and took the car back. He lined the cars up in various orders around the containers and took turns driving each of them on the "streets" he had created, offering his own sound effects as they made their ways across the carpet.

"All sorts of them . . . " Juanita was saying to Thatcher.

How could someone who looked like Juanita possibly have a son? Who would sleep with someone like Juanita? The thought made Ronnie feel queasy.

"See this one?" Bean said holding up a purple car. "This one is super fast."

"Oh," Ronnie said distractedly

Bean had a grandfather, though. That was more than Ronnie had growing up. Vivian's family lived up north somewhere, and she hadn't spoken to them in years. How could it be that some man who walked around like everybody else was her father?

"You want to see it?" Bean handed her the purple car.

"Cool," Ronnie said.

"You want to see it in the kitchen?"

"No, that's okay," she said. "Maybe later."

"Bean, are you pestering Veronica over there?" Juanita asked. "He loves them cars. Veronica, why don't you come and sit with us a minute? Unless you don't want to."

"Oh. I don't mind . . . "

Juanita waved her arm toward Ronnie. "Come on."

Ronnie stood up and walked to the table. Juanita's mouth hung in an open smile as she stared at her. She leaned back against the wall but reached her arm out, rubbing her hand in a half-circle on the table top.

"I was saying to T. that you can really see the stars good out here."

Ronnie pulled the chair out from the table and tried to be casual as she scooted it, as much as she could, toward Thatcher. She sat there and tried not to notice how Juanita filled the room, filled the house, dwarfing everything that was around her. She settled her eyes on the table in Thatcher's direction. His hands were wrapped, unmoving, around a beer.

"He don't know what to think about me . . . about all this. He thinks I'm crazy." She laughed and threw her head back and slapped her hand on the table. Ronnie felt the vibration under her palm. "But he thinks I'm crazy anyway."

Ronnie had missed something. Who were they talking about? She looked at Thatcher, but he was looking at his hands, smiling politely and nodding his head. Ronnie knew that smile—it was the smile he used when he had to do unpleasant things like go to her school for Open House every spring and act polite in the face of the nosey parent who felt no qualm about asking where Ronnie's parents were and why Thatcher was there. It was the smile he gave when he met with her teachers at conference time. It was too polite, and it wasn't Thatcher. Whoever they were talking about was making Thatcher very uncomfortable.

And here, seeing this smile on Thatcher's face, Ronnie felt a glimmer of hope. Maybe Thatcher was regretting his decision to come. Maybe he was realizing that it was all a mistake. She hoped. She hoped he was miserable, and decided that she would tell him that just as soon as they had a minute alone.

"There isn't too much to do here at night," Juanita said. "I'm sorry to say that. Mosquitos are bad, but I got bug spray if you want to sit out and look at the stars. We even got a telescope out there."

"I'm fine," Thatcher replied, though Juanita had been talking to Ronnie.

Juanita looked at Thatcher, then Ronnie, then leaned sideways to get a glimpse of Bean, who was still sitting on the floor, and said, "Well, I'm sorry to say, I'm not fine." She stood up. Her knees just about reached table height, exposing her thighs. "Don't get me wrong. I'm thankful for this place and all, but I can't move in it. I prefer to be outside when I can."

She looked past the light fixture that blocked her view of them.

"You can join me if you want, but you don't have to. I just need some fresh air. You don't mind, do you?"

They shook their heads no. Thatcher raised his beer.

"Well, hey, you help yourself to another one of those if you want one. Veronica, you help yourself to something, too."

As she passed Ronnie, she put a hand on her shoulder. Ronnie's body tensed. Juanita's touch was surprisingly light. She went out the front door, stopping for a second to rub the top of Bean's head. She had to bend low to reach him.

After she'd left the room, Ronnie leaned in to whisper to Thatcher but he pointed his finger at her before she could make a sound.

"Don't start," he said in a low voice. He took a drink.

"Oh, okay. You can just sit and get drunk until we leave, and I'll sit here and be miserable," Ronnie whispered. She looked over her shoulder to see if Bean had heard, but he was in his own little world of fast cars and roads to nowhere.

"Stop," he warned.

He stood up and went to the kitchen. He came back with two new beers and walked past Ronnie without a glance.

She spent the evening sitting on the brown recliner, watching Bean play first with his cars and then with a couple of GI Joes until it was time to go to bed. Juanita showed them where to sleep. She gave them blankets and pillows and shushed Bean along to bed.

Thatcher and Ronnie did not speak. They lay in the dark in the living room. Thatcher was on the couch with his back to Ronnie. Ronnie lay there listening. The sounds outside were so different from home—no traffic noises, no sirens, no neighbors talking or radios playing—and yet it was anything but quiet. The sound of crickets and frogs and who knows what other creatures covered every inch of silence with a noise so deep it was like going under water and not being able to come up for air. Ronnie reached her arms over her head, locking the pillow around her ears, and stared at the white lace curtains that glowed in the light of the risen moon.

CHAPTER TWENTY TWO

Ronnie heard the sound of a door being shut, a gentle quick snap of wood on wood. Her eyes opened wide and as she scanned the unfamiliar room, she was filled with the momentary panic that comes with waking in a strange place. Thatcher laid still asleep on the couch. His body faced the couch back and his blanket was wrapped tightly to his shoulders. She stared at the back of his head, at the swirl of the cowlick that would never stay down. She could hear the sound of his breathing, in and out, a slow and steady rhythm. It was comforting, the sound of his breathing, though she still wanted to go home.

She pushed the foot rest of the easy chair down and sat up. Her neck ached from sleeping in a half sitting position. The quiet house was filled with a hazy blue light, the light of rain. In daylight, the little house didn't seem nearly as awful as it had the night before. Everything was still and quiet. Had the sound of that shutting door only been part of a now forgotten dream? Ronnie stood up and stretched, walked passed Thatcher, through the dining room and to the bathroom with its ceiling high medicine cabinet and mirror for Juanita, and a door mirror next to the sink for Bean. Ronnie was relieved last night that everything else in the bathroom was normal sized. She had wondered if they made giant toilets?

She walked out of the bathroom and peeked into the sunroom. The bottom half of the porch walls were plaster, the tops were dirty windows, screened in, but shut at the moment. A washer and dryer sat in the inside corner of the rectangular room. A card table sat next to them with a stack of folded clothes on top. The floor was a slab of concrete, painted blue with a floor drain in the middle. A huge rocking chair, an end table, and a reading lamp sat on a middle-sized blue and brown braid rug in the other inside corner of the porch. Ronnie stepped outside and saw that at the end of the gravel driveway, toward the back of the yard was a greenhouse—a big greenhouse—with Juanita's old green pick-up parked in front of it. She started to walk toward it, realizing that it was the only other building in sight.

In her neighborhood, everywhere she looked she saw houses and garages and cars and streets lined with concrete sidewalks. But here . . . here the sight and sound of the country had her surrounded. Hazy greens and browns of one sort or another seemed to fill every spot that was not taken by the blue sky. A vibrant green pasture stood before her, and behind that were deep woods with tree upon tree of varying height and density and color. The air was filled with a quiet crispness that made the songs of the birds and bugs especially clear. Ronnie turned away from the greenhouse and walked down the gravel drive, toward the front of the house to where Thatcher's truck was parked. Across the gravel road, a meadow meandered up a few gentle, rolling hills and ended in more woods, all muffled in the soft white cover of morning mist. The beauty of the scene was great enough to momentarily overpower even Ronnie's misery. She caught her breath, but then was startled by the loud and sudden low of a cow. Ronnie jumped and turned around. It was just on the other side of Thatcher's truck, standing next to a tree just inside the barbed-wire fence. She hadn't noticed it when she walked out and wondered if it had been standing there all the time.

"A cow," she said to the morning mist.

It stared at her with its dumb, uninterested intensity, and then stomped its foot and turned its head away. Another cow lowed. Ronnie looked behind the cow and saw that the whole pasture was dotted with black, brown and white speckled cows.

She thought of how she had been afraid to get out of the truck the night before, and wondered if the cows had been there then, watching her, hiding in the dark.

She had never been close to a cow before and as she stepped closer, the cow stepped back from the fence but was still not far off. Its mouth chewed in a slow, crooked motion.

"Come here, cow," Ronnie whispered, reaching out her hand.

She heard a sound to her right and looked down the driveway. A speckled brown chicken stood in front of Thatcher's truck. It walked into the front yard, in a slow, jerky chicken-walk, pecking at the ground every few seconds. The side of Juanita's house was lined in flowers. Their colors glowed in the morning light. What time was it? She turned away from the cow, past the flowers, to see where the chicken had gone.

"You're an early riser, or did you not sleep last night?"

Ronnie jumped. Juanita was standing by the corner of the house, sipping on a cup of coffee. Ronnie looked at the ground and half shrugged her shoulders.

Juanita walked toward her. She had on a long yellow t-shirt that covered a pair of cut-off blue-jean shorts. Ronnie wondered where she got her clothes. She'd only seen her in t-shirts and blue jean shorts so far. Maybe that was all she ever wore. Maybe that was all she could find to fit her. She was outside the realm of all size. She stood beside Ronnie. Her hair was held back from her face by a yellow barrette. Color coordination, Ronnie thought, must be key when you are seven feet tall.

"Your flowers look nice," Ronnie said.

"Why, thank you, Veronica," she smiled down at her. "You drink coffee? I'll get you some."

Ronnie shook her head no.

"Well then come on and sit over here with me." Juanita started walking toward the front of the yard. Two plastic lawn chairs and another giant chair made from worn-looking wood sat next to an old picnic table, all beneath the shade of the tree in the corner of the front yard. The chairs sat in a half-circle and faced the meadow across the road. Juanita went to the wood chair, sat down, and waited for Ronnie. She was patient. She took a sip of her coffee and looked toward the sky. When Ronnie walked over and sat down, Juanita said, "T. told me he had to make you come here."

Ronnie felt a knot in her stomach. Why in the world would Thatcher tell her that?

"It's not that I don't want to be . . ." she began.

"It's all right, Veronica," Juanita said. "I'm just sorry you're here if you don't want to be. I can imagine how all of this must be to you."

"No," Ronnie said. "No, I don't think you can."

Her chin began to quiver and her voice cracked. This was, perhaps, the first truthful thing she had ever said to Juanita. To Ronnie, there was no one on this planet who understood or cared about how she was feeling. All she ever heard about was how she should be *acting*, or what she should be *thinking*. But really, that had to do with what everyone else was feeling and not with her at all. She felt completely alone in this, and no one would listen.

She glanced up at Juanita quickly, wanting to see if she'd betrayed herself. Juanita was looking right at her, and when their eyes met, Ronnie saw that Juanita was considering her in a careful, respectful way, without judgment. Ronnie swallowed the growing lump in her throat and looked at her hands. Juanita didn't say anything, but looked back up at the big tree.

"We were talking last night about maybe taking a day trip to Blue Springs. It's a real pretty swimming hole."

Juanita reached down and scratched her bare ankle.

"You ever been to a spring?" she asked. She sat back up.

"No."

"Do you know how to swim?"

"Yes."

"It's better than any swimming place I know," she said. She stood up, which seemed to take a lot of effort. "I have to get back to the greenhouse." She looked down at me. "You wanna see what I do?"

"I guess."

"Come with me and I'll show you."

They walked around the house, past the flower garden that lined it, and past the cow that stood at the fence, staring. For every step Juanita took, it seemed Ronnie had to take two or three. Juanita mooed as they walked by the cow, and to Ronnie's amazement, the cows answered her. Juanita looked at Ronnie sideways with a dumb grin on her face as a laugh tumbled out of Ronnie's mouth.

"Those cows will answer just about anyone," she said. "Try it."

"No . . ." Ronnie shook her head and waved her hand. She was not going to moo like a cow.

"Oh, go on. It ain't like anyone's going to hear you but me."

"No," she said again. "No thanks."

Juanita shrugged and they continued walking to the green house, past a little red tool shed that sat to its side. Ronnie hadn't noticed it before. The chicken she'd seen earlier was perched on the top. Juanita stepped ahead of her on a short flagstone walkway bordered by short white flowers. She opened the door and stepped aside to let Ronnie pass under her arm, and they stepped into the greenhouse.

The gravel floor crunched beneath her feet as she walked forward, looking at flats and flats of bedding plants that sat on high counters that ran in rows along the greenhouse walls and middle. Potted plants sat on stands and hung down in baskets from a string of wire above that was way too high for Ronnie to ever reach. The greenhouse was big—bigger than two of Juanita's houses put together, and everything in it was big, too. The table-tops were chest-high to Ronnie, but as Juanita walked ahead, Ronnie saw that they were at perfect counter height for her. The air was warm and misty-humid. The light filtering in from the translucent walls and ceiling made everything look crisp and heavy and tinged with a color of blue. Two giant fans sat at each end of the greenhouse. The one farthest away from them was on, sending a soothing hum through the room. It smelled of earth mixed with the color green of plants upon plants dripping wet in a morning mist. Blossoms seemed to reach out, seemed to speak, seemed to compete with each other for the deserved attention and wholehearted admiration of any onlooker gazing into the sea of green. As they walked toward the back of the green-house, the plants changed, became smaller, like she moved them down the counters as they grew. By the time Ronnie got to the end, the counters were filled with flats of seedlings and then empty counter.

"I have to put on some music," she said. She walked down one of the aisles, talking to Ronnie over her shoulder. "You heard of talking to plants to make them grow? Well, I play my plants music."

Playing music to plants. Juanita went all the way to the back of the green house and stepped behind a counter that was even higher still. Ronnie wondered if she would be able to see over it if she stepped behind it. Juanita bent over and suddenly music was playing. Guitar music. Classical. Ronnie raised her eyebrows. She didn't really know what kind of music she had expected to hear—not that she really expected to hear anything—but where was the country music? Wasn't that what everybody listened to in the country?

Juanita smiled. "I usually like cello, but lately, I been playing this for them."

Ronnie listened as the music played. She listened as the music filled the humid air, gentle guitar in gentle waves, mixing with the fragrance of the greenhouse, becoming, for the moment, the sound of color. She started to reach up to touch one of the firm, cool-looking leaves of a plant hanging over the rim of a basket above her, but realized as soon as she'd put her arm up, that it was too high to reach.

She felt like a peon in there, a little squirt in such a big room. She walked toward the back, toward Juanita.

"Everything is so big," she said to Juanita.

"That's funny," she said. "I think it's just right." She laughed.

Ronnie heard water trickling and walked toward the sound. To the right, behind a table of ferns, was a small pond with a small waterfall. Large rocks surrounded the pond with plants growing out between them. A big wooden chair and a couple of regular chairs sat next to it, and beside it was a tall, wooden table.

"That's pretty," Ronnie said pointing at the pond.

"Yep. I just took out a shovel one day and started digging a hole," Juanita said.

Ronnie smiled at her. It was becoming obvious that this was where Juanita spent most of her time, that, unlike the house, this is where she placed her care and that this was the world that was made to her proportions. Ronnie took a step nearer to the pond and peeked over the edge. Orange glints of goldfish flitted beneath slender, floating tentacles of water hyacinth root.

"You can feed them if you want," Juanita said. "They're always hungry." She walked over and put her hand into a sack that hid behind one of the rocks, and pulled out a handful of fish pellets. She held her closed hand out to Ronnie, and Ronnie reached her hand up, open. Juanita dropped the pellets into Ronnie's hand as Ronnie stared at Juanita's thick knuckles, her long fingers and wide fingernail beds. When Juanita drew her hand away, Ronnie was left with a comparison of her own hand that suddenly looked overly-delicate and overly-small.

"Just throw them in," she said. Her lips curled in a half smile. Her eyes were confident and full.

"Hey, I want to show you something," Juanita said after Ronnie had fed the fish. "I got an idea I want you to consider. I got a job to offer you."

Ronnie looked at her skeptically. She had a strange look on her face, her eyebrows raised and her lips pursed.

"What is it?"

"Hold on. Stay there."

She walked down the aisle between a haven of plants on either side. She walked with her arms out-stretched, hovering over the plants on both sides of her, as if she were bestowing them good wishes, encouraging persistence, giving off vibrations of nurturing care. Her movement seemed all at once graceful and light with little hint of cumbersome movement Ronnie had come to expect with every movement Juanita made.

Juanita came back holding a clay pot and saucer in her hands. She handed them to Ronnie, and Ronnie examined them. They were both painted bone-white. A swirl of hand-painted flowers, in purples and pinks amidst leaves that trailed toward the base, flowed around the middle of the pot while leaves, continuing on from the scene above, twined the side of the saucer.

"I paid eight dollars for this at a craft show," she said.

"It's pretty," Ronnie said turning the pot in her hands. She noted the swirl pattern the brush had made to create the base of each flower, the dots of yellow that accented the center, the black that lined the edges of petals as accents. The lines of stem were drawn with a thin brush that wove in and out of the flowers and leaves, connecting them, tying them all together.

She looked up at Juanita and held the pot up, trying to hand it back.

"Murphy sells me plain pots this size for a less than a dollar each," she said. Her mouth dropped open in a stupid grin.

"Who's Murphy?" Ronnie asked still trying to hand the pot back.

Juanita brushed the question away with an open palm and shook her head from side to side. "That's not important," she said. She turned around and sat in the other chair, then leaned over and took the pot and saucer from Ronnie. She held the pot up in front of her. The saucer sat on her lap.

"You paint," she said. "If you wanted to, you could paint for me."

"Paint for you?"

"If you want. I'll buy the pots, you paint the pots, and I'll try to sell them along with my flowers to the markets. After the cost, we can split the profits fifty-fifty."

"I . . . but we live too far away," Ronnie said.

"Well, we could come back and forth," Juanita said. "It ain't *that* far and T.'s willing to make the drive out now and again, and I'll make the drive in, and, hey, I hear you got a new car at home."

"T. knows about this?"

"I talked to him."

"What. Like, I take pots home and paint them and then bring them back?"

Juanita nodded.

"I don't know . . ." Ronnie said.

She sat back suddenly. The pot and saucer clanked on her long lap.

"Well, it's something to think about, right? You like to paint, and this might be kind of nice for you and for me. Like a business partnership, but really, you know, like we could just keep in touch."

Ronnie looked at the pot in Juanita's lap. For Juanita, it wasn't about the painting.

"You could do it, couldn't you?" Juanita asked. "I mean, not that you have to, but it wouldn't be too hard for you, would it? I mean, art wise?"

"No," Ronnie said, defensively. "That's not hard at all." She looked at the pond again.

"Not hard for you," she said, "but I can't paint a lick. I got the business contacts. I sell my flowers to more than half the stores in this town and a few other towns besides. We could make some nice money on them, I bet. And if it don't work out, you ain't lost nothing. I can always get rid of the pots whether they're painted or not. But shoot, eight dollars?

"I tell you what," Juanita said after a minute. "I'll send you home with all the pots I got just hanging around and we can see what happens." She leaned forward, reached her long arm out and touched Ronnie's knee. Ronnie made herself sit still and not flinch. "What do you say? You wanna try it?"

Ronnie looked at the pot again.

"How do I know you'll like what I paint?"

"Oh, I'm not worried about that. I saw what you can do. You're the artist. I'll leave that part up to you."

The artist. Ronnie liked the sound of that.

"I guess we can try it," she said tentatively.

Juanita sat back and clapped her hands together. The pot and saucer nearly fell from her lap. Ronnie leaned forward quickly out of reflex, but Juanita caught them and then laughed her silly laugh.

"Yes," she said, satisfied.

"Hey." Thatcher had come into the greenhouse. He looked rumpled and tired, his cowlick sticking up in the back.

"Look at this little pond, T." Ronnie said standing up.

He raised his eyes at the friendliness in her voice, and Ronnie immediately remembered her anger from the night before. She gave herself a mental check, a reminder that she was angry, that her brother was a jerk. She turned back to the pond as he walked up and when he stood beside her, she took a step away to show him that she was, indeed, still angry, but he didn't seem to notice.

"That's cool," he said squatting down to look into the water. "Did you make it?"

"I sure did," Juanita said. Her arms were crossed in front of her chest.

Ronnie kept her eyes on the pond. She thought of that chicken perched on top of that little red tool shed. She thought of that cow and its stupid eyes peering over the fence. She thought of the oversized chair in the living room. She didn't want to stand there with Thatcher. She walked toward the door on the other side of the green house.

"Where you going?" Thatcher asked.

Ronnie didn't answer.

"I'll make us some breakfast," she heard Juanita say to Thatcher. "Do you drink coffee? I'll make us a fresh pot of coffee if you like it."

Thatcher mumbled something.

"How about flap jacks? Does Veronica like . . . "

"Hey, Veronica . . . "

But Ronnie had stepped outside. The sun had come up and was shining brightly now, clearing away the faint, gray heaviness of the early morning mist, making colors that had minutes ago looked subtle and blended, now look crisp. Ronnie went back to the front yard. She was going to sit in one of the plastic chairs, but changed her mind and sat in Juanita's chair. It was like sitting on a bench. She sat back, testing it, trying it on. The back was slanted in a surprisingly comfortable way. She sank into it and waited for the day to end.

CHAPTER TWENTY THREE

"Here."

Bean held a plate of pancakes. He set them on the table and walked away. Ronnie was still sitting in Juanita's chair, looking across the road at the blur of purples and blues and yellows and greens of the wildflowers that covered various spots of the meadow. Bean came back a minute later, holding a bottle of syrup. He was barefoot and his hair was uncombed and sticking up in the back. He wore a pair of bright print shorts that covered his kneecaps, making his legs look a sawed-off, half-length. An orange t-shirt hung below his hips. The kid was cute, she had to admit. He kind of swaggered when he walked, holding the syrup bottle with both hands.

"You just wake up?" she asked.

"Huh-uh," he said.

He set the syrup on the table and walked away.

"Where you going?"

He didn't answer. Ronnie looked down at the pancakes sitting in front of her, big and golden. She loved pancakes.

"Want some milk?"

Juanita was walking toward her carrying two glasses. Bean was at her side, carrying another plate of pancakes. Were they all going to have breakfast out there? Was she going to have to sit there with Thatcher and Juanita through breakfast?

Would they not leave her alone? Juanita set the glasses on the table.

"Thanks," Ronnie said.

Juanita smiled.

"You mind if Bean has breakfast out here with you?"

Just Bean? Ronnie looked at the kid. His mother had cut his pancakes into neat little squares.

"No, I don't mind."

"Well then, great," Juanita said and walked back across the front lawn, toward the house. Ronnie watched her back, her viscous walk that covered a lot of ground in a single step. At the front porch she turned around.

"Come in for seconds. There's plenty."

Bean was staring at Ronnie staring, she realized, just as Ronnie had been staring at Juanita. They sat for awhile, not talking, just eating their pancakes. She took a drink of milk, and it was so cold and so thick. It was like cream, not like the milk they got from the Quick Shop at all. She took another drink and looked toward the fence, toward the cows.

"You get this milk from those cows?"

He shook his head no.

"No?"

"Not them," he said.

"Where?"

"Gertrude."

"Who's Gertrude?"

"Gertrude the cow," he said.

Ronnie nodded. "Oh, Gertrude the cow." Of course. "Where is Gertrude?"

"At Papa Ray's."

"Papa Ray's?"

"Uh-huh. He has a cow named Gertrude. We get milk from her."

"You mean your Grandpa?"

"Uh-huh."

Ronnie took another bite. She thought of the man walking out the door of the *Pink Lemonade*.

"Is he a nice grandpa?"
"Papa?"
"Yes."
"He's really nice."
"Do you see him a lot?"
"Uh-huh."
"You do?"
"Yep."
"Does he milk Gertrude?"

Bean shook his head yes but said, "I milked her four squirts once. Papa says he'll let me milk her every morning when I get bigger. Then I'll have to wake up really early."

Ronnie's pancakes were gone. She sipped on Gertrude's milk, watching Bean slowly finish his breakfast. To him, his grandpa was just his grandpa. He didn't even seem to understand that it wasn't normal for an aunt and uncle to just suddenly appear out of nowhere like we did. But then, from Ronnie's perspective, he didn't seem to realize his mother was a giant freak, either.

"Momma said we're going swimming today."
"I heard."
"Do you like swimming?"
"Yeah," I said.
"Did you bring your swimming suit?"
"Yes."

The chicken walked past Thatcher's truck.
"That your chicken?"

Bean turned around.

"Daisy!" he shouted to the chicken. He smiled. "That's my chicken, Daisy!"

He took two more relatively quick bites of his pancakes, gulped down some milk, then got up and ran toward the chicken. The chicken saw him coming and flapped its wings, doing a hop-fly-hop to get away.

"You done?" Ronnie called after him.

He chased the chicken around the truck. "Daisy! Daisy!"

"Hey, Bean," she said again, "are you finished with these pancakes?"

She brought the dishes into the house. Thatcher and Juanita were sitting at the dining room table, Thatcher in a chair, Juanita on the floor. Juanita was drinking coffee. Thatcher's back was to Ronnie, but she could see smoke rising from his cigarette. Juanita looked caught off guard when she saw Ronnie. She put her coffee cup on the table with a sudden bang.

"How was breakfast?" she asked.

"Good, thanks." Ronnie looked at the floor as she walked toward the kitchen.

She wondered what they'd been talking about to become so quiet like that. She set the plates down on the kitchen counter. Maybe they were trying to remember things. Maybe they were talking about all of the things that happened before Ronnie had been born. She turned to the trashcan that sat next to the stove. When she leaned over to scrape Bean's plate, she caught a glimpse of Thatcher's face. He was pale, his eyes fixed to a spot on the table. Ronnie could see that he was upset. She took a step back so that he wouldn't see her looking at him.

Ronnie couldn't, for her life, figure out why he was being so open to putting himself—and her—through all of this. It wasn't like he'd spent the last 18 years talking about Juanita and their father. It wasn't like the topic had consumed him all these years . . . or had it? Ronnie began to wonder. Was that what had kept Thatcher so serious all the time, so quiet? Was that what had driven him to work so hard at Oliver's, working so many hours day after day, and coming home exhausted? When people said to Thatcher, "Hey, how you doing?" Thatcher's standard line was always, "Just getting through the day." Maybe that was completely true—true in a way she had never realized. Maybe each and every day was a struggle for Thatcher, that maybe he had lived his days focusing on one thing at a time just to keep himself from thinking about the things that were always on his mind, lurking just under the surface. But it was hard to know with him. It was hard to know anything with Thatcher. If

Juanita hadn't shown up that day, Ronnie doubted she would have ever met her or heard about her.

Juanita cleared her throat.

"Veronica, how was breakfast?"

Hadn't she just asked that? Ronnie looked at her, though, realizing that her voice was shaky this time, realizing that they were both upset about something.

"Fine," Ronnie said. She could tell by the way Juanita looked past her, though, that she wasn't really listening.

"I gotta get this cleaned up," Juanita said. She stood up, unfolding her limbs like the legs to a card table, and walked past Ronnie. She turned on the water and began rattling the dishes around. Ronnie turned back to Thatcher. He was still staring at the table, his lit cigarette hanging between his fingers, his arm resting over the edge of the table. Ronnie watched Juanita as her hands worked beneath the layer of suds in the sink. Ronnie took a step toward Thatcher, but when he looked up at her, she stopped. His eyes looked tired, old and worn out. They rested on Ronnie as if he were day-dreaming—empty, as if he weren't really seeing her at all.

"Hey," Ronnie whispered.

As soon as she'd spoken, his whole look changed, as if he'd been snapped back to the present from a dream. He cocked his jaw out and stood up, took a drag off his cigarette and walked away from her, through the living room, and out the front door.

What could have possibly upset him so? Ronnie looked over her shoulder. Well, at least maybe now he would start to see what a stupid thing it was for them to be there. Maybe now he would finally get what she'd been trying to tell him all along. Maybe now they would go home. She went after him out the front door.

Thatcher stood next to the towering oak tree.

"What's wrong?"

Thatcher didn't answer her. He looked across the road to the meadow and the sky.

"T.," she said. "Can we go home now? I'll put everything in the truck."

He looked at her without expression.

"Come on," she pleaded. "I hate it here."

He kept staring at her and she felt tears welling up in her eyes. She felt helpless and angry and frustrated. She'd lived with him all her life, and yet, in a way, she didn't even know him. He took care of her, and yet—though she had a roof over her head, and though he made sure she went to school and made sure there was food in the house—there was a part of Thatcher that was untouchable, unreachable.

"Listen . . ." Ronnie said. It wasn't just herself she was trying to rescue. It wasn't just herself that she was trying to spare. Whatever was happening there, whatever all of it was about, Thatcher was the one it affected the most. Charles was right. Thatcher was stuck right in the middle. He was shook up. Ronnie had seen it plainly on his face as he sat in the dining room not ten minutes before. And she wanted to protect him; she wanted to protect them both. She wanted to go home.

"Now, you listen," Thatcher said. "We aren't going anywhere."

Ronnie stared, startled by the sharpness of his voice.

"It's time," he said. His voice broke, and when Ronnie heard that, when she heard that crack in him, it was too much. She started to cry.

"Time for what? What is it time for, T.?"

"Stop crying," he said. "Stop."

Ronnie took a step back. He didn't understand at all. He didn't see that he was the one she was worried about. Her jaw began to ache.

"It's not about me," she cried. "It's not!"

She looked for a place to go, but there was none. She looked at the white gravel road and started to walk toward it. This damn place. No shelf of rocks. No Donika. She even missed her mother. This damn place! Ronnie walked hard and fast down the road past the cow pasture. She walked quickly, putting one foot in front of the other, hearing the quick and angry crunch of her feet on the gravel. She saw the wildflowers and weeds that grew thick along the side of the road, the cows that stared at her—she saw it all, yet she saw nothing. Flying bugs buzzed her, cutting sharply into the noise of the surrounding cricket-chatter. She waved them from her face as she walked. Who would live out here like this? She wondered angrily. Who would put up with this?

The road before her curved toward the right, and the woods that lined the meadow across from Juanita's house began closing in, making it impossible to see what was ahead. She kept walking. The pasture on her left seemed to be rising up from the road as she went, separating from it as an embankment that grew higher while the roadside gully grew deeper and wider. Her view was limited so that she saw only what was right in front of her. She looked back toward Juanita's house, but it was gone from sight. She didn't care and walked even faster.

She stayed focused on the road ahead. It seemed to rise again, the pasture on her left lowering steadily toward road level, the gully becoming shallower and less sharp once again. The road came to a dry creek bed. A large drainpipe went under and through the road, making it look like a mini-bridge. She walked over it and looked both ways down the creek bed. Just rocks. No water. A new pasture began on the other side of the bridge, and woods continued on her right. There was nothing here. It was all a bunch of nothing with every step she took. Nothing. Nothing. Nothing. What did people do to get away from it, to get away from the nothingness of it all? She wanted to see a Quick Shop or a McDonalds or something. She wanted to see sidewalks and traffic lights, but suddenly a house came into view up the road, and when it did, she stopped short. She was going onto someone else's property. She looked back toward the direction from which she'd come, realizing all at once that this would be *his* house. She stood still, not sure what to do. She didn't want to go back to Juanita's. She didn't want to see Thatcher or Bean. She looked toward the house up the road, taking a few steps further.

A dog barked, and she stopped again, then heard the voice of another dog's bark. Suddenly, a black Labrador and a German shepherd ran onto the road up by the house. They were a ways off, but Ronnie's heart beat faster. She stoo[d?] they wouldn't see her. She watched them as they started and sniffed around, marking their territory.

She looked behind her again, at the long [...] was nowhere to hide if they saw her. She star[ted to] walk backwards, slowly. They were pretty far away, she kept reminding herself. If she were quiet, maybe they wouldn't see her. She would be around the corner and out of sight. All she had to do was be quiet. She turned around and headed back to Juanita's with a quick step. The gravel crunched beneath her feet. She heard the dogs bark again and looked over her shoulder. They stood still, looking in Ronnie's direction.

"Oh, God."

The shepherd began barking.

"Oh, God."

Ronnie walked faster, trying to look over her shoulder as she went. The lab started forward, and the Shepherd followed, and when they started running, and so did Ronnie.

"Oh no. Oh no," she said with each step.

She ran over the drainpipe bridge, her heart pounding. Big dogs. Running. Behind her. She ran as fast as she could, but heard their barks getting louder and closer. She refused to look behind her, and sprinted with all her might, not looking back until she was nearly to Juanita's front yard. Only then did she realize that the dogs had given up the chase.

She bent over, her hands on her knees, breathing hard, trying to catch her breath, to calm herself. She lifted a shaking hand and a nervous laugh jumped from her throat. She looked out, checking again and again to make sure the dogs were not coming. She heard nothing but the sounds of the crickets and flying bugs. The road was going up again, back toward Juanita's yard. Ronnie walked slow, taking in deep breaths, continuing to calm herself. Her lungs ached. Her legs ached. Her knees still shook.

"Jesus," she said looking behind her and then looking ahead. She couldn't even take a walk. Couldn't take a walk. Couldn't escape.

"Jesus," she said again, looking at the sky. And she realized suddenly and surprisingly that she meant the word as a prayer more than anything, a prayer of relief that the dogs had stopped, and a prayer of pleading for the whole situation, the whole idea of being there and learning about Juanita and her father. Help. That was what she needed—only she didn't know what kind. She was like an escaped prisoner going to turn herself in, willing to give it all up, only there was nowhere to turn herself in to, and no other place to go.

CHAPTER TWENTY FOUR

Juanita led the way to Blue Springs in her old pickup truck and Thatcher and Ronnie followed. Thatcher seemed to prefer the Cabool honky-tonk playing on the radio to any conversation, which was just fine by Ronnie. She stared out the window, out at all of the nothing around them. Juanita looked like a man from the back of her truck window. Her shoulders sat well above the truck seat. Bean was invisible. Ronnie looked over at Thatcher. His shoulders reached just over the top of the bench-back, and Ronnie's neck hit the top of it. She thought of her little red car at home, and tried to imagine Juanita in it. It would be like twenty circus clowns rolling out of a little circus car.

Juanita pulled off the highway onto a gravel road and Thatcher followed. They turned onto a dirt road that was nearly hidden by woods.

"Where is this place?" Ronnie asked.

The dirt road was really just a clearing in the woods, a parking spot, a big circle that went around a brown billboard park sign that said "Mark Twain National Forest." A white car was parked on the right side next to the woods. Juanita parked behind it and Thatcher parked behind Juanita. Bean jumped out of the truck and went toward the woods.

"Wait for us, Bean. I mean it," Juanita said to him as she unfolded herself from the pickup truck's cabin.

The way she said, "I mean it," startled Ronnie. It sounded just like her mother, and Ronnie had given her mother hardly a thought since they'd left home. She walked around the truck and saw that there was a path in front of Bean.

"Veronica, would you mind carrying this blanket?"

Juanita laid a blanket in Ronnie's arms gently, as if she were handing over a baby. Thatcher took two folding lawn chairs from the back of his truck. Juanita carried a small cooler and a picnic basket. Bean stood at the beginning of the path.

"Get my tube," he said.

"Oh! I almost forgot. I . . ." Juanita looked around, at Thatcher, at Ronnie, looking at what they were carrying.

"You think you can carry this too?" she said. She handed Ronnie the picnic basket then went to the truck for two blown up tire inner tubes.

"Here," Thatcher said. He took one of the tubes from Juanita.

Bean smiled and hummed happily as they started down the path. Ronnie went behind everyone else. She thought about the Honda trails. She thought about home, wondering how long they would have to stay there. Thatcher's back blocked the view of anything in front of her. The dirt path began going downhill and suddenly gave way to a gravel bar. Ronnie heard a kid laugh and then the sound of someone jumping into water.

"Oh!" Thatcher said.

Ronnie stepped forward, onto an expansive gravel beach, out of the woods, off of the path, into an oasis of crystal blue water with a back drop of high black bluffs that faded into woods. It was overwhelmingly beautiful. Ronnie's whole body opened to the view. She breathed it in: black rock, blue sky, green tree, crystal water. A slow breeze offered a whiff of fish and algae. Water lapped softly against the bank. The echo of children's voices bounced off the bluffs around and above them.

"Wow," Thatcher said. He was looking up, across the slow running river, toward the bluffs, toward a piece of heaven, his eyes wide and smiling, then looked down. "Look how clear that water is."

"Everyday," Juanita said. "It's here everyday, whether we are or not."

Juanita walked past us and over to Bean who stood at the water's edge and put him in a life jacket. A huge boulder, the size of a small house, sat in the middle of the deep, perfect swimming hole. Ronnie wondered at the splash that giant rock must have made when it fell into the water from above. It dwarfed the two children who were busy climbing up it and jumping off. They jumped into the cool looking water and swam around to the back of the rock, disappearing at the bottom only to reappear at the top again a minute later. They wore tennis shoes on their feet and orange life jackets around their necks that made them stick out against the black rock like ladybugs sitting on a lump of coal.

They spotted Juanita as they reached the top of the rock. The girl nudged the boy on the shoulder and pointed toward Juanita. They hushed, both of them, sitting on the top of the rock, pulling their knees up to their chests. Ronnie looked around. A man was downstream a little ways sitting in a lawn chair with a fishing pole. Juanita was still bent over Bean, tying his life jacket around his waist.

"Hey, lady," the little boy called.

The girl had her hand over her mouth and was pushing on the boy with her elbow. He shushed her arm away like a bothersome fly. Juanita stood up straight and turned around. Thatcher had dropped the inner tube and took a few steps forward, setting the lawn chairs, still folded, on the ground.

"Well," Juanita called back, walking along the edge of the water, one foot directly in front of the other, like a giant circus star navigating over a wet tight-rope. "Say what you're going to say."

The words echoed in Ronnie's mind. Bean looked up at the kids, but ignored them and stepped into the water up to his knees.

"It's cold," he said.

"Are you the giant?" the boy asked. His accent was thick with slow Southern Missouri.

"A what?" Juanita asked.

"Are you the giant that lives in Cabool?"

Ronnie couldn't believe how forward he was. She felt like taking a rock and throwing it at him. Ignorant country bumpkins, that's what she thought. But Juanita was smiling at them. She leaned her head back and laughed.

"Momma, the water is cold," Bean said again.

"Refreshing," Juanita said to Bean. She looked back to the kids. "Yep," she said to them. "That's me. Come down here."

The kids shook their heads no.

"Oh, come on. I ain't gonna hurt you." She turned and looked at Thatcher and me. "I'm a friendly giant. Isn't that right, Bean?" Bean shook his head yes matter of factly. "Come on, now," she said to the kids.

The girl whispered something into the boy's ear and after a minute, they both jumped into the water. The father was standing up now, looking toward them, looking toward his children. He put down his pole and began walking to them. Juanita saw him and waved.

"How you doing?" she called.

He waved tentatively. The kids came out of the water slowly.

"Bean, come here," Juanita said.

The kids stopped in thigh-deep water. Bean walked toward his mother.

"I want you to meet my little boy," Juanita said. "His name is Benjamin, but we call him Bean for short."

"How come you're so tall?" the girl said.

"God made me this way," Juanita said. "It's kind of you to notice."

Thatcher and Ronnie looked at each other.

"Who are you?"

"Tyler! Carolyn!" the man called out. "Don't you bother anyone." He spoke to the children, but was clearly giving them a message of his presence.

"Hey," Juanita said as he came closer. "I'm Juanita. This here is my boy Bean. That's my brother, T., and my sister, Veronica, over there."

The man glanced at Ronnie and Thatcher, but openly stared at Juanita. He was short and tan with skinny legs and sun-bleached hair. He wore an unbuttoned short-sleeved plaid shirt that gave view to a naked beer belly that hung over the top of his cut off shorts.

"You live in Cabool?" he asked this to Juanita, and yet it sounded as if he were testing her.

"Yep," Juanita said nodding, acknowledging that she was the one. "Where you all from?"

"We come over from Willow Springs."

"Oh, yes. I sell my flowers over there at Harp's market."

He smiled at her. "That's what I thought! You're the flower lady." He said this knowingly.

"That's right," Juanita said. She laughed.

Ronnie couldn't believe how the man just stood there, staring at her. He was no better than his rude little kids.

"Hey, kids," he said, "this is the Flower Lady."

"Oh!" The kids seemed to know immediately who he was talking about.

"Where's the flowers?" the little girl asked.

Juanita laughed.

"My wife goes to Harp's," the man said.

"How 'bout that," Juanita said.

"Well, hey. Pleasure to meet you." The man took a step forward and stuck out his hand to Juanita, ignoring Thatcher and Ronnie completely.

"Likewise," Juanita said.

"We've just come for a swim."

"Best hole around," Juanita said.

"Yep."

The man looked at his kids. His voice turned stern. "Go on and play or I'll take you home right now."

Juanita pushed Bean gently.

"You too, Bean."

"Well," the man said. "I best get back to my fishing."

As he walked away, Juanita put her hands on her hips and turned toward her brother and sister.

"I guess I'm kind of like a monument around here," she said smiling humbly. "Everybody round here knows me cuz of my flowers . . . ."

Thatcher and Ronnie looked at each other, wondering if Juanita was kidding, but Juanita shook her head, laughed, and stepped out into the water.

The water was cold and clear. No matter how deep it got, Ronnie could still see the bottom. Juanita led them across the river. They waded. It wasn't very wide, but in the very center they—even Juanita—had to swim. Of course Thatcher and Ronnie were swimming long before Juanita had to. She dragged Bean by the collar of his lifejacket, walking along and pulling him with each easy step as Ronnie fought without footing against the gentle current that tried to persuade her downstream whether she wanted to go or not. When they got to the other side, Juanita took Ronnie up a little ways to a spring coming right out of the ground. Thatcher and Bean meandered behind them, making their way slowly, taking their time, stopping to look under rocks and talking about things like frogs and tadpoles.

Ronnie was surprised when they got to the head of the spring, surprised by the lack of drama—no fanfare, just frigid water coming right out of the ground. She didn't really know what she expected to see, but she expected to see something dramatic. The water created a small, shallow pool that trickled gently down into series of small pools, all leading to the river below. To Ronnie, it was like a quiet miracle.

"Try this." Juanita put her hand in the water.

"It's cold!" Ronnie said.

"Have you swam in a river before?"

"Not like this," Ronnie said. "I've never seen a spring before."

"Ah-ha!" Juanita was pleased to be offering Ronnie something new. She nodded her head up and down, smiling.

"Seems like it would run out sooner or later," Ronnie said.

"Hm," Juanita said. She put her hand on Ronnie's shoulder as they stood at the springhead. Ronnie tensed. She wasn't used to people touching her. Vivian and Thatcher certainly weren't cuddly people. They simply were not affectionate people. The only one who ever hugged Ronnie was Mrs. Wilson, but Mrs. Wilson was different. Mrs. Wilson hugged everybody whether they wanted to be hugged or not. Ronnie had learned long ago to just give in to Mrs. Wilson's hugs. But she was the only one, really.

And though Ronnie tensed at Juanita's touch, she was surprised to find that she didn't really mind Juanita's hand on her shoulder, and that in fact, she liked it there. A kind of softening had come over Ronnie. She didn't know if it was this place or if it was the way Juanita had talked to that man and those children, or if she was just getting used to Juanita, but whatever the reason, Ronnie found herself liking the feeling of Juanita's reaching out. She liked it as she stood next to her giant sister. The feeling caught her off guard, and so Ronnie stood very still, trying to go with the moment, trying to let it happen, but the more she tried to send the message to Juanita that she didn't mind her hand on her shoulder, the more Ronnie's body tensed. It was too foreign, too odd. She knew that Juanita was trying to be kind, was trying to connect, and though Ronnie wasn't trying to send a negative signal, she knew that she was. She couldn't help it. A second later, Juanita took her hand away, picked up a stick and poked at a rotting tree trunk.

Ronnie looked up at the trees hanging high above them, feeling sad that she wasn't able to respond to Juanita's gesture with ease.

"You know," Juanita said, "whole worlds exist around ours, under ours, above ours, between ours." Ronnie stared at the water coming out of the ground. Juanita raised her hand and swept it in front of her. "And all we ever get is a glimpse—of the worlds around ours, I mean. All we ever get is a hint at them. A speck of the real thing. Just watching my flowers? There's a whole little drama going on in each and every one of 'em and I only see a speck of it, but it's all happening whether I see it or not and it's all important whether I'm there to care about it or not."

There was such a peace there, such a peacefulness in the quiet sounds of the birds and squirrels and slither-critters moving about, branches scratching gently together high above where the sunlight shown down, filtering through the leaves here and there. Ronnie looked downstream toward Thatcher. He and Bean were engrossed in their own drama, hunched close together with Bean pointing to something.

"I like that about the world," Juanita continued. "There's so much to know or not to know and we get to decide what we want to pay attention to or not. I mean, I like my flowers. That's what I like paying attention to."

Ronnie was silent.

"What do you pay attention to in life, Veronica?"

"I . . . oh."

The question had surprised Ronnie and as she considered her answer, she realized that she didn't really have one.

She could feel Juanita watching her.

Ronnie looked back downstream toward Thatcher. He was moving farther away. Ronnie didn't know what to say. Wasn't just being alive enough? She suddenly wanted to go to Thatcher, to be closer to where he was, back toward the river, but there she stood, alone with Juanita, pondering a question of life.

"I don't know," she finally said.

"Well, what about your painting?"

"I don't know," she said again. "I just like to do it."

She did not want to be standing there any longer. She was ready to go back, ready to join Thatcher and Bean.

"There's a reason for it, you know. All that painting. There's a reason for everything."

Ronnie tried to nod, tried to show Juanita that she was listening. It became evident, however, that Juanita was going to continue speaking whether Ronnie responded or not.

"And that's how it starts," she said. "I was always growing things. Always planting flowers and making little gardens and picking flowers. It's all in what you pay attention to . . . take frogs for instance."

Ronnie reached down, dipping her fingers into the water, making circles with her hands, feeling the shock of it, the cold invitation of it. As she waited for Juanita to continue, a crawdad that had been sitting motionless at the bottom suddenly made itself known by scooting backwards. Ronnie pulled her hand away.

"Say you like playing with frogs. You always been interested in playing with frogs—just because you like to. You could grow up to devote your whole life to studying frogs, from the time they are tadpoles all the way to the time they die . . . and it would be a good thing, and you would probably never be bored because you like them."

Juanita furrowed her brow and stared out into the woods.

"I don't know," she said, "I just don't believe in accidents, I guess. I don't believe I love flowers for no reason. I don't believe you paint for no reason."

Ronnie didn't know what Juanita was trying to get at. She knew that Juanita was waiting for her to open up, that she was waiting for Ronnie to turn and say something important, but Juanita just didn't understand. Ronnie wasn't made that way. She wasn't made to be open with people, to hug and to talk about things like frogs and the meaning of life. What did Juanita want her to say? She stood up and took a couple of steps in Bean and Thatcher's direction.

"Well, anyway," Juanita said following her, "I can go on and on about nothing, can't I . . . I'm just so glad you're both here. That's all. I'm just glad and . . . and that day I came to Rock Hill and picked up that phone book and all . . . well, I don't think that was any accident either."

"I guess not," Ronnie said, but she wasn't convinced. A part of her wanted to embrace the idea that it was no accident that they were all together there, that there was a bigger plan at work, but if Ronnie believed Juanita, it meant that there would be more still, that this one journey would not be enough—and that thought filled the other part of Ronnie, the part that wanted to run away and just go back home and live her life one day at a time without thinking about it, without analyzing it. To believe what Juanita was saying would take some kind of faith, some kind of courage–things Ronnie wasn't sure she had.

Juanita followed Ronnie as she walked toward the river, toward Thatcher and Bean. Ronnie was grateful when Juanita picked up a rock and admired its beauty. She didn't say anything more about meaning or destiny or fate. They made their way from the spring back to the river, Ronnie's mind turning all the while between resisting and pondering Juanita's words.

By the time they got back to the swimming hole, the other family had left and they were all alone on the water. Bean had Ronnie follow him to the top of the boulder. He knew the rock well, telling her where to put her hands, telling her where to step up to the next spot. Ronnie watched him and followed his directions, and when she got to the top, she stood upon the dark, smooth surface of the boulder. It looked to her like melting chocolate—a giant chocolate melting rock. She surveyed the banks and the trees and the water and the world. Was that a plan too? She wondered half with sarcasm, half with hope. Was she supposed to be standing on that rock that day? Was she supposed to be looking at the tree over on the bank with that broken branch? Was that ordained too? It was nonsense, really, though Ronnie had never really thought about life that way.

"Come on," Bean said, and just like that he disappeared over the edge of the rock.

"Oh!" Ronnie said, moving to the edge and looking down. It was higher than she'd realized, and she was surprised that Bean had jumped so easily. She watched as he came up for air, his lifejacket making him pop to the surface of the water like a fishing bobber.

"Come on," he said waving up at Ronnie. "It's fun."

"It's pretty high," she said hesitantly.

"Just jump. It's fun."

"Don't think about it," Juanita called from the bank.

Ronnie looked at her. Juanita stood with her hands on her hips, watching them. Don't think about it? Ronnie looked down at the water again. It looked far away from where she stood. She considered the jagged looking sides of the rock as Bean swam away.

"Jump," Thatcher hollered. He walked over and stood next to Juanita.

Ronnie shook her head. It was too high, too scary, too far to go.

"I can't," she said.

She felt a hand grip onto her own. She looked down. Bean had climbed up the rock again and was standing beside her.

"I'll hold your hand," he said. "You'll like it. It's scary the first time, but it's fun. You'll like it once you do it."

They stood there for a moment, Ronnie looking down at the blue-brown water with a frown, Bean pulled gently on her hand. There was something about it, something familiar about standing on the edge and looking down like that.

"Quit thinking and jump!" Thatcher called from the bank.

But she was thinking. She was thinking about the men who had jumped into the quarry. She likened herself to them, standing on the edge, gathering courage for the step she knew she wouldn't be able to take back. She looked at Juanita, her face turned upward expectantly. Juanita's forehead glistened with sweat as the sun blazed down, and her dazed-looking eyes seemed half closed. Juanita wanted them to be a family. That was all. And Ronnie just stood there. She could either resist everything Juanita was trying to offer, and stand forever on the edge of the truth, or she could jump. And if she jumped, it would mean really letting go—letting go of everything she knew, letting go of the only life she understood. Ronnie simply didn't know if she was ready for that.

Bean looked up at her, his face all squinty in the sun, his little hand gently squeezing hers. Ronnie shook her head.

"I can't do it," she finally said.

"Why not?"

"I can't." She backed away and let go of Bean's hand. He stood looking at her, not understanding.

"Chicken," Thatcher taunted.

"I can't," she called out, feeling stupid. Her face began to burn.

"It's all right, Veronica," Juanita said.

"Bawk, bawk!" Thatcher said.

Juanita smacked his arm playfully. He threw his head back, laughing.

"Ain't you gonna do it?" Bean asked.

Ronnie shook her head. "Not yet. I can't do it. You go ahead. I'm just going to sit up here and get some sun."

Bean shrugged his shoulders and jumped off the rock. He jumped over and over again all afternoon while Ronnie lay on top, basking in the sun like a red slider on a log. Thatcher razzed her the rest of the afternoon. Every time she climbed off the rock to get into the river and cool off, he made chicken noises. It made Ronnie angry, him teasing her like that in front of Juanita and Bean, and in Thatcher's cruel style, he wouldn't let it rest.

Finally, he was lying on the blanket with his arm draped across his eyes. Ronnie went to the cooler for a soda being as quiet as she could. He didn't stir. She went to the river and stood in the water, up to her thighs as she drank her soda.

Juanita walked by with a good-sized sunfish hanging from her fishing pole.

"Hey," she whispered, "Watch this."

Ronnie raised her eyebrows and watched.

"We girls gotta stick together," Juanita said.

She took the fish off the hook. She put a finger to her lips and then pointed to Thatcher. She went over to him and dropped it on Thatcher's bare chest where it flopped and flailed and caused Thatcher to yelp and jump up so quickly that he fell backwards and landed on his butt, swiping at his stomach with panicked hands.

Juanita grinned at Ronnie, nodding her head in conspiratorial success.

"Ha!" Bean said, covering his mouth with one hand and pointing to Thatcher with the other. "Ha! Ha!"

"You scared of fish, T.?" Juanita said.

"Jesus," Thatcher said, trying to laugh, but still trying to collect himself. "I didn't know what that was. I was asleep."

"Didn't look like you were sleeping to me," she said.

"You were scared!" Bean said joining in on the joke. "Ha, ha! You were scared of a fish!"

"Hey," Thatcher said pointing to him seriously. "You better watch that." But Bean didn't stop until Thatcher jumped up, picked up the fish, and chased Bean into the water.

Ronnie was still laughing when Juanita walked over. "I told you, didn't I?"

Ronnie nodded. "That was a good one."

"Nobody calls my little sister a chicken and gets away with it."

Ronnie looked at her, happy at the sound of being called a little sister.

Later, as Ronnie lay on the rock again, back to her sunning mode, her eyes closed against the brightness of the sun, feeling the heat on her face, on her chest, on her arms and legs, she heard someone coming from behind her. She didn't look, assuming it was Bean, but when a shadow fell over her eyes, she turned her head and looked.

"Hey," Thatcher said.

Ronnie sat up quickly, worried for a second that he was going to pull a prank, going to get revenge, but he was just standing there.

"It's nice up here," he said, squinting into the sun.

Ronnie lay back down and closed her eyes.

"Don't get burned," he said. He plopped down next to her. "The sides are so jagged. I didn't know it was so flat up here."

Ronnie turned her head and looked to the bank. Juanita and Bean were eating oranges.

"Seems like you're having fun," Thatcher said.

"It's nice here," she said. That was the truth, so beautiful, so quiet and peaceful.

She closed her eyes, but when she heard Thatcher sigh, she turned, shading her eyes with her hand so that she could see him. He was looking away, across the water.

"What?" Ronnie said.

He pursed his lips. His hair was wet and sticking to his head. Drops of water ran from his face, dripped from the tip of his nose. He licked his lips then took both of his hands and rubbed his face as if he were washing it. He took a deep breath and looked at Ronnie.

"Um . . ."

Ronnie waited.

"What?" she said.

He stared at her for a minute and then looked to the bank. "Nothing," he said. "I'm just glad you're having fun."

Ronnie waited. He obviously wanted to say something to her. She considered him sitting there. She considered the day. Maybe that was enough. Maybe for today it was enough that they were trying. Thatcher stood up suddenly, and looking back to her over his shoulder, smiled and then turned away, jumping off the rock with a "Geronimo!" Ronnie sat up on an elbow and looked after him, down over the edge of the rock, onto the gravel and the water and the earth below. She waited for Thatcher to break the surface. He came up only to dive right back under. She watched his body glide below the surface of the water as he swam downstream away from the rock.

Ronnie tried to smile—it was a nice sight—but she was suddenly overwhelmed by the sudden shift in her feelings. She closed her eyes and lifted her face to the sun, swallowing the lump of emotion that had formed in her throat.

CHAPTER TWENTY FIVE

"Wanna go to the creek?" Bean said.

He stood next to the recliner where Ronnie sat. It was early evening and wouldn't be dark for another few hours, but the sun was low and the shadows had grown long. Thatcher and Juanita were in the kitchen. Juanita was making spaghetti.

"What creek?"

"Up there." Bean pointed in the direction of the dogs, and Ronnie remembered the dry creek she had crossed.

"Aren't you worn out from swimming all day?"

"Nope."

"Why you want to go up there?"

"To look for rocks."

"Aren't there dogs up there?"

"Just Tracer and Zubin."

Bean stood there, his hands on his hips, rocking from side to side, impatiently.

"I don't know, Bean . . ."

"Come on," he said. He reached out and pulled on Ronnie's hand. His touch was light, yet insistent.

Thatcher came into the room. He looked relaxed or maybe he was buzzed. Ronnie couldn't tell which, but he was holding a beer so one guess was as good as another. He had taken a shower and his hair was still wet. Strands of dry hair separated and flew away from the combed back hair still heavy in wetness. He suddenly looked young to Ronnie, and she wondered if this trip, if seeing Juanita was reversing a toll it had been taking all these years. She watched him walk across the room—tall and lean with just the hint of a smile on his lips. He needed to shave. His short sleeve shirt hung open, showing his hairless chest, his flat stomach. He came and stood behind Bean.

"Hey," he said to them.

"We're going to the creek." Bean looked at Ronnie. "Right?"

"Oh, yeah?"

Bean took her hand again and pulled. Ronnie stood up.

"Mom! We're going to the creek!" he yelled. He didn't look back as he tried to drag Ronnie across the room.

"Go tell her to her face so I know for sure it's okay," Ronnie said.

Bean ran into the kitchen, and Ronnie and Thatcher stood there facing each other.

"*Grandpa Ray* lives up by the creek, you know," Ronnie said.

Thatcher looked at the floor. "So I hear."

"Don't you think it's weird he hasn't come down here?"

"Juanita told him not to."

"How come?"

"Because I don't want to see him." He said it matter-of-factly.

Ronnie frowned. She expected that meeting their father would be the next logical step, that Thatcher would even be the one to push for it once he'd gotten over the shock of bumping into Ray Geisel at the Pink Lemonade.

"I . . . You don't want to see him?"

Thatcher walked to the sofa and sat down.

"Well, I guess in a way I want to see him just to tell him what a prick he is," Thatcher said. He smiled at Ronnie, but his expression was hard and defiant.

"Don't get drunk, T.," Ronnie said.

"I'm not drunk." He stared at her. "I just got nothing to say to him."

"Well . . ." Ronnie stammered as Bean came running back into the room.

"Let's go," he said.

He grabbed Ronnie's hand and tried to spin her around, but Ronnie didn't want to be spun. She wanted to stand there and talk with Thatcher.

"Come on," Bean chattered, pushing and pulling her. "Come on."

"Go on," Thatcher said waving his arm at them. "Bean wants to go to the creek."

He was dismissing her. He was finished talking. Ronnie stared at him for a second longer, but then let Bean pull her out the front door.

They walked down the gravel road, toward the creek. Ronnie's mind stayed on Thatcher and Juanita, though. It was clear that for Ronnie, getting Thatcher to talk was going to be impossible. He was talking to Juanita, though . . . she could tell by the way they became silent whenever she walked into the room.

Ronnie had brought in the breakfast dishes that morning. He was talking to Juanita, and it bugged Ronnie. Why couldn't he talk to her?

Bean jumped off the road and into the dry creek bed. Ronnie followed. He looked at the ground with a treasure-seeker's focus, picking up rocks and then throwing them down, picking up rocks and saying, "How 'bout this one?" He waited for a "yes" or "no," then put the rock aside or dropped it. Ronnie sat on a big, dry rock and half-heartedly picked up rocks herself, pretending to listen to Bean as he chattered about a rock he'd found once that looked just like an ear.

Ronnie had always known that Thatcher wasn't a big talker, but she liked to think that they were close in their own way. Hadn't the car proved that? He'd been good to her. He'd taken her in. He'd rescued her from Vivian. But this . . . now Ronnie was seeing this big locked door sitting between them that she hadn't even realized was there—and it had been there all the time. Thatcher had been locking this part of himself away from Ronnie for 18 years, and now that it was time to open it up, he couldn't do it, not to her, anyway. It made Ronnie wonder about herself, made her wonder if maybe she was just as difficult as Thatcher, if maybe she was the one who was really hard to talk to. It made her sad to think about them living together all that time and not being able to talk to each other when it counted most. What kind of relationship was that?

Ronnie heard a dog bark. Her body tensed and she looked at Bean.

"Zubin!" Bean shouted, standing up and dropping a rock absentmindedly.

"Bean!" Ronnie scolded. "Don't call those dogs!"

He looked at her, surprised by her tone. "They're nice," he said.

Ronnie shook her head. "They chased me."

He stood looking at her for a second as if he didn't understand what she was saying, and then turned and called again. Ronnie heard two dogs barking.

"They don't know me, Bean," Ronnie said. She stood up, her stomach tight with fear.

"They ain't mean," he said.

The barking grew louder and in a flash the dogs stood on the gravel road, hanging their heads down over the bridge that ran over the dry creek, reaching out their noses, sniffing the air, wagging their tails with mouths hanging open and tongues sticking out.

Ronnie wanted to run, wanted to scream at Bean for calling them, but she stood still, frozen at the sight of them. She had never had a dog, and these dogs . . . they were so big. Her knees started to shake.

"Hey, Zubin," Bean said. He walked to the pipe bridge and stretched his arm up as high as he could. The black Labrador bent his head down toward Bean, sticking his tongue in and out, trying to lick a hand he could not reach.

"Hey, Tracer," Bean said to the other dog.

Ronnie stood perfectly still, but the German shepherd began barking when it made eye contact. Ronnie shut her eyes.

"Tell them to go home, Bean," she said. Her voice sounded high and squeaky.

"They won't hurt you," Bean said. He called them down into the creek instead.

"Bean," Ronnie pleaded.

The dogs walked around to the side of the creek, pushing through tall grass to get to them. The shepherd, Tracer, walked straight over to Bean and stood solid in front of him like a rampart of Troy. The black lab, however, went over to Ronnie. Ronnie squinted her eyes, trying not to look at that dog, but not able to stop herself. She tried to will herself into calmness, to push down the rising punch of panic she felt.

"He's nice," Bean said. He stepped toward Ronnie, leaning his whole body onto the dog in front of him.

The lab smelled Ronnie's feet, her legs, her crotch. She stepped back.

"Put your hand out," Bean said.

Ronnie nodded cautiously and did what Bean said. She held her hand out for the dog to smell. The shepherd came up beside her, its huge head rising up nearly to her waist.

"See, they're nice," Bean said.

"They don't know me," Ronnie said. "Bean, tell them to go away."

"Are you scared?"

"Yes."

"What are you scared for? They just want to love you. Look." Bean sat on the gravel and called them to him. They turned. The lab licked his face while the shepherd sniffed his hair and tickled his ear with its whiskers. "See?" Bean said through his laughter. "See how they're kissing me?"

The black dog stopped and came back to Ronnie. It stood still in front of her, and then nudged her hand with its nose. Ronnie reached a hand out, laying it gingerly on the top of the dog's head.

"See?" Bean said.

Her panic broke, but did not disappear. The dogs wouldn't attack with Bean there, but Ronnie wondered what would have happened if they had caught up with her alone on the road. That would have been a different story. The shepherd came to her now as well and sniffed her. Then both dogs began sniffing the ground around Ronnie, walking casually here and there, looking up, looking down. Bean went back to looking for rocks.

When Ronnie realized they had done all they were going to regarding her, she started to relax. She tried to look toward the house down the road—toward *his* house. She hadn't realized it before on her earlier walk, hadn't realized that she had been walking right toward her father's house. She tried to look now, to see the house, but the bank of the creek was high and overgrown with grasses and bushes and trees that blocked her view. These were *his* dogs, dogs that he called by name and fed and petted. When Tracer came near her, she lifted her hand and gingerly touched his soft fur. Sitting there, petting her father's dog, a man she had never met—it was an odd feeling.

"Bean," Ronnie said, "is your grandpa at home right now?"

"I dunno," Bean said.

"Do you ever go down there?"

"Sure. I go there all the time."

Grandpas, moms, dads, aunts and uncles. When Ronnie thought about family, she thought about Thatcher and Vivian. That was it. Then she thought about the Wilson's—that gigantic beautiful family. There were so many of them. And now this, the idea of a sister, a father . . . suddenly Ronnie felt cheated. All this time, she had been cheated out of her own family. Thatcher had his whole family in view now, and it included Ronnie, of course, but it was a family she didn't even know. For Thatcher, the picture was nearly complete, and it made Ronnie furious. It was easy for him to decide that he didn't want to meet their father—he already knew the whole story. For Ronnie though, the picture wasn't even in focus.

"Bean," she said. "Will you take me to see your grandpa?"

"Okay," he said simply and stood up.

Ronnie stared at him, instantly afraid of her own suggestion and of Bean's innocent willingness to take her there. As Bean started climbing out of the creek bed, though, Ronnie followed and found herself charged with a strange and powerful feeling, a feeling of courage and confidence. She would meet him. She would meet him before Thatcher did—if he ever did—and she would meet him whether Thatcher wanted her to or not. She would have, at least, that satisfaction, that advantage. And she would not have to see him through her brother's eyes, as she saw Juanita; Ronnie would see her father with her own eyes, on her own terms, of her own will.

CHAPTER TWENTY SIX

Ronnie walked quickly down the gravel road with Bean skipping and running to keep up.

"Wait for me," he said more than once.

The dogs followed them, running ahead, running back, running around them. They hardly existed to Ronnie now. The two-story white house sat back on a long front yard that was fenced on the front by triple barbed-wire. A double wide steel gate stood open, and the gravel road split into a gravel drive that led to and around both the front and the back of the house and to a big red barn off to the right. A blue pickup truck sat in front of the barn. The barn doors stood open like the gaping jaw of a monster ready to swallow a meal.

Ronnie was on fire with energy, alive and full, her senses taking in every detail as they walked on the road: the spiderwort that grew wild and stood out sharply on a canvas of rock road and grass greens; the zapping buzz of bugs flying and grasshoppers hopping around her and out of her way; the sunlight glaring from behind her right shoulder yet casting its light before her like arms opening in a gesture of presentation; the air hot and humid with a smell of dark, rich earth. Ronnie took it in as she walked along, feeling the earth in her blood. She heard her pulse, steady and strong in her ear. Ronnie was alive and would see her father.

They walked through the gate and started up the drive. Zubin and Tracer ran barking from behind them, bounding through the open gate in unison, racing across the lawn and to the barn. Potted red geraniums sat at the bottom on both sides of the front porch steps. An empty rocking chair sat at the top.

"Grandpa," Bean began to sing over and over. His voice was high and sweet. It lulled Ronnie in its innocence like the song of the siren.

She walked steadily, as if hypnotized in a make-believe world. The dogs reappeared from the barn and stood in front of the blue pick-up truck, watching their approach with wagging tails. Ronnie and Bean cut across the front lawn, right in front of his house and as they came to the edge of the house, nearing ever closer to the barn, Ronnie heard a clanking sound coming from the barn.

"Grandpa," Bean shouted. He ran ahead and into the barn, leaving Ronnie alone, leaving her behind.

The clanking sound came again.

Ronnie's resolve wavered and began to slide, timidity vying for a dominant spot. She took a deep breath and pushed away the fear, struggling to keep her goal before her: to meet her father, to impress Thatcher by her stalwart courage. That is what Ronnie needed to be—stalwart and courageous. She began to walk forward, slowly, but with firm resolution. She stood at the open barn door.

"Come in, Aunt Veronica!" Bean said.

Ronnie walked gingerly. The barn smelled like hay. When she looked to her left, Ronnie saw it, bales of hay stacked above in the loft.

He was standing behind a tractor. Ronnie could see the back of his head and the slope of his shoulders as he faced a lighted work-bench that ran along the wall of the barn. Bean stood near him. As soon as she saw him, she froze. Her resolve? Her courage? Gone. All that was there were shaking knees and sweaty palms. This was a mistake, she realized. She wasn't ready. She looked at Bean who was peeking out at her from behind the tractor. He stared, frowning. She wondered now what had made her think she could just go up there and meet him like that, unexpected, with no preparation? What had she been thinking?

She wanted to turn and walk away, to run back to Juanita's, to run to Thatcher. She looked at Bean who was still staring. What did he realize? He walked over to Ronnie and took her hand. What kind of wisdom was there in that little boy? Ronnie tried to smile at him, him and his dirty little boy fingers squeezing hers, offering her courage just like he'd tried to do when they were standing on that rock, offering her comfort in his quiet little hand. There was a tightness in Ronnie's chest. She wasn't ready to cry, but she couldn't breathe.

She was afraid, but like a quiet push, she was suddenly, simply, putting one foot in front of the other, walking toward the far side of that huge barn, walking toward that tractor, walking toward her father. The palms of his hands were resting flat on the workbench, as if he was having to hold himself up. His head was bowed down. Ronnie stood there. Waiting. Waiting for him to turn.

"I got Aunt Veronica, Grampa," Bean said.

He lifted his head a notch, but didn't turn.

"What do you want?" he said. His voice was thick and low.

Ronnie's breath was completely gone, and when she spoke she sounded winded, like she'd just run a 50 yard dash.

"I . . . I wanted to meet you . . . I . . . ." Why didn't he turn around? Why didn't he face her?

"Grampa?"

"I mean," Ronnie said, "I . . . I'm Ronnie."

She waited for him to turn, for him to greet her, but he didn't. He just stood there with his back to her.

"I know who you are," he said.

When he still didn't turn around, Ronnie took a step backwards, suddenly understanding. He was not going to face her. He was not going to turn. She let go of Bean's hand.

"Grampa," Bean was saying as Ronnie turned and left. "Grampa, it's Veronica."

Ronnie walked out of that barn. She left him. She left Bean, not quite running, not quite walking. And when she got to that dry creek, she went down the steep, dirt bank, falling blindly into it. She went down into it, stepping over and around rocks and logs, breathing hard and crying the whole way. She walked and cried. And while she was forced to stop walking by a giant tree trunk that stretched, thick and impassable across the width of the creek, she stopped moving, but she did not stop crying. She sat and cried. She sat on a big rock and leaned against the trunk of that tree, leaning her arms on her knees and her head on her arms. And she cried. She cried hard and long. Her stomach and throat muscles burned with the strain of tears, so many tears that surely they would fill a dry creek-bed, and Ronnie wished they would. She wished her tears would fill it and that the current would drag her away from this place and these people and dash her against the rocks and pin her under until she drowned.

CHAPTER TWENTY SEVEN

It gets pretty dark at night in the country. No street lights. No house lights. When Ronnie realized the sun was going down, she wiped her eyes, dusted off her legs, and headed back toward Juanita's house. What else could she do? Where else could she go, stuck out in the country?

As she got closer to the road, she heard Juanita's voice calling her name. The pipe bridge came into view. Juanita stood on it, leaning toward the creek.

"Veronica! Veronica is that you? Oh God, Veronica! We've been looking everywhere for you." She stood up straight and turned toward her house down the road. "I found her!" she yelled. "I found her!" She turned back to Ronnie. Her immense hand spread across her chest, as if to hold her heart in place.

Ronnie's legs seemed to drag and her feet stumbled on the uneven rock bed. She reached up to grab hold of the bank so that she could pull herself up when she felt Juanita's hand grab her arm, strong and sure. Juanita helped Ronnie up and even before Ronnie could fully stand, Juanita had bent her looming frame down upon Ronnie and wrapped her tightly in her arms as best she could, pulling Ronnie close to her body and keeping her there. Juanita pulled Ronnie close and did not let go, cooing to her in sounds of soothing. It sounded to Ronnie like Juanita was crying, but Ronnie didn't care. She had seen enough of tears for the day. She was weary. Weary and broken. Everything. It was all too much. And maybe it wouldn't have mattered who was hugging her at that moment because she was so worn down, so worn out from her emotions, but Ronnie found herself melting into those extra long, generous arms, grateful for the comfort they offered in the moment. She leaned into Juanita's body, enveloped.

After a minute, Ronnie tried to say something, but no words came.

"I know, I know," Juanita hushed her. "I know everything."

Juanita guided Ronnie back, down the road, away from the creek-bed that was still dry in spite of all Ronnie's tears, away from Ray Geisel, who Ronnie realized did not care about her. Juanita guided Ronnie, and she didn't let go. She kept her long arm about Ronnie as best she could. The thought would occur to Ronnie later that maybe Juanita was taking advantage of the situation—of Ronnie letting her get so close without a struggle—but the fact was, Juanita didn't let go, not once, until they were back at the house, and then, even there, Juanita did not leave Ronnie's side. Thatcher and Bean saw them as they walked toward Juanita's house, down the road. Thatcher put his hand out to stop Bean from following, and then came to meet them. He walked quickly, sort of a hop-run in spurts.

"It's okay now," Juanita said to him. "Veronica is okay." The three of them stood still for a moment. Ronnie looked at Thatcher. His eyes were filled with concern. She looked at his hands, his fists clenching and unclenching as he stood there. She looked, and then she looked away—the anger was always there within him, always right below the surface. She was tired of it. She was tired of dealing with it along with everything else. But then Thatcher reached out his hand and brushed Ronnie's arm lightly, and though it was just for a second, Ronnie appreciated it. It was the best he could do. When they reached Bean, he said nothing but merely fell in line and walked silently alongside them.

At the house, Juanita led Ronnie to the couch in the living room. She sat with her there, her frame taking up a large amount of the space. Thatcher stood—pacing the room and staring at the floor, back and forth in short, quick steps, his fists still working. Juanita looked up at him and then at Bean who was watching Thatcher.

"Bean," she said, "You go get yourself in the bath."

Bean started to complain, but when he looked at his mother, he fell silent. Now was not the time to argue. He went into the bathroom and shut the door.

"What did he say to you, Ronnie?" Juanita asked gently. "You can tell us. What did he say?"

Ronnie looked at her, shaking her head back and forth. She didn't want to look at Juanita, her face so large and out of proportion, so close to Ronnie's, but when she placed her hand on Ronnie's shoulder, Ronnie found herself looking past the protruding brow bone, past the high and heavy cheekbones, past her thick lips. She winced when she looked into Juanita's deep brown eyes. She winced because as she looked into them, Ronnie saw something she recognized. She saw hurt. She saw pain. And Ronnie realized that she had been just as cruel, just as cold and hurtful to Juanita as their father had been to her. Ronnie had been turning her back on Juanita all along. Her chin started quivering all over again. Juanita nodded toward her, encouraging her to speak.

"He didn't want to see me," she said looking into those wounded eyes and then looking down at her own hands. Ronnie was ashamed of the hurt she knew she had probably caused Juanita, just as she was hurt by the shame her father had caused her.

"Oh," Juanita said. "You don't understand and I'm so sorry. I wanted to tell you but . . . but . . ." she looked at Thatcher.

"I told her not to," Thatcher said.

Ronnie looked up, not understanding.

"It's my fault," Thatcher said.

"No," Juanita said to him.

"Ronnie," Thatcher said ignoring Juanita. The way he stood by the front door made Ronnie think he was waiting for a chance to make a getaway. "He ain't your dad."

Ronnie stared at him, trying to understand what he was saying.

"What?"

Thatcher was shaking his head and looking at the floor. "He ain't your dad," he said again.

Juanita squeezed Ronnie's shoulder and nodded.

"It's true, Veronica."

Ronnie stared at Juanita, her brow furrowing in confusion. Not her father? She sat there, dazed, trying to think, trying to let what they were saying sink in, and yet not quite knowing exactly what it was she was supposed to think about. Not her father? If he wasn't her father, then who was?

"Tell her, Juanita," Thatcher said. "Tell her everything."

"Well, let's just take this all real slow," Juanita said. "Are you all right, Veronica?"

Ronnie exhaled.

"Do you want to hear this now? Maybe you want to, you know, like rest or something. You're so upset already."

"Jesus Christ, just tell her and let's be done with it," Thatcher said. He walked out the front door and stood by the screen. Juanita and Ronnie watched him for a minute, and then Juanita turned to Ronnie.

"He's right," she said. "Listen, it doesn't change anything."

That was a lie, and a part of Ronnie wanted to laugh. Ever since Juanita had shown up, everything had changed.

"But I want you to know something. I want you to know that my dad is a good man." She looked toward the front door and then looked back to Ronnie. "I know T. don't think so, and you might not think so, but he is. He brought me here, and I have a good life here."

Ronnie looked at Thatcher. She knew he could hear Juanita through the screen door. His body remained tense and still as she spoke.

"I . . . I don't know where to start," she sputtered.

"Just tell her," Thatcher said from the porch.

Ronnie felt great disgust for Thatcher at that moment. There he was, still unwilling to talk, still with his back turned. If the sight of that turned back hadn't been so scathingly familiar at the moment, Ronnie would have laughed at the similarity she saw between Thatcher and his father, their backs turned, refusing to look at what was in front of them. But it was not funny. It was angering and hurtful, and while Ronnie didn't know about Ray Geisel, she thought Thatcher was nothing but a coward.

Juanita patted Ronnie's shoulder to get her attention, to get Ronnie to look at her.

"Well . . . you know our mother. Thatcher says she hasn't changed much. But he said she treats you all right. Isn't that right?"

Ronnie shrugged. "I guess . . . for her."

"Yes. See, it's that 'for her' that you're saying. You know what she's like. Can you imagine how she would have been with me?"

Ronnie looked at Juanita, and Juanita looked to the floor.

"She couldn't stand the sight of me . . . I mean . . . she really couldn't." Juanita's voice had become smooth and far away. "I know I'm hard to look at." She looked at Ronnie. "I know that. You want to think your mother will love you no matter what, but that ain't always the case. She couldn't stand the sight of me and made sure I knew it every day, but my Daddy . . . Veronica, he took me away and gave me a good and safe place to live. I want you to know that. I want you to know that he's a good man."

Thatcher was lighting a cigarette and blew a blustery cloud of smoke into the air. Ronnie kept listening.

"And T. . . . well, he's mad at him for leaving, but Momma didn't treat him like she treated me. She loved him. She never laid a finger on him . . ."

Ronnie's mouth fell open in shock. "You mean, like, hit you?" she asked.

"Yes." It was Thatcher who answered. "She hit her."

Vivian was not a good mother, Ronnie knew that, but she had never laid a hand on Ronnie or Thatcher. Of course, Thatcher had been twice Vivian's size for as long as Ronnie could remember, but she'd never even given Ronnie the idea that she would hit her.

Juanita rested her hand on Ronnie's leg and leaned forward. "Listen. I'm over that," she said. "I really am. And the only reason I am over that is because of our father—," she shook her head to correct herself—"*my* father got me out of there and gave me a good place to live."

"But he didn't take T.," Ronnie said.

"No."

Ronnie looked at the screen door again. Thatcher had turned around and was leaning against the side of the porch. He and Ronnie looked at each other through the screen, Thatcher's expression made of granite.

"He's *your* dad, right?" Ronnie said to Thatcher.

"Yes," Juanita said for him.

"But not mine," Ronnie said.

Juanita shook her head. "No."

"And you're not my full sister."

"That's right."

"And T. . . . ." Ronnie looked at the screen again.

Juanita squeezed Ronnie's leg.

"And T. isn't my full brother."

Thatcher opened the door.

"That don't matter, Ronnie," he said. He sounded like he was irritated with her, as if Ronnie would be a fool to even think such a thing.

Ronnie closed her eyes and leaned her head back against the couch. The world swirled behind her eyelids in both back and forth directions.

"Daddy found out that Momma was pregnant and . . . well . . ." Juanita looked at Thatcher for support. "They'd been fighting for years by then, Veronica, and our Daddy was gone most of the time because he was driving a truck over the road then, and there was just no way that baby was his."

"Then whose was it?"

"We don't know that," Juanita said. "I mean, Thatcher and me. We don't know that. If Daddy knows he never said, and I never had the nerve to ask him."

"You don't know?" Ronnie asked Thatcher. He shook his head.

"See," Juanita went on. "I just think Daddy'd taken as much as he could. You know? I think he'd been staying in the picture for T. and me, but I think that when she got pregnant it was the last straw. He'd taken as much as he could, and I think he knew that I had taken as much as I could, too."

"How much of all this did you know, T.?" Ronnie said.

"He knew most of it," Juanita said for him. "But that don't matter either, Veronica. This is not his fault."

Juanita stared into Ronnie's eyes until she had no choice but to look back.

"I was the only one who knew that you weren't his—and I didn't find that out till years later. I mean we were kids when all this happened. We were just kids. T. found out about it just this morning, Veronica. I told him while you were outside with Bean eating breakfast."

"Well then why didn't you tell me when you found out, T.?" Ronnie looked at Juanita helplessly, and then looked back to Thatcher. "Why don't you tell me anything?"

"I tried," Thatcher said. "I tried to tell you."

"When! When did you ever try to tell me anything?"

"On the rock. I came up to tell you."

That was true. Ronnie had known he was trying to say something to her. It was true. Ronnie took a deep breath and was quiet for a minute.

"It's just hard," Juanita said in his defense.

"But you didn't, T. You didn't tell me anything, just like always."

Thatcher moaned and stepped off the porch. Ronnie leaned

forward, looking after him, trying to see where he was going. He stood in the middle of the yard, facing the meadow. His hands were on his hips, his head thrown back. Ronnie seemed to be trying every ounce of his patience.

"It's hard, Veronica," Juanita said again. She patted Ronnie's knee. "I mean . . . we don't have many more answers than you. It's hard for all of us, but you know . . . all I know is we're a family. *We* can be a family . . ."

"This is just nuts," Ronnie said. She stood and went to the screen door. "T., I want to go home. I really do."

She watched him, waiting for him to turn, waiting for him to answer, but he remained where he was, his back rigid. Coward, Ronnie thought. He was nothing but a coward.

Though it took a long time for Ronnie to fall asleep that night, she slept soundly, recliner or not. She dreamed of Blue Springs, of the water, of the big rock, only she was alone. There was no Thatcher, no Juanita, no Bean. Suddenly, a man was there and, though he had no face, Ronnie knew who he was. He stood downstream on the bank of the river watching her, waiting for her. She sat on the big chocolate rock by herself, wondering why she was alone, why only this man and Ronnie existed. He began to walk toward her and she was filled with dread and a painful longing. He was a blur, not even an image. A vague vision. An idea. Ronnie hid behind the rock that was no longer the grandfather rock in the water but was now a rock that sat on dry ground. She hugged the rock, trying to meld herself to it, trying to become invisible, trying to become something else, anything else, trying to become something she was not.

"Ronnie," the man said.

Ronnie hugged the rock with all her strength, her eyes squeezed tightly shut.

"Ronnie."

She felt a tap on her shoulder. She jumped and sat up to a room filled with dusky light. Her heart pounded, and the dark shadow before her spoke.

"The sun's going to rise soon," he said. "Come watch it with me."

Thatcher's voice was a whisper, and Ronnie stepped out of her dream.

"It's still dark," she said.

"Come outside with me."

There was a hint of pleading in his voice, a hint of loneliness, a hint of fear . . . Ronnie wondered for an instant if she were still asleep.

She followed him outside, and they sat under the oak tree in the chairs that faced toward the meadow across the road. A humid mist hung low in the fields, clinging to the grasses, to the bushes, to the trees. The smell was wet and sweet and clean, like the cool breath of pouring rain felt from underneath a covered porch. The dark sky was growing lighter shade by subtle shade, and the waking sounds of early birds, morning crickets and country bugs grew loud.

They sat in silence, waiting for the sun. Light was coming, surely, from behind the hills that backed the meadow. But before it did, before Thatcher and Ronnie were completely out of the dark, he said her name and then the three words that she had never in her life heard him say. He said them quietly, and he said them only once, but his words were clear and crisp.

CHAPTER TWENTY EIGHT

They left for home a few hours later.

Home. Everything felt jumbled in Ronnie's mind. Too much to think about. Too much to focus on at one time. The ride home was quiet. Thatcher and Ronnie had both had their fill, and then some, of heavy conversation. They let everything rest.

The phone was ringing when they walked in the door.

"Well it's about time. Jesus, Ronnie. Where the hell have you been?" Vivian said when Ronnie picked it up.

"Oh . . . hey, Mom . . . "

"Well? How come you haven't been answering the phone? I been looking all over for you. Gayla said you weren't working and Philip acted stupid when I talked to him. Now where the hell have you been?"

As she was talking, Ronnie looked out the front window to see what was keeping Thatcher. He was lifting a big cardboard box from the back of his pick-up and then headed toward the back yard.

"Are you going to answer me?"

"Hang on a second, Mom," Ronnie said.

She put the phone down, though Vivian was saying, "Ronnie! Ronnie!" Ronnie walked to the back door and leaned out.

"Telephone," she said to Thatcher.

He looked up. "Coming."

He set the box on the ground and shut the gate. As he walked past Ronnie, she felt a little jab of guilt, but above that was a greater sense of freedom. He could deal with their mother from now on. Ronnie didn't owe Vivian anything. She'd been lying to Ronnie in one way or another all her life. Ronnie didn't owe her a thing, and she didn't ever have to talk to Vivian again if she didn't want to. As Thatcher walked past her to go into the house, Ronnie went over to the box to see what was inside. She opened the lid. Four stacks of different sized clay pots sat nesting inside with saucers propped up against the sides of the box. She picked up a small pot and turned it around in her hand. She thought about Juanita's hand on her shoulder, about Juanita sitting next to her on the couch the night before. No, Ronnie didn't owe Vivian anything.

"Hey thanks." Thatcher stuck his head out the back door. "I didn't want to miss *that* call."

"Better you than me."

"You gonna paint them?" He nodded toward the box.

Ronnie shrugged.

"Might make some money."

"Whatever."

"Yeah. Whatever." He went back inside.

In spite of all Ronnie's new feelings, it was good to be back home, to be in her own room again. At least this place, this room, this spot in the world was hers. She felt sure of that. She lay in her bed and stared at the mural on the wall, letting herself get lost in the colors and shapes. Maybe now life would go back to being normal. Maybe now that the truth was out, they would all be able to go on with their lives. Ronnie would work hard at it, anyway. She would work hard at just staying in the day. That, she decided, was how she would live. She would handle whatever task was before her and nothing more. That was the way. That is what she decided. She shut her eyes, comforted by her plan, and slept away the afternoon.

CHAPTER TWENTY NINE

When Vivian didn't come around or call for a while, Ronnie figured Thatcher must have told her where they had gone for the weekend, and had maybe even told her about Ray Geisel. Vivian wouldn't like that. She would want to avoid that, and she would want to avoid Ronnie and Thatcher as much as they wanted to avoid her. Ronnie didn't ask Thatcher, but she hoped he had told their mother and that Vivian was suffering over it.

Ronnie didn't exactly ignore the pots in the back yard, but Thatcher must have thought she was because, while he never said a word, he started putting them around the house. Ronnie found the first pot in the bathroom on the windowsill. It was a smaller pot—red, smooth clay on a small, round saucer. Ronnie wondered why he put it there, but at the same time, she liked the way the red of the clay went with the peach colored tile. A day or so later, there was a bigger pot sitting on the floor next to Ronnie's bedroom door.

"Why'd you put that there?" she asked when she saw him.

"I dunno," he shrugged.

When Ronnie had come home from work, there were three medium clay pots on the front porch, two with saucers, one without, one pot on each step up to the door. Inside the house, one of the biggest pots sat in the middle of the kitchen table, taking up entirely too much room, and the windowsill over the sink was lined with small pots the same size as the one in the bathroom.

"Stop it," Ronnie told him the next morning.

"Stop what?"

He was sitting at the kitchen table, eating a bowl of cereal and reading the back of the cereal box. Ronnie got herself a bowl. When she went to look for the milk, she saw that he had set the carton inside the pot.

"Stop this," she said tipping the pot and making a face at him.

He kept eating and turned back to his cereal box.

"I never said I'd do it, you know," Ronnie said.

He didn't say anything.

"I didn't tell her to send all those pots home with you."

Ronnie looked at him, waiting for him to respond, but he didn't look up. She shook her head. "I didn't."

She started with the one on the bathroom windowsill. She painted it while Thatcher was at work, cleaned everything up before he came home, and placed the painted pot back on the windowsill where he had put it. She didn't say a word, and he didn't either—at least not directly.

"You been sitting around wasting time all day?"

He said this hours after he had come home from work and gone into the bathroom to take a shower. Him saying this was nothing new, but this time when he said it, there was a hint of amusement beneath the complaint—and that was all that was needed.

Next, Ronnie chose one of the pots on the front porch and again set it back before he came home. She didn't know if he noticed it when he first pulled in the driveway or if he saw it later that evening when he was cutting the grass, but when he came in he said, "The front of our house sure looks good when I cut the grass," but Ronnie knew he was really talking about the pot.

They were making peace, Thatcher and Ronnie. Without saying a word, they were binding their wounds and reestablishing themselves within the light of all the truth that had been poured on them. And it was a good thing. Ronnie had always been so critical of Thatcher and his unwillingness to talk, but really, she knew that she could be accused of the very same thing. They weren't taught to be open. But through this game they were playing with the pots, Ronnie was realizing something else. She was realizing that all these years, Thatcher and she had been communicating just fine—but that it was just in a different way than words. It was more like they had a secret code . . . like the game they played with the car keys. On the surface Ronnie guessed it seemed silly, but to them it wasn't silly at all, to them it meant that they cared, that they were paying attention.

And this was the way Thatcher and Ronnie had always gotten along. It didn't matter *how* they got their points across, did it? What mattered was that they *got* them across. So they didn't sit down and have heart to heart talks. So Thatcher didn't tell Ronnie everything he knew about their family. Juanita was right. None of that was his fault. He told Ronnie what he thought she needed to hear. They communicated well enough, and more than that, what Ronnie had learned that last morning in Cabool when they were sitting outside and waiting for the sun, was that Ronnie could count on Thatcher to tell her what she really needed to know when it really mattered.

Of course, she was irritated with Thatcher all over again just a few hours later. It was his cup. He had this old mug from his childhood that he never let Ronnie touch. It was junk as far as Ronnie could see. There was supposed to be a picture of Davy Crockett on the front, though the face was all but faded away. The tail of Davy's coon-skin cap had been, at one time, the handle of the mug, but that too was gone. No handle, no face. The cup had a chipped lip and a crack that ran down along what should have been Davy Crockettt's nose. And every so often, Thatcher would drink from it, though it was barely able to hold liquid. Every so often he would take that cup off the windowsill and try to use it.

"Why don't you just throw that old thing away?" Ronnie said to Thatcher. "You're going cut your lip off."

He paid no attention to Ronnie, though, and poured some coffee into it. He said it was his favorite TV show growing up, and that's all he'd ever say.

"Look!" Ronnie said pointing. "Look it's leaking."

Thatcher held the mug up and turned his hand to inspect it. A few small beads of coffee began making their way from the crack.

"It's gonna leak all over everything. Throw it away."

But Thatcher simply took the cup and set it inside this other cracked cup they had—not a special one, just a second cracked cup. Ronnie watched Thatcher take the Davy Crockettt cup and set it into the plain cup and misaligned the cracks. He looked up at Ronnie and smiled, showing her that even though both of them dripped a little bit, together they could hold a cup's worth of coffee just long enough to let Thatcher drink it down. He took a drink and then gave a loud sigh of satisfaction for Ronnie's benefit.

"Nothing like a good cup of coffee," he said.

Ronnie rolled her eyes and went back to washing the dishes. When she turned to take the cup from him, Thatcher pulled his hand away. "Uh-uh," he said. "I can't trust you with this."

"You are so stupid," Ronnie said.

Ronnie sat up quickly and stared into the darkness. It was the middle of the night. She must have been dreaming—what about she didn't remember, but her breathing was quick and her heart was pounding. She heard voices and laughter from outside. A late night party was going on down the street. Ronnie got up and walked to the window. When she pulled back the curtain, she thought she smelled a hint of cinnamon in the air. She heard a long and low sigh come from Thatcher's room down the hall. He was sleeping.

She looked back out the window, to the moon that filtered through the leaves. The sky was a deep, cadmium blue, and it was too beautiful. She breathed in the cinnamon air, thinking how funny it was that the simplest thing could be so beautiful that it suddenly filled every pore with an aching sadness.

She thought about her father, wondering why she didn't have one—especially since her mother was so off center. It didn't seem fair, and she wondered why she didn't get this one thing that everyone else seemed to have—that even someone like Juanita had. But then Ronnie felt bad, thinking about Juanita. She wouldn't change places with Juanita for a thousand fathers. She stood there, staring out the window thinking only about herself while Juanita was living in a nightmare body. No wonder God wouldn't give her a father.

Ronnie sank back down onto her bed and cried softly, only now it was for all of them. It was for her and Thatcher. It was for Juanita and Bean. It was even—just a little bit—for Vivian. They were all broken: chipped, cracked and leaking, like Thatcher's old mug.

Ronnie got up and walked down the dark hallway toward the bathroom. When she flipped on the light, she thought she heard Thatcher say her name. She leaned out of the doorway and looked into his room.

"Thatcher?" she whispered, but his only response was even and rhythmic breathing. Ronnie started to look away when her eyes caught the light of a reflection coming from under Thatcher's bed. She thought of an eye—a monster-under-the-bed sort of eye. She stepped toward it, slowly. Of course it was no monster, but it was the middle of the night and she'd thought she'd heard her name and suddenly she was afraid to take the next step, to go to that reflection, to go to Thatcher's bed where he lay like a dead man in the shadow of night. She was afraid to peek into the darkness to see what was there. She turned away.

Silly her. Silly imagination. She turned from Thatcher's room and went into the bathroom. Who cared what was under Thatcher's bed? After she had cupped her hand beneath the faucet for a drink of water and stood up straight again, Ronnie looked in the mirror, her hair messed, her eyes red from her tears. She thought about that light, that little glint. Maybe it would be gone.

She went back to the doorway, turned off the light, and looked into Thatcher's room, into the darkness, training her eyes to where the light should be. It was gone. She turned the light on again, and the reflection returned. Thatcher groaned. Ronnie crouched down and went into his room, keeping her eyes on the reflection, trying to make some shape come of it. She could see that she would have to get to it, that she'd never figure out what it was from so far away. She'd have to peer into the darkness and maybe even reach out her hand and feel it. She stepped closer and got on her hands and knees. What is it? What is it?

A coffee cup? Ronnie let out a breath. Thatcher's stupid coffee cup. She reached under the bed and stretched her arm long. What was his coffee cup doing under there? He usually rinsed it out and put it back on the windowsill. Why was it in his room? Why was it under his bed?

"What are you doing?" Thatcher said sleepily. His voice made her jump.

"I . . . dropped something," Ronnie whispered. She grabbed the cup and pulled it out from under the bed, and when she looked at Thatcher, his eyes were closed and he was sleeping again.

Ronnie stood in the light of the hallway holding Thatcher's precious Davy Crockett mug in her hands. Then she got an idea. She took the cup to her room and set it on her worktable. It would need a bit of cadmium blue to restore the eyes, but the smile would be easy.

CHAPTER THIRTY

      She was worried that Thatcher would be angry when he saw it, that she'd made a mistake, but every time she held the mug up to the light, she thought it looked pretty good. Ronnie was afraid to give it to him, though. She put it in her top dresser drawer, waiting for the right time, but the right time didn't come that day or the next. Then Ronnie began to worry that Thatcher was going to look for his mug and ask Ronnie if she'd seen it. She didn't want to admit that she'd taken it and painted it. She didn't want to appear sneaky or deceptive. She didn't want to have to confess anything; she was just trying to give him a gift.

      It was late. The house was dark and Thatcher was asleep. Ronnie was lying in bed, staring up at the ceiling and thinking about that mug and how to give it to Thatcher, when it came to her. She crept out of bed, took the mug out of the dresser drawer, and went to the kitchen. She turned on the light and set the mug on the table in front of Thatcher's chair. He would find it sitting there in the morning, and Ronnie wouldn't have to see him because he always left for work before she got up. It was perfect. Ronnie smiled and started back to her room. When she reached for the light switch, though, she turned around and took one last look. Davy was facing the wrong direction. She went back to the mug and turned it to face

Thatcher when he sat down. There. That is how she wanted him to find it. She couldn't do anything about the leak or the chip, but Davy Crockett had a face again.

The next morning, just as she expected, the house was empty when she woke up. When Ronnie saw that the mug was gone from the table, her stomach tightened. She looked around the house: in the sink, on the dining room table, on the bathroom windowsill, by the television, on Thatcher's dresser—she even looked under his bed. She looked everywhere that Thatcher would have normally left it, but it was gone. She didn't know if that was a good thing or not. There was nothing to indicate how Thatcher had felt when he'd found it, whether he'd been pleased or not. The only evidence that he'd been in there at all was the fact that the mug was gone and there was an open box of cereal sitting next to a dirty cereal bowl with a splash of milk and the spoon in it, sitting at Thatcher's spot on the table.

Ronnie cleaned up the mess and went to work a few hours later.

"Has T. been in?" she asked innocently as she stocked Pig-Power Pork Rinds on the snack rack.

"Well, sure, early to get coffee, but I ain't seen him since," Gayla said.

"Oh," Ronnie said, acting hard like she didn't care. "Did he bring his own cup?"

Gayla looked at Ronnie and frowned. "Honey, he could have brought in an empty tin can and used it as a cup for all I know. Why?"

"No reason," Ronnie said and went back to her pork rinds.

She kept expecting him to come over and say something about the mug, and each time the door opened and the bell rang, Ronnie looked up, half hoping, half dreading to see him. She spent her entire shift that way, but Thatcher never came. She didn't see him until later that evening over at the Wilson's. Mrs. Wilson had called Ronnie late in the afternoon and told her that she and Thatcher were to come to dinner. She didn't ask; she told, and Ronnie listened.

"There's Pretty," Mr. Wilson said when Ronnie walked in the door later. Mr. Wilson was sitting in his recliner, reading a newspaper, but immediately sat up when Ronnie came in, which meant that they were waiting on her and that he was hungry. He shouted up the stairs for Donika on his way to the kitchen. Ronnie followed him. It was just an everyday of the week kind of dinner, just the six of them: Ronnie, Thatcher, Mr. and Mrs. Wilson, Philip and Donika. Donika's mom worked nights at St. John's Hospital.

Thatcher and Philip were sitting at the table with their backs to Ronnie and Mr. Wilson as they walked into the kitchen. They were talking to Mrs. Wilson as she pulled a tray of corn muffins out of the oven. Mr. Wilson went to his place at the head of the table. Ronnie glanced at Thatcher, but she looked away before their eyes met. She felt shy and foolish and unsure, seeing Thatcher, and was glad to be surrounded by the Wilson's.

The Wilson's didn't treat Thatcher or Ronnie like special guests when they came to dinner; they treated them like family with a pot-luck of conversations, some involving all of them, some being little offshoot conversations between Ronnie and Donika, or Philip and Thatcher. Sometimes they'd have to listen to Mr. Wilson lecture on whatever topic happened to be stuck in his craw—lately he was talking a lot about the state of social security. Mrs. Wilson always shook her head when she was listening to him, and offered clucking sounds of understanding and support, but she'd change the subject to something else, like what needed to be fixed around the house, just as soon as she saw an opportunity. Philip and Thatcher talked about the customers they had that day or the challenges of whatever cars they were working on. Mr. Wilson always tried to act like he understood everything they were saying, but it was clear he didn't know anything about cars. Philip and Thatcher humored him, though. Sometimes no one said anything at all except for things like, "Pass the salt," or "Could you get the milk?" Being with the Wilson's was like being under a big, soft blanket.

Thatcher and Ronnie always sat across from each other. It wasn't like they usually talked much anyway, but on this day Ronnie was particularly careful not to look at him, and when Donika came in the kitchen and sat down, Ronnie focused all of her attention on her. Thatcher reached across the table and took Ronnie's glass.

"You want some milk?" he asked Ronnie.

She looked at him. His expression gave nothing away, but it was unusual for Thatcher to offer Ronnie anything unless she asked for it first. It was a gesture, and Ronnie nodded yes. She looked down at her bowl. Thatcher set the milk in front of her. "There you go," he said. Ronnie tried to hide her smile at this particular attention, but she knew what he was really saying. She knew that he was telling her that he liked her gift. Ronnie couldn't look at him, but she knew that she had, indeed, done a good thing after all.

They heard the front door open, and then shut.

"Oh, hey," Vivian said peeking around the corner and into the kitchen. "I didn't know my own children were over here." She must have seen their cars in front of the Wilsons' house because not even twenty minutes after they'd sat down, there she stood.

Who was she trying to fool? Thatcher glanced at Ronnie, but then looked toward the kitchen sink, like it made no difference to him whatsoever that Vivian had just walked in the door. Well, it may not have mattered to Thatcher, but it mattered to Ronnie. She was still angry with her, angry with all of her lying, angry for keeping her from the truth about her own family, angry about the way she had treated Juanita, angry about her father—whoever he was. Ronnie thought Vivian was cruel and fake and selfish and pathetic and Ronnie couldn't stand the sight of her. She wondered how a person could really be like her, how a person could be so far off. And more than that, she wondered how a person like that could be *her* mother?

Ronnie was thankful to be on the other side of the table, far from Vivian's grasp in case she felt like hugging her to show the Wilson's just how close they were.

"Well come in and join us, Vivian," Mr. Wilson said casually.

Ronnie took a deep breath, the breath that comes before submersion, the breath that comes before drowning.

"Oh, well, I only have a little bit of time. I got to work, you know."

Mrs. Wilson got up and pulled out a chair.

"Nonsense," she said. "Sit here." She brought out another plate, a bowl, and a spoon, and set it next to Philip and said to him, "Scoot over." Philip scooted his chair closer to Thatcher who scooted his chair closer to Mr. Wilson.

Ronnie looked across the table at her mother. Vivian flipped her hair and smoothed the front of her tight-knit shirt. She seemed nervous. Ronnie liked that. She decided that she would not say a word to Vivian, even if she spoke to her directly. She would not listen to Vivian and she would not talk to her. She watched her with a distance, as if Vivian belonged to someone else, as if she had come to entertain them all during their dinner, only she didn't know it. If only Ronnie could say to her, "So, Mother, who's my father? Who were you sleeping with way back then?" That would have been sweet. That would have set the mood all right. But Ronnie wasn't speaking to her, and knew that even if she were, she would never have the nerve to say something like that. Ronnie wanted to, though. She wanted to say that and more. She wanted to point her finger; she wanted to humiliate; she wanted to make Vivian feel the weight of her sins. She wanted everything Vivian had ever done to topple over her and cover her like boiling water. She wanted to make Vivian confess that it was all her fault—this family of theirs—that *she* was the one who had made their lives a huge mess, that she was the one who had been cruel to Juanita, that she had driven Ray Geisel away, not that there was any reason for Ronnie to care about him anymore, but Ronnie wanted to convict Vivian for it all. She glared across the table.

"Well," Vivian said, oblivious to Ronnie. "How are things up at the car shop?"

Thatcher didn't answer, and Ronnie looked at him. Maybe he was feeling the same things. Maybe he had decided to convict her with silence as well.

"Everything's going just fine, Ms. Geisel," Philip said. Vivian cleared her throat. "And, Marvin, I seen your tomatoes are coming up nicely."

"They sure are," Mr. Wilson said.

Vivian spoke in a stilted, proper tone, as if the entire room depended on her presence—and in a way, it did. As soon as she'd walked in the door, no one said a word that wasn't some sort of response to her. Though Ronnie was attentive to every word around her, to every breath, every glance anyone took, she kept her outward interest directed at her dinner, taking small, particular swallows of soup and pulling tiny crumbs off of her corn muffin as Vivian made chit-chat, talking to everyone but Thatcher and Ronnie.

"Donika, have you decided what you're going to do now?"

"Uh . . . I'm going to manicurist school," Donika said, throwing Ronnie a glance as if to apologize that she was answering.

"Well, now, isn't that great? You must be proud of her, Constance," she said leaning toward Mrs. Wilson.

"Of course, of course. We're proud of all our children and grandchildren," Mrs. Wilson said.

Ronnie looked up quickly, wondering if Mrs. Wilson had meant that as a slight against Vivian, wondering if Mrs. Wilson was talking about how Vivian had treated Juanita and Bean. It wasn't like Mrs. Wilson to play games like that, but still, Ronnie wasn't sure. Thatcher reached for another muffin.

"Well, of course, Ronnie and I have to get on making her plans for the future," Vivian said.

Ronnie's mouth dropped open, but she shut it quickly. Vivian was such a liar. They had never talked about Ronnie's future—not even once.

"You know you better start thinking about deadlines if you're going to apply to a college, Ronnie," Philip said.

It was clear to Ronnie that she was supposed to be contemplating her future now, preparing to move on, making big decisions, and big plans about her life and what she would do with it, but the truth was, since Juanita had shown up, Ronnie's mind was stuck—not on the future—but on trying to figure out the past. Why didn't anyone understand that? All the guidance counselors at school had tried to push Ronnie into making decisions about college, and now that she had graduated, everyone else seemed to assume that she was, indeed, making plans, but they didn't get it. If Ronnie couldn't answer even the simplest question about her own family, about her own past, how was she supposed to be able to make any decision about the future? Weren't they connected somehow, the past and the future? Didn't one have a direct bearing on the other? Why couldn't people understand that? Why couldn't they just leave her alone about the future—she didn't know. She didn't have a clue, and the more people asked about it, the more irritated she became.

She didn't care what Vivian had said, but when Philip started in on her, Ronnie stared at him evenly to show him that she didn't want to talk about the future, but she decided that she had to say something just to shut them all up and to show Vivian that she didn't need her help.

"Well," Ronnie said, "I was thinking of maybe just working full-time for a year until I decide if I even want to go on to school. And, you know, maybe getting a place of my own, like an apartment or something."

"What?" Donika gasped.

Ronnie jutted out her chin and looked around the table.

Mr. Wilson took a long, slow drink of milk. Mrs. Wilson had her head cocked, her eyebrows raised. Philip coughed. Thatcher's spoon clanked noisily back to his bowl. Vivian leaned back and crossed her arms over her chest. Ronnie's heart raced. She looked down at the table.

"Well now," Vivian said. "That's quite a statement, Ronnie. I thought you were happy living with T." Her voice was syrupy with concern, but the corners of her mouth curled in a smirk.

Ronnie realized her mistake immediately. She had forgotten she was dealing with Vivian—the master at turning a person's arrow around, mid-air, and shooting it right back, or in any other direction she chose. This time she aimed not only for Ronnie, but for Thatcher as well. She threw her words like a javelin, hitting her targets with ease. Ronnie winced at her carelessness. She looked at Thatcher, but he was staring ahead at a spot on the table, not at Ronnie, not at anything.

"I didn't say that . . ." Ronnie said, but Vivian cut in, closing the subject.

"You know, this soup is just delicious, Constance." She babbled on for five minutes about how she had tried and tried to learn how to make navy bean soup, but just didn't have the knack.

"Isn't this the best soup, Thatcher?" Vivian asked. "You want me to get you some more?"

She reached in front of Philip, intent on taking Thatcher's bowl to fill it, but Thatcher pulled it away from her.

"I'm fine," he said looking her in the eye.

Vivian sat back down immediately and looked around the table. "Oh, well. Okay then," she said. She fluffed the back of her hair and smiled, looking like she'd won some sort of contest. She looked at her watch. "Oh my," she said. "Oh, I really *do* have to get to work. It's been so nice, though, having dinner together like this, like one big family." She was nodding first toward Mrs. Wilson and then toward Mr. Wilson. "Where would we be without neighbors like you?" She stood up.

"Ronnie, I'll call you," she said as if they had talked before, as if they were a couple of pals making plans, and then she left.

They sat in silence after she left, not quite knowing how to carry on until Mrs. Wilson said, "Well, that was strange." There was an inaudible, yet tangible exhale in the room. Mrs. Wilson looked at Thatcher.

"T., you children talked to her at all since you been back?"

"Just for a minute," Thatcher said.

"You?" She was looking at Ronnie.

Ronnie shook her head no.

"You plan on talking to her?"

"Now, Connie . . ." Mr. Wilson started to say, but Ronnie cut in.

"I don't have anything to say to her," she said.

Ronnie looked at Thatcher. Had he told Mrs. Wilson that Ray Geisel wasn't Ronnie's father? Did she already know? Did everybody already know that?

"You be easy on these children," Mr. Wilson said to Mrs. Wilson. "They can't help how that woman is."

"I hear that," Philip said.

"You hush," Mrs. Wilson said to him.

After dinner, while they were cleaning up, and while Donika was taking out the trash, Ronnie decided to ask Mrs. Wilson about Ray Geisel.

"Did you know . . . you know . . . that he wasn't my father?"

She handed Mrs. Wilson a plate to put into the dishwasher. Mrs. Wilson put the dish into the washer and stood up slowly. She nodded.

"Yes, I did," she said. She looked at Ronnie thoughtfully.

"You knew?" Ronnie said.

She nodded again.

"You know all that happened?"

"Pretty much, baby."

Ronnie stood there, not sure what to ask next, but not wanting to stop talking. Donika came in the back door and plopped down at the table.

"Hey, sweetheart, we're talking," Mrs. Wilson said. "Can you please go on out of here for a while?"

Donika looked at Ronnie. "Sure," she said. "I'll be in my room, Ronnie."

Mrs. Wilson reached out and took Ronnie's hand and pulled her over to the table.

"Talk to me," she said to Ronnie.

"I . . . I don't know . . . I just feel like everybody's been keeping all these secrets from me and . . . and . . . I don't know. I feel like . . . like I don't know anything."

Mrs. Wilson put her hand on Ronnie's arm.

"You know, when I was in Cabool I tried to meet him—only I still thought he was my dad—and he wouldn't even turn around and look at me."

Mrs. Wilson patted Ronnie's hand, but was silent.

"I meant it, you know," Ronnie said, looking at Mrs. Wilson.

"Meant what, baby?"

"I think I need to move out."

"Oh. You think running away will take care of everything?"

Ronnie shook her head. "I'm not running away. I'm just growing up."

"If you really want to grow up, you'll stick around—for awhile anyway."

Ronnie looked at Mrs. Wilson and frowned. That was not the answer she wanted to hear.

"You just gonna leave T.?" Mrs. Wilson said.

Her question made Ronnie think of Juanita and her father. That's what they had done. They'd just left him. Ronnie started to object, to explain that it was different for her, that she was just growing up, but Mrs. Wilson shushed her.

"Listen," Mrs. Wilson said. "You got all these questions, all these secrets coming out. Seems to me only one thing's going to make any difference."

"What?" I asked.

"The truth." Mrs. Wilson stood up. "And how you going to get at that if you go running away?"

"I'm not running, Mrs. Wilson . . ." Ronnie said, but Mrs. Wilson held up her hand. Ronnie smacked her own hand against the table in frustration. "Well then *you* tell me," she said, "Because no one else will."

Mrs. Wilson smiled. She cupped Ronnie's chin in her hand. "Now you know, honey, that isn't for me to say. This is something you got to figure out with your family."

Ronnie stared at the table and frowned.

CHAPTER THIRTY ONE

After work the next day, Rochelle was leaning against the kitchen sink, waiting for Thatcher to take a shower. Donika and Ronnie were sitting at the kitchen table. Donika was flipping through Vogue.

"You know," Rochelle said, "I could do your nails for you, Ronnie."

She was a manicurist up at Digits over on McKnight Road. Of course, Donika liked her immediately because of that. Ronnie had her reservations, though. Rochelle was nice enough, but that didn't matter.

"I'm not really the type," Ronnie said.

"You could do my nails," Donika said to Rochelle.

Rochelle gave her a teasing look of disapproval.

"They don't have to be long, you know. I could make them nice and natural looking, or give you a French manicure—that's one of my favorites."

"Oh, me too," Donika said. "You could do that to me, and teach me how, because you know I'm going to school for it."

"Well, if you're going to school for it, you won't be needing me," Rochelle said. She looked at Ronnie. "What do you say, Ronnie?"

Ronnie shook her head. "No thanks," she said. She didn't want to be indebted to one of Thatcher's girlfriends.

The truth was, however, that Ronnie was beginning to worry about Rochelle. None of Thatcher's other girlfriends had ever come over in the middle of the week and waited for Thatcher to take a shower. He always picked the girls up and took them out; he didn't bring them home. None of his other girlfriends had ever eaten with them either, but Rochelle did. She came over on a Tuesday night and ate a pizza with them, and then was there again the next Friday, standing at their kitchen making some broccoli dish while Thatcher barbecued chicken out on the patio. None of his other girlfriends had ever done that. And it wasn't like they expected Ronnie to disappear so they could have a romantic dinner either. When Thatcher ordered the pizza, Rochelle had asked Ronnie what she wanted on it, and the night they had barbecued, Rochelle asked Ronnie to help her tear lettuce for salad and even taught her how to make the broccoli that Ronnie thought ended up tasting pretty good.

Rochelle asked Ronnie about her job and asked her about her friendship with Donika and asked her about all the pots she'd been painting. If Ronnie didn't know better, it was almost like Rochelle really cared. But Ronnie did know better and tried to keep her distance.

And Thatcher, he lit up when Rochelle was around in a way Ronnie had never seen before. He wasn't as crabby as usual and was even sort of talkative when Rochelle was around. She drew him out somehow. Ronnie had never seen a girl do that before.

It was just one more thing that didn't make sense, just one more thing that threw everything off. Ronnie looked at Rochelle. She was leaning over Donika's shoulder, looking at her magazine. Thatcher walked in, looking handsome, dressed in a plaid button down shirt and new looking blue jeans. His hair was combed and he had on his cowboy boots.

"Ready?" Rochelle said standing up and smiling at him. "See you later, Ronnie," she said.

Ronnie nodded but didn't respond. She stared at them as they left, watching the way Thatcher put his hand on the small of Rochelle's back as they walked to the door.

CHAPTER THIRTY TWO

Ronnie was going to Cabool—alone. She had finished painting the pots, and when Juanita called her to see how it was coming along, and then asked her to think about coming down to deliver them, Ronnie couldn't think of any good reason to turn her down, but could think of lots of reasons for why she should go.

She didn't have any luggage. She had all her stuff packed in a couple of laundry baskets along with all her paints and brushes and sponges and pattern books. She'd even packed up the easel and canvas that had been sitting in her room for so long, untouched, thinking that maybe she'd try to paint something out there. Painted pots were stacked in the pumpkin seat of her VW—that's what she called the little trunk-like space in the back—painted pots were stacked there and on the floor of the back seat and the front seat of the passenger side. Ronnie had left her favorite pot—the bigger one with the flowers and bees painted on it—on the front porch. Rochelle had planted a red geranium in it.

"See you later," Thatcher said to Ronnie. He was looking down at her, but squinting from the light of the morning sun. He reached out his hand and rested it for a minute on the sill of her open window. His fingernails were clean and filed straight. Rochelle had given him a manicure the night before as they sat on the living room floor watching a movie-of-the-week. Thatcher had acted like he was doing her a big favor by letting her do such a girlie thing to him, but it was apparent to Ronnie that he had enjoyed the attention. Thatcher patted the window sill. "Be careful," he said. "You got the hang of driving this clutch all right?"

Ronnie nodded, though stopping on a hill was still a bit nerve wracking for her.

Rochelle stood next to Thatcher and when he stood up straight again, his arm went around her waist as naturally and easy as a hand went into a pocket. The way they stood there, they looked like newlyweds, but Ronnie knew it was just a matter of time. She'd start getting on his nerves and Thatcher would stop calling her, or stop taking her calls. Ronnie looked at Rochelle again, at the way she was smiling. It wouldn't surprise Ronnie if Rochelle were out of the picture by the time Ronnie got back. She shifted the car into reverse.

"You got the directions, right?"

Ronnie nodded, picking up the scrap of an envelope that he'd scribbled the directions on and waved it for him to see.

"Well, call me when you get there so I know you made it," he said.

"I will," she said.

She was nervous about driving so far on her own and about staying in Cabool, but she was ready, too. While she didn't understand it all, she did understand that everything was changing in her life, everything seemed to be out of her control. Going to Cabool was, at least, her decision, and it was as good as anything else she could think of at the moment. It was a plan, wasn't it? Even if only for a week. It was a plan. She was to deliver the pots to Juanita, stay down there long enough to paint another batch, and then bring a new load of plain pots home with her. No big deal. And maybe by the time she came back, it would be clear to her what she needed to do, whether she should go to school or work or move out or what.

She drove off, down the street, onto the highway and realized as she drove for a few miles out of St. Louis, with the warm wind blowing through her hair, and the sun shining, out toward the country, out toward something new, that she felt free. She was leaving everything behind, if only for a short while. She turned up the radio and smiled, not really knowing what to expect, but certain of one thing: whatever was going to happen, she was on her way.

She drove down highway 44, paying attention to the landmarks she had seen before, past Wet Willies water slide, past Six Flags, past the town of Pacific. She felt free and dangerous, free and wild, somehow. Here she was on her own, driving away from everything she knew. Past Catawissa. West until Rolla—west then South. She looked at her directions frequently, watched the billboards trying to remember them from the trip before: "Meramec Caverns—See Jesse James' Hideout!"; "Onondaga Cave—See the Natural Wonder." She watched the clouds. She watched other cars as she passed them or they passed her. She watched the people in the cars. She watched the reflections of truckers in their side mirrors as they glanced in her direction. It was all just like before, only this time she was driving. This time, she was free. Free and moving.

By the time she pulled onto the white gravel road that led to Juanita's, though, her stomach was a ball of jitters—nervous, but excited—and when she pulled up into the driveway, she found herself praying.

"God," she said, "I don't know what I'm doing here, but help me out, would you?"

Bean was sitting on the front porch with a box of sidewalk chalk.

"Aunt Veronica," he said, jumping up and running to the car. "Hey!" He stood next to her car door, smiling and fidgety.

"Hey, Bean," Ronnie said.

"I'm the lookout," he said. "I gotta tell Mom. I'm the lookout!"

And he dashed away behind the house. "She's here! She's here," he yelled as he ran.

Ronnie got out of the car and stretched, looking over at the meadow. The sun was moving to the other side of the sky, casting its bright light on the meadow in retrospect, one last glance before moving on to the west for the day. Ronnie looked over at the pasture and smiled at the cow who had walked over to the fence.

"Hey, cow," Ronnie said. She started walking toward it when Juanita and Bean came down the drive. Ronnie sucked in her breath. She had forgotten how tall Juanita was, and wondered if she would ever get used to that first sight of her?

"Veronica!" she said, her long arms reaching out.

Ronnie smiled and took an unsure step forward.

"Hi," she said shyly.

"I'm so happy to see you." She looked like she was going to cry. She put her hand on Ronnie's shoulder. "I'm so glad you're here!"

Ronnie nodded. "Thanks," she said.

It was odd. She was glad to be there too, though she couldn't say it. It was more like a feeling in her—a lightness that had taken over her since the moment she'd left home. Something was happening there—something new. Juanita had set it up for Ronnie to come back, but it was Ronnie's decision to be there.

When Juanita saw that Ronnie had to pull out all the pots before she could get to her laundry baskets, she said, "Oh, bring them out one at a time and hold them up! We'll make it an art show!"

Ronnie raised her eyebrows. "There's a lot," she said.

"What's the hurry?" Juanita smiled.

Ronnie handed the pots to Bean one by one, who handed them to Juanita, enjoying their reactions, the oohs and ahhs, like each pot was a work of art, like each pot was important.

"Look at this one, Mom," Bean would say. "It looks like the sky!"

"Like a starry night," Juanita said taking it from him and holding it up. She took them and set them in rows across the lawn for display.

"Oh!" she said. "Oh, they're beautiful!"

They stood in the yard and watched Bean as he wove himself through the pots, stopping and pointing out things he liked about specific ones. Ronnie looked up at Juanita. Her arms were crossed over her chest, and her smile was open, happy, and satisfied.

"You sure are talented, Veronica," she said.

"Oh, I'm not that good," Ronnie said, but, of course, she was pleased. "Oh, I forgot one," she said and went back to her car. There was a special pot that she'd kept separate, that she had put at the bottom of one of the laundry baskets that held her clothes. It was for Bean. She didn't know if he'd like a thing like that. He was a kid, after all, and she doubted he would care about a flower pot, but when she was painting that particular pot, her brush had slipped and when she looked at the mark she'd left, it made her think of a dinosaur. That's when she decided to paint the pot for Bean. All kids liked dinosaurs.

"Bean," she said bringing it out, "I have a special one just for you."

And his eyes lit up, and he ran to her.

"Cool," he said, holding it up and turning it around. He held it up for his mom to see.

"I hope you like it," Ronnie said. "Even if you don't put flowers in it. Maybe you can keep it in your room and put your special rocks in it or something."

"Oh, cool," Bean said again and ran into the house with the pot.

"Veronica," Juanita said. She was holding back her tears. "That was sweet." She sighed, and gained control of her voice. "I always wondered what it would be like to meet you, to know you . . . and here you are. And you're sweet."

Sweet. Ronnie had never been called sweet before.

They delivered pots to stores and shops around town that afternoon, and everywhere they went Juanita and Bean were known by name, like a couple of local celebrities. People waved and called out to them in friendly voices, but even before Juanita and Bean could wave back and call them by name in return—and they always did—the eyes of the greeter would fall on Ronnie, and on Ronnie their eyes would remain.

"Who's that with you?" A woman asked. She was sweeping off the sidewalk in front of her shop door as they approached.

"This is my sister, Veronica," Juanita said happily.

The woman stared at Ronnie, suspiciously.

To the kid on a street corner who was stopped on his bike and sucking on a purple popsicle, Bean said, "'This is my aunt. This is my Aunt Veronica."

Everywhere they went people stared: the old barber who was sitting outside of his shop and reading the newspaper, the cop who was driving down the street, and everyone in between.

"This is my sister," Juanita said to the old geezer who was standing at the counter of the hardware store, buying a bag of black oil sunflower seeds. "This is the girl who painted them pots." Juanita pointed to the pots they had just brought in.

"Your sister, you say?" the old guy asked. He squinted his eyes, looking Ronnie up and down. "She don't look like you," he said as if Ronnie weren't there.

"She's my aunt and she's a artist," Bean told him.

He looked at Ronnie skeptically.

"What'd you say your name was?" he asked.

"Ronnie," she started to say, but stopped herself. "Veronica."

"Yes," Juanita smiled down at her. "This is Veronica."

Everywhere they went it was the same thing. Every one of them. "Your sister?"

Juanita might have been over seven feet tall, but it was clear that in Cabool, Ronnie was the oddity.

CHAPTER THIRTY THREE

She was almost never in the house, and Ronnie could understand why. It was just too small. It was even smaller than their place back home. Juanita spent most of her time outside or in the greenhouse, or, if she wasn't doing something with Ronnie and Bean, in the afternoon, she took a cat-nap. She had odd sleeping patterns. No matter how early Ronnie got up, Juanita was already out working in the greenhouse. She seemed to sleep in spurts instead of long stretches like everybody else, and when Juanita did sleep, she snored. Ronnie peeked into her room the second morning she was there. Juanita had a queen-sized bed, but at the bottom of it, butted up to it, was another bed, a twin bed. It made her bed look huge. Ronnie guessed she needed it to keep her feet from hanging over the edge. The rest of the room was normal enough, though, a dresser, a night table. It was odd, a giant trying to live in a world that was too small for her.

The greenhouse was big enough, though—big and comfortable. But there was something else about it, something that went beyond size. There was something about the light in there that seemed brighter, a cool-ish blue, cooler than the greens and yellows outside. There was something comforting about the heavy, moist air that carried the smell of earth and life.

Ronnie liked it in there, too. It was pleasant, almost magical. Juanita had set up a table for Ronnie made out of sawhorses and a sheet of plywood. It was comfortable, both of them doing what they liked to do. Bean would come along later when he woke up. He'd chirp around them, playing here and there, or playing outside, or playing in the house. He had his "chores" to do in the greenhouse, chores that amounted to nothing more than keeping him busy. He'd water plants, or feed the fish in the pond, or fill starting trays with dirt.

Juanita hardly stopped talking from the moment Ronnie got there. At first she talked about her plants or asked questions about Ronnie's painting. But after a while her questions became more direct. She asked Ronnie about growing up, about living with Thatcher. And what Ronnie was surprised to realize was that she didn't mind answering. Juanita had a way of asking things, and a way of following the things Ronnie said that was so unassuming and filled with such a genuine interest that Ronnie found herself wanting to tell Juanita anything she asked.

Ronnie told Juanita that her favorite color was blue, and that she hated eating fried fish. She told Juanita about the good teachers she had in school, the bad ones, and which subjects she had liked and which ones she hadn't. She told Juanita about working at the Quick Shop. When she told Juanita that Donika was Sharon Wilson's daughter, Juanita got all teary.

"That family," she said. "They were so good to me." She tried to say all their names, and could have, but ended up being speechless because of her tears. Ronnie said the names for Juanita while she nodded, "Yes, that's right," her lips quivering and her eyes all glassy.

They talked about growing up in Rock Hill, and when Ronnie told her the stories she'd heard about the quarry Juanita said, "I been to the bottom. Thatcher and me and Charles and Philip used to go down there. It was such an adventure. Mrs. Wilson would have killed us if she knew about it. Most people only look in, but it's something else to be at the bottom of it and look out."

Juanita talked about "the old house," which was Vivian's house, and they compared their memories of it. Ronnie talked about Thatcher and Philip and their business, and Ronnie even talked a little bit about Vivian. It didn't seem to matter, though. It didn't seem to matter what she was saying. Juanita hung on every word. She seemed dying to know what kinds of vegetables Ronnie liked, like it was truly important to her whether Ronnie had always worn her hair long or if she had ever cut it short. She wanted to know everything.

At first it was odd for Ronnie, having someone ask so many questions, but the truth was, she liked it. No one ever really asked her about herself. And when Ronnie thought there was nothing more to say or when she thought she'd said enough, Juanita would ask another question or add something of her own. They drank in everything the other had to say and, over the course of a couple of days, Ronnie began to see that even though they had always been apart, and even though Juanita was so different, they had things in common; they had shared a lot of the same places and same kinds of experiences—just at different times. This was how they discovered themselves as sisters.

The only topics they tended to avoid were Vivian and Ray—until the third night.

Bean was asleep in the house, and Juanita and Ronnie sat outside in the backyard, lying on lounge chairs and looking out for shooting stars. Ronnie could live in the vision of those stars in the country night sky, they were so numerous, so billiony. Juanita's legs splayed out on either side of her lounge with her feet touching the ground flat. It was a moonless night with no clouds, and so dark, that Ronnie could just make out the outline of Juanita's brow bone.

When Ronnie asked her about that night—about the night she'd left home with Ray, Juanita sighed and for a minute there was silence. Ronnie winced, thinking she had crossed the line, but slowly, Juanita started talking.

"I didn't know what was happening at the time, why they were fighting, but Daddy was packing his bags."

Ronnie thought of Juanita's features, distorted even more in her mind because of the dark, and for a minute Ronnie was scared. Her body stiffened and she felt her thighs sticking with sweat to the seat of the lounge. She had the urge to get up and run, but of course she didn't. She breathed and waited. She knew that it wasn't really Juanita that scared her as much as what Juanita was about to say. Her voice was soft and low and when Ronnie looked back up into the night sky, into the dark canvas pierced with a zillion points of light, she felt like she was falling.

"You know he drove a truck back then," Juanita said, "so seeing him pack wasn't an odd sort of sight. But the things he took . . . I followed him around . . . when he started taking stuff off his dresser I knew he was leaving for good. I was afraid when I saw that. Momma was in the kitchen, crying at the table and I went in there. I said, 'Where's Daddy going, Momma?' And she looked up at me and . . . and . . . I ain't never seen so much hate in a person's eyes as I saw in hers when she was looking at me. And she screamed at me. She said, 'Get out of here, you goddamn freak! Get out of here and leave me alone!' That's exactly what she said to me."

Juanita stopped and Ronnie heard her take a deep breath. She didn't sound like she was crying though. She sounded like she was reporting on something she'd seen, like she was watching something from far away, like an old movie reel was running through her head and she was merely reciting the words.

"I got scared then. Daddy was gonna leave and I was gonna be left behind with Momma, and she hated me. Ronnie, she hated me so much."

"Where was T.?"

"He was right there," she said. "He was right there only he didn't say nothing, and he didn't move. He just stood there over in the corner of the living room and watched them."

"What'd you do?"

She made a sound, like a laugh, only there was no humor in it.

"I went back to Daddy. I went to him and I begged him to take me with him. And at first he said no. At first he said I had to stay, that he didn't know where he was going, but I begged him, Veronica. I told him she'd kill me if I stayed there. And that stopped him. I don't know if he thought I meant it or not, but he stopped packing and turned to me and just stood there, staring, and I was crying and saying over and over and over again, 'Please don't leave me here. Please don't leave me here.' And I tell you, I knew he was there, I mean I was standing right in front of him, but it was like he wasn't and . . . and he reached out and took my hands . . . I must have been grabbing at my hair . . . when he opened my fists, my hands were full of it. I'd pulled out two fistfuls of my own hair, and I didn't even feel it."

Ronnie tried to see Juanita in the dark, but couldn't. She imagined Juanita was staring up at the stars too, only she was falling into the memory. The vastness of the sky enveloped Ronnie, made her wonder, made her think. Where had God been on that night? And where was He now? Could He hear Juanita? Did He know what kind of pain she went through in life? Maybe they were all just too small—even Juanita. They were nothing more than a couple of specks in the universe, smaller than a couple of ants. Ronnie didn't get it. She didn't understand the point of all the pain and turmoil.

"Daddy untangled the hair from my fingers and closed his hands around mine the best he could, and he said, 'No, Drink'—that's what he calls me sometimes, you know, like a tall drink of water—he said, 'I won't leave you.' And he didn't."

Juanita was quiet, and this time Ronnie thought she heard Juanita whimper.

"But what about T.?" she asked.

"I'm telling you, Veronica, wasn't any one of us thinking straight that night. I didn't even think about T. I mean, I did but . . . no. No. I was thinking about me and that's all I was thinking about. When Daddy told me to pack my things as quick as I could, that's just what I did. That's all I did."

"He didn't say he wanted to go with you too?"

"It all happened so fast and he was in the living room the whole time. It was like . . . it was like it wasn't real or something. Like none of us had time to think. Daddy said come and I came and all I thought about was leaving her—I didn't pine a second on that."

"So you just left T. behind?"

"I . . . yes. We just left. And it wasn't like I thought I'd never see him again. I mean I don't know what I was thinking. It was like a storm, Veronica. I guess I just figured we'd go back. In the back of my mind I figured we'd go back for T. later."

"But you didn't."

She shook her head no.

"I don't remember much after we got in the car, really. I only know that we ended up in Cabool, and this is where we been ever since."

CHAPTER THIRTY FOUR

Ronnie thought she had dialed the wrong number when a woman answered. The voice on the other end was slow, like she'd just woke. Ronnie was poising to hang up when the voice said, "Ronnie?"

Ronnie looked at the clock on the wall. It was 7:30 in the morning. "Rochelle?" she asked.

"Yes," she said. "How's it going?" Her voice became clearer, more awake.

"It's okay . . . I . . . ." Ronnie was confused. She thought she would catch Thatcher before he went to the shop.

"Is T. there?" she asked.

"Sure, hang on . . . "

Ronnie heard her say, "T., . . . T., it's Ronnie." Ronnie could tell by her tone of voice that Rochelle was waking him up.

"Hey," T. said in a sleep-laden voice. "How's it going?"

"What'd she do, move in just as soon as I left?"

"Huh?" Thatcher said.

"And how come you're still in bed?"

"Did you call here to yell at me?"

Ronnie didn't say anything.

"Is everything going okay?" he asked.

Ronnie had just wanted to talk to him, to tell him about the people in town and how everybody thought she was the strange one. She had wanted to tell him about the greenhouse in the morning and about all the pots she was painting. She had wanted to tell him about the stars last night, about the beautiful sky, about Juanita's big bed. She had wanted to tell him that it was good there, that it was a good place to be, but now she didn't want to say anything.

"Ronnie? You there?" His voice was sounding clearer. "Ronnie? So how's it going?"

"Okay."

When she didn't say anything else he said, "You want to come home?"

"No," she said defensively.

"What's wrong then?"

"I . . . nothing. I didn't mean to wake you up."

"It's okay."

"I was just . . . checking in."

"Oh. Well what are you doing?" he asked.

She wanted to get off the phone. She looked around the quiet house. Juanita was already out in the greenhouse, and Bean was still asleep on the couch. "I don't know," she said, "painting and stuff . . . well, listen . . . I'm going to let you go. I was just calling to say I'm fine."

"Oh," he said. "Well, okay."

"Okay."

"Hey," he said. "You set up your easel yet?"

"What?"

"You using that easel and canvas yet?"

Ronnie was surprised that he knew she had taken it. "No," she said. "No, not yet."

"Hmm," was all he said.

"Well, okay. So I'll talk to you later, all right?"

"Okay," he said.

And Ronnie hung up. She didn't move, though. She just stood there staring at the phone and feeling suddenly very alone.

That afternoon Ronnie sat in the shade under a tree by the driveway. The greenhouse was too warm in spite of the two huge fans Juanita had blowing in there. Ronnie took her paints and pots outside and sat in the grass, under the shade of a tree. She was thinking about that easel, about Thatcher's question of whether she had set it up or not. She was always so hard on him. It wasn't hard to believe Rochelle had spent the night there; it had just taken her by surprise was all. Thatcher had asked about the easel. He had been watching.

"Can I try one?" Bean said, walking over to Ronnie.

She had a brush in her hand, and another one clenched between her teeth. She set down the pot and looked up. The sky surrounded Bean like a frame. She took the brush from her mouth.

"Where's your Mom?"

"She's laying down. She has a mean headache."

"A mean headache?"

He shrugged. "She always gets 'em, but sometimes they really hurt."

Ronnie stood up. "Should I do anything for her?"

He shook his head no. "She just needs some quiet."

Ronnie looked toward the house.

"So can I?" Bean said, pointing to the pot.

"What?"

"Can I paint one?" Ronnie could tell by the way he started shifting his weight from foot to foot that he was getting irritated with her. She smiled.

"Yeah, yeah," she said. "Go get one of the little pots in the greenhouse."

He ran off and came back a minute later holding a pot. Ronnie gave him a clean brush and he sat next to her. "I'm gonna do a dinosaur on mine."

"Cool," she said. "It will match your other one."

They sat there, not talking, just painting. He was pretty confident, and seemed happy with the dinosaur he was painting even though to Ronnie it looked more like a green and black blob than it did a dinosaur.

"I'm gonna get yours in my room," he said. He jumped up and ran toward the house with a brush in his hand, only to come back a second later, looking unhappy.

"What's wrong?" Ronnie asked.

"I got paint on my mom's truck."

His hands were smeared with red paint.

"Oh," she said standing up. "Let me see."

The side of Juanita's truck had a red splotch and it was clear the Bean had tried to rub it off, but had ended up doing more harm than good. Ronnie studied the splotch.

"Wait here," she said. She got her brush and some red paint and came back.

"What are you gonna do?" he asked.

"Just watch," she said. "It will be okay." She turned the splotch into a flower, a sort of uneven flower, but a flower nonetheless.

"Now don't say anything about it," she told him. "We'll let it be a surprise."

"She's gonna be mad at me."

"How could she be mad? This old truck needed a flower." The flower needed more color. Ronnie went and got some orange and pink to give the petals some depth and life, and some black and green to make a stem and some leaves.

"You see? Now who could be mad about that?"

Bean stared at it seriously.

"It'll be okay, Bean," Ronnie said. "I promise."

"Ronnie!" Juanita said later. She was up and seemed to be feeling all right. She stepped around the side of the house, "You put a flower on my truck!"

"Oh . . ." Ronnie said. Bean jumped up and started walking toward the house.

"I'm . . . uh . . . I got a little splotch of paint on your truck and I didn't know what else to do, and you were resting and so . . . I'm sorry, but . . ."

"I love it. I love that flower there, Veronica. It's perfect."

Bean stopped walking and turned his head a little. Juanita was watching him, and then she looked at Ronnie.

"What do you think about it, Benjamin?"

Ronnie had never heard Juanita call Bean Benjamin before. He didn't move, and without turning around said, "Yeah, Ma. It's good."

"Well, now I've got an idea."

Bean turned to face us, nervously biting his bottom lip.

"Ronnie, I want you to paint my whole truck in flowers."

"What?"

"I mean it. I want you to paint flowers all over it!" She spread her arms in a generous sweep. She nodded and smiled at them. "It's like marketing or something."

"Well it seems like everybody already knows you, Juanita," Ronnie said. She thought of that guy and his kids at Blue Springs. She thought of the people waving to Juanita and saying hey to her wherever they went as they drove plants and pots around town. "I mean it's not like you need a new gimmick or anything."

Juanita realized Ronnie was teasing her and grinned. Ronnie smiled. She had never teased Juanita before.

"Well, sure everybody knows me, but this would be something new. This would give them something to talk about."

"Well, how do you want it?"

"I don't care," she said. "Just cover it. Fender to fender."

"That's crazy," Ronnie said. "And it would take a lot of paint."

"They sell paint in Cabool, you know," she said.

She insisted that Ronnie start painting right away—only if she wanted to, of course—and pulled the truck into the front yard so that they could sit under the shade of the big oak tree. It was fun, Ronnie had to admit, the idea of painting that truck. She just started at that rose and kept adding flowers outward from it.

"This will take forever," Ronnie said.

"Yes," Juanita answered from her chair. "That means you'll have to come back again."

Ronnie looked at Juanita and then looked at the ground.

"It's true," Juanita said, watching Ronnie. "I'm crafty, but look here, I got my own sister sitting with me in my front yard." She nodded proudly.

Bean was busy playing with Tonka trucks in a sandbox that sat on the side of the house. Juanita brought a radio out and sat in her chair and they listened to music as Ronnie painted. Painting flowers on a truck . . . it made Ronnie smile. As she worked, Juanita acted as her audience. She sat there drinking iced tea and making comments like, "Oh that's a good one, Veronica," and "Oh, I like that color yellow right there." Ronnie called Bean over every once in awhile, telling him she needed a new blob of paint in a certain spot, but that she needed a professional for the job and did he know of anyone who could blob paint well. Once he realized she was kidding, he reached for the brush she held out.

"Well, I'll do it," he said.

Ronnie stopped him just as soon as the brush hit the truck. "Perfect," she said. "Just perfect. Go on back and play. You are a master and I'll call you when I need a new blob."

He smiled and ran back to his sandbox, looking up every so often, waiting for Ronnie to call him back.

They heard the sound of a car coming down the road. It was from his direction, and as the truck came nearer, Ronnie saw it was, indeed, Ray Geisel. Her heart began to pound. She did not want to see him again—she did not want to see the back of him. When she had decided to come back to Cabool, she knew there was a chance that she would see him, but Ronnie had decided then that Ray Geisel would never have the opportunity to turn his back on her again.

Bean came running from the side of the road. Juanita stood up and she and Bean walked around the hedge to the edge of the road to greet him. Ronnie watched them. The truck stopped in front of Juanita. He looked straight ahead, though she was talking to him. He looked straight ahead, though she was leaning down to his open window and saying something to him.

Ronnie stared hard, saw him shake his head no, and when Juanita turned to look at Ronnie, turned to see if she had seen the offense, Ronnie looked right past her. Though her heart pounded in her ears, she looked right at him, but he didn't even see her. He kept his eyes straight ahead, looking through the bug-splattered windshield, his hands firmly wrapped around the top of the steering wheel. Thatcher was right, Ronnie thought. He was a prick. She stood up, casting a pointed eye at the truck, at him, showing him that the opportunity to offend no longer existed, and she walked into the house.

Her hand shook when she picked up the glass and filled it from the kitchen faucet. She stood there, drinking water even though she wasn't thirsty. The screen door opened.

"Ronnie?" It was Juanita.

"I'm in here," she said. She didn't want to move in case he was with her. She would not go to him again.

Juanita came to the kitchen and leaned up against the opening. She looked weary, her eyes heavy and her mouth turned down at the corners. She sighed.

"I'm so sorry for the way he's acting."

Ronnie shrugged. "I don't care."

"Of course you care. I don't understand why he's being so awful to you."

"What's not to understand? I'm not his," Ronnie said. "It doesn't take a brain surgeon to figure out why he doesn't like me."

"Oh, but he would like you," she said. She took a step forward. "He would like you if he stopped acting so bad."

Juanita stepped closer. "I know you don't believe me about him. I know T. don't either, but if you could get to know him . . ."

"Well, that's really not my problem, is it?" Ronnie said. "I tried that."

"No . . . I mean . . . I know. You're right. It's his fault. He shouldn't have treated you that way. But I'm just saying . . . I'm just saying that if there's any way . . ."

"You're talking to the wrong person," Ronnie said.

Her mouth opened to say something, but then she closed it again. She nodded. "You're right." She stared at Ronnie for a minute. "I *am* talking to the wrong person."

They went to the Pink Lemonade for dinner that night—just Juanita and Ronnie. Bean had gone off to spend the night with his grandfather. Juanita waved and nodded to the two families in the restaurant. They all said hey back to her, but then, as usual, their eyes fell on Ronnie. Ronnie walked behind Juanita, her eyes trained timidly on the floor. They went in the smaller room where Thatcher and Ronnie had been before, where Juanita's bench-seat and high table sat against the wall. Ronnie remembered the cute guy that had walked in and wondered what the chances were of seeing him again. After all, it was a small town.

"Hey, Juanita" the waitress said. It was Katie. She pointed to Ronnie. "Hey, I remember you. Only last time you was here with that cute brother of yours." She looked over her shoulder. "Where's he tonight?"

Juanita gave one of her goofy laughs. "He didn't come this time," Juanita said. "It's just me and Veronica here. T.'s back in St. Louis."

"Too bad," she said. "You bring him back. He's cute."

"I will do my best," Juanita said nodding.

"Oh, you sit over here," Katie said to Ronnie. She reached over and grabbed a barstool that was in the corner and brought it to Ronnie and placed it on a platform that was built on the floor at the end of the table. Ronnie hadn't seen it the last time she had come in. "Now you can sit at the same table but be high enough. Sorry it don't have a back to it, though."

"That's okay," Ronnie said stepping up on top of the platform. She felt like a queen sitting on a loft until Juanita sat down

"You want two pinks?" Katie asked.

"That'd be nice," Juanita said. "Did you have a pink lemonade last time you were here?"

Ronnie nodded.

"Yep, then," Juanita said. "Two pinks."

The waitress took Ronnie's order and then walked away.

"She didn't get your order," Ronnie said.

Juanita waved her hand. "I always get the same thing: shredded pork sandwich, fries and a piece of peach pie. I just love peach pie."

As they were eating their dinner, Juanita said, "You know, I'm going to have a talk with Daddy about all this." She held up her hands to stop Ronnie from any protest. "I mean, you two are going to have to come to some sort of terms."

"I tried . . ." Ronnie started to say again.

"I know, I know. That's why I'm going to talk to him. I just want you to know it. I ain't going behind nobody's back here." She looked at Ronnie sternly.

In the middle of her pink lemonade, Juanita said, "Tell me more about your mother."

Ronnie wasn't sure what she meant.

"Well, she had red hair the last time I saw her," Ronnie said. "That was new."

"She ever been a red head before?" Juanita asked.

"She's been everything. Light brown, dark brown, black, blonde . . . I don't know if I've ever seen her natural color now that I think about it."

"Not even in old pictures?"

"Oh, well . . . brown I guess."

Juanita nodded yes, sucking on her straw, but kept her eyes on Ronnie.

"You seen old pictures of T." she said, making a statement rather than asking a question.

"Yeah," Ronnie said.

"But no pictures of me."

Ronnie looked up, thinking, realizing, of course, "I . . . no. I never."

"But you knew about me?"

"Kind of."

"What did you know? I know you didn't know I was tall like this."

Ronnie shook her head. "No, I didn't know that. I didn't know anything. I just knew I had a sister, and I wasn't supposed to talk about her."

Juanita rubbed her large hand over her mouth, covering what comment, Ronnie didn't know, but Ronnie realized that this was the same thing, what Ray Geisel had done to her, Vivian had done to Juanita, only longer, only in a much worse way. Vivian had wiped Juanita out of their lives completely. Ronnie would have certainly remembered seeing a picture of Juanita, but there were none that Ronnie knew of. Vivian had always kept all of her photo albums in the bottom drawer of her dresser, and Ronnie had spent many a bored afternoon lying on her stomach, looking at pictures. Juanita was not there, and neither was Ray for that matter.

"Do you . . . do you want to see her?' Ronnie asked.

Juanita raised her eyebrows and pursed her lips. "I . . . I don't know. I guess maybe one day . . . but . . . no. I don't think so. I don't think there's too much to say there."

"Well, what about Bean?"

"What *about* Bean?"

"I just . . . I'm wondering . . . about his father? Where is he?"

Juanita put her fork down and Ronnie looked at the window, biting her bottom lip, hoping she hadn't gone too far.

"Oh," Juanita finally said. She took a deep breath.

"I'm sorry," Ronnie said. "I shouldn't have asked. It isn't my business and didn't mean anything by it."

Juanita was shaking her head back and forth. "No, no," she said. "I'm glad you asked." She patted Ronnie's arm. "It just took me by surprise is all, but that's okay. I mean, it's only logical you'd be wondering."

"Well, I was just wondering and since you never said anything about him and Bean never said anything about having a father..."

Juanita looked at Ronnie as if she were a puzzle piece. "I never really thought about it," she said, "but you two got something in common, don't you?"

"What do you mean?"

"With your fathers, I mean, growing up without knowing your fathers."

"So he doesn't know his father?"

Juanita shook her head no.

"It was... it was stupid. I mean, I didn't know it at the time, of course, and I don't really blame him too much." Juanita looked up at Ronnie and sort of laughed, only it wasn't a laugh. "Hm. This is a hard question to answer."

"I'm sorry. You don't have..."

"No, no. I meant it. I meant it when I said now wasn't the time to be timid, and you want to know, and that's fine. Really. I'm just having a hard time thinking about it, but it's okay, because one of these days it's gonna be Bean sitting here asking me this, isn't it? So this will be good practice, won't it."

"Well, I..."

She shushed Ronnie with her hand. "So anyway, there was this guy there. He had come from Arkansas, and worked at the mill for awhile—I worked at the sawmill over on Jackson Road for a good long while when I was younger—and I don't know... I mean, I didn't really know him, know what he was like, and to everyone else I was just one of the guys, but... well, he paid attention to me, I guess and I sure ain't used to that kind of attention. And I guess if I had it all to think over again I would have been smarter, but I wasn't. I slept with him. Just once. And that was my fault, you know. I mean, I was stupid because the truth is all I amounted to was some kind of weird trophy for him, you know, but I wanted to believe something else. I wanted to believe a man could really be attracted to me that way . . ." She tried to look over at Ronnie, but lowered her eyes instead, embarrassed. "I was foolish about that."

She traced a circle onto the table-top with her index finger as she spoke. "And then I found out I was pregnant and of course I couldn't believe it. And he left lickety-split. Went back to Arkansas or something, which was okay by me." She looked up. "I don't hold nothing against him because something good came from it. I got Bean, and he is my gift straight from God. I ain't ever sorry about that—I was scared at first. I mean, I didn't know what I was gonna do—but I ain't ever been sorry."

Suddenly, Juanita slammed her palm down onto the table, making her lemonade glass rattle. "Oh my gosh! I just figured it out."

"Figured what out?"

"He's scared."

"Who?"

"My dad!" Juanita smiled at Ronnie, her eyes welling up with tears. "He's just scared is all."

CHAPTER THIRTY FIVE

Ronnie stepped out of Bean's bedroom and into the living room, yawning and scratching the back of her neck. The front door was open, and when she looked toward it, she saw the sun trying to shine in through the big oak tree out front—and then she saw him. He was standing just outside the screen door, leaning against the house like he didn't have a care in the world. She jumped when she saw him. For a second, she thought it was Thatcher standing there. He must not have heard her come into the room because he didn't move, and he must not have been able to see into the house through the screen because she was standing directly in his line of vision. All it would take was for him to turn his head toward her. He wasn't looking in the door, though. He was looking toward the meadow.

Ronnie took a step backward, toward the doorway of Bean's room, but then she stood perfectly still. What was he doing there? She watched him, not making a sound, not wanting him to try and peer into that screen, not wanting him to see her. She felt like a deer that had been passing by innocently only to look up and see the hunter in a tree stand, waiting, yet looking in the wrong direction.

If he were looking for Juanita, she would be out working in the greenhouse by now. Surely he would know to look for her there. He didn't appear to be waiting for anyone to answer the door, though. Maybe he was bringing Bean home, but Bean was nowhere in sight. He just stood there leaning, his shoulders slightly hunched, his face turned toward the meadow. His shirtsleeves were rolled up, revealing thick, strong looking forearms. If he were Thatcher, he'd be smoking a cigarette. If he were Thatcher he would just be standing on the porch smoking a cigarette and looking at the meadow. But he was not Thatcher, and he was not smoking, and this was not his porch.

Ronnie didn't know what to do. She could go back into the bedroom and wait until he left. Then, even if he knocked, she could ignore him. She could walk quietly to the back of the house and go out to the greenhouse and tell Juanita that her father was there. She could walk to the front door and ask him what he wanted, ask him why he was standing there that way. She wanted to do all three things; she wanted to do none of them. She heard a sound and looked toward the door. He was gone. Ronnie took a step forward, peeking her head round, in case he was still there, but he wasn't. When he didn't come into view as she approached the door, Ronnie grew brave and went right up to it. She put her hands on the screen and pushed into it as she looked out, only to see the back of him walking across the yard, walking off toward the gravel road.

Ronnie's breath caught in her throat and when she cleared it, he stopped. His back stiffened and he turned around. Ronnie didn't know if he could see her or not through the screen, but they stood like that for a good minute. She saw that he looked a lot like Thatcher—or rather Thatcher looked a lot like him. It was startling, like seeing a ghost of what Thatcher would look like in the future. He squinted toward the door.

"You there?" he said.

Ronnie knew he couldn't see her then, though perhaps he could see her hands as they pressed against the screen. When he took a step forward, Ronnie took her hands from the screen.

"You there?" he said again.

Ronnie cleared her throat again and answered yes. Her voice was thick and unfamiliar to her own ears.

"Well come on out here, won't you?"

His voice sounded firm and Ronnie didn't like it. What did he think, that he was going to boss her around, that she was going to listen to him and do what he said?

"I can see you from here," Ronnie said.

He blew out his breath and bent his head sideways, just like Thatcher always did, and looked toward the screen, taking a couple steps forward.

"Yeah," he said, shoving his hands in his pockets. "Yeah well. I just . . . uh . . . I just wanted to say something to you."

Ronnie stayed still. She was afraid that whatever he was going to say would dissolve her, dissolve her anger and fear, dissolve everything she'd been living on. He waited, but when Ronnie didn't move, he took his hands out of his pockets and stepped forward.

"I can't see you from here, you know, and I'd like to say this to your face."

Ronnie considered him for a minute more, and then opened the screen, but only part-way. She stood halfway in the house and halfway out. His eyes were on her, and though Ronnie wanted to be brave enough to take him on and stare him down, she couldn't. She looked in his general direction so that she could see him and not see him at the same time.

"I'm sorry for how I treated you," he said.

She looked up. Their eyes met for an instant, but then he turned away. "Um . . . Uh . . ." he said. "Yeah. That's all I wanted to say."

"Oh," Ronnie said.

He tried to look back at her, but couldn't. He looked over at the tree in the front yard.

"Well, that's it then," he said. He started walking away.

Ronnie stood still, watching him. He didn't look back and as he got further away, Ronnie came further out of the house until she realized that she was at the bottom of the porch and half way across the lawn.

"Oh," she said, snapping back to attention. The grass and ground felt cool and dry and solid under her bare feet.

"I didn't say a word to him," Juanita said. "I was going to, though." She pointed at Ronnie. She was in the middle of loading flats of flowers into the back of her truck. "Huh," she said standing there and looking at Ronnie. "Well, that's a good thing, ain't it?"

Ronnie shrugged. She wasn't so sure. She wasn't so sure anything about him was good.

"See, I told you he was a good man."

"Are you sure you didn't talk to him?"

"Of course, I'm sure, silly girl." Juanita frowned for a minute, thinking, then threw her head back and laughed. "My little Bean!" she said. "That's who it was. I should have known. He's been up there chattering a mile a minute about you, I bet. Ha! Ha! Sweet little Bean-boy!" She reached for another flat of flowers from the wheelbarrow. "You know what? I'm going to tell him to come down for supper."

"No!" Ronnie said.

Juanita straightened up. "Why not?"

"Because . . ."

"But he said he was sorry . . ."

"So?"

"So, when somebody says they're sorry, you're supposed to forgive them."

Ronnie humphed, thinking of Vivian and all the times she's apologized to Ronnie for one thing or another—apologies that meant nothing. Ronnie shook her head.

"You don't forgive?" Juanita asked.

"Forgive what?" Ronnie said. "Forgive that he's been a jerk to me every time he's seen me, and that he hates me? Or am I supposed to forgive him for everything . . . you know . . . for deserting Thatcher and my mom, and even though I didn't belong to him, for . . . well, am I supposed to forgive him for everything just like that?" Ronnie swiped some potting soil off the truck's tailgate. "You know, you can't go messing with people and then say, 'oh, sorry,' and expect it all to be okay. If you think that, then you're crazy. I mean, what if Mom came up to you today and said she was sorry. Would it all be okay? Just like that?"

Ronnie had hit a nerve—she could see it in the way Juanita's brow furrowed and in the way Juanita's mouth hung open, and Ronnie thought she looked stupid, like an idiot. Juanita put the flowers down and faced Ronnie. Ronnie looked away, looked at the side of the truck, at the flowers she had painted. When Juanita didn't say anything, Ronnie looked up at her, and when she did, she saw sadness in Juanita's eyes, but what else could Ronnie have said? Juanita was refusing to see the truth.

"You know," Juanita said, "it don't matter how you feel. All I know is that when somebody says they're sorry, you got a choice to make. You got to decide if you're going to forgive them or not, and if the answer is no, then you're the one who has to carry around the burden—and the burden ain't just the hurt anymore, now it's the hurt plus your not being able to forgive—and that's even heavier. You only have to carry the burdens you won't let go of, Veronica. When you forgive? Even when it's hard? Well, that's when you get your chance to be free of it all."

Ronnie shook her head no. "Well, if that's true, then I guess a person can do just about anything they want then, can't they?"

"Make a choice," Juanita said and turned back to the greenhouse without another word.

CHAPTER THIRTY SIX

Ronnie watched them walk across the yard. Even the way he walked reminded her of Thatcher. She had pleaded with Juanita not to ask Ray over for dinner, but Juanita did it anyway.

"He's my daddy, after all, Veronica. I mean, it ain't unusual for us to have dinner together. We do it all the time."

"But *I'm* here," Ronnie had said.

"Just try your best. That's all you got to do."

But Ronnie's best wasn't very good. She could hardly look at him. He nodded at her, mumbling hello, and started to reach out his hand to shake hers, but then dropped it awkwardly and rubbed his palms on the tops of his thighs instead.

Juanita wrung her hands together and shifted her weight from one foot to the other, reminding Ronnie of the first time she had seen Juanita in their back yard.

They stood there, awkward and silent until Juanita said, "I want to show you the pots Veronica's been painting."

"Oh," Ray said in an overly interested voice and looked up at Juanita.

"You coming?" Juanita said as she and Ray walked toward the greenhouse.

Ronnie shook her head no.

"She's real talented," Ronnie heard Juanita say to Ray as they walked away from her.

She sat there waiting for them to come back from the greenhouse, fidgeting and worrying about how she'd get through the afternoon and evening. Maybe he wouldn't stay long. Maybe he would be so uncomfortable that he would leave early. Bean was inside. She could always go hang out with him, though Ronnie had the feeling that Juanita would never stand for that.

When they came back, Ray piddled around the barbeque, taking an extraordinarily long time to build a fire, and then standing there and watching it too closely. He pretty much ignored Ronnie, though he kept throwing glances in her direction. He asked Juanita how things were going in the greenhouse. Juanita was the only one who seemed at all comfortable. In fact, after that tense moment of introduction, Juanita became ecstatic. She smiled at Ronnie and smiled at Ray and nodded to them, saying things like, "Oh, this is so good."

"Daddy come and sit down here," she said.

Ray's shoulders straightened and he turned around. He looked at Ronnie, his lips in a straight, tight smile, and sat down.

"You know what?" Juanita said, "The only way this could be any better was if T. was here." She looked at the sky as if she were wishing on a star. "Oh! I wish T. was here."

Ronnie did too. Ronnie wished he were there too because then *he* would be the one Ray was looking at and Ronnie would be able to make herself scarce. If Thatcher were there, everything would have been okay.

Ray took a deep breath and looked at Ronnie matter of factly. "Well, how is he?"

"T.?" Ronnie said. "I . . . he's fine."

Ray nodded. "You know," he said after a minute. "I could use a beer. You want one?" He looked at Juanita, and then at Ronnie in passing.

"I'd sure like one, Daddy," Juanita said.

She turned to Ronnie and raised her eyebrows.

"You know what? Bring two. Ronnie might like one."

When Ray came back, instead of sitting down with Juanita and Ronnie, he went back to the barbeque pit.

"Fire's coming along," he said to no one in particular.

"Ain't those pots pretty, Daddy?" Juanita said.

"Uh-huh." He didn't turn around.

Juanita went into a speech about what she and Ronnie had been doing, how they were selling the pots all over Cabool, what shops they were putting them in, and how much they expected to make. He nodded every so often, like he cared, though she was prattling on and it was all just a bunch of nothing, just a bunch of words filling the air so that there was something to be found hanging there in case anyone looked. By the time Ray finally sat down again, Ronnie's beer was gone.

"How's your mother?" Ray said.

Ronnie felt a shock of heat in the pit of her stomach. "She's okay." She couldn't believe he asked her that, like it was no big deal. She looked at Juanita, who was watching her carefully. "Um . . . I'll be right back," Ronnie said.

She walked inside the house and let out a deep breath. She threw away her beer can and went to the refrigerator. She wanted another. She wanted to be loose. She wanted to be relaxed. All she had to do was to get through the evening and then everything would be fine. Tomorrow she would wake up and Juanita and she would be out in the greenhouse again, and Ray would be gone. Ronnie looked around the corner. Bean's eyes were fastened to the television. She opened the beer and guzzled. She burped and smiled, peeking around the corner to see if Bean had heard her. She got another beer and walked back outside. Loose and relaxed. That's all she needed.

"Oh," Ray said like he'd just remembered something. "Look here." He stood up and reached into his pants pocket, pulling out a long rock. He held it up. "Found this in my field yesterday."

Juanita reached out and took it. "Oh!" she said excitedly.

"What is it?" Ronnie asked.

"It's an arrowhead," he said.

Juanita admired it. "It's perfect," she said and handed it to Ronnie. "We find 'em every so often out here. It's always so exciting. I'll have to show you. Bean's got a box up in his closet with at least five of them—of course they aren't all perfect. Some's only chips, but you can tell."

Ronnie ran her finger along the chipped edge. "Daddy, you ought to show Veronica all yours." She looked at Ronnie. "He's got a bunch of 'em, don't you, Daddy?"

"I got a few," he nodded.

"He's got a bunch. He's got a knack for finding them, too. One time we were out fishing—I was pretty young, I guess 14 or 15 at the time—and I didn't feel like fishing that day and so I's just walking along the bank, you know, looking real hard for one. You know, it's always a good place to look for arrowheads around rivers and stuff. But anyway, I spent all day looking. All darn day, and Daddy comes walking by me and says, 'What you doing?' and I say, 'I'm looking for an arrowhead,' and he bends down—I'm not kidding," Juanita looked at Ray, who was smiling, "and he reaches down and picks up a rock and says, 'Why, here's one,' just as easy as pie, just like it was the most natural thing to just look down and find a arrowhead. Ha!"

"Oh, you were mad," Ray said.

"I was spitting mad," Juanita said. "Ha! But I kept looking, didn't I?"

Ray nodded.

"Did you find one?" Ronnie asked.

Juanita waved her hand. "I ain't ever found one. Not ever. And it's irritating because I know they're out here. Bean's found some; Daddy's found some. I guess I just ain't lucky when it comes to that."

Ray stood up and went back to the fire. "You're just too tall, Drink," he said. "You can't see that far down."

"I guess so," she said. "I guess so."

Ronnie took a long drink from her beer. She was beginning to feel good. "I know how tall you are," she said suddenly.

At first, when they both turned and looked at her, Ronnie thought she'd said something wrong, but then Juanita smiled.

"You do?" Juanita said.

"Shoot, everybody knows that," Ray said.

"I didn't until I came here."

Ronnie told them about talking to the men at the Pink Lemonade. She looked at Ray to see if he remembered bumping into Thatcher, but from where she was sitting, his expression seemed to remain the same.

"Well, how tall did they say?" Juanita said.

"Eighty-seven and a half inches," Ronnie said.

Juanita threw her head back and laughed.

"Isn't that true? Isn't that right?"

"You better get Bean out here," Ray said.

"Oh, no Daddy," Juanita said rolling her eyes. "No, no, no."

"Yep," he said. "I gotta get the meat on the grill anyhow. I'm getting Bean so's we can be sure."

"Be sure of what?" Ronnie said to Juanita after he'd gone into the house.

Juanita waved her hand. "They . . . oh it's so silly. I hope he don't do it."

"What?"

Ronnie was working on finishing her third beer, was thinking that maybe the evening wouldn't be so bad.

A minute later, Bean came out of the back door carrying two beers. He handed one to his mother and one to Ronnie. No one knew it would be her fourth. She set the unopened can in the grass. Ray came out with a platter with hamburgers and a beer for himself. After he put the meat on the grill, he turned to Bean.

"Okay, Beanie, let's go." Bean ran to Ray. He stood in front of him, but then put his back to him. Ray picked him up with a "hoo-wee" sound and set Bean on his shoulders. Bean was laughing, his mouth open and his head thrown back, just like his mother.

"You boys leave me alone now," Juanita said, though it was clear she didn't mean it.

"Stand up tall, girl," Ray said to her. "Stand up tall and be proud of who you are."

Juanita looked over at Ronnie and rolled her eyes. "They're silly is what they are," she said. "They're just plain silly." But she stood up, and as she did so, Ray reached into his pocket and pulled out a little tape measure and handed it to Bean.

Ronnie's mouth dropped open. They were going to measure her right then and there!

"Come on, come on," Bean was saying to Juanita.

She walked over and stood next to them. Ronnie found herself laughing out loud. Juanita smiled. She looked embarrassed, but not in an awful way.

Ray held onto Bean's legs as Bean leaned toward his mother.

"Let her down," Ray said.

Bean began to lower the tape. Down, down, his fingers awkwardly pulling out the tape. He let it go and it whipped back up into the holder.

"You forgot to push down the yellow button," Ray said. Bean pushed the yellow button on the holder, his tongue sticking out of the side of his mouth as he concentrated, and let the tape down again.

"Hold still, Ma," Bean said.

And Juanita wiggled purposefully, waving her great arms and moving her hips to the left and then the right like a giant hula dancer in slow motion.

"Hold still!" Bean said.

It was a scene. Ronnie opened that beer, though she knew she shouldn't, and watched Ray. He looked straight ahead but had a grin on his face. This, Ronnie thought, was the man that Thatcher didn't want to see. This was the man who had turned his back on her, the man who had treated her coldly. Ronnie watched his smile, the way the right side of his mouth curled upward higher than the left side. She watched the way he was looking at Juanita, the way his eyes sparkled at her. She was supposed to be hating him—and maybe it was just the beer, maybe she was too loose, too relaxed, but she was beginning to feel something else. Not like. No, not exactly that . . . she felt confused. She took another drink of her beer, watching them. Just watching.

Bean and Ray finished measuring and decided that Juanita was, indeed, eighty-seven and a half inches tall.

"My mom is the tallest person in Cabool," Bean said to Ronnie, and he reached out to Juanita as he sat atop his grandfather's shoulders, grabbing her head and pulling her to him.

Juanita's eyes shined. "Silly, silly," she said.

They all sat back down, except for Bean. In light of Ray's new find, Bean was out on an arrowhead hunt.

"The whole town is good to her," Ray said to Ronnie.

Juanita nodded.

"They all try their best to make things easier."

"Like the table at the Pink Lemonade," Ronnie said.

"Yes," Ray said. "Things like that. You keep your eyes open, you'll see that all over this town there's things been made just for my Juanita." He looked at the ground and shook his head. "This town helped me raise her. I mean, without them . . ." He looked up at Ronnie. "Lady in town makes most of Juanita's clothes," he said. "And them doorways inside? Ed Jones helped me do that so's Juanita wouldn't have to duck down in her own house when she went from room to room. And when she was still in school, they had a special desk made for her."

Juanita nodded. "Made me a whole lot more comfortable," she said.

"And the greenhouse . . . seems like everybody came to help, and it's the biggest greenhouse around here."

"Not the biggest," Juanita corrected.

"No, no. It ain't a huge greenhouse. I mean the largest scale-wise."

Juanita sat quietly, nodding. "I've had it good here," she said. "No doubt about it."

Ronnie looked down, and her eyes falling on the half drank beer in her hand. She set it in the grass next to her chair. "People don't bother you here," Ronnie said.

"Not too much. Oh, well, you know, they stare and all, and when I go out of town—like when I took Bean to the zoo—I drew a considerable crowd there." She shrugged. "I just ain't the kind of person you see everyday is all, and I guess that's okay, but I guess that is why I like it here."

"You're just one of a kind, honey," Ray said tipping his beer at her.

When they were eating dinner, Ray said out of the blue, "I don't guess Thatcher'll ever want to see me."

When Ronnie looked up, she realized that he was talking to her, looking at her.

"Oh, I don't know," she said, though she knew full well.

"Veronica," Juanita said to Ronnie. "It's okay. You ain't going to hurt Daddy by being honest."

Ray nodded. "That's true. I understand. Too much time . . . I don't blame him."

"Now, Daddy, don't say never. Why look at here! You and Ronnie and me and Bean are all sitting here having a fine time! Who would've thought it? It's all just a mess waiting to unfold, but T. will come around, right Veronica? He's just afraid is all, just like you was afraid to see Veronica. Right Veronica? Tell him."

But Ronnie couldn't look at them. She couldn't wear hear heart on her sleeve the way Juanita did, the way Ray sort of seemed to do. It was too different. The way they talked, the way they just said whatever they were thinking or feeling . . . it threw Ronnie off.

"I suppose that's right," Ray said to Juanita. "I'm . . . I'm sorry about that again," he said to Ronnie, but she looked at the ground, not knowing what to say.

"I tried to get him once, you know," Ray said. He stood up from the picnic table and went and sat in one of the lawn chairs. "Not too long after we came here and got settled in, I went back. Remember when Mrs. Alison come over and took care of you for a few days?"

"I . . ." Juanita's brow wrinkled. "I don't . . . " but suddenly her mouth fell open, and she nodded yes.

"I went back, and I tried to talk to . . . to your Mom and all . . . and . . . I couldn't do it," he said, shaking his head. "I wanted to, but it would have killed her. So I didn't. I guess I should have, but . . ." he looked at Ronnie, " . . . but it turned out all right for you, didn't it? Having Thatcher with you? Everything turned out okay, didn't it?"

He expected some kind of an answer from Ronnie, but she was imagining what life would have been like without Thatcher, what it would have been like to grow up with Vivian all by herself.

CHAPTER THIRTY SEVEN

Ronnie left Cabool the next morning.

"Please come back," Juanita had said to her. "Please become a part of our lives."

Ronnie had thought about that on the way home. She thought about Bean and about that tape measure. She thought about that table at the Pink Lemonade and about the truck, only partly painted with flowers.

When Ronnie got back to Rock Hill, Rochelle insisted that they all go to La Casa Mexican Restaurant to celebrate her homecoming. Ronnie was still a bit miffed at Thatcher, still a bit hurt at that phone call, but she had stayed in Cabool for eight days, and in that time she had come to see that knowing Juanita was a good thing, that forgiveness was a good thing, that family could be a good thing.

Thatcher seemed happy listening to Ronnie talk about what she did, about Juanita and Bean, but when Ronnie started to talk about Ray, when she told Thatcher that Ray had apologized and that he had come over for dinner, Thatcher became sullen.

"I don't want to hear about him," he said as if to brush off a pesky subject. "Tell me about everything else."

"All I'm saying is, there's another side," Ronnie said.

"Yeah, well, I don't want to hear that."

"Oh, you're being stubborn," Rochelle said. She raised her margarita glass and licked a spot of salt from the rim before taking a sip. Her long, purple fingernails clicked against the glass.

Ronnie watched Rochelle, but said, "Yeah, T. You're just being stubborn."

Thatcher pointed at Ronnie. She knew he was going to tell her to shut up, but then he looked at Rochelle and stopped. Instead, he stood up like he was going to leave, but then looked around, remembering that he wasn't at home. He wasn't the sort to throw temper tantrums in public. They could see that he was getting angry. Ronnie looked at Rochelle. She was just sitting there smiling at him, undaunted.

"Sit down, T.," she said gently. "You can't run away from us."

Thatcher looked around for a way of escape, but ended up sitting back down. Rochelle reached across the table and took his hand.

"Isn't this what you said you wanted?" she asked him. "Didn't you tell me that you wanted Ronnie and Juanita to get along?"

Thatcher glanced at Ronnie awkwardly.

"This is a good thing happening," Rochelle said.

The waitress stopped at the table. "You all need anything?" she asked.

Ronnie thought of Katie and the Pink Lemonade, and she almost started to tell Thatcher about Katie's asking about him, wanting him to come back to see her, but then, of course didn't. Thatcher ordered another beer and pointed at Rochelle's glass. She waved her hand and shook her head no. Ronnie still had half a soda. When the waitress left, he said, "Look. I don't want you both harping on me. Just leave me alone because I don't want to see him." Thatcher stood up and looked at Rochelle. "Now. I am not running away, Rochelle. I am going to the bathroom, and I'll be back in a minute, so you can just stop your worrying."

"Who's worried?" Rochelle said, holding her hands up and shrugging.

"He's very stubborn, isn't he?" she said to Ronnie when he'd gone.

Ronnie nodded, staring at Rochelle, trying to figure out why she was different, trying to figure out what kind of hold she had on him. He listened to her.

"He'll come around," Rochelle was saying.

"Don't count on it," Ronnie said.

"He's just scared."

Juanita had said the same thing about Ray. Ronnie watched Rochelle pick a tortilla chip from the basket. "It'd be scary giving his dad a chance. It pretty much means that in one way or another he's got to deal with everything he's been ignoring all these years."

Ronnie thought about that. Thought about Ray.

Thatcher came back, sat down, and smiled overtly at Rochelle.

"So," he said turning to Ronnie "Gayla's wanting to know when you're coming back to work."

Rochelle winked at Ronnie and sipped her margarita.

It was good to be home again, but by Ronnie's third day back in the Quick Shop, stocking shelves and checking people out, she found herself thinking about Cabool more and more, missing the greenhouse in the morning, missing Juanita and her silly laugh, missing the way Bean flipped his bangs out of his eyes. Cabool became a taste that lingered in her mouth.

She was putting quarts of oil on the bottom shelves in aisle three when she heard the bell on the door ring. Ronnie heard Philip's voice and stood up. He said hey to Gayla, and then went over to the soda machine.

"So, I hear you had a fine time in Cabool," Philip said when he saw Ronnie.

"It was okay," she said.

He raised his eyebrows. "You going back?"

"If I can get off work again."

Gayla was reading a *National Enquirer*.

"You know," she said without looking up, "normally I'd say you were a pain, sweetheart, but considering the circumstances, you just let me know ahead of time and we'll work it out."

"Thanks," Ronnie said.

Ronnie followed Philip to the cash counter. He set his large soda and a pack of donuts down for Gayla to ring up.

"I want T. to go back there," Ronnie said.

"Oh yeah? Well, I'm guessing he will."

"His dad wants to see him."

"I heard that," Philip said. "He'll come around."

Ronnie leaned onto the counter so that she could be more in front of Philip. "Help me talk him into going back."

"I don't need to. He'll go," he said.

"How do you know that? Did he tell you that?"

"Don't have to. The ball's rolling."

"But he told me . . ."

Philip sucked soda from the straw but shook his head to stop Ronnie from going on. "Don't matter what he says."

"Sounds like he just needs a push," Gayla said, hitting the cash register drawer button at just the right moment to emphasize the idea with a ding.

CHAPTER THIRTY EIGHT

"Let's go!" Rochelle called, leaning out the window of Thatcher's truck.

Ronnie opened the passenger door, and Rochelle scooted to the center.

"Where's T?"

"He's locking the backdoor," Ronnie said.

"I'm excited. This is an adventure," Rochelle said, bumping her arm into Ronnie's playfully. Thatcher got into the truck. He looked at Rochelle and gave her one of his little half smiles before starting the engine.

Rochelle was the map keeper. Thatcher had just written the directions down on a piece of paper for Ronnie, but Rochelle had a state map and tested Ronnie and Thatcher to see if they could remember the names of the little towns before they saw any signs for them: Sullivan, Bourbon, Doolittle, Newburg . . . Ronnie didn't remember any of them until she saw them.

"Oh my gosh," Rochelle said.

"What?" Thatcher asked.

"We're passing through a town called Licking?" She laughed and tried to lick Thatcher's ear and when he squinched his neck, she licked his arm instead.

Thatcher was too cool to really react, but Ronnie watched as he kept giving her sly looks from behind his sunglasses every so often, shaking his head in amusement as he listened to her banter. Ronnie looked at something Rochelle was pointing out on the map, and when she looked up, she saw that Thatcher was watching the two of them, looking at the road, looking at Ronnie and Rochelle, looking back to the road . . . Ronnie couldn't see his eyes behind the dark lenses, but when he smiled at her, it caught Ronnie off-guard. Thatcher, she realized, looked happy, and happiness was a new look for him.

Ronnie walked into the greenhouse first thing and saw Juanita standing there, tending to her plants. Her size was no longer shocking to Ronnie. And when Juanita turned and saw Ronnie and her face lit up and she held out her arms, Ronnie went to them. She went to her arms and though it was like trying to hug something the size of a grizzly bear, it was a good and perfect hug to them both.

"Where is he?" she said.

Ronnie followed Juanita back out of the greenhouse to where Thatcher and Rochelle stood waiting. Thatcher had taken off his glasses and when he saw Juanita he smiled at her. It was so different from that first meeting when Juanita had tried to hug Thatcher.

"This is Rochelle," Thatcher said.

Rochelle looked up into Juanita's face, and if she was at all shocked by Juanita's size, Ronnie thought she hid it well, because Rochelle smiled widely and held out her hand.

Ronnie watched the scene unfold and found herself in a wide smile all her own.

CHAPTER THIRTY NINE

Whenever Ronnie took walks in Cabool—whether she was alone or with Bean or Juanita—for some reason she always went to the left, always went in the direction down the road that led toward Ray's house. She didn't know why, really. It wasn't a conscious thing. Even before she'd met him, even before she had ever actually seen his house, whenever Bean and she had gone wandering, or when she had wanted to get away from Thatcher and Juanita, Ronnie went in that direction. She thought that maybe it had something to do with the sun. Walking to the right, she was covered by a canopy of trees with no sky visible and only shade. It felt deep and dark. She found she preferred the airiness of the open pastures and meadows, the white sunlight and the spacious sky. And so, when Bean and Rochelle and Ronnie headed out for a walk late in the afternoon, quite naturally they went down the road toward Ray's house.

Bean buzzed up in front of Ronnie and Rochelle, then lingered behind them, then walked with them. A couple of times, he slipped his hand into Ronnie's hand—just for a minute—but each time he did, a tenderness pushed on her that she had never really felt before.

"It's so beautiful here," Rochelle said. She spread her arms out, embracing the air, then walked over to the side of the road. "Look at this. These beautiful flowers just grow here wild." She cupped a pale blue flower gently in her fingers, bending down to smell it.

"That's a spiderwort," Ronnie said.

Rochelle turned. "How do you know that?"

"I know everything," Ronnie said, smiling.

"Nuh-uh," Bean said. "My mom told you!"

"You tattle-tale!" Ronnie said. She raised her fingers toward him and wiggled them, threatening to tickle him. Bean laughed and ran ahead, just out of Ronnie's reach, daring her to chase him, daring her to just try and catch him.

Rochelle smiled at them. "She sure knows a lot, doesn't she?" she said to Ronnie.

"About flowers? Yeah."

"I think she knows a lot about everything."

Ronnie thought it was an odd statement for Rochelle to make, as she'd only met her a few hours earlier, but Bean piped up to agree.

"She does," he said proudly. "My mom knows everything." He was still in front of Ronnie, but was walking backwards, keeping a keen eye on her in case she made any sudden moves.

"My Grandpa knows everything too. He knows even more than my mom. He knows all about cows."

Rochelle and Ronnie smiled at each other, and then Ronnie took two giant steps toward Bean, reaching out to catch him only to send him running up farther away.

"Hey, take me up there." Rochelle said. "Do you think he's home?"

The memory of that first meeting with Ray rapped on the pit of Ronnie's belly, and she stopped walking, trying to remember that she was over that, trying to remember that he had apologized, that they were now on friendly terms. She knew that. She surely did, and yet that first meeting . . . it was hard to forget.

"I'm not sure that's a good idea," Ronnie said honestly.

Bean nodded, as if he understood, and Ronnie wondered if he was thinking about that first meeting as well.

"Oh. Well, okay. I was just thinking that it might be easier later, you know, not so awkward if we can get T. to meet him later."

Ronnie bit her lip, unsure of the idea.

"You think your granddad's home?" Ronnie said to Bean.

"I dunno." Bean shrugged.

"You think it's an okay idea?" Rochelle was looking at Bean.

"I guess so," Bean said, but he was looking at Ronnie, looking to see if it was a good idea or a bad idea.

Ronnie looked back at him and nodded her head up and down. "I think that it will be okay this time," she said.

And so Bean grabbed both of their hands and pulled them along down the gravel road toward Ray's house. Ronnie and Rochelle swung their arms, lifting Bean along and letting him take giant hops down the long gravel road.

Ray sat on his front porch, as if he had been expecting them. When Bean ran up ahead of Rochelle and Ronnie, Ray scooped Bean into his arms. He stood on the porch, watching as the two girls walked toward him.

"Hello, Veronica," he said.

Ronnie had not heard him say her name before, and was oddly touched. He didn't reach out to hug her or anything like that, but he called her by her name, and it felt good.

"This is Rochelle," Ronnie said. "She's T.'s girlfriend."

"Nice to meet you," he said. He cleared his throat and gave Bean a jostle on his hip.

"Uncle T.s' here too, Grandpa."

"He is?" Ray said it lightly, as if it didn't matter. But he set Bean down and took in a solid breath. He looked at Ronnie again. "Okay then," he said, shaking his head.

"I think it's just wonderful," Rochelle said, reaching out her hand to shake Ray's.

Ronnie believed Ray looked like a man who was getting ready to step off a ledge into something new below—serious and careful and very aware.

"Veronica," Juanita said, "You are like a Christmas present. Do you know that?"

She and Ronnie were in the kitchen making lemonade. They had left Thatcher and Rochelle outside, standing by the barbed-wire fence by the cows.

"A Christmas present?"

"Yes," Juanita said. "Look what you done. You got us all here. All here together again and this time even with T.'s girlfriend."

"Oh," Ronnie said humbly. "It wasn't just me."

"Well, whatever. Daddy's coming over later and Thatcher and he's going to meet again."

"Aren't you nervous?" Ronnie said. "I mean, I think it's good and all, but . . ."

"Hey, whatever happens, happens, Veronica. The first time they see each other is just going to end up being the first time they see each other. That's it. Might as well get it over with as quick as we can because once they get past that, they can get to the next meeting and the next meeting. You see? It's just the first time."

"But what if there isn't a next time?"

"Oh, you got to have some faith, Veronica. Look at us. I didn't come to your house worrying about the next time, did I? One thing at a time, that's all you got to think about."

Ronnie frowned.

"Quit your worrying," Juanita said.

Juanita didn't seem to be concerned, but when Ray was an hour late, Ronnie began to question her. Juanita waved her hand. "It's okay," she said.

Juanita was happy—so happy that she could barely contain it. She walked around grinning and chit-chatting with Rochelle and Ronnie and Bean and Thatcher, talking about anything, talking about nothing. As big and cumbersome as she was, right then Juanita seemed to be floating on air. Ronnie wished she felt the same. She could see that Thatcher was trying to be open in his own way—there was no doubt about that. But Ronnie was worried about him. She could also see the way he avoided any length of eye contact with her or anyone else. She could see the way he kept biting his nails and biting the inside of his lip. Ray was coming, and Thatcher was trying to be ready. Ronnie heard him offer a beer to Rochelle a couple of times, but he wasn't drinking. That surprised Ronnie more than anything. Hardly a day went by that Thatcher didn't at least have a couple of beers, and he would never consider being at any kind of a gathering without drinking.

"Aw, you silly," Ronnie heard Rochelle say to Thatcher. She leaned over him attentively, held his chin in her hand and looked in his eyes. "You're okay right now, aren't you?" And he looked at her and nodded, and after she kissed him lightly, he smiled up at her like she was some kind of angel.

Ronnie wondered, was he trying not to drink on purpose? That would sure be a first, but then it was clear, as each day had gone by since Juanita had shown up, and since Thatcher had started seeing Rochelle, that he was changing. There was no doubt about it. More than a couple of times, as they sat in the backyard waiting for Ray to show up, Rochelle had stood behind Thatcher and laid her hands on his shoulders. She whispered something in his ear, something to psych him up, and he nodded. Thatcher. New-and-Improved, Ronnie thought.

Juanita stood up and walked into the house, and when she did, Ronnie stood up and followed her.

"What if he doesn't come?" Ronnie said.

Juanita turned to her, exasperated. "Look you," she said in mock sternness, "I thought we already had this talk. Just let it happen."

"I . . ."

She shook her head and put her enormous hand out to block Ronnie from view. "No, no, no. I'm not listening!" She laughed at Ronnie, dropping her arm.

Ronnie laughed in spite of herself.

"Come on, now" Juanita said. "Get on outside. T. needs us to help him along."

"Juanita," Ronnie said. She was going to ask if Thatcher was trying not to drink, but when Juanita looked at Ronnie, Ronnie thought better of the idea. "Never mind," she said.

She stepped out the back door and as she did so, Ray was walking up the drive. He stopped and looked at Ronnie. He tried to smile at her, but Ronnie could see that he was afraid. She walked toward him.

"Hey," Ronnie said. "I . . . um . . . T.'s back there." She pointed toward the back, around the corner of the house that was blocking their view of where Thatcher and Rochelle were sitting.

Ray looked in the direction that Ronnie pointed, but then stopped and looked back toward the road—a man with a second thought, or a man planning an escape. Juanita came out of the back door.

"Hey, Daddy," she said. She was trying to sound casual, but her eyes gave her away. They were sparkling with happiness. "You look like you seen a ghost already." She laughed and leaned down and patted his back with her giant hand.

Ray looked like he wanted to say something, but nothing came.

"We're here with you," Juanita said. "Come on back."

He looked up at her, and she smiled.

"Stand up tall, Daddy," she said. "Stand up tall and be proud of who you are."

Ray took a deep breath, trying to smile, but the way his chin was moving . . . for a second Ronnie thought he was going to cry.

Ronnie let them go ahead of her, staying a few steps behind. She knew that she was a part of this whole thing—she knew that now—but this was Thatcher and Ray's moment, and a part of Ronnie felt like she was intruding to be part of it, like maybe they all were. Juanita was right, though, they needed to help Ray and Thatcher along—at least for now.

Juanita put her hand on Ray's shoulder and sort of walked him forward encouragingly.

Thatcher was standing with his back to them as they walked toward him. He was turned to Rochelle and Bean. Rochelle was sitting in a lawn chair with Bean standing beside her, leaning against her leg. Thatcher was showing Bean a trick with the yo-yo he'd brought as a gift from St. Louis.

"Look here," Juanita said.

Thatcher turned, and when he did, when he saw Ray, the yo-yo jerked and immediately went dead at the end of the string. He took a step back, but he was so close to his own lawn chair that he ended up stumbling. Without missing a beat, Rochelle stood up and held his arm for a second to steady him. "Hey, Ray," she said, "Nice to see you again."

"Hey," Ray said. He tried to look at Rochelle, but his eyes were glued to Thatcher.

Thatcher just stood there, his arms so stiff and straight they looked like they were attached to his body. He didn't look at Ray. He didn't look at anybody. His chin jutted up, making him look tough and proud. His chest moved up and down, like he'd been running and was trying to catch his breath. Rochelle reached out her hand again and touched the back of Thatcher's hand. It was a small motion, but when she did, his hand opened wide and when she put hers inside of his, he held onto it tightly.

Bean stood between Thatcher and Ray. He looked at his grandpa and his uncle—first to one, then to the other—with open curiosity.

"Look at this," Juanita said. Both hands were sort of covering her mouth and her eyes were teary. "Look here." She lowered her hands. "Daddy and Thatcher, together. Both in the flesh." But then her hands went back to her face, back to covering her mouth.

All these moments, all these steps . . . the scene felt so familiar now, like when Juanita had first shown up, like when

Ronnie had tried to face Ray in the barn, like when Ray had tried to face Ronnie behind the screen door. Always, it seemed, there was something in their way, and yet there they were—taking the first steps anyway, over and over again, taking the irretrievable steps that would change things forever, only it all happened a little at a time. It made Ronnie think as they stood there together; it made her think that they were all very brave, each one of them in his or her own way willing to take a giant leap of faith.

"Grandpa," Bean said looking up, "This is Uncle T."

Juanita smiled at Bean. "He knows that, silly goose," she said. "Grandpa is his Daddy."

Bean's mouth dropped open as something big dawned on him, and they all laughed. Even Thatcher's expression softened a little.

"It's been a long time, hasn't it?" Ray said.

Thatcher nodded.

There was silence for a minute that lasted forever. Ray took a deep breath and blew it out loudly.

"Well, this is hard," he said.

"You know," Juanita said, "Veronica and Rochelle made some lemonade out of real lemons this morning."

"Oh yes. Good idea," Rochelle said nodding. She patted Thatcher's arm. "We'll be back." She made him look into her eyes when she said it, nodding to him that all would be just fine. Juanita held her hand out to Bean, and he went to her, and the three of them started walking to the house.

"Ronnie," Juanita said, "Hey, why don't you come help us?"

Ronnie had been frozen in her spot, transfixed, and mesmerized by the sight of them together, but Juanita's voice jerked her to attention and she instantly headed for the house.

Of course, all that Rochelle and Juanita did once they got into the house was to stand at the window that looked out past the screened-in porch and into the back yard. They spied out the window while Bean got out glasses. Ronnie got out the ice and lemonade, watching the women's backs. Rochelle leaned on the counter, standing on tip-toe with a straight back, while

Juanita stooped down, her shoulders rounded, her neck bent to see out the window.

"They're sitting down," Rochelle whispered in Ronnie's direction.

"T. don't look too happy," Juanita said.

Juanita and Rochelle watched Thatcher and Ray, and Ronnie watched Juanita and Rochelle. The room was quiet—the only sound was the clink of Bean dropping ice into empty glasses.

"Daddy's saying something," Juanita's said. "I wish I could hear them."

"This is so hard for T.," Rochelle said quietly. She looked up at Juanita. "Maybe this wasn't such a good idea. I mean, he said he was ready . . . but look at him."

Juanita nodded, but didn't say anything.

"You think we pushed him too hard?" Rochelle said.

"Kind of late to be asking that, isn't it?" Ronnie said from her spot by the sink.

Juanita turned around.

"You think this is the wrong thing, Veronica? You think this is gonna hurt T.?"

Ronnie shook her head. She didn't know what to think.

"T.'s saying something back," Rochelle said.

Juanita turned back to the window.

"Look at him," Juanita said.

Ronnie went to the window and tried to squeeze between them. They each took a step aside to let her in. Thatcher was talking all right, but his face was expressionless. Ronnie knew that look. That was the kind of look he gave when he had reached his limit. She had seen it before—directed at her, directed at Vivian. Ronnie couldn't hear his words, but she knew what his voice would sound like no matter what he was saying: it would be controlled—a monotone that tried to cover the truth of what he was feeling with even-sounding syllables, the quiet before the storm.

"We gotta go out there," Ronnie said.

Rochelle and Juanita looked at Ronnie. She shook her head again. "Now," she said taking hold of Juanita's hand, pulling on it just a little. "Go stop them. Stop them!" Ronnie said when they didn't move. She looked up to see Juanita staring at her with an alarmed expression. "Can't you see?" Ronnie said pointing to the window. "Can't you see him?"

"Yes. I see them. It's okay, Veronica," Juanita said.

But Ronnie wasn't listening. "Stop him," she pleaded.

"Stop who?" Rochelle said. "They're just talking, Ronnie."

"Look at him," Ronnie said. She looked out the window at Thatcher. Her breathing was too fast and she was having trouble catching her breath. "Can't you . . . can't you see how upset he is?"

Juanita and Rochelle didn't seem to understand. They were staring at her, watching her with dumb expressions. Ronnie turned and started walking toward the door, but realized that she was too afraid to go out there.

"Please," she said turning back to Juanita and Rochelle. "Please."

"Oh," Juanita said walking toward Ronnie. "Oh, Veronica, come here. Come here, honey."

"No!" Ronnie said. And she was crying, suddenly sobbing. "We can't just stand here," she tried to say.

"It's okay," Juanita said.

"What is wrong with you?" Ronnie's eyes were blinded with tears and her voice came out thick and cracked. "You're going to make him stay out there all alone?"

"Veronica," Juanita whispered. "Honey," she said. "It's okay," she soothed. "It's all right." And she pulled Ronnie to her as she cried, and for a moment, Ronnie let her. She buried her head in Juanita's middle trying to gain back control, trying to stop the overwhelming sobs that had taken hold of her. Juanita drowned Ronnie in soothing sounds and words of comfort, and after a minute, Ronnie began to calm down. Rochelle was still at the counter, watching Ronnie. Bean was standing by the sink, biting his bottom lip, looking worried. Ronnie wiped her eyes and nodded to him, trying to show him she was okay.

Juanita smiled down at her with compassion.

"I'm sorry," Ronnie said. "I'm sorry . . . I just . . ."

"You know what?" Juanita said, looking down at Ronnie. "You're right, honey. You're right. I'm going to go out there with them. You stay here and I'll go out, okay?"

Ronnie nodded, wiping her tears away with her fingers.

"We'll take care of T.," Juanita said. "Don't you worry."

Ronnie nodded again, feeling stupid, but feeling grateful. She sniffed and wiped her eyes again.

"You want to sit down?" Rochelle asked.

"No." Ronnie shook her head. "I'm okay. I'm sorry. I'm okay now."

Rochelle came over to Ronnie. She didn't say anything, but led Ronnie back toward the sink. Ronnie tried to smile at Bean, but he was frowning. She had upset him. She patted his head when she got to him, and he hugged Ronnie's waist, burying his face in her waist just like Ronnie had done minutes before to Juanita, only Bean wasn't crying—he was trying to comfort Ronnie, and she almost started crying all over again.

Juanita went outside. Rochelle helped Ronnie and Bean get the lemonade, but they both kept glancing toward the window, and after a second, they were back at it, looking out. Thatcher looked relieved when he saw Juanita. Ray stood up and said something to her. He started to turn away, but Juanita reached her arm out to stay him and said something. She was saying something and whatever it was, Ray and Thatcher were listening, neither of them looking at her or at each other, but both obviously listening.

Juanita made a gesture toward her father, and then sat down in her big chair next to Thatcher. Ray shook his head and said something in their direction. He stood there for a minute, but then he sat back down.

Juanita sat back and smiled.

Rochelle and Bean went outside and served them all lemonade and then sat with them, but it was too hard for

Ronnie. It was too hard to think about sitting out there and feeling all that weird energy in the air. Ronnie just couldn't do it. She stayed inside awhile, trying to figure out what to do, and finally decided to get her paints out of the greenhouse and to work on Juanita's truck. That way she would be out there, but she wouldn't be too close—she wouldn't have to sit with them. She was relieved when no one bothered her, though she saw Juanita look in her direction. Ronnie sat on a stool by the driveway, near enough to everyone so that she could sort of hear them when they spoke loud enough, but at the same time far enough away that she didn't have the burden of being a part of any conversation.

Rochelle had smiled and Thatcher had laughed when they first saw what Ronnie was doing to Juanita's truck. They agreed that it was a good idea, though, that it was perfect for a flower delivery truck.

Of course, when Bean saw Ronnie get her paints out and move toward the truck, he came over—but that was okay. Ronnie would let him help. She gave him a brush and let him fill in petals, or paint leaves—and he always made a mess. It made him so happy to be helping, though, and Ronnie liked the challenge of having to "fix" his unintentional strokes without hurting his feelings. A blob of yellow became a dandelion; a smear of orange became the base for a zinnia. The whole driver's side of Juanita's truck was nearly finished, and Ronnie was getting ready to turn the corner and work on the front. She looked toward the yard. Thatcher looked more relaxed than he had been a little while earlier. Juanita was saying something, though Ronnie couldn't hear what. Thatcher was listening, and Rochelle was smiling. Ray had his back to Ronnie, so she couldn't tell what he was doing, but seeing them all sitting there together . . . seeing Thatcher there and not even drinking . . . to Ronnie, it seemed like they were all getting ready to turn a corner.

CHAPTER FORTY

"Come to the store with me to get some groceries," Thatcher said.

He looked down at Ronnie as she sat on the couch. He wasn't asking. He was telling. Ronnie raised an eyebrow, but started to put her shoes on anyway.

"Why isn't Rochelle going?"

"I want you to go," was all he said. "Hurry up." He waved his arm in a circle to hurry her.

"Can I go?" Bean asked.

"Next time, buddy, okay?" Thatcher said.

Ray hadn't stayed very long the night before, but as soon as he left, Thatcher and Rochelle had taken off in the truck. Juanita told Ronnie they were going to dinner and then going up to a lookout point to watch the sun go down and then see the stars.

"It's good," she said. "He needs time to let things sink in."

Ronnie got into Thatcher's truck and they bumped along down the road, gravel dust leaving a white cloud behind them. Ronnie waited, wondering what it was he had to say, wondering why he wanted her to go with him. When they pulled off the gravel road and onto the main road leading into town, the big message came: "I just want you to know," he said, "that I'm okay with this. It's all okay."

Ronnie wasn't sure how to respond. "Okay," she said.

He glanced at her. "I mean it," he said.

Ronnie nodded. "All right." What did he want her to say? "I'm glad," she added.

And that was all they said about Thatcher meeting his father.

When they got back, Rochelle and Bean were sitting out on the front porch, but when the truck pulled up, Rochelle stood up and met them.

"What's going on?" Thatcher asked.

"Juanita's sick," Rochelle said.

"What do you mean?"

"She gots migraines headaches," Bean said. He stood next to Rochelle.

Ronnie knew that about Juanita, that she sometimes got headaches, but in the time Ronnie had spent with her, Juanita, had only had one that she was aware of.

"She's pretty out of it, T.," Rochelle said. "I'm worried. I mean . . . I don't really know what to do."

Bean tugged on Rochelle's shirt. "I told you. She just likes it real quiet and dark."

Rochelle ran her hand over his head. "Yes," she said. "You did." But she looked at Ronnie and Thatcher and said, "I called Ray."

Thatcher told Ronnie to get the groceries and went toward the house, but Ronnie followed him instead.

The house was quiet except for the steady whir of the window fan. Juanita was in her room, lying on her back, on top of the covers. The bed, that looked so enormous when she wasn't in it, looked suddenly small. Her eyes were closed, but Ronnie knew that she wasn't sleeping because she wasn't snoring. Her face was pale and waxy looking. Ronnie thought of the Halloween mask again and wondered what her skin felt like, what the ridge of that massive brow bone felt like beneath a person's fingertips.

"Juanita?" Thatcher said. He took a step closer, but Ronnie stayed at the door.

"Juanita?" he said again.

She opened her mouth but not her eyes.

"Daddy?" she whispered, but her voice sounded far away.

"No. It's T. Are you okay?"

"T." she said his name softly, like she was dreaming about something good. "I'm . . . I'll be okay," she said.

"Can I get you something? A bag of ice or something like that?"

"Yes," she said.

Ronnie stood at the foot of the bed, not quite knowing what to do or what to say. She didn't think Juanita even knew she was there.

"Here you go," Thatcher said when he came back. He sat next to her on the bed and gently held a bag of ice wrapped in a kitchen hand towel to his sister's head.

Her mouth opened and her face seemed to relax. A tear ran from her closed left eye and she sighed.

"Is that helping?" Thatcher asked.

She whispered yes, but her lips barely moved.

It hurt to see her lying like that, lying in so much pain that she couldn't open her eyes and couldn't speak. Ronnie just stood there at the end of the bed, watching them, watching Thatcher take care of Juanita, watching him be so gentle, so tender. He was taking care of her. Ronnie would have just left her alone. She would have just let her rest, but Thatcher . . . he was there, sitting beside her, holding a bag of ice to her head. Ronnie had never thought to ask if there was any way to help. She had never thought to just sit by her side and offer her comfort. It made her feel ashamed. Ronnie was always complaining about him, always accusing Thatcher of not caring and not talking when all the time he had been proving, over and over again, that he was the one person that would never let her down—and not just her, but all of them. There he was taking care of Juanita, showing her the very same thing.

Ronnie looked up and saw that Ray had come in and was standing at the bedroom door. He was completely silent and when their eyes met, Ronnie saw that his were filled with tears. He shook his head at her, shook it like he was saying no, but Ronnie didn't know what he meant, didn't know what he was saying.

"It's like that sometimes," he said when Ronnie and Thatcher came out of Juanita's room.
"What do you mean?" Thatcher said.
"I mean with her condition"
"What is her condition?" Ronnie asked.
He looked at Ronnie for a minute. "She's got a tumor on her pituitary. It's what made her so big . . . well, sort of . . . and . . . it puts pressure on her brain."
"A tumor? Is it growing?" Ronnie said.
"Yep." He squinted at Ronnie, like what he said was hurting him somehow. "I mean, not quick, but . . . . " He went over to the dining room table and sat down, Thatcher stood at Juanita's bedroom door, listening. Ray looked up and saw Thatcher.
"So, like what, she has cancer?" Ronnie said.
"No, no. It's benign." He was still looking at Thatcher, but then turned to Ronnie. "It's not cancer. It just made her pituitary gland go crazy."
"Can't they do something about it? Can't they take it out or something?"
Ray shook his head. "She ain't a candidate for that. We tried other things, drugs and all. We looked at all the options."
"What options?" Thatcher said. He peeked back into the bedroom, back at Juanita, but then came full into the room and stood at the table.
Ray set his jaw straight, and for a minute, he looked just like Thatcher when Thatcher was mad. "Look," he said. "Juanita and me been through all this. We seen the doctors and know all our choices. She's made her decisions."

"I'm not judging you," Thatcher said quickly. "I just . . . I just don't know."

"You know," Ray started to say. He looked toward the front door. Rochelle and Bean were sitting on the front porch, out of hearing range. Ray lowered his voice. "People like Juanita don't live long. You got to realize that."

He was silent for a minute. "It's made her real happy to see you both," he said. "Real happy."

"What are you saying?" Thatcher whispered. "Are you saying she's gonna die soon or something?"

Ray looked toward the door again. "No. I'm not saying that. I'm saying . . . I'm saying that you got to enjoy a person like Juanita while you can because you never know." He stood up. "That's all I'm saying."

CHAPTER FORTY ONE

Thatcher leaned over and rested his hand on Juanita's arm. "You need anything?"

Juanita smiled at him, looking up from the oversized wooden lawn chair where she was sitting. They were in the front yard, sitting under the big oak tree. Juanita was wrapped in a king-sized, flowered sheet, though it was warm outside.

"Oh, T. I'm fine. Really. You're spoiling me."

Something had changed. Sometime between Ray's visit the night before and now, Thatcher had turned into a considerate, caring, and open person. Ronnie had never seen this side of him before—at least not to this extent.

"Well, just call if you need me," he said and went into the house to help Rochelle.

Ronnie stared at Thatcher as he walked away, thinking she hardly recognized him. He and Rochelle were making dinner for everyone. That wasn't surprising—that was just Rochelle's influence more than anything. Earlier, Rochelle had insisted that Ray stay for dinner. "As long you go home and pick some of those home-grown tomatoes you were bragging about last night," she teased. Ray had taken Bean to help him and promised to be back before long. That was Rochelle. But this—

Thatcher taking care of Juanita—the way he was doting on her, Ronnie had never seen Thatcher act so openly considerate.

Ronnie always thought of Thatcher as being angry and irritated. He was her grumpy brother, a guy who seemed irritated with life and with everyone around him. He drank too much and smoked too much and he didn't talk. He took care of business and kept to himself. He worked hard. He provided. If a job needed to be done, he did it. He didn't complain and his expectations were simple—live and work hard. That was the Thatcher Ronnie knew. Thatcher did things out of duty, not out of love. He did things simply because they needed to be done.

But then there were moments like her birthday party. Maybe, beneath the demands of the day, beneath the many hours of work at the shop, beneath the many responsibilities Thatcher had taken on in his life—including raising Ronnie—maybe Thatcher had always been this way but had simply never had the opportunity to show it. Maybe the burdens of responsibility and duty—qualities that Ronnie had always seen clearly in Thatcher—had veiled other truths about him: that he was compassionate, that he was considerate, that his actions were born, for the most part, out of love. Then again, Ronnie thought, maybe she had been so focused on herself, so focused on what she wanted and thought should happen in their lives that she had been blinded to what had truly been in front of her all along.

Ronnie looked at Juanita.

"You okay?" Ronnie asked.

Juanita smiled, but her eyes looked tired. "You two are the sweetest. I'm fine."

"Hey," Juanita said in a confidential tone. "We done all right here, haven't we?"

"Yeah . . . I . . . yes," Ronnie said smiling.

Juanita nodded her head slowly. "You see, Veronica? Things work out. Just gotta take a chance and have a little faith."

Ronnie watched Thatcher closely the rest of the day, trying to really see him for the first time—and she had never seen him act as charming as he did then. He took care of Juanita's every need. If her tea glass was empty, he filled it. If she said she was hungry, he brought out a bowl of grapes. When the sun started to peek through the trees on their side of the yard and landed on Juanita, Thatcher made her stand up so that he could move her big chair to a shadier spot. Was this a new Thatcher, or had this been Thatcher all the time? Ronnie just didn't know.

And it wasn't just Juanita that he fussed over. It was all of them. When Ray came back with Bean and a bowl full of beautiful, red tomatoes, Thatcher took one and held up.

"That's a good looking tomato there," he said, nodding to his father and smiling.

Smiling! Ronnie thought. Thatcher is smiling at Ray! She watched as Thatcher bragged about Rochelle's cooking and brought out an appetizer she'd made—some artichoke dish.

"You put it on crackers," he told them knowingly. He spread some on a cracker and handed it to Juanita.

"Oh," she said. "That's delicious. Rochelle, that's delicious."

"See?" he said. "I told you she was a good cook." He made a cracker for Ray and then even made one for Ronnie.

Every once in a while Ronnie thought that maybe it was all just a big act, that Thatcher was trying to impress Ray, that he was trying to make Ray think he had it all together. It reminded Ronnie of Vivian. But it wasn't an act, and though Thatcher had a couple of beers, he really wasn't drinking much. On that day, Thatcher had something else going on. He held all of them captive—even Bean when he was hanging around. Thatcher was so animated and so open that, for a long time, Ronnie just sat and watched him in amazement. She listened to him during dinner as he told stories about working with Philip and about the customers and about the strange things that have happened over the years, like the time a car had been sitting at the shop overnight and that when he had opened the hood the next morning, a squirrel jumped out at him.

"Remember that, Ronnie?" he said. "You were there. Remember?" And she answered yes, thinking to herself what a beautiful person Thatcher was sitting there like that, just talking.

Ray was laughing at Thatcher's story, and when he tilted his head back and smiled, Ronnie saw both Juanita and Thatcher in his expression. She looked around the table, suddenly aware that she was no longer sitting with strangers, that she wasn't angry, and that she wasn't afraid. She was with family—*their family*—and it was good. Thatcher had to be feeling it, too. What else could be making him act so . . . so happy?

That was it—Thatcher was happy, and Ronnie was seeing it in the open for the very first time. She gazed at the sky and laughed. She'd heard a saying that you never realize how dark a room is until someone turns on a light. She thought she'd seen him happy before, but it was nothing compared to this. It was darkness compared to this light. And she wondered how Thatcher would have been all these years if Vivian hadn't gone and screwed everything up—if this wasn't the kind of person he was supposed to have been all along.

Of course, Ronnie wouldn't be there if Vivian hadn't been the way she was—and that, of course, tied to the black thought that Ronnie only half belonged there, that she could lay no claims to Ray as her father. But for Thatcher, something in his life was now complete. Ronnie saw that clearly. And whether he had intended to or not, whether he even knew it or not, Ronnie realized that Thatcher had given up something for her and Vivian all these years. He had given up a good measure of happiness.

"You play horseshoes, T.?" Ray asked.

"Oh boy," Juanita said. "Don't answer him, T. He's like a hustler or something. Just tell him no."

"Hey, now" Ray said, pointing at Juanita.

"Tell him no, T.," Juanita said, but she was smiling. "He's trying to trick you."

"I am just asking a question," Ray said. He looked at his son. "Do you?"

Thatcher looked from Ray to Juanita and then back to Ray again. "I played before . . ."

"You up for a game?"

Juanita leaned forward, making a ruckus, saying, "No, no! Don't let it happen." Bean came running from the side of the house where he'd been playing in the sandbox.

"What's a matter, Mom?"

"Grandpa's trying to get your uncle to play horseshoes," she said.

Bean squinched up his shoulders and started to laugh, covering his mouth. His shoulders shook up and down like a fish bobber getting a nibble. Thatcher grabbed Bean around the waist and pulled him close.

"What's so funny?" he said, tickling Bean's middle.

Bean struggled to get free, but not too hard. "He'll beat you!"

"How do you know that?"

"He's a champ-een."

"A *champ-een*, huh?"

Thatcher looked at Ray and Ray waved his hand dismissively.

"Ain't anyone in this whole town that's beat him more than once," Juanita said. "He's in a league."

"I didn't know there were horseshoe leagues," Rochelle said.

Juanita nodded. "Oh, yes."

"I'll give it a try," Thatcher said.

Ray's eyes lit up, and he stood. "Well, let's go. There's a pit out behind Juanita's greenhouse."

Ray turned to Ronnie. "You and Rochelle interested? We could play doubles."

"Oh . . . I . . . no," Ronnie looked at Rochelle.

"Yeah, you both go on," Rochelle said. "I'll play the winner." She smiled coyly at Thatcher.

"Ha!" Juanita said. "You'll be playing Daddy."

"Hey, now," Thatcher said.

He sounded just like Ray had a minute before. They are similar, Ronnie thought. Similar and yet they'd been apart all these years.

"Tell 'em you'll play the loser," Juanita said.

Rochelle laughed. "Okay, then. I'll play the loser."

"I could win," Thatcher said, though he didn't sound convincing.

"Sure you could," Ray said as they walked away.

The women and Bean watched the two: the same build, though Thatcher was a little taller and Ray was a little huskier; the same walk, though Thatcher was a little slower moving.

Rochelle started to pick up dishes.

"You did all that work," Ronnie said turning to Rochelle. "I'll clean up the dishes."

Rochelle started to fuss, shooing Ronnie with her hand.

"Really," Ronnie said. "I want to do this."

Rochelle looked at Ronnie with a puzzled grin and set the plate down. Ronnie wanted more of this feeling, was all. She wanted more of this happy family idea. So she cleared the table and went into the kitchen, feeling for the first time, Vivian aside, that everything in their family was finally the way it was always meant to be.

CHAPTER FORTY TWO

Juanita gave Ronnie a check for $107 before they left to go back to St. Louis.

"That's your earnings so far on the pots that we sold."

Ronnie smiled. "Really?"

"You really got a good talent there, Veronica."

"Thanks."

Ray came down to say goodbye. He and Thatcher started to shake hands, but then Ray reached out his other arm, and they embraced in an awkward, quick, and manly hug. Ronnie never knew what kind of understanding they had come to. She never knew what they said during that first meeting, but it was clear—they were putting the past aside.

They drove home, not really saying too much. Ronnie guessed they were all just . . . satisfied—even Rochelle. They had gone to Cabool in search of something, and something had been found—something good. They weren't like the Wilsons. They weren't like any other family Ronnie knew, but that was okay. Ronnie had never felt this way in all her life, like there were people she could claim, and people who could claim her. Good people. And because of it, everything was easier. Everything was lighter somehow.

And when Vivian came into the Quick Shop for a pack of cigarettes a few days after Ronnie, Thatcher, and Rochelle had come home, Ronnie smiled at her—not a fake and forced smile, but a real one.

"Hey, Mom," Ronnie said.

"What's wrong with you?" Vivian said, eyeing her daughter suspiciously. She plopped her cash down and drummed her long nails on the countertop. Ronnie thought of Rochelle and her long fingernails.

"Nothing," Ronnie shrugged. "I'm just in a good mood."

Vivian stared at her for a minute longer and then looked at Gayla and raised her eyebrows.

"What was that all about?" Gayla asked after she left.

"What?" Ronnie said.

"I ain't never seen you act so friendly toward your momma before. What gives?"

"Nothing," Ronnie said. "Can't I be in a good mood?"

"Well . . . your family ain't exactly known for its good moods, if you know what I mean," Gayla said.

Ronnie laughed.

Now Ronnie knew the truth about her family. She knew that there were people who didn't spend their days getting drunk and hurting each other over and over again. She knew she didn't have to keep her guard up all the time. And that made her know something else: she didn't have to pin all her hopes on trying to please or appease Vivian. Ronnie saw Vivian for what she truly was—a sad woman who had rejected any sort of truth of love in her life. Vivian had turned her back on everything that could have been good. Up until that moment, regardless of how awful she could be, Vivian had been an idea that Ronnie clung to, the best she could get, the best she could hope for. If Ronnie lost Vivian, what then?

But the truth had cast its shadow so that, standing in the store, looking at her mother, Ronnie saw shades of possibility that had never before existed. Truly, Ronnie did not need her mother in her life, but could keep Vivian at whatever distance she chose.

It was a sorry feeling, but also an oddly freeing feeling. Ronnie didn't have to invest herself any more into an account that had long before gone bankrupt; she didn't have to look to Vivian with hopes of happiness—no matter how dim those hopes had been. Ronnie had other options as far as family was concerned. The truth had, indeed, set her free.

Vivian's mouth opened in surprise when Ronnie showed up at her house a week later. Vivian stood at the front door, wearing her robe, though it was nearly ten thirty in the morning.

"What's the matter?" Vivian asked.

"I just want to ask you something."

"Well, I gotta get ready for work so you'll have to come in here," she said. She turned and walked down the hall toward the bathroom. Ronnie followed her and leaned against the bathroom door and watched her. She opened the mirror to the medicine cabinet, her back to Ronnie. She talked to Ronnie's reflection.

"I gotta work the lunch shift because Jessica can't do it—again. I swear, I told them a year ago I want off these lunch hours and I mean it, but first time somebody wants off, they come calling me. If I have to cover for her one more time, I'm gonna tell them to fire her ass. They'll listen to me too, I been there so long."

She picked up the curling iron that had been heating on the bathroom sink and began curling her hair. Ronnie watched Vivian pull long strands of hair and wind them around the iron. She held her position, curling the hair at the top of her head, her arms hovering above her head like a ballerina. She tapped her fingertips along the wound hair, tap-tapping, checking for heat. She let the coiffed strand loose and picked up the next.

Ronnie imagined the ballerina who spun around in a jewelry box. She didn't know how other people saw the little ballerinas, but to Ronnie they were tragic figures, dancers trapped in a dance with only one song, in a box that remained shut and dark most of the time. Who knew what Vivian's box was—if it was the drinking, if it was pursuit of men and beauty, if it was winning a Worst Mother contest . . . Ronnie didn't know. All she knew was that her mother was primping for some gig in the dark and tiny little box that was her life.

Suddenly Vivian's hand stopped in mid-air. She looked at Ronnie's reflection directly. "Well, what is it? Jesus, you're acting weird."

"Mom . . ." Ronnie said, trying to find a delicate way, "I know Ray Geisel isn't my dad."

Vivian's mouth dropped open for an instant, but immediately she corrected herself. She shut her mouth tightly, her jaw becoming taught, and stared at Ronnie's reflection. Ronnie could see the wheels spinning. She could see Vivian trying to recover, trying to decide how to respond.

"Well shit," Vivian said, trying to laugh. "Everybody knows that." She tried to go back to curling her hair, but fumbled with the strand.

"That's not true, Mom. *I* didn't know," Ronnie said. "And Thatcher didn't know either."

Vivian turned and faced Ronnie straight on. "What in the hell have they been telling you?" She cocked her head back, offended, angry.

Ronnie blinked. She had to think about it, had to think about what she knew under the condemning glare of her mother's eye.

"The truth," Ronnie said. "They've been telling me the truth."

"The truth? I just bet that's what they're telling you. Who the hell do they think they are talking about?"

"They're . . . " Ronnie found herself floundering. She took a step back, wanting to back down, wanting to walk away, but she knew she couldn't. This time she would stay. This time she would wait for the truth no matter what. The truth—that was the thing to rely on. "They're my family."

Vivian threw her hand back and laughed, shaking her

head incredulously. "Oh, Jesus," she said. She turned to Ronnie, laughing as if the amusement were too much for her. "Darling, you wouldn't know the truth if it came up and bit you on your ass." She frowned in pity.

"Because you never told me," Ronnie said. "How could I if you never told me?"

"Told you what? That your sister is a freak? You should thank me for that, Veronica." She pointed at Ronnie's reflection. "You should thank your lucky stars I saved you from that."

"Saved me from what? From knowing her?"

"You don't know what you're talking about." Vivian's voice got quiet. "You didn't see how people treated us, treated *me*. Being a damn freak show wherever we went." Vivian laid a hand across her stomach as if she were ill, and closed her eyes. "She didn't even have to be with us after awhile. Everybody knew us, boy." She opened her eyes and took a step toward Ronnie. "Is that what you want? Answer carefully, Ronnie, because you don't know anything. You want to be known as the freak's little sister?" Vivian crossed her arms over her chest and waited.

"That's what I saved you from," she said, satisfied by Ronnie's silence.

Her eyes filled with a blackness that in Ronnie's mind went way beyond color. There was nothing to say to Vivian about Juanita—Ronnie could see that. Nothing would change her in that regard.

"What about my father?" Ronnie said.

"What about him?" Vivian raised her hands and shrugged her shoulders as if Ronnie were wasting Vivian's time.

"Who is he?"

She blew out a breath and turned back to the sink.

"I . . . " She grabbed the hair at her scalp like she was trying to hold something in, like she was trying to keep from exploding. "You little bitch," she said turning. "Jesus Christ what is wrong with you?"

"You're the one with the handle on the truth, Mom. Tell me."

"What gives you the right to come over here and judge me? What gives *any* of you the right to judge me?"

"I just want to know," Ronnie said in a firm voice.

"Bullshit!" Vivian pushed past Ronnie and walked into her bedroom. Ronnie followed. Vivian shook off her robe and started dressing hurriedly.

"I just want to know," Ronnie said again, trying to make her voice quiet, calm. "You owe me that."

"I owe you?" Vivian stood in her lavender colored bra and matching panties, looking at Ronnie. She laughed. "*I* owe *you*?" She went to the closet and rummaged through her clothes. "I don't owe you shit, Ronnie."

"Mom." Ronnie walked toward Vivian. "Just tell me. That's all I want to know. Just tell me who my father is and I'll leave you alone."

Vivian spun like a soldier, ready to fight.

"Oh, you'll leave me alone all right. Wouldn't be anything new about that, now would there?"

"No, no, no," Ronnie said shaking her head and holding up her hand. "Don't start that. Just answer my question."

Vivian picked some clothes out of the closet, looked at them, and then threw them at her bed, turning back to the closet where she rummaged again, stalling, trying to divert herself from the question.

"Mom," Ronnie said, consciously lowering her voice, consciously downshifting, wanting to calm Vivian instead of confront her, wanting to calm herself as well, wanting to remain reasonable. "I'm not judging you. I'm not. I just want to know the truth. That's all."

Vivian stopped moving and stood, staring into the dark closet. Her shoulders sank. She turned toward Ronnie, slowly, her angry eyes softening into sadness, dissipating toward defeat. She didn't say anything, but sank onto the bed, sitting on top of the blouse she had thrown in anger, holding onto a teal colored shirt that she crumpled in her lap.

"You want the truth." She looked across the room, away from Ronnie.

Ronnie stood quietly. Watching. Waiting.

Vivian looked at Ronnie. She set her jaw and narrowed her eyes—a different sort of defiance than she had shown a minute before. "The truth," she said, her eyes on Ronnie's, " is that I don't know."

Ronnie felt no sense of triumph when she left. She didn't feel like she'd broken Vivian or accomplished some great task in getting her to admit the truth. She didn't feel angry. She didn't feel surprised. Really, she didn't feel much of anything. It was just a question. Ronnie was just the listener. Ronnie got into her red beetle and drove down the street. The important thing had not been the answer. Ronnie hadn't known what to expect from Vivian, but in a way, that didn't even matter. What mattered was that Ronnie had asked. What mattered was that she wasn't afraid of the truth anymore, whatever it turned out to be.

CHAPTER FORTY THREE

Ronnie was working at the Quick Shop when the call came. Gayla answered, and by her silence Ronnie knew that something was wrong. She didn't suspect it had anything to do with her until Gayla looked up, until she looked Ronnie in the eye. That was when Ronnie saw it. Her first thought was, "Mother."

Gayla was nodding into the phone, saying, "Okay. Yes. Okay." Her hands were shaking as she hung up. She leaned into the counter, and for a second, she looked like she would crumple right there onto the floor.

"Gayla, what's wrong?" Ronnie said, walking to her.

Gayla looked up, remembering that Ronnie was watching her. She stood up straight.

"Gayla," Ronnie said.

"Ronnie," she said. Her voice was thick and her mouth was twisted in an odd sort of way. "Philip is coming over to get you."

"Why? What's going on?"

"He . . ." Gayla glanced at the customer who had just stepped up to the counter.

Ronnie ignored him.

"Why is Philip coming? What happened?"

When Gayla saw the man only had a cup of coffee, she said, "Buddy, that one's on the house. I need you to get out of here."

"Oh," the man said, confused.

Gayla walked around the counter and ushered the man out. She locked the door behind him and turned the 24 Hour neon sign off.

"Gayla come on. Is she all right? What happened?"

Gayla looked at Ronnie, confused. "Who?"

"My mom. Did something happen?"

"Oh honey," Gayla said. "Oh honey, it ain't your mom."

She led Ronnie back toward the storeroom and sat her on the straight-backed wooden chair. Not Vivian? What Ray had said about Juanita flashed through Ronnie's mind. *People like Juanita don't live too long.*

"Oh my gosh. It's Juanita, isn't it." Ronnie's heart began to burn in her chest, squeezing the breath right out of her lungs until she found herself.

"Ronnie," Gayla said. "Ronnie look at me. Philip's coming to get you, honey. I . . . I don't want to say. It isn't Juanita. Ronnie. Ronnie, look at me. Oh! It's T. He's been in an accident, and . . . and Philip's gonna come and take you to the hospital."

"The hospital?" Ronnie looked at Gayla trying to understand what she was saying. "T.'s been in an accident?"

Gayla leaned forward, putting her hand on Ronnie's knee. "It ain't good, honey . . . that's all I can say. Philip's going be here in just a minute. Let's just sit here and wait for him, okay?"

When the back door to the storeroom opened and Philip walked in and Ronnie saw him, when she saw the look on his face, she knew that it was much worse than not good. Philip's eyes were red. He'd been crying, and it was easy to see that he was holding himself back from crying as he stood in front of her. Ronnie tried to stand up, but the sight of Philip looking like that made her legs suddenly go weak.

"Philip?" she whispered.

He shook his head back and forth, biting on his bottom lip. Tears spilled from his eyes. He took a deep breath and opened his mouth. "You got to come with me," was all he said. He stood there crying, his arms hanging listlessly by his side.

Philip squatted down in front of Ronnie, and when he looked into her eyes, he began to sob. " Ronnie, he's . . . T.'s hurt." He lowered his head and hid his face in his hands, his shoulders shaking. Ronnie reached out her hand and put it on Philip's arm. She looked at Gayla who was biting on the back of her finger and breathing hard. Tears were running down her face.

"Ronnie," Philip said, gaining some control over himself. "T. was in an accident, and he didn't make it."

"What do you mean he didn't make it?"

Just then, Mrs. Wilson came through the door along with Donika. They were crying too. Ronnie watched them. Mrs. Wilson hugged Gayla and then hugged Philip, who held on to her for the longest time. Donika went to Ronnie. She bent down and started to hug her, but Ronnie pushed her back. She felt a hole, burning in her chest. And suddenly she felt cold. And suddenly her teeth were chattering and her body was shaking. And she knew that she was supposed to be thinking something, but she was too cold and her mind wandered to that arrowhead Ray had found out in his field. And she wondered if she'd ever be lucky enough to find one, and then wondered why everyone was there in that storage room. And that was the last thing she remembered.

Mr. Wilson was kneeling in front of her.

"It's okay, baby," Mrs. Wilson said.

Ronnie sat up, confused. She was in the storage room and everyone was surrounding her, but she couldn't remember why.

"Everybody hush now," Mrs. Wilson said, putting her face right in front of Ronnie's. "Baby, you're going to come with us, okay? We're going for a ride."

They led Ronnie to the car and put Ronnie inside with Philip on one side of her, and Donika on the other. Ronnie remembered. He was hurt. Thatcher was hurt.

"T . . ." Ronnie said, looking at Philip, her eyes squinched into a question. Philip put his arm around Ronnie.

"What happened?"

"He was at Jamie's."

"Who?"

"She's one of Rochelle's friends. He was helping her out, working out in the driveway. The car fell off the jack."

"What do you mean?"

"He was fixing her car in her driveway."

"So what?" Ronnie said.

"Things weren't right," Philip said.

"What things?"

"It slipped," he said. "It just slipped."

"And he's hurt," Ronnie said leaning toward the front seat, leaning toward Mrs. Wilson. "I mean . . . I mean . . ."

Mr. and Mrs. Wilson exchanged glances. Donika put her arm around Ronnie's shoulders and pulled her back. Philip buried his face in his hands.

Vivian and Rochelle were already at the hospital when Ronnie and the Wilsons got there. They were in the emergency waiting room. Rochelle sat with another girl who Ronnie guessed was Jamie, though she didn't know. And there were three older people there with Rochelle, too, more people Ronnie didn't know, people who looked like maybe they were parents. A woman feeding a baby a bottle sat in the far corner. A middle-aged man sat near the woman, but he didn't seem to be with her. He was drinking coffee from a paper cup. He looked up at Ronnie and the Wilson's as they walked into the room, but then went back to his coffee. Vivian was across the room, sitting in a chair, crying loudly, her arms crossed, her body rocking back and forth.

"My baby. My baby," she was saying over and over. "No, no, no . . ."

A man whom Ronnie had never met was sitting close to her, trying to put his arm around her shoulder, trying to hold her hand, and Ronnie realized it was probably Vivian's boyfriend. Ronnie tried to remember his name, but for the life of her couldn't. She tried to hear in her own mind Vivian saying his name, but she only heard silence.

Vivian stood up when she saw Ronnie and walked toward her, holding out her arms, wailing loudly. The way she looked and sounded was frightening, and Ronnie took two steps backward, but Vivian caught her by the wrists and held onto her like shackles.

"Oh God, Ronnie," she said. "Oh God." Vivian pulled Ronnie to her, clutching her so tightly, her fingers dug into Ronnie's back. Ronnie's lungs began to burn, objecting to Vivian's constrictive hold. Ronnie tried to push her back, tried to get some space for herself. Vivian was the last person Ronnie wanted so near her, but Vivian didn't notice. She was hysterical and Ronnie's movements to put herself at arms-length only made Vivian hold on to her all the tighter.

"Mom," Ronnie said. "Mom, stop."

"My baby," she wailed. "Oh God, my baby! He's gone."

Ronnie managed to pull an arm free from Vivian's grip. She put her hand on Vivian's shoulder.

"Mom," Ronnie said sharply, looking Vivian in the eye. "Mom, you've got to stop."

But Vivian's eyes were glassy and unfocused. Panic rose in Ronnie's throat and suddenly she didn't care about upsetting Vivian any more. She just wanted Vivian off of her, off and away. Ronnie pushed Vivian back and must have made an odd noise because suddenly the Wilson's and Vivian's boyfriend were surrounding them, pulling Vivian and Ronnie apart. Mr. Wilson directed Vivian to her boyfriend, and Mrs. Wilson took Ronnie's hand and led her to a chair. The Wilson's led Ronnie and Vivian away from each other, to chairs that sat across from each other, like boxers being led to opposite sides of the ring. Suddenly a nurse was on the scene. She went to Vivian, who was still sobbing uncontrollably. Ronnie could hardly stand to look at her, to see her acting this way when it was Thatcher who mattered, when Thatcher was the issue.

"Mrs. Geisel," the nurse said. "Mrs. Geisel you need to calm down."

And for a minute, Vivian looked at her, looked to see who was speaking to her so directly, so sternly in her lost moments. "I don't have to calm down. My boy is dead. Don't you even try to tell me to calm down." She pointed at the nurse and tried to stand up, but her boyfriend pulled her arm to make her stay. "You don't know," Vivian went on. "Don't you tell me anything."

Something inside Ronnie was cracking. It was white and hot and hard to hold. Mrs. Wilson held onto Ronnie's hand, and Donika stood by her, helpless, yearning to comfort but not quite knowing how.

Philip sat in the corner on the opposite side of the room, his head buried in his hands. Rochelle watched Vivian from where she sat. Ronnie wondered what she was thinking, wondered if Rochelle had ever even met Vivian, had ever seen her in action. The nurse handed Vivian two pills. Yes, Ronnie thought. That's the ticket. Drug her. Drug her up to shut her up. That would work. That was what she needed. Vivian took the pills.

"Oh God," she said as she swallowed them.

The room seemed to sigh in relief, a hope given that Vivian would stop her moaning and wailing. The pills wouldn't really help. Ronnie knew that. Vivian might shut up for a while, but nothing would ever stop her—there was no help big enough for that. Why couldn't she see how she acted? Why couldn't she see that Thatcher was dead and that all of her wailing and acting crazy was just making it worse on all of them?

"There you go," the nurse cooed in practice compassion.

"I'm fine. I'm fine," Vivian said, crying, but fine was as far away from the truth as things could get.

"Ronnie," Vivian said. "Oh God, Ronnie. He's gone! Ronnie, he's gone!" And her mouth opened, but then nothing came out. Ronnie closed her eyes. When she opened them, she looked at Mrs. Wilson.

"Where is he?"

"He's here, baby," Mrs. Wilson soothed her.

"Where?"

Mrs. Wilson squeezed Ronnie's hand and Donika rubbed Ronnie's shoulder.

The nurse took them all to a room, a place where they could have some privacy, a place where their grief would not disturb others, a place—Ronnie thought—where Vivian could act crazy. Ronnie looked at Philip as they walked down the hall. His face looked puffy and his eyes drooped in despair. He looked at her, but when their eyes met, it was too raw for Ronnie, and she looked away. The nurse led them down a short hall, and except for Vivian, they followed in silence. Vivian's boyfriend had her by one arm, and Mr. Wilson had her by the other. She moaned and groaned the whole way. Even now, Ronnie thought, even now she acted absurd. Even now she was ridiculous.

His heart had been crushed. Broken ribs had punctured his lungs.

Ronnie stared at the wheat brown walls with meaningless photographs of flowers hanging all around. The couches and chairs were all color coordinated. Sterile. A meaningless room made only for mourning. No one said a word, and so the room was filled only with sounds of stifled crying and heavy sighs. Mrs. Wilson had abandoned Ronnie and was sitting next to Vivian now. They were holding hands, just sitting there, holding hands with pained expressions on both of their faces. Vivian's boyfriend wasn't in the room, and Ronnie wondered where he was and wondered again what his name was.

The chaplain came, and Ronnie was surprised to see that Vivian seemed to know him. Another scam, she thought. Thatcher is dead, but Vivian would be sure to claim righteousness in the presence of a priest. It made her sick.

When the priest came to her, he asked Ronnie if she wanted to see Thatcher, to see his body. He told her that it was okay if she did, and that it was okay if she didn't.

Ronnie nodded yes, trying to grasp exactly what she was consenting to. Look at my dead brother? Did people really have to do such things? Did people really have to suffer so? She looked at Vivian, watched her mother biting at her knuckles as Ronnie walked past.

He was a kind looking man. Short. Older. Balding. He looked Ronnie in the eyes when he spoke to her. He brought Ronnie down a long hallway and a half flight of stairs to a set of heavy steel doors.

"Take a minute now," he said. "Steady yourself. I'll be with you, okay?"

Ronnie leaned against the wall. No one was around. Just Ronnie and the priest. And he didn't say anything. He just stood there, his head bowed. His hands were folded in the middle of his stomach.

"I'm scared." The words came out broken and scarred.

"I'll stay with you. I'll hold your hand if you want," he said.

That white-hot feeling was back again, only now it wasn't anger. Now it was something else, something worse. Fear mixed with sadness, sadness that Ronnie knew was going to fill her life forever from this moment forward.

The priest pushed open the door and led Ronnie into the room. A man in a lab coat was standing next to a covered body. Ronnie heard the drum of her heart beating in her ear. Her knees shook. She squeezed the priest's hand so hard that he pried her fingers up a bit with his other hand. "I'm here," he whispered. "Take your time."

They walked to the body. Ronnie stared at it, the shape of it. It was not real. It couldn't be. But the man standing there looked at Ronnie, and the priest looked at Ronnie. The priest nodded to the man, and he uncovered the face and shoulders of the body.

Ronnie sucked in her breath.

"Breathe," the priest said.

CHAPTER FORTY FOUR

His dresser was dusty. She took things off of it, one by one. She didn't leave the house, but she didn't have to. People came to her. Donika came. Mr. and Mrs. Wilson came. Vivian came. Even Gayla came. They came and they went. They brought food and answered the phone when it rang and sat with Ronnie and with Vivian. In all her life Ronnie had never felt anything like this, a pain so deep and sharp that it took away everything else completely. She stayed in the house, afraid to leave, afraid that if she did, it would somehow disappear too. Vivian walked around the house when she was there, touching things, muttering, sighing, crying, smoking. She walked into his room and smelled his pillow. She looked in the bathroom and picked up a comb. It was like a cloud. Thatcher was everywhere and nowhere at the same time.

Mr. Wilson and Philip helped them with the funeral director, and helped them with the dreadful details of picking out a casket and burial clothes. She didn't speak, but only nodded, wondering if she'd ever be able to speak again. Words stuck in her throat, gagging her with their unimportance. What did any of it matter now? Mr. Wilson and Philip spoke for her, spoke for Vivian, walking them through, walking them forward.

On the day of the funeral, Ronnie waited in the living room, sitting on the living room couch, twirling the frayed fringe on the couch cover around her index finger, staring at the television without seeing, without hearing. Ronnie jumped when Andrew tapped on the front door and then opened it, sticking his head in. Seeing her, he stepped into the room, tentatively.

"Ah, Ronnie. Your mom and I are here."

She followed Andrew out the door.

It wasn't until they got to the funeral home, until Vivian stepped out of the car that Ronnie had a chance to take a good look at Vivian. Ronnie never knew what to expect, and she never hoped for much regarding her mother's ideas about style and what was appropriate and what was not, but that day, Ronnie was shocked to see that Vivian looked stunning. She wore a plain, short sleeved, short length black dress with black stockings and black stiletto sandals that strapped gracefully around her delicate ankles. Her hair was swept up in a French twist, and she wore hardly any makeup—merely a hint of plum colored lipstick. Ronnie stared. She looked beautiful and elegant and Ronnie didn't know this version of her.

"Come on," Vivian said, taking Andrew's arm and walking into the funeral home.

"Mom . . . "

Vivian turned.

Ronnie wanted to tell her that she looked beautiful, but the words got stuck in her throat. Vivian waited for a second.

"Well?" Vivian said. She looked nervously toward the building, and when Ronnie didn't answer, turned and started walking. The funeral director tried to take them to the parlor where Thatcher was laid out, but Vivian shook her head. "Where's the lounge?" she asked. The director pointed. Vivian looked at Andrew. "Let us have a minute, would you?" she said to him, grabbed Ronnie's wrist and pulled her along.

In the lounge, Vivian sat Ronnie at a table, and then started digging through her purse until she found what she was looking for. She rattled a bottle of pills at Ronnie.

"Dr. Neston gave this to me," she said. "He told me to only take one, but I took two." She opened the bottle and dumped some of the pills into her palm. She looked around and saw a water cooler in the corner. She pushed two pills into Ronnie's hand and then got her a cup of water. "Take them," she said. Ronnie looked at her. "Go on," Vivian prodded. "Take them and let's get this over with." So Ronnie did. She took them both.

Mrs. Wilson stuck her head into the room. "How are you, honey," she said to Vivian. She walked in and reached in both directions, giving Vivian a hug with one arm and reaching out and squeezing Ronnie's hand with the other. Donika came in behind her.

"How're you doing?" she asked, sitting next to Ronnie.

Ronnie shrugged.

"You want me to go with you? Be with you when you first walk up there?"

Ronnie nodded.

"You two go ahead. I'll be there in a minute," Vivian said. She lit a cigarette and plopped down on a mauve colored loveseat. Mrs. Wilson stayed with Vivian.

Charles and Mr. Wilson were already standing at the casket when Ronnie and Donika walked into the viewing room. Mr. Wilson reached toward Ronnie and pulled her to him, tucking her closely to his side, then pulled Donika to his other side.

"Oh, Pretty Girls," he said sadly.

Ronnie tried to smile at him but ended up looking at the burgundy carpet instead. She tried to concentrate on the pills she had just taken and anticipated the pain and everything else going away. She kept her eyes on the carpet, trying to avert them from the open casket before her, but once she looked at him, she couldn't look away.

It was just like it had been with Thatcher lying on that cold metal table in the hospital—unreal. She sucked in her breath sharply and put the back of her hand to her mouth to stifle a sob. *Be still, be still*, Ronnie thought, trying to calm herself, but her hand went out from her as if on its own and started to reach for him though she knew that what she was reaching for was long gone and that she did not want to feel the coldness of what was left behind. Mr. Wilson plucked her hand from the air, pulling it to his chest—a chest alive and warm and beating with life. Ronnie's throat tightened even more.

"Breathe," a voice whispered in her head. It was the voice of the priest in the hospital. "Breathe," she heard again, and so she did. She took a long, deep breath, in and out. Then another. Until those magic pills kicked in, Ronnie decided to concentrate on that.

Her concentration, however, was soon broken by the sound of Vivian entering the room. She was crying loudly. Ronnie turned.

"My baby," Vivian moaned as she made her way to the casket. "Oh my baby!"

Ronnie's mouth dropped open slightly when she saw her. Vivian—who had looked so beautiful just minutes before—had put on a long black lace veil, a veil that hung all the way down to her waist. "My poor T.," she wailed.

Ronnie watched her mother lament her way into the room, and she found herself oddly comforted by the spectacle walking toward her, even cheered by it. This is what Ronnie had been looking for, waiting for: that step too far, that taking of something that was just right and turning it into something foolish. It was comedy, is what it was, the over-exaggeration of everything. And it was a good sight because no matter how terribly the world had shifted, no matter how much things had gone askew, Ronnie saw that Vivian was the same. There was joy in that, wasn't there? There was comfort in that.

"Oh, look at my baby," Vivian was saying, and then she laid her hand on Thatcher's hands.

Ronnie put her hand over her mouth in horror, but then suddenly it was more than that. Suddenly the sight was more than Ronnie could contain. A burst of laughter escaped from her lips. Ronnie looked up, shocked and appalled by her own lack of control. She covered her mouth harder and looked at the floor, hoping her laughter had sounded like grief. She didn't mean to laugh, didn't want to laugh. It was just that Vivian and the pills and the veil and Thatcher lying there like that . . . it was all some sort of silliness. Philip put a hand on Ronnie's shoulder.

"Easy," he whispered leaning down toward her.

Ronnie shook her head, wanting to explain, but all she could do was stifle another giggle. Vivian stared at her for a minute, looking annoyed and dismayed.

"Come over here," Philip said, taking Ronnie by the arm. He bent down as he led her toward the back of the room. "What's the matter with you?" he said, but Ronnie couldn't stop laughing. It was funny. Was she the only one who saw that? Who realized what a joke the whole thing was? Philip made her sit on the gold-weave fabric couch and sat beside her.

"What are you doing?" he said.

Ronnie shook her head. "I don't know," she said. "I don't know," and she started to cry. Philip's look softened. He put his arm around Ronnie's shoulder and pulled her close to him. Donika stood in front of them, looking lost and helpless.

"Look at her," Ronnie said to them. She wiped her eyes with the back of her hand. "She's enjoying herself up there."

"No," Philip said.

But it was true. Ronnie knew it. Vivian was having a moment in the spotlight. It was her final show for Thatcher. If Thatcher were there . . . if Thatcher were alive . . . he wouldn't let this get to him. He would just ignore her. He would pull Ronnie aside and roll his eyes or something. He would just let her go on and on and not say a word. Ronnie and Thatcher had watched Vivian put on shows all their lives, and Ronnie didn't know why she expected Vivian to stop now, but for some reason she did. She expected Vivian to know better—to see the limit, to understand for once that there was a line she didn't need to cross. Thatcher was dead. All her moaning and arm waving wasn't doing a thing about that.

Ronnie sat on that couch, watching Vivian as she moaned and carried on, but the worst thing by far was the way Vivian wouldn't stop touching Thatcher's hands. Ronnie was truly horrified by it. Vivian patted them, held them, touched them, and each time it made Ronnie's stomach grow queasy. Andrew could not stop her. Mr. Wilson could not stop her, though he tried to pull her aside at one point.

People came and went. Ronnie watched them approach the casket. Of course they wouldn't stay there long with Vivian circling Thatcher's body like a buzzard. When Rochelle walked into the room, she was with the same man and woman and girl Ronnie had seen at the hospital. Rochelle looked pale. She didn't have any makeup on her eyes, and they were red from crying. The man led her to the casket. She stayed a good ways away from Vivian, who was still touching Thatcher's hands. Mrs. Wilson whispered something to Andrew, and he went to Vivian and was finally successful in getting her to sit in a chair a few feet away.

Ronnie wanted to go up to Rochelle, but she was afraid. She was just beginning to feel like she had some control over her emotions. But Philip went, leaving Donika to stay with Ronnie. He walked right up to Rochelle and wrapped her in a hug.

Gayla came in, a few minutes later. She went right up to Vivian. Ronnie smiled. Gayla wasn't afraid of Vivian. And then she kneeled in front of Thatcher's casket and bowed her head, though Vivian stood right next to her, resting her hand on Thatcher's hands as if she were trying to keep him from moving. Gayla didn't seem to mind. She bowed her head, and after a minute, Ronnie could see Gayla's shoulders shaking.

Gayla was sitting on the gold couch, talking to Ronnie when Juanita came through the door. The room became instantly quiet. Ronnie sucked in her breath. She was happy to see her—all 83 and one half inches of her—but Vivian was there . . . Ronnie started to stand up, but Gayla held her arm to stop her.

"Wait, honey," she said. "Don't go stepping into a hornet's nest if you can help it."

Ronnie's mouth opened to argue, but Gayla's expression was stern. "Sit down."

Vivian's back was turned. Juanita walked toward the casket. Ronnie looked to the door to see if Ray or Bean were there, but Juanita had come into the room alone. When Vivian heard the sound of Juanita's sob—so thick it was like hearing a record played in slow motion—Vivian turned around. Her mouth dropped open and she gasped, taking a quick step back to recover her space.

"Oh no. Oh no," Ronnie whispered over and over.

"Oh my God," Vivian said loudly as she backed away. "Oh my God." Her face crinkled, and she threw her hands back as if to avoid contact with some kind of contagion.

But Juanita was looking at Thatcher. A sound came from somewhere deep within her, and she put a hand over her mouth, trying to stop it, trying to keep it in. She reached out toward Thatcher, but then looked at Vivian.

"No!" Vivian said shaking her head from side to side as she reached backward toward Thatcher. She backed up and bumped into the casket, making the spray of flowers that sat on top shake. She turned and grabbed again at Thatcher's hands. "Get out of here!" she said to Juanita.

Juanita shook her head from side to side, her face streaked in tears as she looked at Thatcher. She reached a hand toward Vivian's shoulder. "Mother," she said in a thick voice, but her mother recoiled.

"Don't touch me!" Vivian shouted.

It all happened within the space of a minute, and yet it was long enough for Ronnie to see, to understand. This was the defining moment. She had been wondering what would ever happen if Vivian and Juanita saw each other, wondering what they would say, what they would do. And Ronnie had been coming to terms with her mother. She had been letting go of her expectations of Vivian all this time, trying to just accept her as she was, but here . . . seeing Vivian react, seeing her reach for a cold, dead hand over a warm, live one . . . it was too much . . . but Ronnie also understood that it was Vivian's way, that she was only fooling herself. She had never touched Thatcher in life, never offered a hug or a word of encouragement that didn't come with some kind of price. Yet here she was willing to reach out now, when it was too late, when there was nothing to risk losing.

"Stop it!" Ronnie shouted from her spot on the gold couch. "Stop touching him! Just stop it!"

Juanita turned.

Donika put her hand around Ronnie's shoulder, and Gayla put a hand on Ronnie's arm again, but she shook them off and went to Juanita. Juanita looked down at Ronnie, tears ran down her face, down her sharp cheekbones, dripping off of her square chin. She frowned as she looked at Ronnie, trying to control herself, but at the same time offered Ronnie a nod of encouragement, a nod of comfort even then.

"No," Vivian said, now looking at Ronnie. "She needs to stay away from us." She looked back at Juanita, repulsion on her face. "You stay away!" But suddenly she faltered, staring at the floor.

"I . . ." Vivian said in a suddenly slurry voice.

"She's going to faint!" Mrs. Wilson said.

Bodies jumped into motion as Vivian began to crumple toward the floor—Mr. Wilson, Andrew, Mrs. Wilson, Charles— all leapt forward to catch her. She fell backward, knocking into the casket, causing the lilies to fall to the floor.

Andrew reached her first and she fell into his arms. Mr. Wilson pulled over a chair and Andrew placed her in it. She sat slumped and motionless.

"Vivian," Andrew said, patting her cheek. "Vivian, honey."

She came to and looked at him, confused. "It's okay, Viv. It's all right."

"I'm alright," she whispered. "I'm all right."

Ronnie and Juanita stood motionless, watching her.

"Let's see if we can't get her to the lounge," Mr. Wilson said to Andrew. And together they helped her stand and walked her toward the door. Vivian did not look back. The room fell into hushed whispers, everyone stunned, not only by the harsh words and drama of Vivian's reaction, but by the spectacle of Thatcher's oldest sister towering before his open casket.

Juanita had stopped crying. She looked down at Ronnie, whose small fingers clutched Juanita's enormous hand. Juanita tried to smile. Ronnie looked up at her, trying to do the same. Mrs. Wilson stepped forward, motioning toward Philip to help her pick up the flowers and place them back on the casket. Ronnie and Juanita stepped forward and stood, side by side, hand in hand, in front of the casket of their dead brother.

"I've lost him all over again," Juanita said.

Ronnie felt a tug on her sleeve. Bean was suddenly standing next to her. Ronnie looked for Ray, but he wasn't there. Juanita leaned down, over Ronnie, and touched Bean's head.

Ronnie didn't see Ray until a while later, until she went to look for Vivian. When she peeked into the lounge, she saw them together, Ray and Vivian, sitting there alone. It was not a scene Ronnie would have expected had she thought of them actually meeting. Vivian was on a couch, and Ray sat on a chair, pulled up close in front of her. Leaning in, elbows on their knees, leaning toward each other and holding hands, so close that the tops of their heads almost touched. They were crying, both of them, Ray whispering something to Vivian as they sat there. Ronnie did not stay there. She went outside, past the gentlemen in suits who opened the doors for each visitor, past the people who knew Thatcher, and who knew her. She went outside and walked around to the back of the building and sat alone on a concrete ledge, not crying, not thinking, not doing anything but fixing her gaze on the fact that Thatcher was gone.

CHAPTER FORTY FIVE

The cup was sitting on his dresser. Ronnie picked it up, turning it over in her hands. She half expected Thatcher to walk into the room, to say, "Put that down." Of course, that wouldn't happen. She ran her finger along the crack, remembering the way he had lined up the two broken mugs that together would be solid enough to do the job.

She went out into the living room. Juanita had been calling Ronnie every day, not having a whole lot to say, just pretty much saying hey. And when she had asked if Ronnie wanted her to come to St. Louis and visit, Ronnie said yes and started to cry. She left Bean with Ray in Cabool and drove up the very next day.

She was sitting on the floor with her back against the wall when Ronnie came out of Thatcher's room. She went and sat on the floor next to her.

"T. loved this," Ronnie said, holding out the mug.
Juanita took the cup and as she examined it, as she turned it over in her large hands, she sucked in her breath. "Oh my goodness," she said. "I forgot all about this."

Ronnie nodded. "I think you should have it."

Juanita looked at Ronnie, then pulled her to her side, swallowing her up, sheltering her beneath the huge cave of her embrace. Ronnie closed her eyes. If she could have, she would have stayed there forever.

After a few minutes Juanita said, "I had one, too, only I dropped mine about a week after I got it. Shattered into a hundred pieces." She was looking at the cup again. "Only mine was Calamity Jane." Ronnie looked away so that she wouldn't start crying. These tearful moments, she had learned, snuck up at the least likely moments, and Ronnie didn't like it. She didn't like feeling in control one minute and feeling out of control the next.

"When Daddy gave them to us, T. said he was keeping his forever."

Ronnie cocked her head in surprise. "I thought *you* gave it to him."

"No. That was from Daddy. He was gone over the road a lot, and sometimes he'd bring us stuff, you know? Never big things. Just things like this," she said nodding toward the cup and then handed it back. "You should give this to Daddy," she said. "It'll mean the world to him."

And it did. Ronnie gave it to him a few weeks later when she went to Cabool for the weekend. He shook his head back and forth, and his chin quivered. "What a waste," he said. "All this time." He tried to smile. He looked so much like his son that it made Ronnie's stomach ache to watch him.

CHAPTER FORTY SIX

Vivian leaned in the doorway that led to the living room. She stared at Ronnie as she lay on the couch. Ronnie knew she looked like hell. Her hair needed washing and she was still in her pajamas, though it was the afternoon. Vivian's lips puckered in disdain. She had been going through Thatcher's papers for two hours.

"Where else does T. have any papers."

"I don't know," Ronnie said without looking away from the television

"Would you sit up when I'm talking to you?"

Ronnie fluffed her little green pillow and laid her head back down.

"Ronnie!" Vivian walked across the room and stood in front of the television.

"What?"

"Don't be difficult with me. You could help me in there, you know. We got a lot of shit to figure out here."

"I don't want to do it."

"Oh you think I do? Listen to me," she said, walking into the room. "You got to realize some things, Ronnie. You ain't going be able to stay here. I been talking to a lawyer, and he said chances are slim to none. You hear?" Vivian stared at Ronnie. Ronnie shut her eyes.

"Sit up," Vivian said.

When Ronnie didn't move, Vivian walked over and smacked her on the hip.

"I mean it. Sit up."

Ronnie sighed and sat up reluctantly, pulling the green pillow to her lap. Her head hung low, and she looked at the floor. Vivian sat down next to her.

"You ain't gonna be able to stay here. Even if the government doesn't tax it to death—and hell you know they will—you won't be able to afford the payments, and it ain't in your name anyway, and I don't know how all this works, but here's what I do know—you're gonna have to leave here." She waited for Ronnie to respond, but the only sound was coming from the television. Gilligan was in a cave, fending off a huge spider.

"Are you listening to me? Do you hear what I'm saying?"

Ronnie tapped her fingers on her thigh and looked at the television.

"Ronnie!"

"I hear you!"

"Well what are you going to do?"

"I don't know," Ronnie whispered.

"You can't ignore this, you know."

"I know! Leave me alone."

Vivian raised her hands in helplessness, but then let them fall back into her lap with a thud. They both sat for a moment, staring straight ahead. Skipper was calling to Gilligan, calling him Little Buddy.

Vivian blew out a big breath and looked at the ceiling. "Shit!" She stood up and looked down on Ronnie. "You want to come home?"

Ronnie shrugged, though she knew there was no way, no way, no way she would live with Vivian ever again.

"Get your act together, Ronnie. If you want to come home, come home. If you got some other magical plan then bring it on, but you're going to have to get off this couch and make up your mind." Vivian walked to the table and pulled a cigarette out of the pack that sat there.

"I'll figure it out," Ronnie said, though she didn't have a clue and didn't even know where to start.

CHAPTER FORTY SEVEN

Ronnie pulled into the driveway and got out of her car carrying a bag of McDonalds. She went to the garage. Philip and Mr. Wilson had come over early that morning to clean out the garage, but when it got too hot, Philip sent Mr. Wilson home. Philip followed Ronnie inside.

"Whew, it's hot out there," he said. Sweat poured from his face and his gray t-shirt was soaked. He walked over to the sink and got a glass of water. He chugged it, refilled, and chugged it again.

"I got something I want to show you," he said.

After they ate, Ronnie followed Philip out to the garage.

"I know you ain't a baby," he said. "But look what I did. See this toolbox? It's got everything you need, stuff like screwdrivers and a hammer . . . look here. Pliers, tape measure . . See?" He held up the pliers and then let them fall back into the box with a clink. "So I'm putting it over there." He pointed to the workbench. "You keep it."

"Okay," Ronnie said, trying to be business like.

"But you can always call me, and I'll help you if there's something you need done."

Ronnie nodded to show him she understood, but he shook his head at her, like she wasn't understanding.

"You always been like a pesky little sister to me anyhow. That's for sure."

"Hey," Ronnie said at his teasing, but he wasn't smiling.

"Well, now it's for real. You hear? You're my little sister for real now, like I inherited you, and I'll help you just like T. always did."

"Thanks, Philip," she said, trying to look at him, trying to smile at him, feeling shy and thankful.

"Loose ends," he said walking back over to where he had been sweeping. "That's what this is."

CHAPTER FORTY EIGHT

Donika wanted to move in with Ronnie.

"I can't stay here," Ronnie said.

"Why not?"

"I don't know. My mom is handling everything, and I don't have any money. I can't pay for this house."

"Well, then where are you going to stay?"

"I don't know," Ronnie said. "I mean . . . I don't know what to do."

"I think I should move in here with you. I bet we could afford it if we split it. Or maybe we could get a third person too."

Ronnie looked at her.

"I mean, if you want and all. But I'm telling you what, I need to leave Gram's and Gramp's, you know? I been thinking about renting an apartment, but I can't afford it all on my own. And I was hoping that you would rent one with me, before . . . you know, before all this. And I think if you're going to stay here, you should just take me in as a roommate. We'll be living like sisters."

Donika had been staying with Ronnie off and on for the past few weeks, trying to keep Ronnie from being by herself too much. Ronnie had slept in Thatcher's bed since the accident, and decided to make his room hers.

Rochelle had come by a few times. She came to check on Ronnie. She came by a lot at first, crying, and talking about Thatcher.

"I think I would have married him," she said.

Ronnie wanted to tell her that she was the first girlfriend of his she had ever liked, but she stayed quiet. It was hard to talk about any of it. All Ronnie said was, "That would have been good." She didn't look at Rochelle when she said it, though she meant it.

Rochelle gave Ronnie a big hug when she left.

Later that night Ronnie smashed the painted pot that had been sitting on the bathroom windowsill. She was just standing there, not doing anything, really, just looking at herself in the mirror . . . and she looked over and saw that pot—the very first one she'd ever painted for Juanita. Ronnie picked it up, turning it in her hands, thinking about Thatcher, thinking about how he'd gotten her to paint those pots . . . his odd ways of encouraging her . . . and then thinking about him being gone forever . . .

When it hit the ground, Ronnie was startled by the sound it made—startled that it was so pleasing to her ear, almost like music—a chalky, satisfying clap. She looked at the floor, at the pieces of the pot, splayed on the floor like a broken heart. Five pieces. Five pieces to a broken pot. She stared at them, knowing the pieces would never go back together again, even if she tried.

Forever is a pretty long time.

The days came and went like that, whether Ronnie cared about them or not. She went back to the Quick Shop after a week. The hardest part about that was passing by Oliver's. Philip was still there, though. He was there early in the mornings until late at night. Ronnie wondered if he was hoping to capture a wisp of Thatcher's ghost, though she knew herself there was none of him to be felt or found. In the end, Mr. and Mrs. Wilson helped Philip buy Thatcher's half of Oliver's, and life went on, whether anyone liked it or not.

CHAPTER FORTY NINE

"I went to the community college today."

Ronnie was talking to Juanita. "They got this art program there . . ."

"Oh Veronica! Oh that's a good thing. Are you gonna do it? Are you gonna sign up?"

"I think so," Ronnie said. "Only I have to wait until January. It's a two-year deal. I'm going to go talk to an advisor there later this week."

"Well, I'm proud of you, Veronica," Juanita said. "You got so much talent. Good for you. Good, good for you."

"Everybody's always talking about my truck. I bet my business doubled now. I should give you a percentage of everything I make."

Ronnie smiled, thinking of that truck.

"It's still only halfway done, though. When are you gonna come and paint the other side?"

"Soon," Ronnie said. "I promise."

"People been asking where you are and how come you ain't been around."

"Really?" Ronnie said. She liked the sound of that. She liked the sound of being missed.

"You could work out here whenever you want," Juanita said. "You can live out here if you want."

Bean's voice was suddenly in the background and Ronnie could hear the phone being tugged on.

"Hi Ronnie!" he shouted in the background.

Ronnie laughed.

"Tell Bean 'Hi,'" Ronnie said. "Tell him I'll be out there to visit real soon."

Ronnie knew she would probably have to leave Thatcher's house eventually, but she wasn't ready for that yet; she wasn't ready to leave everything she'd known for so long. That house was like her last real connection to Thatcher, the only thing she could actually touch. She thought of what Mrs. Wilson had said when Thatcher was still alive, when she had threatened to chuck it all and move out. Mrs. Wilson had said that if Ronnie really wanted to grow up, she wouldn't leave, that she wouldn't run away, that she'd find out the truth and deal with it. Truth was, there were people who loved her. Thatcher was gone, and Ronnie was lonely for him, but Ronnie also knew that she wasn't alone.

CHAPTER FIFTY

Ronnie looked over at Ray in the passenger seat, leaning back into the headrest, lazily looking out the window. She looked over her shoulder at Bean who sat scooted up close behind his grandpa, his eyes closed and his chin lifted, enjoying the feeling of the air on his face like a dog looking out of a car window.

Almost a year had come and gone since Juanita had shown up on that patio, and by the time the daffodils were blooming again, Ronnie's entire life had changed. She had finished up her first semester of community college, and before summer even started, one of her teachers had helped her get a part-time job painting stage props at the Muny Theater. Ronnie was still painting pots for Juanita, but that was for fun more than anything. She wouldn't have believed it was possible, but Ronnie was doing okay.

She had never given much thought to it until recently, but the way things had worked out—looking back—the way that she had found the rest of her family just in time . . . Ronnie had never really given much thought to the idea of there really being a God, but when she looked back—not only over the past year, but over her entire life . . . it made her wonder. Even when things were hard, when things happened that Ronnie couldn't explain or that just plain hurt, in one way or another, she always ended up with what she needed, when she needed it. Thatcher. The Wilsons. Juanita. Bean. Ray. When Ronnie looked at it, when she thought of everything, she couldn't help but think that it was all some sort of masterful plan . . . some sort of taking the bad and turning it to good.

"We're here," Ronnie said pulling the little red VW off into the gravel road.

At first they weren't going to go. Juanita wasn't feeling well, but she insisted that Ronnie, Ray, and Bean go on without her. Ronnie packed a picnic lunch, and Ray tucked a couple of fishing poles and a tackle box behind the seat. Ronnie watched Bean splashing in the water, and smiled. She closed her eyes and lifted her face to the sun. She knew she would take care of him one day. She thought of that quarry, that big mysterious hole she'd grown up with, and decided that mysteries usually ended up getting solved and empty things usually ended up being filled. That's just the way life was.

She went into the water and swam to the big chocolate rock, climbed up the side and stood there, taking in her surroundings. Ray and Bean stood on the bank, each holding a fishing pole. They were watching her. Ronnie looked down at the water below, and realized, suddenly, that she wasn't afraid.

"Stand up tall, Veronica," Ray called to her. "Stand up tall and be proud of who you are."

Ronnie looked at him, and she looked at Bean, and she sucked in her breath, and she jumped.

The End

ABOUT THE AUTHOR

Janet Goddard, Master of Fine Art in fiction writing from the University of Missouri-St. Louis; Creative Writing Certificate and a Bachelor of Science in English from Washington University. *Shake the Middle Tree* is Janet's first novel. Janet has been teaching English and writing courses in a variety of venues for the past 15 years. Presently, she teaches English and creative writing full time at Visitation Academy in St. Louis.

Made in the USA
Charleston, SC
14 December 2011